THE
GIRL WHO
SURVIVED

Center Point
Large Print

Also by Lisa Jackson and available from
Center Point Large Print:

You Will Pay
Ominous
One Last Breath
Liar, Liar
Willing to Die
Paranoid
Last Girl Standing
The Third Grave
Afraid

THE
GIRL WHO
SURVIVED

LISA JACKSON

CENTER POINT LARGE PRINT
THORNDIKE, MAINE

The text of this Large Print edition is unabridged.
In other aspects, this book may vary
from the original edition.
Printed in the United States of America
on permanent paper sourced using
environmentally responsible foresting methods.
Set in 16-point Times New Roman type.

ISBN: 978-1-63808-473-0

The Library of Congress has cataloged this record
under Library of Congress Control Number: 2022940557

CHAPTER 1

MOUNT HOOD, OREGON
TWENTY YEARS EARLIER

Creeeaaak!

Kara's eyes flew open.

What was that?

She squinted into the darkness.

"Don't say a word."

She started to scream.

But a hand came down over her mouth.

Hard.

"Shhh!"

Marlie? Her sister was holding her down, forcing her head back against the pillows?

She started to struggle.

"Stop it! Just listen and don't say anything!" The warning was whispered against her ear. Hot breath against her skin. "Listen to me." Her voice was urgent. This was no joke, not the kind of prank Kara had grown up with due to the antics of three older brothers. "Handfuls," her mother called them. "Delinquents," her father had said.

Now, though, it was just Marlie, and she was freaked. "Just do what I say," Marlie warned. "No questions. No arguments. This is serious, Kara-Bear, so don't make a sound."

Why?

As if she read Kara's mind, Marlie said, "I can't explain now, just trust me. You're a smart girl. That's what all the teachers say, right? That you're way ahead of kids your age? So just do as I say, okay? Now, come on."

Kara shook her head, her hair rustling against her pillow, her eyes adjusting to the thin light. Whatever had scared Marlie so much could be handled. Mama would know what to do.

"You can't make any noise, okay? Got that?"

Marlie lifted her hand and Kara couldn't help herself. "What's—?" she started to whisper and Marlie's hand returned. Firmer. Pressing Kara back against the sheets.

"Just listen to me!" Marlie insisted through clenched teeth. Her sharp, desperate plea stopped Kara cold. Though Mama, at times, had accused the older girl of being a "drama queen," this time was different. Marlie was different. Scared to death.

Kara sensed it. She lay still.

"You have to hide. Now."

Hide?

"*Right now.* Do you understand?"

Wide-eyed, Kara nodded.

"And it can't be here." Marlie started to take her hand away from Kara's face.

"Why? Where's Mama . . . ?" Kara said in a whispered rush. She couldn't help herself.

"Shit! Stop! Kara, *please!*" Marlie's hand was over her younger sister's mouth again. Harder. Forcing Kara's head back into her pillow. "No questions! They'll hear you!"

Who? Who would hear her?

Kara's heart was beating crazily. Fear curdled through her blood.

"Just come with me and don't say a word! I mean it, Kara. There are bad people here. They cannot find you. If they do, they will hurt you, do you understand?" Marlie's face pressed closer and even in their dark bedroom, Kara saw that Marlie's blue eyes were round with fear. She was dressed, in jeans and a sweatshirt, her blond hair pulled into a single braid.

Kara shook her head violently.

"Okay. Now, this is the last time," Marlie warned. "Got it?"

Kara nodded slowly. Scared out of her mind.

"Promise you'll be quiet."

Kara swallowed against the growing lump in her throat, but nodded again.

"I love you, Kara-Bear. . . . I'll come get you. I promise." Marlie hesitated just a second, then withdrew her hand.

Kara didn't speak.

"Okay." Marlie glanced out the window, where moonlight played on the thick blanket of snow, then grabbed Kara's palm. "Come on!" She tugged, but Kara didn't need any more encouragement. She scrambled to get out of the tangle of bed clothes. They crept past Marlie's bed, where even in the darkness Kara could see several neatly stacked piles of clothes piled over the rumpled coverlet. Even Marlie's boots were on the bed. Now, though, she, like Kara, was barefoot.

So her footsteps wouldn't be heard.

Kara's blood turned to ice. This was wrong. So wrong. She stepped on a toy, probably a Barbie shoe, but held her tongue as Marlie cracked open the door to the hallway.

Along with the scent of wood smoke from the dying fire, the faint sounds of a Christmas carol filtered up from the floor below.

"Silent night . . ."

Marlie peered into the darkness.

"Holy night . . ."

Taking a deep breath, Marlie squeezed Kara's hand and whispered, "Let's go." She pulled her younger sister into the dark, narrow corridor, past the closed doors of the boys' rooms toward the far end of the hall, where the stairs curved down to the first floor, light curling eerily up from below, the massive doors to Mama and Daddy's bedroom just beyond the railing.

"All is calm . . ."

For a second, Kara's heart soared. Marlie was taking her to get Mama and—but no. She stopped at the last door before the staircase leading down,

8

to the door that was always locked, the doorway leading upward to the attic and the warren of unused rooms above.

What?

NO!

"All is bright . . ."

Kara balked. She wasn't going up there! *No, no, no!*

She started to protest when Marlie caught her eye and sent her a look that could cut through steel.

Bong!

Kara jumped at the noise, her heart hammering.

But it was only the grandfather clock near the front door, striking off the hours, drowning out the music.

"Jesus," Marlie whispered under her breath and pulled Kara behind her as she slowly mounted the narrow wooden steps.

Bong!

"Marlie, no," Kara whispered, feeling the temperature drop with each step.

"We don't have a choice!" Marlie snapped, her voice still hushed as they reached the third floor.

Rather than snap on a light, she pulled a small flashlight from her pocket and switched it on, its thin beam sliding over draped furniture and boxes, forgotten lamps and stacks of books, open bags of unused clothes. Her family used the extra space for storage, though according to Mama it had once been servants' quarters. "I wish," Mama had added, lighting a cigarette as she warned all of her "patchwork family" that the area was forbidden, deemed unsafe. "Don't go up there, ever. You're asking for serious grounding if you do. Hear me? Serious."

Her threat hadn't stuck, of course.

Of course they'd all sneaked up here and explored.

Though the area was declared off-limits, her brothers were always climbing up here, and Kara had poked around the rabbit warren of connected rooms often enough to know her way around. But tonight, in the darkness, the frigid rooms appeared sinister and evil, the closed doors standing like sentinels guarding the narrow corridor.

Bong!

"Where's Mama?" she asked again, fighting panic.

Marlie glanced at her and shook her head. She placed a finger to her lips, reminding Kara of the need for silence, then pulled her anxiously along the bare floor of the third story.

This was wrong.

Really wrong.

At the far end of the hallway was another staircase, much narrower and close. Cramped. It wound downward and ended up in the kitchen. For a fleeting second, Kara thought they were

10

going down the back way, which seemed stupid since they'd just ascended, but Marlie had other plans. She stopped just before they reached steps, at the small cupboard-like entrance to the attic.

Kara's bad feeling got worse. "What are you do—?"

Marlie pulled a key from the front pocket of her jeans and slipped it into the lock. A second later, the attic door creaked open. "Come on."

Kara drew back and shook her head. "I don't want to." Marlie surely wouldn't—

"Don't care." Forcefully, Marlie pulled her through the tight doorway and yanked the door shut behind them.

"What the hell is this?"

"Don't swear."

"But—"

"Look. I'm saving you. Us." A loud click sounded as she flipped the old switch. Nothing happened.

"Shit," Marlie muttered as they stood in the darkness.

"Don't swear," Kara threw back. "And saving us from what?"

"Shhh. Quiet. You don't want to know."

"Yes! Yes, I do! Tell me!"

"Look, it's . . . complicated." Marlie hesitated.

"And scary."

"Yes, and really scary." She clicked on her flashlight again so that they could see the stairs winding upward. The steps were steep and barely wide enough for Kara's foot, a rickety old staircase winding to the garret under the eaves. It was freezing in the tight space and dark as pitch.

"I'm not going up there."

"Of course you are. Come on."

This was bad.

Kara's skin crawled and though she wanted to argue, she didn't. The tone of Marlie's voice, so unlike her, made the ever-rebellious Kara obedient as she was prodded up the stairs. Marlie was holding the small flashlight, its weak beam illuminating the path.

At the top of the stairs, under the sloped ceilings where Kara was certain bats roosted, Marlie stopped, leaving Kara standing on the floorboards of the attic, while she hesitated on one step lower, so they were eye to eye, nose to nose. She shined the flashlight near her face, distorting her features in shadow, causing the small dimple on her chin to shadow and creating an eerie mask much like their brother Jonas's face when he held a flashlight beneath his face for a macabre effect as he told ghost stories.

But tonight was different.

Tonight wasn't a game. That much Kara knew.

"You need to stay here and wait for me to come back."

"No!"

"Just for a little while."

Kara shook her head. "I want Mama."

"I know, but I already told you that's not going to happen."

"Why?" Panic welled in her heart. "You're not leaving me here alone."

"Just for a little while."

"No!"

"Kara—"

"I'm not staying here. Why would you even say that?" Kara demanded.

"I just have to make sure it's safe, okay—?"

"No, it's not okay."

"Then I'll come get you. I promise."

"Safe from what?" Kara cried, freaking. Anytime her siblings added an "I promise," it was because they weren't telling the truth. "You said there were bad people here. Who?"

"I-I don't really know."

"What're they doing?"

"I'm not . . . I don't . . . I'm not sure, but I know this, there's something . . . something really bad, Kara."

"What . . . what's bad?"

"I don't know."

"And it's here."

"I . . . yes . . . please, just do as I say."

Kara suspected her sister was dodging the truth. "Where're Mama and Daddy?"

A beat. "Out."

"Liar." Why was Marlie lying to her?

"Kara—"

"What about Jonas and Sam and Donner?" Kara asked frantically. Her older half brothers. They'd all been here earlier. She'd seen them at dinner and after. Donner and Sam had been listening to music and playing video games, maybe even drinking, and Jonas, the loner, had been in his room practicing his ninja moves or whatever it was he always did. Sam had kidded him, calling him Jonas Joe-Judo. Which Jonas hated.

Marlie said, "Everyone's gone."

"Gone?" On Christmas Eve? That didn't seem right. "Then what're you afraid of?"

Marlie licked her lips nervously. Her voice was the merest of whispers. "As I said, there's someone here. Someone else. Someone bad."

"Who? How do you know?" This was crazy. "But you just said everyone was 'out' and now . . . You're scaring me."

"Good."

"I want Mama."

"I told you she's not here!" Marlie's voice was still a whisper, but there was an edge to it. Like Mama's when she got mad or frustrated with Kara's brothers. "Just listen to me, okay? You're going to stay here for a little while, until it's safe, and then I'll come back and—"

"No!" Marlie was going to leave her here, in the middle of the night, all alone?

14

"Just for a while," Marlie was saying again, but Kara was violently shaking her head.

"No, no! You can't. Don't leave me!" Frantic, Kara clawed wildly at her sister. Why was Marlie doing this? Why? At seven, she didn't understand why she was being left. Alone. Here in this dark, horrid attic that smelled like mold and was covered in dust and probably home to spiders and rats and wasps and every other gross thing in the world. "I'm not staying up here alone, Mar—"

"Shh. Keep quiet!" Marlie's hands tightened over Kara's forearms.

"Please—"

"Listen!" Marlie's voice was sharp. A whisper like the warning hiss of a snake.

She gave Kara a shake. Her fingers dug through the long sleeves of Kara's pajamas.

"Ow!"

"Don't say a word, Kara-Bear. Keep quiet. You hear me? I'm serious."

"But you can't leave me here." Not in this cold, drafty space situated under the eaves of the peaked roof. "I'll freeze!"

"You won't."

This wasn't right. Kara might be almost eight years old, but she knew this was wrong. All wrong. "You're lying!"

Marlie gripped her forearm so hard Kara dropped the flashlight and it rolled down the steps. "Damn it," she swore. "For once, Kara, just do as you're told." And then she was gone, nearly tripping over the flashlight as she fled down the stairs.

Kara took off after her but was a step behind and Marlie reached the door first, slid through and shut it.

Click.

Kara grabbed the door handle, but it wouldn't move.

Locked? The door is locked? Marlie has locked me in?

Fury and fear burned through her as she heard Marlie's swift footsteps as she hurried away.

No, no, no! "Marlie!" She rattled the door handle and pounded on the door, then as her rage eased a bit, thought better of it. This was no prank. Something was wrong. Seriously wrong. Something . . . evil. She swallowed back her fear and brushed aside the angry tears that had formed in her eyes. Her arms ached in the spots where her sister's fingers had clenched.

She wanted to scream, to yell, to beat her fists against the door so that someone would hear her, so that she could escape this sloped-ceilinged jail and breathe again.

But she didn't. Marlie's words, whispered like the sound of death, ran through her head. "It's complicated . . . and really scary."

Shivering, she bit her lip and stared at the door, a dark barrier to the rest of the world. She couldn't just sit here and wait.

What if whoever it was Marlie thought had come into the house came up the stairs and found her?

What if he hurt Marlie? What if he *killed* her? Kara's heart wrenched.

Again she wished for her mother and father. They would know what to do. But they were gone, according to Marlie, and she wouldn't lie. Not about that.

Or would she?

Teeth chattering, heart knocking erratically, Kara grabbed the flashlight and stared at the door, shivering and trying to hear something, anything over the wild beating of her heart. Her skin crawled.

She sat on the lowest step, clicking the tiny flashlight on, then off, watching its yellowish beam illuminate the back of the door for a second before she was swallowed in darkness again.

On.

Off.

On.

Click, click, click.

The light growing fainter each time she turned the flashlight on.

She couldn't just sit here and wait while the batteries in the flashlight died. What if Marlie never came back?

Kara wanted to rattle the door handle frantically, to scream and flail at the door. She reached for the handle again, her fingers curling over the cold lever. But she stopped herself. It would do no good. And probably cause unwanted attention. No, she had to be smart. She had to find another way to escape.

Determined, she climbed up the rickety steps again to the attic, where a single round window mounted high above and the faint moonlight cast the dimmest of light through the dusty, forgotten boxes piled everywhere. The boxes and crates were marked with words scribbled on them, some of which Kara could read: *Books. Clothes. Office.* Or marked with names: *Sam Jr. Jonas. Donner. Marlie.* Her sister and brothers. No box for her, the youngest, the only child of both mother and father. Not yet. She heard the rustle of something, something *alive* in the far corner. Tiny claws on the wood floor. A squirrel? Or a mouse . . . or a rat?

She shivered and was sorting through a box when she heard it—a horrid, bloodcurdling scream rising up from a lower floor.

"AAAAHHHHHGGG!"

Kara jumped. Nearly peed herself. She sucked in her breath as the horrid wail echoed through the house.

What was that? *Who* was that?

Marlie?

Mama?

Or someone else?

Thud!

The house shook.

Something really big had fallen.

Kara's mouth turned to dust and she blinked against tears.

Was it a body?

Someone hurt and screaming, then falling?

Marlie?

"Mama," she mouthed around a sob.

Don't be a baby.

Pulse pounding, fear nearly paralyzing her, she forced herself to sweep the flashlight's thin beam over the boxes again and spied the one marked *Office*. It was closed, cardboard flaps folded but gaping. She shined the light inside and saw yellowed papers, an old stapler, envelopes, a tape dispenser and a pair of dusty scissors. She picked up the scissors and a paper clip that held some papers together, then silently made her way down the stairs to the door.

As she'd seen Jonas do at the locked bathroom door when she'd been spying on him, she took the paper clip, straightened it as best she could and slid it into the small hole beneath the lever. She'd tried it once before on Sam Junior and Donner's room and it had worked and now . . . she wiggled the tiny wire, working it inside the lock as she strained to hear any other noise coming from the other side of the door.

Come on, come on, she silently said to herself,

pulling the wire out once before sliding it back through the hole and twisting gently . . . feeling it move. With a soft *click* the lock gave way and fighting back her fear, she took a deep breath, held her scissors in one hand and pushed the door open.

CHAPTER 2

The hallway was empty.

And nearly dark, the only light coming from the far end, where a shadowy illumination crawled up the staircase.

I don't think we're alone. . . .

Kara licked her lips, as she had a hundred times before when she was sneaking around this old house. She made her way to the smaller staircase and crept down the steps in the darkness, her skin feeling too tight for her body, her lungs barely able to draw in a breath.

She slipped onto the second floor and was vaguely aware of the music again as she crept into her bedroom. It was empty, but as she shined her flashlight's beam over the room, she noticed the pile of clothes were still on Marlie's bed. Folded clothes and boots near her open suitcase. Her own bed was as she'd left it, the covers thrown back and crumpled.

But her sister wasn't inside.

She bit her lip.

Fought fear.

Heard the strains of the same Christmas carol seeping through the house.

". . . All is calm, all is bright . . ."

Barely breathing, she made her way along the

hall to Jonas's room. It was the smallest of the bedrooms and even messier than usual. The bed unmade, junk on his desk, clothes and games tossed over the floor and . . . Oh, God! An unblinking eye reflecting her flashlight's beam.

She dropped the flashlight and bit back a scream. Shrinking backward to the door just as she realized she was looking at the stuffed head of a deer that had been mounted on the wall and now lay on the floor, antlers propping it up.

Crap!

Her heart felt as if it might fly out of her chest.

It was just the deer. Long dead. Stupid dead animals were mounted all over this house and they'd always creeped her out. She snagged the flashlight and swept the beam over the rest of the mess. Not far from the stag's head, pushed against a half-drunk bottle of Gatorade, an eagle was sprawled, feathers everywhere, and she realized the bird hadn't just fallen from its perch on the wall but had been sliced and . . . beheaded. The body with its curled talons was still attached to the stand, but the head was separate, the sharp beak digging into the carpet, glassy eyes condemning.

Her insides turned to water and she raised the beam of the flashlight to the wall over Jonas's closet, to the spot where a sword had been mounted. The weapon was a relic from some long-ago war. The weapon was never supposed to be handled, never to be taken down from its spot on the wall.

Never.

Now it was missing.

Kara wasn't surprised by that.

Just this afternoon as Kara had passed by his room with the door ajar, she'd spied him with the sword in his hand, and he had been swinging it and lunging with it like he was in some kind of fantasy battle. A ninja or something.

Idiot, she'd thought at the time.

Now she was scared to death.

Her fingers tightened around the handle of the scissors.

The next room belonged to both of her older brothers. Donner. He was really Marlie's brother, both of them Mama's kids. Mama had them before she'd married Daddy. And Sam Junior and Jonas were brothers, too. Daddy's sons. They had a different "real" mom. That left her, Kara, the only child of both Mama and Daddy.

Not that it mattered.

At least not to her.

And certainly not now.

She only wished she could find any one of them.

The older boys' room was the same as it always was—a mess of rumpled sheets and coverlets sliding to the floor to tangle with clothes, shoes, boots and candy bar wrappers and cans. Sam

23

Junior's backpack was pushed against the foot of his bed, his new Nokia cell phone on the dresser. He was always the neater of the two and never without his new phone. So why had he left it?

Her throat tightened as she swung the dying beam of her flashlight over the room. Donner's area was a wreck. With a small pizza box long empty, a pack of cigarettes only partially hidden under his pillow.

Nerves stretched to the breaking point, she crept into the hallway again and heard the music once more.

"Glories stream from heaven afar . . ."

Coming from the CD player downstairs.

Heart in her throat, Kara inched to the servants' stairs again, avoiding the huge carved staircase that curved up from the massive entry and living area. Instead, she crept noiselessly down the back steps to the kitchen, where no lights burned. The only illumination came from outside, where moonglow reflected on the snow. Quietly she slipped past the freestanding island, then under an archway to the dining area, where a massive table stretched from the butler's pantry to the French doors leading outside. Through the paned windows, she saw a thick mantle of snow on the veranda beyond which the lake glimmered, partially obscured by sparse stands of snow-crusted firs and pines.

Inside, the table had been set for the next day, crystal glasses glinting red with light from the remaining embers of the fire Daddy had lit in the fireplace earlier. She'd watched him stack wood that he'd taken from the built-in cupboard near the firebox and light old newspaper and kindling until flames caught and crackled. The smell of smoke was stronger here and something else . . . something odd, sweetly metallic. In front of the big window, the Christmas tree stood at an angle, white lights blinking, branches broken.

Not like it had been.

The back of Kara's neck twitched.

And then she noticed the walls.

The dark spots that drizzled downward.

Red.

Thick.

Blood!

Staining the walls in scarlet rivulets that pooled almost purple on the floor.

She let out a scream and her stomach threatened to hurl. She took two steps into the living room and screamed again. There, lying on Mama's white carpet, was her brother Donner, his throat slashed, his skin pale as milk, his blond hair streaked red, his eyes staring upward and unblinking. She stepped backward and her heel rammed into something soft, only to turn and find Sam Junior, curled up, his hair matted red with blood, his mouth open, eyes open and

25

vacant. "Noooo!" She screamed again, gasping and sobbing, her stomach cramping.

She dropped the scissors and flashlight and started to turn when she noticed Jonas, partially hidden by the Christmas tree, his face and shirt covered in blood, a hank of black hair falling over his face. Eyes open.

Hyperventilating, she stared at him and screamed when she saw him blink.

He was alive?

But how?

"K-k-k-k-k-a . . . karrrra . . ." he said, his voice a garbled whisper.

She could only stare at his blood-smeared face.

"Get . . . he . . . he . . . get . . . help . . ." He tried to lever himself up but fell back. "Go . . . run . . ." he whispered, his words sounding wet. His eyes rolled up in his head and she backed away, her feet slipping on the blood that seemed everywhere—on the walls, on the floor, sprayed to the ceiling.

"Marlie!" she yelled. Where the hell was she? "*Mar*lie!" Choking out her sister's name, she stumbled from the room and forced herself to the short hallway that led to her parents' bedroom.

Sobbing wildly, Kara gasped for breath as she pushed open the door and saw the horror within. "No!" she cried, breaking down completely. "No, no, no!" Both of her parents were in their bed, Mama in her silk pajamas and her father in only

26

his boxer shorts. Both of her parents were covered in the blood that stained the sheets and spattered the bedstead and wall. Mama's blond hair was mussed, her eyes glassy and set, and Daddy's face was a scary bluish color, blood sliding from his gaping mouth. Over his naked torso, huge, ugly gashes exposed his flesh, and blood matted the curling hair of his chest.

In a daze, she backed out of the room.

Dead.

They were all dead.

Except Jonas.

She started back to the living room, to her brother, when she thought of the phone.

She had to call and get help.

9-1-1.

But she couldn't go into Mama's bedroom again, she couldn't see her parents that way . . . no, she backed up, scrambling to her feet. There was a phone in the kitchen and Sam Junior's new cell phone upstairs. She'd call the police. Get an ambulance. But as she raced through the living room, she saw Jonas had collapsed again. She was probably too late!

She started for him.

The front door swung open.

Marlie?

No!

Not her sister.

A man.

A big man filled the doorway.

The killer!

She knew it.

Oh. God.

She let out a short scream and spun, her bare heel sliding in a pool of sticky blood.

"Holy shit! What the fu—?" the man said.

He'd seen her!

She took off at a dead run.

As fast as her feet would carry her, she flew through the dining room, knocking over a chair before she sped across the short span of the butler's pantry to the kitchen.

"Hey!" The voice was deep and male. Commanding. "Hey! You! Stop!"

She yanked the door open, sprinted across the porch and jumped from the steps to the snow-covered backyard.

"Stop! Little girl!"

No way!

His loud voice only propelled her farther and faster through the drifts. From the corner of her eye she saw his massive shape on the porch.

"Stop! Hey, little girl—"

Without thinking, she ducked under the lowest limbs of the fir trees and cut to the back path, the one that led to the lake. The snow here was packed, as if someone else had trod on it, and it felt like ice between her toes. Still she raced unheeding as branches slapped at her face and

28

berry vines clawed at her pajamas. She heard her sleeve rip, felt the prick of a thorn, but she didn't stop, didn't dare chance a look behind her. Her lungs were starting to burn, her breath coming out in a foggy mist, but she didn't slow. Her heart was pounding and she kept her head down, skimming through a copse of trees, feeling snow fall onto her shoulder as she brushed against the branches.

What had happened?

Who had killed Mama and Daddy?

Why? She felt the tears start to freeze on her cheeks as she ran through the thickets and she saw in her mind's eye her family, bloodied and slashed, horrid images flashing through her mind, appearing behind the trees that were a blur. Her parents unmoving as they lay in their own blood. Sam Junior and Donner with their hair matted in blood, eyes glazed as they lay next to each other. Jonas raising up, telling her to *run. Get help.* And Marlie, ghost white, peeking from behind a long-needled pine, urging her to keep going. *Run, Kara!* she yelled over the pounding in Kara's ears.

All in her imagination, she knew.

All ghosts.

Her vision blurred with tears, but she forced her legs to keep moving, her near-frozen feet to fly through the snow.

She heard him coming after her, the heavy

footsteps pounding on the path, the crack of a brittle branch as he passed.

Faster. Run faster!

Kara was breathing hard, but she saw the glitter of the lake. Through the forest, the icy surface gleamed in the moonlight, beckoning. On the far shore, lights of a few houses glowed like beacons.

If she could make it.

She could!

She would!

Faster. Run faster!

She slammed her toe into an exposed root and flew forward, crying out. Pain pulsed through her foot and she stumbled a few steps, temporarily hobbled, and she wanted to give up, to fling herself into the snow and cry.

No! Keep running. Get help. Jonas is still alive!

She plowed forward.

The killer was closing in.

She heard his ragged breathing, felt his footsteps shake the ground. But he, too, was struggling and when he called out, he was gasping. "For the love of God, girl, stop! I'm not . . . I'm not going . . . I won't hurt you."

She didn't believe him for an instant.

Move! Her mind was screaming at her and she was nearly panting.

She reached the bank, her feet sliding out from under her as she slipped downward toward the lake.

"Stop!" the man shouted. "Jesus Christ, stop!"

She hurled her body forward, tumbling onto the glassy surface, skidding away from the shoreline.

"Hey!" he was yelling again, his voice raw.

She ignored him and sliding and spinning, she finally made it to her feet, but she couldn't get traction and had trouble running. She should have run around the shore. But it was too late.

The killer was on the ice.

No!

She threw herself forward, her feet sliding wildly as she willed herself across the icy expanse toward the winking lights, where she would find someone to help her, someone in one of those cabins. She had to.

"Don't! Oh, shit!"

He followed, slipping out onto the ice.

More panicked than ever, she scrambled forward wildly only to fall flat and bang her chin.

"Stop!"

He was making his way across the frozen surface.

Getting nearer!

She had to outrun him! Had to get away!

Another glance over her shoulder and she saw him in the corner of her eye.

He was too close! Only a few steps away.

Kara redoubled her efforts as he took a swipe at her.

Crrrrraaaacccck!

She felt a shifting and saw, to her horror, the ice fissuring beneath her feet. First a single jagged line, then cracking like a giant spider web beneath her.

He froze. "Shit!"

The web splintered.

"Oh, God," he said. "Stop!"

In the back of her mind, she thought about the fact that she could barely swim. She didn't move.

But it was too late.

Another loud, ominous crack, almost a moan, reached her ears.

Then, in an instant, the ice beneath her feet shattered.

Screaming, Kara fell through, plunging deep into the frigid depths that swallowed her whole.

She sank like a stone into the darkness, into the lake's frigid grasp.

Flailing wildly, fighting panic, she tried to swim through the air bubbles and chunks of ice to the surface, where she spied the moon through the layer of ice above. Lake water swirled around her and filled her throat.

Still, if she could reach the surface and—

More of the thin ice splintered, the water around her roiled and she was tossed about as the man fell through, his huge body, so close to hers, creating waves that pushed her away from the dark space free of ice, away from the air she so desperately needed.

No, no, no!

She tried to bob up, kicking to get back to the ice-free surface, while he, too, was struggling to get to air, his heavy clothes and boots like dead weight on him. But he saw her and reached out.

He reached for her and she slipped out of his grasp, trying to swim, flailing frantically, panicked as she searched desperately for the surface, for the moon riding high in the night sky. Instead, she found darkness. Water all around her. Her lungs on fire.

Swim, Kara-Bear. Swim!

She heard Marlie's voice in her head.

But it was no use.

What little air she had in her lungs escaped in a rush of towering bubbles, and her lungs ached and burned.

This dizzying black world of the lake was spinning around her.

She coughed only to lose air and gain water.

She kicked and flailed, but it was no good. She couldn't find the hole in the ice, didn't know what was up and what was down.

Don't give up, Kara, don't!

Marlie's voice. Distant and faint.

Kara's lungs were near bursting when she let go. Her panic subsided as she spun in lazy circles and was only vaguely aware of arms surrounding her in the gathering darkness. The world turned

eerily black and surreally quiet and then . . . then, as if from a faraway place, she heard the slow, sure strains of the music again.

"Sleep in heavenly peace."

CHAPTER 3

TWENTY YEARS LATER

"You know what they say, Kara," Dr. Zhou suggested, her thin eyebrows raising a bit as she sat in an overstuffed chair in her office on the second floor of a historic house set in northwest Portland.

"No, but 'they've' always got something profound on their minds. I'm guessing that hasn't changed," Kara responded, then asked, "Ever wonder who 'they' are?"

"Oh, I know who they are. The sages. The wise ones through the ages." Dr. Zhou's dark eyes sparkled a bit, catching the afternoon light slanting in from the window. She was a small woman. Petite. Jet-black hair, intelligent eyes and a lean body from running marathons.

"Well, they've got an advantage, don't they? You know, the benefit of hindsight and all that." Kara's gaze slid to the window. The December sun was peeking through high, rolling clouds that promised more snow, sunlight gleaming on icicles hanging from the eaves. Like crystal daggers. She'd heard on her Jeep's radio that more snow was predicted, a foot on Christmas Eve. Kara shuddered at the thought. There was no dreaming of a white Christmas for her. More like a nightmare.

"You're right."

"So, what great insight are they offering today? Enlighten me."

"That guilt is a jealous lover."

"Oh, save me." Kara didn't want to hear it.

"She doesn't leave room for any other emotions, chases them away, guards her position in a person's heart feverishly."

"And guilt is a woman? Of course." Kara let out a bitter laugh. "So now, you're not just my psychologist. Now you've graduated to philosopher?" She couldn't keep the edge from her voice.

"Just a gentle reminder."

As if Kara could ever fight the survivor's guilt that was her constant companion and had been for two decades.

Twenty years of therapy, of becoming an adult, of facing the trauma that had left her scarred for life, and she wasn't anywhere near to being "okay." She knew there was no cure, but she had been told there was a life out there for her, a "normal" life, as she'd been told by a child psychologist, a teen counselor and now Dr. Zhou, the third professional she'd seen as an adult.

Kara wasn't sure that "normal" was in the cards for her.

"You said you aren't seeing any more ghosts," Dr. Zhou said. "Right?"

"I should never have told you," Kara said. "It was just a silly dream."

"A silly *recurring* dream."

"Yeah, but nothing for a while now," Kara lied. "Not for two, maybe three months."

Dr. Zhou's eyes were assessing. She leaned back in her chair, tapping a pencil to her lips. As if she didn't believe her patient. "What about the feeling that you're being watched? That someone might be stalking you?"

Kara lifted a shoulder. "That's better, too."

"Is it?" More disbelief as she dropped the pencil into a cup on a small table.

"Yes!" Kara said.

Frowning thoughtfully, the little lines appearing between her eyebrows more distinct, Dr. Zhou said, "Look, Kara, I know this is a rough time of the year for you, and that makes my going away for the holidays difficult, but you've got Dr. Prescott's number and my cell if it's an emergency."

"Isn't it always an emergency?" Kara asked, half joking. She wasn't going to call a different psychologist, wasn't going to have a session with a new person in a new office. Wasn't about to start over, or bring Dr. Zhou's associate up to speed. No, she was comfortable here in this room with its icy green walls, soft furniture and framed watercolors of fields of flowers. And with this shrink. Finally. She'd gone through her share of others.

"Comes with the territory." Dr. Zhou stood and stretched out a hand. Then when Kara tried to take it, Zhou hugged her instead. The doctor was a few inches shorter than Kara, but that didn't stop her from patting Kara's back. Then she straightened. "I'll see you January seventh. Yes?"

"Unless I'm all better."

"Uh-huh." There was more than a note of sarcasm in the psychologist's tone. They both knew that not only were the holidays the worst time of the year for Kara, but this year there was an added wrinkle: Jonas, her surviving brother, was getting out of prison. In two days.

Oh. Joy.

"Merry Christmas," Dr. Zhou said.

"Merry Christmas to you, too." Kara's voice caught and she felt she might break down, so she gathered her coat and scarf and left rapidly before the stupid tears fell. As she hurried down the carpeted hallway, past a few other doors with nameplates for a variety of medical offices, she slipped her arms through the sleeves of her long coat and wrapped her scarf quickly around her neck.

She pushed her way through the glass doors of this building, originally a three-story house, and crossed a small parking lot, where her dirty Jeep was waiting near an ice-crusted pothole, and unlocked her SUV remotely.

The snow had been shoveled and salted away,

but now the sky was threatening again, the clouds overhead turning steely and dark, night fast approaching. She checked the interior.

No one hiding.

Once inside, she fired up the engine. By habit, she locked her doors, then checked her mirrors. No one appeared in the reflection, no deranged killer out to get her, but she did catch sight of her own worried eyes, a hazel color that threatened to fill again with tears. "Stop it!" she said, then turned her iPhone off of silent mode, set it in her cup holder and hit the gas. The Jeep squirreled backward before she rammed the gearshift into drive.

Her cell beeped and she glanced at the screen.

Aunt Faiza's name popped up on the screen.

"Nope," she muttered, "definitely not now. Maybe not ever." She wasn't going to deal with the woman who had so eagerly agreed to raise her only to tap into her inheritance—an inheritance that she would finally be able to claim when she turned twenty-eight in two weeks' time. Nor did she want to hear any of Faiza's nosy questions or her wearisome recriminations. That part of Kara's life was over. The fact that Auntie Fai still lived in the family home, a mansion in the West Hills overlooking the city of Portland, should have bothered her; by rights Kara would inherit it. But she didn't care. The grand home with its seven bedrooms, sweeping staircase and breathtaking views was only a painful reminder of a life of which she'd been robbed. Aunt Faiza had been her appointed guardian, and she and her musician boyfriend had taken over the place to care for Kara, but their lack of attention had been palpable, and Kara had spent most of her growing-up years with Merritt Margrove and his second wife, Helen. Their small home on the east side of the river, a bungalow tucked into the narrow streets of Sellwood, had been more of a home than the big house on the forested hills.

Hitting the gas, she sped into the flow of traffic and cut off a lumbering pickup. For her efforts she earned an angry shake of the red-capped driver's fist and an angry blast of his horn, but she didn't care, just kept driving. The phone rang again. Aunt Faiza wasn't giving up.

"Great." She took the next corner at the last minute, backtracking slightly to wheel into the crowded parking lot of the liquor store. "Bad idea," Kara said under her breath, but cut the engine, stepped out, locked the car and pocketed her keys as she walked inside.

The territory was familiar, the transaction easy.

Two bottles of Merlot and, for good measure, a fifth of vodka.

After all, the holidays were fast approaching. And her brother was being released from the big house. Time to celebrate, and God knew Kara needed a little Christmas cheer. Well, make that *a lot* of Christmas cheer.

The woman at the register was in her fifties and smelled of cigarettes and breath mints. Her face was lined prematurely, and her orange-tinged hair was partially covered by a jaunty elf's cap complete with a bell that jingled as she moved her head.

Merry Christmas.

Kara paid in cash and ignored the curious look the cashier cast as she handed back change and bagged the bottles.

Damn. The woman was trying to place her.

Kara loved her anonymity.

Which, she knew, was about to be shattered.

As if to reinforce her thoughts, she noticed a newspaper on a nearby rack. The headline screamed: KILLER IN COLD LAKE MASSACRE TO BE RELEASED. And in smaller letters: JONAS MCINTYRE TO BE SET FREE.

Kara's stomach soured. Bile rose up her throat.

As the next customer, a sixtysomething woman in a long red coat and matching beret, set her bottles of wine on the counter, Kara grabbed the top copy in the stack of papers and said, "I'll take this, too." She dropped a five on the counter.

"Wait a second," the patron said in a snooty, put-upon voice, her lips, the exact shade of her coat, turning into a tight frown. "I was next."

"You were. But I was here first. Merry

41

Christmas." As the woman gaped at her insolence, Kara told the cashier, "Put the change in there," and pointed to a jar for donations to a local dog rescue.

"Well, I never!" the customer said.

"I'm sure you never did." Kara tucked the newspaper under her arm, leaving the woman in the beret glaring after her.

Not smart, Kara. Remember: You want to blend into the shadows. Remain anonymous. "Yeah, right."

Bottles clinking in the bag, she hurried outside, where night had fallen, darkness settling in, streetlamps glowing while snow began to fall again.

She checked the back, then dropped the bag on the passenger seat and pulled out of the lot, the woman in the beret sending her a dark look as she slipped behind the wheel of a white Mercedes.

Once more, with a little less speed, Kara melded into the traffic streaming out of the downtown area. Stop and go. Brake lights and headlights even though it was only four in the afternoon, evening closing in quickly this time of year. The newspaper, unfolded on the passenger seat, mocking her with its headlines and picture of the family's mountain cabin vacations sprawled across the front page of the *Register*. Well, if you could call a three-storied house built by a famous architect a hundred years earlier a "cabin."

42

Her parents had. Ornate and grand, ordered to specific design by her great-great-grandfather, the "cabin" still stood, rotting and rusting, a FOR SALE sign still in place, she assumed, though there were no takers for the rambling old home where an entire family had been slaughtered. The tragedy had earned its own names: the Cold Lake Massacre or The McIntyre Massacre, each one equally chilling to her.

As she slowed for a red light, Kara's cell rang again and she saw only a local number. No name. No caller ID. "Forget it."

Since the announcement of Jonas's imminent release, she'd been besieged by reporters calling her, and she refused to talk to them. Even that irritating Wesley Tate. No, make that *especially Wesley Tate*. He was too clever. Too charming. Too good-looking and too close to the story.

His father, an off-duty cop, had saved Kara from drowning. And he'd died in the process. Again, she felt more than a modicum of guilt. She probably owed his son some of her time, to tell him her side of the story.

But no. Not a good idea. No matter how close Tate was to the story, how emotional it might be to him, he was first and foremost a reporter, a male reporter.

And Kara was definitely in her man-hating mode right now. Because of Brad Jones, whom she'd kicked to the curb just two weeks earlier.

Brad, like the few boyfriends she'd had before him, had proved to be more interested in her because of her brush with infamy than in Kara as a woman. And, of course, there was her inheritance, what was left of it, the portion Auntie Fai hadn't had a chance to squander.

"Big surprise." She switched on the radio to chase away any lingering regrets over Brad and heard, of course, Christmas music. Worse yet, the strains of "Silent Night" filled the car.

". . . *yon Virgin, tender and mild—*"

"Nope. Don't think so." God, where was "Rockin' Around the Christmas Tree" when you needed it? She clicked off the radio, then drove the next hour in relative silence until she passed the WELCOME TO WHIMSTICK sign, which announced that the population was just over twelve thousand.

Kara skirted the main section of town, easing through side streets and alleys until she finally turned down the quiet street where her home was located. She barely knew any of her neighbors, just the way she wanted it. Three doors down, just below the crest of a small hill, she pulled into her drive. Thankfully there were no news vans or reporters clustered on the snow-covered street. But just wait. That would happen. The second Jonas McIntyre was a free man.

With a touch of her finger to the remote, the garage door started rolling upward and before it was completely open, she drove inside. She hit the button again, closing the garage tight. Less than a minute later she was in the house, turning on lights, adjusting the heat, and being greeted by Rhapsody, her rescue dog who was probably a little terrier, probably some Labrador retriever, and certainly some pit bull, but that was all just a best guess. Until she did a canine DNA test on the dog, Kara would never know. And she wasn't about to put out money to unlock the secrets of Rhapsody's muddled lineage. Who cared? All Kara knew was that this shaggy fifty-pound mutt with her wise gold eyes loved Kara as no one else had since she was a child.

"Yeah, you're a good girl," she said, ruffling the dog's ears and smiling as Rhapsody spun in excited, tight circles until she was little more than a caramel-colored blur. "Okay, okay, I get it. You get your treat," she said, retrieving a bottle of red wine from the bag. "And I get mine. Sit."

Rhapsody sat, eyes focused on Kara until she was tossed a bacon-flavored biscuit. Leaping, the dog caught the treat on the fly, then trotted to the living room to crunch it on her bed while Kara found a corkscrew in a top drawer and went to work.

By the time Rhapsody returned to stand by the door, Kara was pouring wine into a stemmed glass. Sipping the Merlot, she unlocked the door and stepped outside to watch as Rhapsody flew across the patio, startling a winter bird from its perch on a branch. The dog was her best friend— make that her only friend. Her fault. She never trusted any acquaintance she'd made over the years. Too many people had just wanted to get close to her because they were: a) curious about her past, b) wanted something from her, or c) all of the above. Friends just weren't worth the trouble. Dogs, especially Rhapsody with her undying affection, were so much better. And boyfriends? Ugh. Forget it.

Snow was falling again, tiny, powdery flakes that promised not to let up as another downy layer was added to the four inches that had already accumulated. Rhapsody galloped from one end of the yard to the other, letting off pent-up energy and cutting a new trail in the white mantle. The snowy lawn was long and narrow, giving the dog enough room to run, but surrounded by a fence and barrier of thick, impenetrable arborvitae, rhododendrons and laurel. Enough privacy that Kara couldn't see her neighbors, nor could they spy on her. Which was perfect. Now the greenery was covered in snow and reminded Kara of the firs and pines flanking the cabin and that horrid night she ran through the woods, the night of the tragedy that had changed her life for—

"Stop it!" she said so loudly that Rhapsody, nose buried in the snow near the corner of the house, looked up suddenly, her ears cocked, her eyes ready to focus on an intruder. "Sorry," Kara said to the dog, then, "Come on. Finish up out here. It's freezing."

She took another long swallow of wine and felt herself beginning to warm from the inside out while the dog romped and played in the snow, kicking up white clods and shaking the icy powder from her nose. Oh, to be so carefree, Kara thought wistfully as she heard the faraway sound of a jet engine. She looked skyward, trying to peer through the thick clouds. Somewhere high above was a plane full of people going somewhere, skimming through the night sky to destinations unknown. She blinked, snowflakes catching on her lashes.

What she wouldn't do to fly away.

To forget.

But she'd already tried that. A trip to Europe years ago. Didn't help. All the tours and exhibits, the castles and art galleries and the throngs of people couldn't keep her thoughts from turning back to Cold Lake. The Eiffel Tower, Louvre, Notre Dame in Paris, Big Ben and Buckingham Palace in London, the castles on the Rhine, a villa on Lake Como, a room over a bar in Belfast . . . all was now a blur and the pain still resided, the guilt still held fast. And all the moves she'd made, Portland with Aunt Faiza, then a junior college in California, a transfer to Denver, and finally graduating from LSU in Baton Rouge, and still, she hadn't been able to shake off the memories. New friends, new places, fresh starts. To no avail.

Had she really thought she could outrun the past?

How foolish.

And how ironic that the one job she'd been able to land had been here in Oregon, less than an hour from the shores of Cold Lake and the home where all of the horror had happened. Her life had come full circle, the perfect opportunity to "face the past" and "confront her demons," as she'd been advised for years, but to what end? She was still a hot mess. Probably would be for life.

And the house she'd grown up in? The one in Portland that she'd inherited, or would inherit in less than two weeks. Currently occupied by Aunt Faiza, who had moved in within a month of the tragedy. She had proclaimed to the court that Kara needed "stability," "a home she knew," "a place that would anchor her." But the old house high in the West Hills was anything but her home, a place she avoided, even going so far as to live with Merritt Margrove and his second wife rather than stay in that huge house overlooking the city, a place that seemed to harbor ghosts of the past. Though the bloody massacre had occurred sixty miles from the hillside home with its incredible views, it had never felt like home to Kara. Not after what had happened. She felt her throat tighten and her eyes burn at the long-ago memories of a happy childhood that had been severed by a maniac in the mountains one Christmas Eve.

"Oh, get over your bad self," she said aloud, and noticed she'd drained her glass. Time for another. And to end this pity party. After all, who said those memories were so happy, anyway? Her own recollections were clouded, riddled with holes, and all those bits of nostalgia were just that, bits and pieces, maybe even dreams, patched together, but still ragged. Right now, she didn't want to think about it. "Come on, Rhap," she called to the dog.

She walked inside and Rhapsody trotted after her, shaking snow and water from her furry coat. "Yeah, go ahead. Clean floors are overrated anyway." After locking the door, Kara peeled out of her coat and scarf, hanging them by the back door, then unzipped her boots and kicked them to a spot next to her umbrella stand. "Dinner?" she asked, and fed the dog before refilling her glass.

As she headed upstairs to her bedroom, she glanced at her watch. Barely after six. "Good enough," she said, and changed from jeans and a sweater into her favorite baggy PJs.

She caught sight of herself in the mirror, looking pale and wan, the flannel pajamas at least a size too large, her teeth discolored from the red wine.

49

"Pathetic," she told her reflection. Where most twenty-seven-year-olds would just be gearing up for the night, she was shutting herself in. She'd tried the party scene, frequented clubs, met others her age, but since college, she hadn't had a lot of interest in going out. Probably one of the reasons she and Brad hadn't made it work. One of many.

She returned to the main level, topped off her glass and, in the living room, glanced at the bookcase flanking the fireplace and saw the one photograph she had of the two of them. Standing together, hoisting up champagne glasses in front of palm trees, while the Florida sun set behind them. A large crack had split the glass, evidence of their last fight, but Kara thought it appropriate to display the picture, fissure and all, even if it did remind her of the splitting ice on Cold Lake all those years ago.

Don't go there. She closed her mind to that train of thought.

And to Brad.

He was, as they say, history. She switched on the gas fire, sat on the couch and patted the cushion next to her so Rhapsody would join. The dog hopped up. Remotely she turned on the TV, a flat-screen mounted near the fireplace. From habit she channel-surfed, past the shopping network, cooking channels, home improvement and the likes of *Gator Busters* and *Real Gold*

50

Diggers until she found the news where the Cold Lake Massacre was front and center, relevant once more due to Jonas McIntyre's reversed conviction and imminent release. "Awesome," she muttered, and listened as a reporter recounted well-known facts while pictures of her family and the mountain home they'd shared filled the flat-screen. "Just . . . awesome."

The reporter recounted the story of that bloody night.

The facts, summed up, were:

Four people murdered: Samuel McIntyre and his wife, Zelda McIntyre, and two of their children, Samuel McIntyre Junior and Donner Robinson. Also dead at the scene: Detective Edmund Tate, a cop who had been vacationing for the holidays at a nearby home and who was credited for saving the life of Kara McIntyre, youngest daughter of Samuel and Zelda.

And still missing? Marlie Robinson, daughter of Zelda McIntyre and Zelda's first husband, Walter Robinson. Marlie hadn't been seen since late that night.

The elder Samuel McIntyre's second son, Jonas, who had miraculously survived the attack himself but had been severely injured, had been tried and convicted for the heinous crimes.

Now, due to new information, Jonas McIntyre's conviction had been overturned. He was being released after spending nearly two decades, over half his life, behind bars. Jonas, the reporter noted, had always sworn his innocence.

The police were reopening the very cold case.

Any information from the public would be appreciated.

"This just in," the anchor said, glancing down at his desk, then looking up sharply. "We have breaking news. We've just got a report that Jonas McIntyre was released this afternoon. Our reporter at the prison is standing by . . . Marilyn?"

"What?" Kara whispered, staring at the screen, and sure enough a female reporter bundled in a red ski jacket with the station's logo slashed across one shoulder was squinting against the falling snow. Behind her loomed the stark walls of Banhoff Prison.

Kara stared at the screen, at the huge concrete structure that housed some of the worst criminals in Oregon's history. She'd been in that building, visited Jonas there, noting the guard towers and razor wire atop the cement walls. She swallowed hard, her heart pounding in her ears. Jonas was out? Already? And no one had told her?

A red chyron with the words: JONAS MCINTYRE, CONVICTED IN THE COLD LAKE MASSACRE, HAS JUST BEEN RELEASED FROM PRISON.

CHAPTER 4

Oh. God.

Kara's knees went weak.

The reporter was speaking and Kara tried to concentrate. "That's right, Elliot, we just learned that Jonas McIntyre walked out of this prison earlier this afternoon. He'd been originally scheduled to be released later this week, and we don't yet know why the date was changed but—"

The rest of the report was a blur.

Kara stared at the screen, not seeing the news desk or reporter or even the prison, not hearing the report. Instead, she was caught in the web of images of that frigid, horrid night. Her mind spun to what she did remember: the red and blue lights of the police vehicles strobing to reflect on the snow. Jonas, bloody and unconscious on a stretcher, being carried to an ambulance. Her own chattering teeth, wet hair and near-frozen skin as she was wrapped in a towel by a woman police officer. Cops—dozens of them surrounding the house. Yellow tape, one end flapping beneath the low-hanging branches of a snow-laden fir.

She'd been in shock but unhurt, a doctor in the ER had said to a kind, heavy-set woman from Child Services who wore a hand-knit stocking cap and smelled of lavender. Aunt Faiza had rushed into the police station, her face red. She tried not to cry but had failed miserably. Shaking and sobbing, she'd held a numb and silent Kara tight.

Now Kara blinked, realizing tears had drizzled down her cheeks. Angrily, she swiped them away.

Jonas was free?

How had she not known?

Why hadn't someone contacted her?

Oh, right? How many calls did you refuse to answer and delete?

Absently she took a swallow from her glass. Saw that her hand was shaking, the wine sloshing wildly.

Calm down. So he's out. So what?

You don't think he's a killer, do you?

She bit her lip.

Oh, Kara. Have you been lying to yourself all this time?

"Shut up!" she said, and stood, spilling some of the Merlot as she walked to the sink and poured the reminder of the wine down the drain.

She glanced out the window, to the dark night beyond, and saw not only the flickering images of the TV in the glass, but her own stark reflection, her face pale as death, her eyes large and sunken, her cheeks hollow.

Who was she kidding?

Not Aunt Faiza. Not Dr. Zhou. Not even herself, if she were truthful. She was the same terrified girl who had been locked in the attic twenty years earlier, the girl who had witnessed the bloody aftermath of her family's slaughter.

Though Jonas had been the one on trial, Kara had felt as if she, too, were being judged.

It had been long ago, and yet close enough that she felt as if she could reach out and touch it. As if it had been just yesterday.

At eight years old, she'd sat on the hard chair in the witness stand, a waif of a girl. Terrified. Afraid she would say the wrong thing. She'd been coached and was smart, "older than her years," Auntie Fai had said, but still . . .

The judge, a dark-skinned woman in black robes and rimless glasses, had been seated high above her, sharp eyes assessing as the attorneys asked questions she barely understood, but knew the answers, had been primed with the right way to respond. They had approached her, had smiled, had outwardly appeared to be friendly, as if they were just curious, but she'd known better. Instinctively. Had sensed a darker purpose in their questions. She remembered forcing herself to meet their gazes, to appear calm while her fingers, as if of their own accord, had rubbed together endlessly.

It had seemed to go on forever.

Now, two decades later, Kara tried to shake off the feeling of being trapped that had been with her on that witness stand, to put it behind her and concentrate on the television screen. As an adult, she knew a lot more about what had happened and understood that she, a shell-shocked eight-year-old, had been manipulated, played by the prosecutors, by the defense attorneys, by her aunt. By every damned one.

She reached for her empty glass in the sink, thought better of it, and walked back to the TV area. She backed up the program, starting over again, with the reporter standing at the gates of the prison.

Mesmerized, she watched as the jacketed reporter on the screen was wrapping up and signing off. "Back to you, Elliot," she said, snowflakes collecting in her hair as the prison loomed behind her.

Kara's stomach twisted.

Banhoff Prison had been Jonas's home for all of his adult life.

Her cell buzzed and she tore her gaze from the TV to check the phone's tiny screen. Aunt Faiza's name appeared. Again. "Great." She wasn't in the mood to talk to the woman who had raised her, a woman as different from Mama as night to day. It was hard to believe they had been sisters.

"Stubborn as a mule," Mama had confided once while lighting a cigarette on the wide back porch of their city home, "and determined. Let me tell you, Kara, don't try to talk her out of anything.

It's a waste of breath." She'd taken a deep drag from her Virginia Slim, then exhaled and waved the smoke away. "I tried to tell her about Roger, but would she listen? Hell no." Mama's eyebrows had pulled together then as she'd smoked. Mama had never liked "Uncle" Roger, Faiza's boyfriend. Kara hadn't understood it then. At the time Roger had been tall and slim like Daddy, but he'd had thick brown hair and pale blue eyes that flashed in his perpetual tan, while Daddy had black hair that curled a little and light brown eyes that had seemed to look past everyone's façade and see right to the heart of them. But then Kara had lived with Faiza and Roger all of her preteen and high school years. And she'd seen Roger for what he really was—a man who could never hold a job, a man with huge appetites and, Kara suspected, even bigger secrets.

The phone rang in her hand again and Kara snapped back to the present and, gritting her teeth, said, "Faiza."

"There you are! I've been calling all after-noon!"

"Yeah, sorry." Then asked, "I just caught the news. Is Jonas really out of prison?"

"Why do you think I've been trying to reach you?" Faiza asked frantically. "Why didn't you pick up?"

"I've been busy."

"Doing what?" Faiza asked suspiciously. "What

could be so important that you couldn't answer the phone or text me back?"

What did it matter? Jonas was out of prison! But Kara answered. "Working." Not really true, but . . .

Faiza let out a soft, "Humph." A brassier blonde than Mama had been, Faiza wore her hair curly and sprayed so that it fanned out around her face, where she'd always applied what Kara's mother had referred to as extreme makeup. "She never got over the ultra-glam of the eighties," Mama had confided. "If Faiza had her way, she'd have curly hair to her shoulders, out-there bangs and jean jackets with huge shoulder pads." She hadn't toned it down much over the years. "Working," she repeated with more than a little edge of doubt.

She knew Faiza didn't think her working as a substitute teacher was a serious job for a woman in her late twenties, and had said so often enough. Too bad. Kara had learned after college that she wasn't cut out for an elementary classroom; too bad she'd learned that sorry fact while student teaching and already had earned her degree, another fact Faiza hadn't understood.

"Why didn't you change your major?" she'd asked a hundred times over.

"Why didn't I?" Kara had always thrown back at her, not ever explaining that once she'd been on a path, she wanted to just get done with it, through college as quickly as possible. The

58

degree had been a requirement for her to inherit her portion of her parents' estate, and she'd earned it in three years rather than four because college life hadn't been for her. She'd holed up in her dorm room, then apartment, and studied, unable to ever get into the swing of campus life, and even put in the extra hours and another year for her master's. Another requirement to gain her inheritance according to her parents' wills.

Now wasn't the time to dwell on it. Not with her brother out of stir. "So Jonas is . . . where?"

"Unknown. So far. But he'll turn up, let me tell you. Like a damned bad penny."

"But—"

"Listen, you probably would have been the first to know if you'd taken the time to pick up the damned phone." Faiza sounded put out. "You must've seen that I called, heard my message. Or read my damned texts!"

"I've also had a few appointments." At least that wasn't a lie. Before Dr. Zhou, Kara had visited her accountant and learned just how badly her once-healthy trust fund had dwindled. Significantly.

Yeah, it had just been a stellar day.

Kara's stomach twisted, she peeled herself from the couch and with Rhapsody at her heels made her way to the kitchen, where she poured herself another big glass of wine. No restaurant pour for her, not while dealing with Faiza.

Faiza said, "I tried to let you know, to warn you that Jonas was getting out."

"I knew he was going to be released. You'd have to live in Outer Mongolia not to know that," Kara snapped.

Faiza ignored her sarcasm. "I meant today."

"I thought it was scheduled for next week."

"So did I . . . but that was wrong. But it got changed somehow. Who knows? Now he's a free man, your half brother." She said it distastefully, as if the words were bitter. "And believe it or not, he had the nerve—the nerve, mind you—to call me. Your mother's sister. That murdering son of a . . ." She stopped herself, and Kara heard her take in an audible deep breath. "He was, I mean, he *is* your brother."

"Who claims he's innocent."

There was a snort on the other end of the line. "That's what they all say."

Kara kept sipping as her aunt added softly, "He wanted your number."

"What?" Kara choked on her wine, spilling the red liquid on her pajamas and the kitchen floor. "You didn't give it to him," she sputtered. She wasn't ready to face Jonas, not without a wall of thick prison glass between them.

A pause.

"Faiza?" Kara prodded.

"What was I supposed to do?" her aunt asked rhetorically. "He was going to get it anyway."

60

"I don't want to talk to him."

"Who does?" But Auntie Fai, as Kara had called her while growing up, did sound a little contrite. "Okay, okay. Look, I'm sorry. Really. But you know, one way or another, you're going to have to face him. Face what he did. He's the reason, Kara, for everything that happened."

"I don't believe it."

"You never have, but I'm serious here. Okay? Despite the fact that he's out due to a police screwup, Jonas McIntyre is an insane killer."

"He's your nephew."

"No, honey, I'm not related to him at all. My sister was married to his father for eight years, but I never liked that kid. Never. Always thought there was something wrong with him. His mother . . . well, *that* has nothing to do with this, I suppose. Look, I've got to run now, but I just wanted to give you a heads-up."

"Wait—" Suddenly Kara wanted more information from her aunt.

"Seriously, Roger's in the car waiting. Oh, Christ. He just honked the damned horn!" Her voice was suddenly muffled. "I'm coming, I'm coming, hold on to your frickin' horses." Into the phone she said, "Later, hon. Gotta go." Before Kara could object, Faiza disconnected.

Kara wiped the wine from the floor with a wet paper towel, dabbed at the stains on her pajamas, and took another drink. The bottle, now close to empty, was sitting near the newspaper she'd left on the counter.

Eyeing the front page, Kara cringed. The page one story above the fold was all about the grisly murders twenty years earlier. Pictures had been included, the largest being the mountain cabin as it had been the night of the tragedy, shots of cops swarming the frozen grounds. A second photograph was Jonas's mug shot, him staring sullenly at the camera, his dark hair slicked away from his face, the grim countenance of a would-be family annihilator. The last shot brought a catch to Kara's throat as she stared at a familiar picture of her mother and father's wedding. The tall groom was surrounded by his preteen boys, all in tuxedos, all with slicked-back dark hair. The bride was flanked by a light haired son in a matching tuxedo, while his younger sister was in a long silver dress, her pale blond hair pinned atop her head. The bride was dressed in a flowing ivory gown that effectively hid the early months of her pregnancy. Yes, Kara thought, she had been at the wedding, too, a small baby bump that was the reason for her parents' quick marriage after hasty divorces from their previous spouses.

She stared at the photograph, skimmed the article, then as the spots dried on her pajamas, tossed the newspaper into the trash.

She didn't need to read about the Cold Lake Massacre.

She'd had the bad luck to live through it.

"Son of a bitch!" Wesley Tate threw his cell phone onto the chair across the room. He'd called the number he'd gotten for Kara McIntyre three times, each getting a toneless voice mail response asking him to leave his number. He had twice. But no more. There had to be another way to get through to her.

Get a grip, he told himself and walked to the window of the cabin to stare through the trees to the lake, iced over as it had been all those years ago.

So Kara McIntyre was avoiding him. So what?

It wasn't exactly a news flash.

She'd been avoiding him, and practically cutting herself off from the whole damned world, all of her life.

And now, just because her brother was being released from the two decades of incarceration, would she suddenly open up? Grant him an interview?

"You're dreaming."

Not that he blamed her.

The horror of that night hadn't been washed away over the years.

He, himself, had been a part of it.

He imagined his father standing about where he

was when he'd heard noises from the neighboring property that had propelled him to attention.

If Kara knew anything, even if there was something locked in her subconscious, he had no way of asking her. She wasn't about to open up to him. And he couldn't really blame her.

Would he want his whole life turned inside out and upside down after living through the terror of the Cold Lake Massacre, a tragedy that had involved every member of her family?

Would he want to relive the terror of that night?

Would he want to remember the trial where her testimony put her brother behind bars for what should have been life?

Would he want to face said brother?

Hell no.

But he wasn't about to give up. If he put her through her own private hell again, well, as they used to say, *Dem's da breaks.*

A story was a story.

Besides which, it was more than just a story to him.

This one cut close to the bone, seeing as his father had given his life to save the freaked-out only child of Samuel and Zelda McIntyre.

Tate figured Kara owed him.

Big time.

He remembered her as a kid, all gangly arms and legs, mussed hair, and even then showing an attitude through the innocence of childhood.

She'd snuck up on him once, watching from the shadows of the tree line as he'd been skipping stones across the water.

He'd caught her eye. "Wanna try?" he'd asked, and expected her to run like a frightened fawn into the underbrush. Instead, she'd stepped from the umbra, grabbed a smooth round stone, hauled her arm back, released with a flip of her wrist and sent the rock sailing, bouncing easily over the silvery surface. Ten firm skips, water rippling in circles from the spots where the stone had bounced. With a startled series of quacks and wild splash, two wood ducks flapped out of the water and took off into the high, thin summer clouds.

"You're pretty good," he'd said, unable to hide his surprise.

"Well, what is it?" She'd cocked an insolent eyebrow. "Pretty or good?"

"What?"

"I'm pretty," she'd asserted. "*And* I'm good. Better than you."

Damn.

After drilling him with a stark, knowing stare, she'd taken off, leaving him speechless. She'd been what—seven or eight at the time? Precocious. Older than her years because of all of her older half siblings. Probably had known things no seven-year-old should. Even before witnessing the aftermath of the slaughter of her family.

Now, he walked to the kitchen, grabbed a bottle of beer from the old refrigerator, cracked it open and looked around the living area, left as it had been years before, his father's presence still evident. A family picture still hung over the mantel and nearby the antlers of a deer he'd shot with a bow, and in the short hallway leading to the bedrooms, a framed military shadow box with a collection of Edmund Tate's patches, badges, ribbons and medals from his years in the Marine Corps. A true hero, Wesley thought as he headed out to the back porch, where the floorboards were rotting and the brisk winter air cut like a knife. This was the very porch his father had stood on all those years ago. Edmund had been smoking a cigarette when he'd heard the commotion at the neighboring house, gone over to investigate, and found a freaked-out little girl in the middle of the carnage of a family slaughter.

Wesley had been eleven at the time, old enough to be fascinated by the horror, young enough to blame the victim and, like everyone else, vulnerable to feel the loss of a father dying while helping others. Edmund Tate had been off-duty. Yet he'd sacrificed his life for the girl, running onto the ice as it cracked and gave way beneath his weight. Edmund had been able to save her, dragging her kicking, screaming, and choking from the freezing water before having a damned heart attack and collapsing on the snowy shore.

Thinking of it now, Tate's jaw turned rock hard, his eyes narrowing, the anger that had been with him for twenty years festering. He'd never gotten to say goodbye to his dad. Edmund had barely spoken a word before coding in the ambulance as it screamed its way to the nearest hospital, where Edmund Tate had been pronounced DOA, one more victim of the bloody massacre.

Even today in what seemed a lifetime later, Wesley felt his own heart twist and his jaw set. He'd been robbed of the father he remembered all too clearly. Edmund had been a big man, overweight and a smoker, but only forty-seven years old when he'd taken that fateful plunge into the icy water.

Tate's hands clenched over the bottle. He stared at the ice-covered lake, its smooth surface stretching for half a mile, though tonight the view was cloaked by falling snow. The houses on the far shore were indiscernible, no lights from windows piercing the whispering veil.

He tipped up his bottle and took a long swallow, a cold wind rattling the trees and swirling the icy flakes.

That damned lake.

He'd loved coming here as a kid with his parents and younger sister. It had been a sanctuary, a haven away from the city, a place to explore in times when their small family had bonded and his father's work was miles away.

He'd fished from the old dock, hunted in the surrounding woods, played one-on-one at the rusted hoop planted in the sparse gravel. How many times had the old man let him win?

Of course, that was before the night that had changed everything, he thought, shivering in his stockinged feet. His love for this place had soured, the sanctuary turning to a hated place—heaven turning into hell in the space of a heartbeat.

"Nothing in life is fair," his mother had reminded him when he'd complained. "He died doing what he loved—protecting others." Of course Selma Tate had been devastated, too, hiding her bitterness from her children, standing proudly in the icy rain at her husband's burial, and forcing a smile she didn't feel when she was presented with a flag as Edmund had served in the marines before becoming a cop and marrying his high school sweetheart.

But, late at night, Wes had heard her crying in her room, over the sound of the country music she played loudly. He, lying on the top bunk in his bedroom, had been able to make out her sobs through the thin walls and hollow-core doors of their condominium.

He rubbed the back of his neck and turned toward the McIntyre estate, but he saw only dark forest looming through the swirling snow. During the day, part of the roof of the big house was visible between the tops of the firs and pines, and when the sun was setting, one could catch the glimmer of fading sunlight on the old panes of the window cut into the top floor, the attic where Kara had sworn she'd been locked.

But tonight it was dark.

Lost in shadows.

While the snow fell softly, an opaque veil hiding the rotting shingles and cracked glass.

God, he hated that place.

He didn't doubt that Kara McIntyre felt the same.

CHAPTER 5

Detective Cole Thomas was pissed.

Pissed, pissed, pissed.

No way that murdering bastard Jonas McIntyre should be out of prison. No friggin' way. McIntyre was the single worst murderer to have ever set foot in Hatfield County, and he should have been locked up for the rest of his natural life. But no. Once again the system had failed.

"Son of a bitch," he muttered under his breath as he glared at the computer screen mounted on his desk and swore a blue streak just as he heard footsteps, the sound of his partner as she approached.

"Good day?" she asked, sliding her arms through the thick sleeves of a ski jacket as she paused at his office. The department was slowing down for the night, only a few day-shift cops still hanging out while the night crew was taking over.

From somewhere near the break room he heard a ripple of laughter and farther off the sound of a heavy door banging shut.

"Yeah, right. The best," he growled, setting the coffee back on his desk. "Just fuckin' awesome."

Aramis Johnson sent him a wry grin and shook her head, black hair scraped into some kind of

70

bun gleaming under the harsh overhead lights. Tall and slim, her features sharp, her mocha-colored skin flawless, she could have been a runway model, he thought, not for the first time. Instead, Johnson was a cop. And, he had to admit grudgingly, a good one. Those gorgeous near-black eyes didn't miss much. He didn't know why she'd joined the force, but he suspected it might have something to do with her special needs child who didn't seem to have a father, at least not one he knew about. "Let me guess: You're not happy with Jonas McIntyre being released."

"You must be a detective."

"Lighten up." She flashed him a quick smile as two uniforms passed by his open door, their conversation low and intense, the taller scratching his crown before squaring his cap on a head of short cropped hair.

"Lighten up? Really? Even though a family annihilator is now walking free—no wait"—he held up a finger—"make that a *convicted* family annihilator." Thomas's desk phone rang. He recognized the number. Didn't answer. Within seconds his cell phone buzzed. Same number. He ignored it.

"You under the radar?" Johnson asked, leaning a hip against his desk. "Not picking up?"

"Reporter."

"On your cell, too?"

"Yeah. Somehow she's got my private number."

"Somehow?" Johnson repeated, arching a suspicious eyebrow. "She?"

"Yeah." Of course he knew how. Didn't go there. Sheila Keegan could stand in line and talk to the PIO with the rest of the TV and newspaper people. That's why the department had a public information officer, wasn't it? To deal with the press.

Far better than for detectives who'd crossed that invisible professional line and gotten involved with a reporter. He closed his mind to that way of thinking. Turned his thoughts back to Jonas McIntyre, who, in Thomas's opinion, was a merciless killer who had murdered his entire family. He flipped open the file, the folders and pages within yellowed with age and smelling of years gone by.

"This is all on computer, you know," Aramis pointed out.

"Yeah, pulled it up." He hitched his chin toward the screen, where Jonas McIntyre's mug shot was visible: a gaunt kid of eighteen with sunken eyes as dark as night, mussed hair and pale skin. Traces of acne were barely evident in his thin beard shadow. More apparent was the attitude, visible in the tight, challenging set of his jaw and the compacted lips. Cruel thin lips.

"What motivates a kid like that?" she said, eyeing the monitor.

"Don't know. Whatever he told to his psychiatrist, it's privileged. Same with his lawyer, so we're left to guess."

"Is he dangerous?"

"You tell me." He glanced up at her from his desk chair. "A teenager who murders nearly everyone in his entire family? You think he's gotten better after spending half his life in the big house with convicts?"

She lifted a shoulder. "He found God."

"Don't they all?"

"Oooh," Johnson said. "Bitter, my man."

"Am I? I wonder why? This guy." Thomas tapped the image on the screen with an index finger. "Hacked up his whole damned family with a sword. His father, his stepmother, his brother, and his stepbrother."

"Not his whole family."

"Okay, fine, one little girl survived."

"And another went missing. The sister Marlie, right?" Aramis picked up the file and rifled through it. "She was what—? Oh, here it is. Seventeen. Jesus."

"Stepsister." Thomas turned away from the computer and the dead look in Jonas McIntyre's eyes. "It was a *Brady Bunch* kind of family. The old man, Sam, came into the marriage with two kids. Sam Junior and Jonas. Zelda was wife number three. The first one was his high school sweetheart—"

"Leona."

73

"Yeah, that's right. They had a son whom they named after Sam and a baby who died at two. A girl. Betsy."

"Wow. Does this family ever catch a break?" she asked, her eyebrows drawing together.

"Not since that time—well, that I know of." He didn't have to look at the file again. He'd already tucked the information about Sam Senior's family away. "So then, as that marriage is crumbling by the loss of the baby, *Sam* gets involved with Natalie, who becomes wife number two."

"Before divorcing number one?"

"That seemed to be his MO. Both times."

"Ouch," she said. "I don't imagine that went over well with the exes."

"Probably not."

"And Jonas? He was from the second wife?"

"Yeah, Jonas is Natalie's kid." Even saying the killer's name left a bad taste in his mouth.

"What happened to the previous Mrs. McIntyres?" Johnson picked up the worn manila file.

"Remarried, I think."

"Both of them?"

"Not sure."

"So, Zelda Donner Robinson was number three." Johnson was flipping through the musty pages of the file, her eyes skimming the notes, her hip balanced against the edge of his desk as the old furnace rumbled from ducts overhead. "And she came with her own kids."

"Right. She was the mother of Marlie and Donner Robinson."

"Along with Kara, the only kid they shared between them." She glanced up as he nodded.

"Right. Zelda's first husband was Walter Robinson."

"And how did he take being tossed over for a new model?"

Thomas shrugged. "About the same as Samuel's ex-wives did, I think. As far as anyone knew, they all got along."

"Got along?" she repeated. "You mean as in they didn't make waves, were cordial, but didn't hang out and go on vacations or spend holidays together?"

"Right." At the mention of holidays, he thought again of that final bloody Christmas but didn't have to mention it. He suspected Johnson was on the same wavelength.

She scanned a few more pages. "In this blended family, all the kids were really close in age. Basically teenagers, it looks like."

"Except for the littlest daughter," he reminded her.

"The one supposedly locked in the attic."

"Right," he said, conjuring up the image of a small girl in the witness box, all blond curls, big eyes, and wan cheeks. Kara had answered each question in a tiny voice, chewed on her lip, and kept the courtroom rapt, Thomas remembered.

The usually noisy chamber had been silent as a tomb, not so much as the rustle of a paper or a shoe scraping as that tiny waif of a girl had recounted what she'd seen in a thin, whispered voice, her answers prompted by the DA. Kara, white-faced, had stared at Jonas, her chin trembling, as if she was about to break down and desperately wanted his forgiveness.

Cole Thomas, himself, had been in the second row of the courtroom, a rookie cop who still believed that only bad guys were sent to prison, that the system never failed.

Now, years later, he wasn't sure.

Johnson was still reading. "Kara insisted her older sister locked her on the third floor and she somehow escaped only to find her family slaughtered." Johnson's eyebrows drew together. "She said she thought the intruder came back into the house, so she took off through the kitchen, ran out the back door, and down a path that dead-ended at the lake. She tried to cross the ice, ended up falling in, and the intruder she'd been running from turned out to be a cop coming to see what all the screaming was about."

"Edmund Tate. Off-duty. A good one. Had been a marine. Hero type." Thomas nodded. "Saved the kid."

"And ended up having a massive heart attack himself and dying." She was slowly pacing in front of his desk, absorbing all the information in the old file, the wheels in her head obviously turning.

"Uh-huh. Despite what the paramedics did, he was DOA at the emergency room."

"Sweet Jesus." She shook her head, dark hair glistening under the light. She looked up, skewering him with those near-black eyes. "So no intruder?"

"None found."

Aramis fingered her cross as she skimmed through the reports. "Kara always claimed her brother was innocent."

"But no one bought it."

"Because of her testimony?" Her eyes narrowed and she chewed on her lip.

"Yup, that's the conundrum. What she witnessed and testified to didn't jibe with what she felt or thought about Jonas."

"Probably she just couldn't believe her brother could be so savage and brutal."

"And a murderer."

"Right." She quit fiddling with the cross and stopped pacing. "His prints were all over the murder weapon."

"Uh-huh." Thomas leaned back in his chair until it squeaked in protest. "You see the motive?"

Frowning more deeply, she nodded. "Jealousy."

"Of his older stepbrother. Donner."

"Dear God. Testosterone at its worst," she

77

muttered with a long-suffering sigh. "So Donner was involved with Jonas's girlfriend?"

"Apparently."

"How involved?"

"Intimate."

One eyebrow arched a little higher. "Let me guess: Jonas was not cool with it."

"Who would be?"

"Lord Almighty . . ." And it seemed a prayer, barely audible over the sound of air whooshing through the vents and conversations in the outer hallway.

Thomas knew what she was reading because he had nearly memorized the case file, and as she skimmed the documents they played over in his mind:

Jonas McIntyre, who miraculously survived the deadly assault, swore to this day that he was innocent of any homicides that were pinned on him. Yes, he'd admitted when the cops had arrived, he had picked up the old sword mounted in the wall of his bedroom. Jonas claimed that he'd been "messing around" with the weapon earlier in the day and had left it on the floor of his room. According to Jonas, Marlie had even walked past the bedroom earlier and had spied him with it. That's why his fingerprints were all over the hilt.

Of course, she had conveniently gone missing, so that fact couldn't be proved.

In his telling of it, Jonas had asserted that later that night he'd been in his room again when he heard something going on in the living room. A "ruckus," that's what he'd called it in the single statement he'd given police before his attorney had shut him up for good. Jonas told the cops he'd "sensed something bad was up," so he'd hauled the sword with him and followed the noise to investigate, because, he'd said, he planned to scare his older brothers if they were up messing around or, alternately, ward off an intruder, "a bad dude," if he discovered a burglar in the dark. Which he did.

And then all hell broke loose. Startled by the guy, Jonas had swung the heavy weapon and missed his target as the intruder spun away. Instead, Jonas had struck the mantel and cut a chunk out of it. The intruder got the better of him and he was injured. Cut and conveniently knocked out. When he woke up, his family was slaughtered, Kara was screaming, and a man he didn't recognize, probably the killer, he'd thought, chased her out of the house.

When the cops arrived at the scene, they'd immediately zeroed in on Jonas. His story didn't ring true, and later they discovered that the fingerprints on the hilt were his and his alone.

As for motive, Johnson had hit on it. The running theory had been that Jonas McIntyre had been royally pissed at his parents for grounding him—he'd been caught earlier in the week by the police for getting into a fight with his stepbrother, Donner Robinson. The parents had declined to press charges, but Donner, like Jonas, had been grounded.

Not good enough. Jonas, a troubled, violent eighteen-year-old, had been furious and smoldering in the days following the fight with Donner, so he decided to kill his father and stepmother, along with his stepbrother, whom he'd learned had slept with Lacey Higgins. Whether Jonas had been just trying to threaten and scare Donner or if he'd really intended to harm Donner, the upshot was that things went horribly, murderously wrong, and Jonas, in a fit of rage, ended up killing everyone who walked into that room on Christmas Eve. Only he and Kara had survived, while Marlie had vanished into thin air.

The police thought the murders of Sam Senior and Zelda McIntyre may have been premeditated.

Jonas may have slaughtered them as they slept first, before hunting down Donner—at least that was the prosecution's theory. Why else wouldn't they have awakened, even in their drugged state, during what had to have been utter, hellishly loud and savage chaos?

Later, after autopsies and lab work, it had been discovered that massive amounts of Valium were in both of their bloodstreams.

That was one of many parts of the story that

didn't ring true to Thomas. What parent ingests massive doses of a serious sleeping aid on Christmas Eve?

The reigning theory was that Sam Junior had tried to stop the slaughter and had been brutally killed in the attack. Marlie, too, was a victim, some of her blood found at the scene. The fact that Donner Robinson's wounds were massive and that his jugular was severed convinced the police that he was the intended victim, the source of Jonas's rage. Sam Junior hadn't had as many wounds, but his femoral artery had been nicked and he'd bled out, possibly had just gotten in the way and Jonas, already out of his head, killed his brother in the frenzy of the attack. Yes, Jonas suffered wounds himself, but they had not been life-threatening. The DA had painted a clear picture that the defense couldn't dispute completely or muddy sufficiently.

Though Jonas had sworn that Marlie saw him with the weapon as she passed by his door that day, she ended up going missing and had never been located, her blood identified through DNA matched with what had been extracted from hair on the brush she'd left behind. Even though Jonas's own wounds were real, they could have been self-inflicted according to the prosecution's expert witness.

"I can't believe he was convicted," Johnson said, closing the file. "All twelve jurors?"

"His juvenile records came into play. Unsealed."

"How?"

"Severity of the crime. The fact that the records were never expunged. Certain information was kept confidential, but the offenses leaked to the press. He had two prior incidents of violence on his record. Then, of course, there was the fight with Donner after he turned eighteen. Jonas pulled a knife."

"Jonas assaulted his brother?"

"Mainly threatened, but somehow in the struggle, Donner ended up with a slit on his forearm, not deep, but required stitches and was bad enough for Zelda to call 9-1-1." Thomas glanced up at her. "Less than a week before the massacre."

"Holy crap." She let out a sigh and shook her head just as noise from the outer hallway, voices and laughter, rippled through the open doorway.

"Yup. The real tipping point in the trial was Jonas's girlfriend at the time."

"Lacey Higgins. I saw." She tapped the file with a long finger.

"Right." He downed the remainder of his now-cold coffee, then crushed the paper cup in his fist and tossed it into the trash can he kept near his file cabinet. He remembered Lacey taking the stand. Dressed in white. Pale and doe-eyed, seeming positively virginal. All part of the theater that was the courtroom. On the stand,

Lacey kept her eyes downcast for the most part, but admitted to sleeping with Jonas's stepbrother, Donner.

When Jonas had found out, she'd said, he'd confronted her at her parents' house in Portland.

"Did he threaten you?" the DA, a tall woman with sleek blond hair and sharp features, had asked.

"Yes," had been the meek reply.

"What did he say?"

Lacey had bit her lip and then whispered, "That he would kill me."

"He would kill you?"

"And anyone I . . . I was with." Lacey swallowed hard. Fingered the collar of her white dress.

"What exactly were his words?"

"Uh . . . that . . . that if he ever caught me, um . . . you know . . ." She'd visibly swallowed and bit her lower lip.

"If he ever caught you doing what?"

Lacey took a deep breath. "If he caught me with someone else, like, you know, sleeping around, that he, um, he would kill me."

"Those were his exact words?"

Lacey had looked up at that moment, her slim shoulders stiffening, her dark eyes suddenly cold, as she'd stared across the courtroom to the spot where Jonas McIntyre, dressed in a suit and tie, sat motionless next to Merritt Margrove. She cleared her throat, then spoke. Clearly. Crisply. "He said, 'If I ever find out you were fucking someone else, I'll take an axe to him first and you next. That way you can watch him die before you go to hell.' "

An audible gasp had come from one of the jurors, a woman with a tight white perm who'd been wearing a pink pantsuit. The other jurors had been somber and tight-lipped, a thin man glaring from behind horn-rimmed glasses, a fortysomething woman turning ashen.

Lacey's quote, coupled with Kara's testimony and Jonas's own past acts of violence, had sealed his fate and become a part of every newspaper report, book, television true crime movie, blog and podcast since. Even though Jonas's own wounds were real and shown in graphic display to the jury, the DA's expert witnesses claimed those cuts could have been self-inflicted, and they paled in comparison to the sickening crime scene and the sliced bodies of the victims. Blood had stained the carpets, run on floorboards, glistened on the tile near the fireplace, splattered against the wood that had been stacked in the firebox and even smeared some of the branches of the toppled Christmas tree. The dead bodies had been strewn in two rooms, the leftover carnage of a brutal, barbaric attack. His own family members butchered. Jonas's violent temper, sparking several times in the courtroom, didn't help, and his prior convictions were the nails in his proverbial coffin.

"So the DA really thought Jonas managed to stab himself with a sword?" Clearly she was skeptical. "His wounds—"

"Were superficial. Hands, forearms, one leg. A weapons specialist showed the court how it could have happened, how he could have been injured in the struggle."

She flipped through the file again and scoured a page. "In his original statement, Jonas said the intruder pushed him and he hit his head, was knocked out for a while." She looked over the edge of the worn file. "But no one believed him?"

"No one who mattered. Not the jury. None of the cops. Not even his family with the one exception of his younger sister."

"Who testified against him?" With another sigh, she closed the file.

"No one knows for certain what really went down that night, and Jonas didn't help himself by not testifying. His wounds looked like they came from the same weapon, and all the victims' blood was found on the blade, even Jonas's." Thomas rubbed a hand around the back of his neck, remembering. "His attorney, Merritt Margrove, advised Jonas to take the Fifth."

"He thought Jonas would incriminate himself?"

"Probably. McIntyre was shell-shocked. No surprise there. Barely spoke to anyone pretrial after his initial statement. My bet is that the lawyer thought the jury wouldn't convict because of his age and his wounds."

"But they did." She straightened and zipped her jacket as a burst of laughter echoed down the hall. "You think the jury got it right?"

"Not a doubt." The phone vibrated across his desk. He caught the number. Sheila. Again.

He didn't pick up.

"So what do you think happened to the other sister?" Aramis asked. "The older one. Marlie."

"That," he said, reaching for his jacket and slipping his arms through its sleeves, "is the million-dollar question, now isn't it?"

"She's never been seen since?"

"Nope."

Johnson appeared skeptical. "Not a trace?"

"Nuh-uh. And no remains ever found."

He checked that his keys were in his pocket, then snapped off the light as they walked into the hallway, where wood paneling had aged yellow since the 1950s and decades' worth of smells from cigarette smoke, body odor or stale coffee couldn't be erased by any amounts of pine-scented Lysol. Closing the door behind him, Thomas added, "Some of her blood was found at the scene. Not a lot, but she had obviously been injured."

"Confirmed by DNA?"

"Oh, yeah." He glanced at Johnson, her jaw set, her black hair glinting beneath the flickering fluorescent lights in the hallway. "There were 'sightings,' of course, way back when, in the first six months or so after the murders, but nothing panned out. Lots of calls came into the department, but, over time, they dwindled." They clattered their way down the stairs, walking single file to allow those bustling up the steps—uniforms and plainclothes officers and administrative workers as well as visitors—up the flight.

At the metal detector near the side entrance, he added, "A lot of the calls that came in were just nutcases looking for a little publicity."

"Always."

"A few seemed legit. You know, people who *thought* they recognized her. But nothing solid ever materialized."

Shouldering open the exterior door, he felt the blast of frigid December air as it rushed through the streets, snow flurries dancing between the buildings, while cars, trucks and vans inched through the town, moving slowly beneath the streetlights. A bus idled at the corner, belching exhaust beneath a corner lamp as passengers dressed in heavy coats, hats and boots tromped into the idling behemoth. A woman hurrying to catch the bus raced by, the edge of her umbrella brushing against Thomas's sleeve.

"Oh, sorry, sorry, sorry," she said without looking his way, and flagged down the driver as she closed her umbrella.

At the station's lot, Johnson hit the remote on her key fob, then checked her messages. Her lips tightened as she read a quick text while her SUV, a Honda CR-V, chirped, its lights blinking to reflect on the snow piled along the edges of the parking area. "So now what?" she asked, her thoughts returning to the McIntyre Massacre. "You still think Jonas McIntyre killed his family?"

"Butchered," he corrected.

"Okay, butchered, and now he's out. Double jeopardy. He can't be convicted again."

"Not for any of those murders."

She opened the SUV's door and slid inside. "Wait." She turned. "You think he'll do more— kill again?"

"Didn't say that."

"Then . . . ?" She drew out the word.

"We wait. See if he's really found Jesus."

Her phone buzzed again and she muttered something under her breath, pulled it from her pocket and let out a sigh that fogged the cold night air. Snowflakes collected on her black hair.

"Everything okay?" he asked, and her chin inched up a notch.

"Fine."

"You're sure?"

"I said it's fine. Now what about Jonas McIntyre? You're obviously not buying into his newfound spirituality."

He slid her a glance as snow collected around his collar and he heard the bus rumbling away. "The truth is, I don't think there's a chance in hell that Jonas McIntyre is on the road to redemption. Not one single chance."

CHAPTER 6

He couldn't let it go.

Wesley Tate shoveled snow from the short walk to the converted warehouse where he owned a condo, but his thoughts were on the Cold Lake Massacre and Jonas McIntyre, who was, by all accounts, a free man again. If not absolved of the brutal murders of his family, at least not behind bars. He threw his back into his work, the broad, flat blade of the shovel scraping against the cement below. He was breathing hard, his breath visible in the darkness, and his thoughts were on a twenty-year-old murder scene. He tried to take himself out of the situation, attempted to ignore the fact that his father had given his life saving that of Kara McIntyre, but, of course, that proved impossible.

Another push on the shovel's handle, another toss of heavy snow into the tiny garden by the walkway. And more thoughts about the case. His jaw clenched and he was beginning to sweat beneath his flannel shirt, gloves, and down vest, but he kept at it, working his muscles as his mind swirled in the recent developments.

Merritt Margrove, that has-been attorney, finally found a way to get his client out. According to what Tate had read, the lawyer had found someone, a cop with a newly scrubbed conscience, who suddenly, after all this time, admitted there had been a problem with the evidence found at the scene. The murder weapon, an old sword from the previous century, had gone missing for over forty minutes in the confusion that was the crime scene.

Tate had a call in to the cop, Randall Isley, now retired, who lived in Omaha, but Isley hadn't answered. Tate had left a message.

He also had joined a Facebook fan page for Jonas McIntyre. He'd used a fake name—no reason to tip any of Jonas's apparent legion of fans by giving his real name. They were so rabid, they'd put two and two together if he logged in with the same last name of one of the victims who'd died that night.

All the same, they were a weird group, dedicated to the belief that Jonas was innocent, and had posted their thoughts, along with links for donations, to the Free Jonas McIntyre Go Fund Me page, which hadn't reached its fifty-thousand-dollar goal but was close.

What was that all about?

There were the names of three women who seemed to be the ringleaders or, at least, were the most vocal on both sites, so he was looking into Brenda Crawley, Simone Hardesty and Mia Long. There was also one guy who was pretty vocal, too. Aiden Cross made a lot of noise online about injustice in general and Jonas in particular, though a cross-check of his profile indicated that Aiden was involved in over ten antigovernment causes.

What was their connection with McIntyre?

The women obviously communicated with the object of their cause as all three had posted what Jonas was thinking about his release, the horrible night he'd found his family slaughtered and almost died himself, as well as who he thought was responsible for the heinous crimes. Cross was out of that loop; never commenting on what Jonas McIntyre thought, but always championing his case. It seemed a little off. But didn't everything?

Tate had created a fake online identity as Jessica Smith, thirty, divorced, no kids, self-employed as a web designer who was into all kinds of causes, Jonas McIntyre's case being one. He'd bought a picture of a thirtysomething woman online and posted it for "Jessica's" profile. Average looking in a hat and scarf that obscured most of her features, Jessica Smith, two of the most common names for her age, lurked, gaining information and giving none.

The group was elated that Jonas had been set free.

Several had commented that they hoped to meet him.

Most of those who commented frequently

agreed that he was not only innocent and wrongly accused and convicted, but "hot."

One woman compared his likeness to Jesus on the cross, the white people's vision of the Son of God depicted in so many pictures, but other than the short beard and long brown hair, the resemblance was lost on Tate.

Then again, people saw what they wanted to see.

There was one member, though, whom he found intriguing. Her name was listed as Hailey Brown. She didn't offer much in the comment section and she was just one of thousands on the site, but the site allowed him to see who was "on" the site at any given time, and there were less than fifty who seemed always to be online, specifically logged into the Save Jonas McIntyre site. He'd been through them all, wondering why they were so connected. Most of the people forever on the site, like Aiden Cross, Simone Hardesty, Brenda Crawley and Mia Long, could be found easily and confirmed as actual people. Several had seemed sketchy at first, but by process of elimination over weeks and months, there had been several dozen who had no connection to other online causes about freedom and liberty and social justice, and he'd checked them out. But Hailey Brown from Modesto, California, was different. An online search had proved her profile picture was a stock image. Cross-checking, using identity searches online, he couldn't locate any Hailey Brown that matched any information he could dig up. The name was so common. An alias. He felt it in his gut.

Not that her fake identity meant anything.

Wasn't he, like she, a faux person?

But why? The question gnawed at him.

Two more thrusts of the shovel and the short walkway to the cavernous building was cleared. He stood and leaned on the handle, watched as a teenager in ski gear and a cap, ear buds visible, cruised down the street on a skateboard. The kid hurdled a pile of plowed snow at the corner before continuing down the hill at a breakneck speed.

Tate shouldered his shovel and walked into the foyer. He clomped the snow from his boots before walking up two flights to his loft on the top floor, where windows climbed to a soaring ceiling. Once in his living space, he kicked his boots to a spot under the hall tree and peeled off his vest. In the kitchen area he cracked open a beer, took a swallow, then dropped into his favorite chair in front of the TV already tuned to an all-news channel.

He'd taken a break from his deep dive into the case that had consumed him for most of his adult life. Well, really since he was eleven. A helluva thing, losing your dad like that. His mother had remarried a few years after the tragedy, and her new husband, Darvin Williams, was a good enough guy. Another cop, now retired. He had stepped into the role of father without too many problems, especially in dealing with Wesley's younger sister, who had ended up adoring her new "Papa-D." But Wesley had been another story, always ended up comparing Darvin to his father. Of course Darvin came up short each and every time, an earthly man being sized up against a martyr, a saint.

So the whole father-son thing hadn't really gelled between them.

Now, all things considered, it never would.

Faiza Donner sat in her Mercedes SL450, a convertible that was impractical in winter in Oregon, but she'd always lusted after this model and had decided, just three months earlier, to indulge herself. Why not? she'd asked herself, though she'd known all the reasons leasing the vehicle might be a mistake.

Now she was parked in the circular driveway staring at the house she'd called home for nearly twenty years, a huge Tudor in the West Hills. Her sister Zelda's home once upon a time.

Oh, Faiza had been jealous then, envious of this house, the boat, the cars, the trips, the mountain "cabin" on Mount Hood—even that house had been a mansion—Zelda's "second home." And most of all Faiza had been envious of the fact that her sister had been a mother, not just once but three times, not counting the stepchildren, which Faiza definitely did not.

But then . . . well, fortunes had changed, hadn't they? She rolled down the driver's side window of her sleek car, then lit a cigarette, her last Parliament, she silently swore, as she'd given up the habit three years earlier and picked at the pack she kept in her glove box only when she was particularly stressed.

Like now.

Taking a deep drag, she stared at the house, festooned as it was in Christmas lights that illuminated the peaks and valleys of the roof line. Cedar garlands sparkling with fairy lights framed the double doors where matching wreaths hung, red bows and sprigs of holly visible. Lights glowed from within, and even the curved walkway was glowing with the soft illumination from the landscaping lamps reflecting on the snow.

Picture-perfect.

And soon to be gone, wrested from her as Jonas was released from prison and Kara's birthday was about two weeks away, that special day that had seemed eons away when Faiza had first become her guardian.

What a joyous day that had been.

Soon after the court gave her custody, Faiza and Roger and their menagerie of pets had claimed this home as their own with Kara as their would-be child and, of course, source of all their income. And it had been wonderful, she thought, smoking and fighting tears at the thought of everything she'd worked so hard for disappearing, like snowflakes melting on her palm. It just wasn't fair.

She thought of what she would lose, including her beloved red 450. She blew a stream of smoke out the window and wished she'd listened to that nagging voice in her head reminding her that she was running out of time, that everything she loved so dearly would be wrenched away.

If only she hadn't let Roger influence her, but then, didn't he always?

His mantra of "Don't worry. It'll all work out," had eased her mind, but, of course, hadn't changed things.

"Crap," she said, taking another puff before jettisoning the butt through the open window. She watched as the red tip arced in the night before dropping the snow-covered azaleas to sizzle and die. Scrounging in the console, she found a box of Altoids, shook two into her hand and popped them. As she did, she caught sight of her reflection in the rearview mirror. Her blond hair had been lightened to platinum, and her complexion was still flawless, she worked hard to maintain it, but her blue eyes were shadowed, worry evident in their depths.

"Pull yourself together," she told herself. "You've been in tighter spots." And that was true. She didn't want to think of her younger years, the ones in which she struggled so hard while Zelda seemed to live a charmed life. Zelda had married young, had two kids with Walter Robinson, then got involved with Samuel McIntyre and found herself pregnant. Zelda had always claimed it was a mistake, that she hadn't planned on her third pregnancy, but Faiza had never bought it. Faiza still believed the conception had been planned, that Zelda, still married to Walter, wanted a way out and the new baby was her avenue.

Smart move.

Faiza hadn't blamed her sister one bit.

Besides, Walter Robinson was a prick, someone who saw everything in black and white, when everyone knew the world revolved in shades of gray. Walter and Faiza had never gotten along, and she was thankful he was out of her life.

But things hadn't turned out as anyone had expected.

"Deal with it," she told herself as she turned on the engine and hit the electronic garage door opener. Her car purred into the garage where she parked in her usual spot, next to Roger's huge black pickup, a Dodge Ram TRX that barely fit into its bay.

Once inside the house, she heard guitar music and smelled the musky scent of marijuana, both of which were emanating from Roger's studio, a room near the back of the house that had once been Samuel McIntyre's den.

Faiza found him seated on the old olive-green couch, the one piece of furniture she hadn't replaced. The heel of one booted foot rested on a coffee table where notepads and sheets of music that had been scribbled upon were scattered around a glass bong. He looked up and the music stopped. "Hey, lady," he said around a smile as she stood in the wide hallway, just outside the open French doors. "I wondered when you'd come back."

"Traffic," she lied, not going into the fact that she'd sat for half an hour outside the house just staring at it and already grieving for its loss.

Satisfied, he turned his attention to his guitar again and she noticed, not for the first time, that his once-lush brown hair was now graying, his narrow face starting to show lines that went beyond crow's-feet, his pale eyes beginning to peer from behind the deep folds of his eyelids. Once a charmer, a little rough around the edges and tough as nails, he'd weathered as he'd aged.

He strummed, then looked up again. "Come sit." He patted the lumpy cushion next to him. "I'm working on a new song."

Nothing new there, but she took her spot and listened as he plucked the strings and hummed an easily forgotten tune. "Don't have the lyrics yet," he said. "Maybe you could be my inspiration."

"Maybe," she said. "But we have to talk. We've got a problem."

"Such as?"

"You know Jonas was released."

"Mmm, yeah. Bummer."

"It's more than that. Because Kara's turning of age," she reminded him, slightly irritated that he wasn't taking this monumental change seriously. "Pretty damned soon."

He plucked another note. "So?"

"We're going to have to move."

"Don't think so." He hit a chord that was purposely off-key, then set the guitar on the floor next to the couch.

"Seriously, Roger."

"Oh, come on, babe. Possession is nine-tenths of the law."

"Take it up with the courts."

"I will." Then he grinned and winked at her. "I mean you will."

"Don't," she said. "I'm not in the mood." She leaned back on the old worn cushions. "Besides, I've thought about it. Margrove has worked hard for this, Jonas's release. He can't be charged again for the same crime. He's free as a bird and, as such, will want his inheritance. All of it. And probably more."

"But he's only out until he fucks up. Right? Then he's back in the slammer." He winked again, which was really beginning to annoy her. "It won't be long. The kid's got a temper. Never could control it."

"He's not a kid anymore, but you're right about him being a hothead," she said, having always considered Jonas arrogant and violent. He'd been a teenager with a cruel streak that bordered on savage. She doubted it had diminished in prison, despite what those idiot Internet fans of his thought. "Lord knows I never liked him," she admitted, trying to find a way not to change her lifestyle. "But until he ends up behind bars again or . . . God forbid, dies, he has legal rights to his inheritance, and that includes this house, the mountain place and, if he pushed it in court and sued us, he could possibly take everything we own."

"Nah, don't think so." He sent her a sly look. "Won't happen."

"I'm just saying, it's possible." She crossed her arms over her chest, stretching the seams of her designer jacket. A Prada cashmere that was worth a small fortune. No, she thought, she wasn't ready to lose it all. Not yet. And if she could come up with some way to keep what she'd grown accustomed to, she'd buy a new couch to celebrate—something in leather, maybe even a sectional in a soft pearl gray. But, first things first: how to stop the inevitable.

Roger pulled at his lower lip, just as he always

did when he was turning a particularly thorny problem over in his mind. Obviously he wasn't ready to give it all up either.

Finally, he said, "We'll find a way out of this."

"How?"

"You'll think of something," he said, nodding as if in agreement with himself. "You always do." Then he reached for the bong and took a hit, holding his breath. When he finally exhaled in a cloud, it was in a smile, the smoke wisping between his teeth and gums in a grin that reminded her of the damned Cheshire Cat in the Disney film. He reached for his guitar again and wrapped calloused fingers around the neck. "You know that, don't you, babe? You always find a way to get what you want."

The wine had gone to Kara's head.

Big time.

Beyond buzzed, she scrounged in the kitchen for something, anything to eat. She hated to cook, rarely had anything of significance in her refrigerator and settled for some kind of crackers—Artesian, the package claimed, and some kind of cheese with no package to give it a name as she'd tossed it into a ziplock a week or so ago.

Didn't matter.

It would work.

After slicing off and discarding a bit that

showed mold, she cut herself three wedges and took twice that many crackers on a plate into the dining area, where her laptop lay open. Now that the wine had kicked in and she'd mellowed out a bit, she googled herself and found dozens of pictures of her as a child and a handful of her as an adult. Her infamy was fading. Or had been. Until now.

She'd gone from a coltish girl of seven with teeth too big for her mouth and a halo of messy blond curls to a thinner teenager with light brown hair that she'd spent hours straightening. There were even pictures of her dressed in black, her hair dyed a dark ebony, her thick eyeliner and heavy mascara at odds with her pale complexion made more so with the ivory-colored makeup she'd so feverishly applied. Her clothes had been black rags, one layer upon another. Fortunately, she'd outgrown her whole hiding-from-the-world-in-plain-sight Goth stage.

Now, though she holed up in her small home—a cottage in the suburbs—often with the shades drawn and the blinds snapped shut, she at least blended in, her brown hair usually piled in a messy bun, her only makeup a touch of lipstick and a bit of mascara. Good enough.

She glanced over her shoulder to the windows, saw that the shades were half open and quickly crossed the living room to snap all three of them shut. Tight.

It was a phobia, she knew, the thought that someone was always watching her, observing her from the shadows, ready to pounce on her the second she turned her back. "Stupid," she said aloud, but then shrugged, as if physically shucking off the unseen gaze. "Get it together."

She nibbled at the cheese and crackers and placed a call to Merritt Margrove, the lawyer who had defended Jonas for the murders. At the time he'd been a famous defense attorney and he'd taken the case to bolster his already impressive career, but he'd lost and Jonas, hands cuffed behind him, had been escorted out of the courtroom and to prison and, despite all of Margrove's promises and appeals, had remained there. The case had been a turning point for the attorney, the first of a string of losses and a downward spiral from which he'd never recovered. Married three times, scandal-riddled himself, he was a shell of the bright young lawyer with a keen mind, quick tongue and a swagger to match.

Nonetheless, Kara waited, listening to the voice message and leaving one asking Merritt to return her call.

She shouldn't think about the tragedy; it was best to let it go. But she couldn't. Never had been able to forget or forgive. And now that Jonas was once again a free man, she couldn't resist looking backward.

To that night.

That horrid, deadly, and oh-so-bloody night.

She saw the photos online, even black and white photos of the crime scene, bodies draped, Christmas tree tilted, fireplace yawning, and all the bloodstains, on every surface.

The murder weapon had been located, of course, the sword that had been mounted over Jonas's bed, a relic from the Spanish–American War, one, she knew now, that had been carried by one of her relatives, a great-great-great uncle or something. She couldn't remember the right number of greats and the wine didn't help. At that thought, she poured herself "one last glass" and sipped it slowly as she read through the articles about the Christmas Eve her family was so mercilessly destroyed.

The sword, it now seemed, was the reason Jonas was getting out of prison. Margrove had never given up on his client, even after losing the initial case.

The prosecution had been ruthless, certain that Jonas, the second and rebellious son of Samuel McIntyre Senior, was the killer. Jonas certainly had fit the profile: a teen who had always been at odds with his family, a loner who had been in and out of trouble with the law. An eighteen-year-old who'd had girlfriend and anger issues. Jonas McIntyre had "flipped out," the assistant DA had said before explaining what that meant in professional terms, a psychotic break that had turned tragically violent. Jonas had killed his family not by intentional premeditated murder, but because of a violent burst of anger where he was totally out of control. And the wounds he'd sustained? Either because one of the victims had fought back or they'd been self-inflicted. The DA had gone to great lengths and detail, showing how Jonas, an athlete and gymnast, had been able to contort and slice himself.

Even so, the jury might not have been convinced except that Jonas's fingerprints had been discovered all over a sword that was not only over a hundred years old but also the murder weapon.

But now, that key piece of evidence was in dispute.

A cop who had worked the scene, Randall Isley, had admitted that there was a screwup that night, that the sword in question had been lost for a bit, that in all of the hubbub of the scene, there had been a crucial forty-five minutes when the sword had been misplaced, and as such the chain of custody of a valuable piece of evidence broken, and that little fact had been covered up by the department.

Isley, now retired, had given a sworn affidavit to Merritt Margrove, who had taken it to a judge.

The end result was that after serving only a portion of his sentence, Jonas had been released.

Kara felt a headache starting to form. She

rubbed her temples and from her chair in the kitchen noticed Rhapsody staring at the back door. Not moving, just looking as if she could see through the panels.

"What?"

The dog gave a low growl.

Kara's heart clutched. "Oh, Jesus."

Throat suddenly dry, she scraped her chair back and walked into the kitchen. "Stop it," she said.

Rhapsody didn't move.

The hackles rose along the back of her furry neck.

Pulse jumping, Kara slid to the window and peered through the blinds into the night. The backyard was as she'd last seen it. Empty. Nothing changed. The night still. Peaceful. A light snow falling.

Slowly, she let out her breath, took steps backward and reached for the wall switch, cutting the lights, hoping her silhouette was no longer visible. Still she saw nothing. "You're scaring me," she told the dog, but kept her gaze riveted to the backyard.

Was there movement near the arborvitae? A rustle of leaves in the laurel near the corner of the property, a spot in the fence line where some of the collected snow had been disturbed? And were those footprints along the hedge line, a path made by someone, now covered in snow? Or the product of her oh-too-fertile imagination?

She swallowed back her fear. There was no one in her backyard. No one watching her. No footsteps, just a spot in the yard near the fence where the ground dipped beneath the snow-flocked arborvitae. She reached for the blinds over the sink and snapped them closed, then as Rhapsody whined, Kara went through her usual routine, counting the doors as she made sure they were locked. Garage to kitchen. "One." Back door from kitchen. "Two." Through the dining room, the living area and front door. "Three." Using the remote, she switched off the fire and whistled to the dog, then mounted the stairs to the second floor and her bedroom tucked tightly under the eaves. With sloped ceilings and old pine floors, there was just room for a double bed.

Cozy and tight.

Safe.

She didn't bother with the lamp but walked to the window and looked again to the snow-covered yard. Ice glazed the bird bath, snow covered the pots where last summer's geraniums had died, the only break in the white blanket caused by Rhapsody earlier.

She saw no dark figure lurking in the shadows, no killer hiding in the shrubbery.

Still, she pulled down the shades before snapping on a bedside light and the dog, having given up her post at the back door, padded noisily up the stairs and entered the bedroom. "Okay, you ready to settle down?" she asked as Rhapsody leapt onto the bed.

Kara closed the bedroom door and threw the dead bolt she'd installed herself. "Four," she said, and despite the wine stain on her PJs, slid between the covers.

She thought about the sleeping pills in the top drawer of her nightstand but didn't bother and instead picked up the book that had dropped to the floor. Nonfiction. All about facing one's demons and women's empowerment.

Dry. Lofty. And guaranteed to make a person drowsy.

Except it didn't.

She read for nearly an hour, put the book aside and drew her duvet to her chin, then closed her eyes, hoping for sleep, silently praying that if slumber came, the nightmares wouldn't.

She didn't turn out the light, but closed her eyes and finally drifted off.

The nightmare roared through her brain, a huge, ugly beast from which there was no escape. She was seven again, unlocking the attic door, and running down the stairs that curved around and around, spiraling downward to the sound of music—Christmas music. It was faint and there was conversation. Her father arguing with someone. A door slamming. Her mother's screaming. Marlie's warnings insisting that she keep quiet and stay in the attic. Faster and faster Kara ran, always downward along the never-ending staircase, her bare feet stumbling on the wetness, her fingers grazing the rail that was slick. "Mama," she called. "Daddy . . ." But her voice was muffled over the sound of thuds and shouts and shrieks and that song, that carol echoing loudly as the grandfather clock resounded up the staircase.

Bong, bong, bong.

She lifted her hand from the rail.

It was red with blood.

And her feet? They, too, were red, slipping in the blood that dripped from one step to the next.

"Mama!" she cried as the clock's tolling and the horrid Christmas carol echoed through her brain.

"Sleep in heavenly peace . . ."

"Mama!"

Kara's eyes flew open.

Her heart raced.

Her back was covered in sweat.

She blinked, found herself in her own bedroom.

"Oh, God," she whispered, struggling to a sitting position in the tangled sheets. The nightmare was so real. Always. Every damned time.

She swallowed against a dry throat and thought about calling Dr. Zhou, then immediately discarded the idea. It was a dream. So what? It wasn't the first time that the night of the massacre came roaring back into her subconscious and it wouldn't be the last.

With an effort, she pushed herself from the bed, her head pounding, and made her way into the bathroom, where she stopped at the sink, turned on the water and dipped her head to drink, then splashed her face with the cold stream.

As she twisted off the tap, she caught sight of her face in the mirror. She looked like hell. Her hair tumbled around her white face and shoulders in messy brown strands wet near her face from tipping her head under the faucet, her hazel eyes appeared sunken and haunted, her cheekbones severe. Water dripped from her chin, and she grabbed the hand towel from its ring and swiped her face.

Pull yourself together. For the love of God, Kara, pull yourself together.

She dropped the towel on the counter and returned to the bedroom, where Rhapsody snored softly and the digital clock glowed. 2:57. Would she ever go back to sleep? Probably not. She walked to the window. Stared out into the quiet darkness.

The snow had stopped falling, a deep blanket glittering from the muted light of her window. She shivered, pulled on the terry cloth robe she'd left on the back of a side chair covered in other wrinkled clothes. Cinching the belt tight, she dropped back onto the bed and dropped her face into her hands.

This had to end.

This torment.

There had to be a way to make it go away.

Maybe once Jonas's release faded to the background, becoming just another forgotten news story when some other tragedy took control of the press, maybe then she could find a way, somehow, to finally put this all behind her.

Oh, sure.

What are the chances of that?

"Shut up," she said aloud, hoping to still that horrid little voice in her head, the one that reminded her she would never be normal, always be labeled a freak, forever looked at as the survivor of an unimaginable event.

Her cell phone vibrated, humming beneath the twisted bedding. She tossed off the duvet and found it in a tangled sheet.

A text.

From an unknown number.

Kara read the message and the hairs at her nape stood on end. She dropped the phone onto the floor, but it landed faceup.

Across the small screen, the words glowed bright:

She's alive.

CHAPTER 7

Kara stumbled back from the bed, tripping on a pair of boots and catching herself against the wall. Who? Who was alive?

It's just another prank.

Immediately she thought of Jonas. He was out now, right? Had he texted her in the middle of the night?

No way.

Quivering inside, she returned to her bed and picked up the phone, noticing a voice mail from the same number, a call she'd missed when she'd been asleep.

You mean passed out, don't you?

Ignoring her stupid conscience, she picked up the phone and listened to the voice mail message.

For a few seconds there was nothing, just some ambient noise. The wind? Air rushing outside a moving car? Labored breathing?

She swallowed hard and pushed aside her racing thoughts as a whisper-thin voice came onto the call.

"She's alive," the person said, the voice a raspy whisper.

Was the caller male?

Female?

Impossible to tell.

Click!

Whoever it was had disconnected.

An hour later, the text had come in.

Heart hammering, she texted back.

Who is alive?

She waited.

One minute. Two. After three, she wrote again.

Who are you?

She was sweating though the room was cool. Rhapsody snored softly, and she heard the quiet thrum of the heater pushing warm air through the house over the pounding of her pulse in her ears.

No response.

She looked at the clock. 3:17.

Her stomach knotted as she punched out the number, held the phone to her ear and closed her eyes. One ring, two, three . . . no voice mail box where she could leave a message. Just ringing over and over in her ears.

She imagined the caller on the other end of the connection, staring at the ringing phone, seeing her message and not even bothering to pick up.

Her eyebrows drew together.

Why?

It's Jonas. You know it is. He's out and he's still angry with you, so he's playing a game. Get ready, Kara, this is going to be bad.

"No," she whispered aloud, and clicked off the phone. Lying on the bed, her head propped by pillows, she stared vacantly to the wall where the picture hung, a photograph of her entire family, caught in a moment in time. They had all been gathered at the cabin, and Mama had insisted they sit for a family picture, outside near the lake, a professional photographer hired.

It was supposed to show the blended family as happy. Normal.

But it hadn't been. Nor would it ever.

She blinked against a spate of tears and studied the photo that she knew by heart.

Backdropped by the lake in summer, the entire family was strung out on a log.

Mama standing behind Donner and Marlie, who sat next to each other on the mossy downed tree. Daddy had his hand on his two sons' shoulders, a relaxed left hand over Sam Junior's, while the fingers of his right were tight over Jonas's upper arm. Kara was seated in the middle between Jonas and Marlie, and everyone smiled at the camera while the sun set. Everyone but Jonas. Even then, he was somber, his eyes, beneath the shag of dark hair, narrowed, his lips compressed, his arms crossed over his chest. He looked as if he would rather be anywhere else in the world.

Her eyes returned to her only sister. What had Marlie known? Why had her clothes been folded neatly on the edge of her bed when she'd never been particularly tidy? Why had she spirited Kara up to the attic? She'd been scared. Frightened out of her mind. And yet she hadn't hidden with Kara up in that dark garret. Instead, she'd insisted she'd return.

But she hadn't.

Not ever.

A lump filled Kara's throat and she felt the sting of tears behind her eyes. What had happened to her sister? And could it be worse than what had happened to her brothers? She remembered inching down the stairs, the dread pounding in her brain, her fingers trailing along the railing as the Christmas carol whispered up the stairs—

"Stop it!" she screamed, and felt her heartbeat pounding in her skull. This was insane! She couldn't do it anymore. "You are *not* a victim. You survived. Remember. You are *not* a victim."

Shaking inside, Kara climbed off the bed, pulled the picture from the wall, and shoved it facedown in her bottom drawer, stuffing it beneath her seldom-worn sweatshirts. She'd never liked the picture in the first place. It had always served as a painful reminder of her life before the tragedy, but Aunt Faiza had insisted she keep it.

"Someday, you'll be glad you have it," Auntie Fai had said.

"Not today," Kara said out loud, and thought silently, *not ever,* as her cell, left precisely where she'd dropped it on the bed earlier, began to ring.

Across the room in an instant, Kara scooped up the phone. The same unknown number. "Who is this?" she demanded as she clicked it on.

Again the sounds of wind rushing.

"Who are you?" More loudly and she realized she was shaking. Head to toe.

"She's alive," came the same whispered reply.

"Who? Who's alive?" Marlie? Was the person talking about Marlie? Who else?

No response.

"Marlie? Are you talking about Marlie?" Kara demanded of the silent connection.

"Who the hell are you?" she demanded, unable to keep the panic from her voice.

Nothing.

"Why are you doing this? Who—?"

The phone went dead in her hand.

"Oh, God," she murmured, backing up, staring at the screen. Who had been on the other end of the call?

Jonas.

It wasn't a coincidence that the texts and calls started tonight, less than twenty-four hours since he was released.

Her throat was dry as cotton.

Her hands shook.

She told herself she had nothing to fear from him, but she remembered her testimony all too clearly, how the female attorney with the pinned-up blond hair and bright blue eyes had asked her questions, twisting her words, making it seem like Kara thought Jonas had actually killed the family. And she remembered the way he had stared at her

117

throughout her time on the witness stand, his eyes focused on her, his jaw tight. She'd shredded a tissue as she'd answered the questions, twisting the fragile paper until it disintegrated in her sweaty hands as she described how she'd come down the stairs and into the living room and her parents' bedroom, the horror she'd discovered and the bodies, only Jonas surviving.

Worse yet, the man sitting beside Jonas, Merritt Margrove, had tried to change her story, to suggest that someone else, possibly even Marlie, had hacked the family to pieces, to level questions to push the jury to a little doubt, enough to clear his client.

It all came rushing back again, the horror movie in her head replaying over and over. "Stop it!" She stomped a foot and balled her fists.

Rhapsody lifted her head and gave off a worried "Woof." Bright eyes focused on Kara.

"Sorry." *Calm down. Just calm the hell down!* Taking a long breath, she stopped to pet the dog, who thumped her tail and yawned, showing a pink tongue, black lips, and sharp white teeth before closing her eyes again. "It's okay," she said, but didn't believe it for a second.

Scooping up her phone, she flopped back onto the bed again and speed-dialed Merritt Margrove, only to have the call go directly to voice mail. So, what did she expect? That he was bent over his computer, working, phone nearby? It was 3:36 in the morning for God's sake.

Great.

"It's Kara," she said when prompted. "Is Jonas with you? Do you know where he is? Call me." She disconnected, then, carrying her cell, walked through the house again, counting the doors again to make certain they were still locked and slamming the dead bolt of her bedroom.

Click!

Merritt Margrove opened a bleary eye.

What the hell was that?

A sound out of the ordinary.

He blinked twice to the eerie, undulating light cast from the television across the small room. His head pounded and his neck ached from his unnatural position on the futon. With a groan, he sat up and then paused as the late-night movie, *Fallen Angel*, a 1940s film noir, resumed after a commercial.

Rubbing his eyes, he focused on the near-empty glass of scotch sitting by a messy pile of his notes, his glowing iMac, his cell, and an overflowing ash tray. A half-eaten pepperoni pizza was on the counter separating the kitchen from the living area, still smelling of spicy tomato sauce and nearly burned cheese. Here, in the trailer, he could partake of all his vices without his watchful wife remarking on lung cancer, emphysema, or cholesterol. No doubt

Celeste knew what he was up to. How many times had he heard her singsong, "When the cat's away, the mice will play"?

"Too damned many," he said, and twisted his neck until it popped and loosened. He should go to bed. He'd lost track of the movie's plot as he'd dozed, and he couldn't work any longer. And the storm outside had become a rager. Wind tearing down the canyon and rushing through the pines. He glanced at his notes, the pages he'd printed off of his laptop, worth, he hoped, a fortune. His insight into the McIntyre Massacre and the fact that, even after all these years, he'd gotten Jonas McIntyre off should be worth a small fortune. Maybe even a large fortune. He envisioned a book deal and maybe a movie or series about what was a horrific crime. Oh, yeah, a couple of books had already been published, but not with his insight, not with interviews from the man falsely accused, not with the secrets Margrove knew.

He felt a zip in his bloodstream that he hadn't experienced in years. The book was destined to be a best-seller, the movie a goddamned blockbuster. And his career would be back on track.

Merritt V. Margrove was back, baby.

Or would be soon. Very soon.

The first stumbling block of getting Jonas out had been accomplished, even if it had taken two damned decades.

He reached for his lighter and pack of Camels

on the coffee table. Lighting up, Margrove let his thoughts spin to the future. He could see it all now—the book tour and television and newspaper interviews. In the interviews he'd talk about the legal ins and outs of the case, how he'd worked the court system and discovered the damning mistake in the evidence chain regarding the murder weapon. It would lead to how he, through perseverance and hard work, had sprung his client. Yes, it had taken nearly twenty years, but Jonas was still a young man, on the good side of forty, and he had dozens, no, hundreds of fans. Jonas knew. He'd been the one to keep the websites and social media accounts active, made sure Jonas was never far from the public eye, and it didn't hurt that he'd grown into an Adonis. Well, maybe that was a stretch, but he was good-looking in a brooding, bad-boy way that kept the girls and women interested.

Oh, yeah, things were going to be fabulous.

He took a drag on his cigarette, leaned back, and blew smoke rings at the ceiling of this used, dilapidated single-wide. All that was going to change. No more hiding up here from Celeste. Nope. As a matter of fact, maybe no more Celeste. His wife was getting under his skin and not in a good way. She was into health food—something called "clean eating" that didn't include any of the foods he liked. No beef. No nachos. No pizza. And booze? Forget it! Cigarettes? Tantamount to poison! Celeste couldn't abide the smell of them, though when he'd met her, she smoked like a chimney. What was it his mother had said, "There's nothing worse than a reformed sinner." Well, amen to that. Celeste was his third and, he vowed, last wife, twenty years younger than he, a hairdresser, and much too serious these days with her interest in yoga, green tea, and fake hamburger. How "clean" was faux meat?

Another advertisement flashed onto the television screen, this one for Cialis—boner medication—and he paid a little more attention. Lately his dick wasn't what it had been, not as super sensitive and hard as it was in his heyday. But he blamed Celeste for that, too. She was just impatient, or tired or . . . whatever.

Click.

He heard the sound again. Over the announcer telling him how to put a little juice in his love life and the whistle of the wind cutting through the woods.

So what the hell was it?

No one knew he was here.

Hell, no one even knew about this place.

Just Celeste.

Well, and Jonas. But that was a given.

Still . . . he picked up his baseball bat, the one he kept near the front door—just in case. He'd been a defense lawyer for most of his adult life and had dealt with some nasty characters, so he made sure his Louisville Slugger was always nearby.

Flipping on lights, he made his way down the short hallway to the bedroom.

Empty.

He paused and felt the air. Did he sense a breeze? A draft of cold air over the heat waving from the old baseboard heaters? Probably nothing—the place was drafty.

Still, the skin at the base of his neck prickled.

A warning.

But he saw nothing.

Heard no one.

"Too much booze," he chided. In the bathroom, he stopped to take a leak and caught a glimpse of himself. His thinning hair long enough to pull into a ponytail, his jowls fleshy despite the facelift he'd had fifteen years earlier, his thin skin showing veins beneath the surface.

Once a good-looking, smartly dressed, much-sought-after lawyer who could demand exorbitant fees for which he did exemplary work. The days when he had six assistants at his beck and call, when the staff boasted three knockout female clerks who never resisted him. When celebrities called him to take care of their indiscretions. Those had been the days.

Wasted.

Long gone.

But maybe, just maybe, they would be back

and he'd make things right. A chin and neck lift, maybe a few hair plugs as he was getting a little thin over his crown and he'd be back at the top of his game. Again.

Returning to the living area to shut things down and turn in for the night, he noticed the light over the stove was out.

Hadn't it been on earlier . . . or had he shut it off? Maybe the ancient bulb had finally burned out.

He waited.

Nothing moved.

He was getting paranoid in his old—make that later middle—age. He had to think of the future. He left the bat on a side chair, close at hand, then finished his scotch and thought he had time for one last smoke, so he lit up and started straightening his notes despite the headache starting to pound at his temples.

He felt something odd.

The air stirred.

He glanced toward the kitchen again.

Had he left the broom closet door open? Shit, no. When was the last time he'd reached for a broom or a mop or—

He felt the barrel of a pistol press against the back of his head—a deadly ring of cold steel through his thinning hair. *What?*

He froze.

His cigarette fell onto the carpet.

He nearly lost control of his bladder.

"Don't move" was the command.

Click.

The sound of a pistol being cocked.

All of the spit dried in Margrove's mouth. He nearly peed his pants.

"Wh-what do you wa—?"

"Shut up!"

He did.

He tried to think over the panic rising like a rocket inside him. Who the hell was this? Why was he—or she?—here? What the fuck was the gun all about?

"I-I don't have any money."

"I said shut the fuck up."

Shit. Shit, shit, shit! Margrove tried to think, to come up with some idea of what to do. He'd been in tight places before. Tons of them. But he'd never in all of his fifty-nine years had the barrel of a gun pressed to the back of his head. *Think, Margrove, think. Talk your way out of this! There has to be a way. Maybe this is just a robbery. Someone, a vagrant who had seen the lights of the trailer through the near-blizzard conditions outside—*

Then why the gun? So close.

Stay calm. You can handle this.

Frantic, his heart thundering, he eyed the bat. Too far away. And if he moved? Oh, shit!

He had to get out. And fast. Get away.

Zzzzt!

What the fuck was that? The swishing noise

sounded like a belt being pulled quickly from loops or—

From the corner of his eye, he caught sight of steel. Sharp metal that reflected and distorted the television screen.

Jesus Christ, the guy had a knife? He'd unsheathed a fucking knife? While he already had a gun pressed hard against Merritt's skull? Why the hell would—

Oh, fuck!

The blade slashed down.

Fast.

From his ear, one side to the other before he could think, could move.

Thin steel sliced quickly through skin and muscle and cartilage.

Blood spurted, thick and red.

Stunned, Margrove dropped to his knees. Sputtering and gasping, gurgling and coughing, he knew he was drowning in his own blood. He wobbled for a second, then his head landed on the floor. He registered for just a second that he was dying. Murdered. His eyes were wide as he tried to see this cruel son of a bitch who had done this.

But his gaze fixed on the TV.

For the last fleeting seconds of Merritt V. Margrove's life, as he bled out onto the old shag carpet, feeling little pain and even less regret, he watched the final credits of the black and white movie as they rolled slowly over the screen.

CHAPTER 8

Head pounding, Kara eased her way downstairs to let the dog out into the still-dark yard, then hit the button on the single-cup coffeemaker on the kitchen counter and ignored the grit in her eyes and the headache starting to bloom at the base of her skull.

Margrove hadn't called back, though, to be fair, it wasn't even seven. Most of the world just waking up. Yawning, she glanced through the dining area to the front window, where, peeking through the blinds, she noticed the streetlights casting a vaporous glow, snow now gently falling from a black sky fighting the coming dawn.

She thought she hadn't slept a wink the rest of the night, but somehow the hours had passed, so she had to have dozed. In the cupboard near the sink, she found a bottle of ibuprofen and shook out the last remaining tablet.

The coffee machine sputtered and steamed, spitting out a shot of espresso to which she added a healthy stream of Baileys.

Just to take the edge off. A bit of "the hair of the dog," as Daddy had once told her years before when she had no idea what he was talking about.

As she popped the pill and washed it down with a hot swallow of the doctored coffee, the TV was blasting, news of Jonas's release still the top story.

So where was he?

Why hadn't he tried to contact her?

More importantly, why was she torturing herself when her head already felt twice its normal size? She found the remote and snapped the sunny-looking reporter right off the screen. "Better," she said, hoping her headache would shrivel as she sipped from an oversize cup.

She opened the door and Rhapsody bolted into the kitchen, waiting eagerly, tail slapping the side of the counter as Kara added dry food to her empty bowl.

Already showered and dressed, with minimal makeup and more than one drop of Visine in her eyes, she decided she'd waited long enough. She needed to see Jonas, and the only way she knew how was to talk to the attorney who lived across the river.

She dismissed last night's prank call for what it was. A stupid joke. Jonas, by all accounts a new man, certainly would phone her directly, right? He already had her number, a gift from Aunt Faiza. Wouldn't he just call her instead of playing some ridiculous high school game in the middle of the night? Or was he that cruel?

So the caller had to have been someone else, someone who wanted to bug the crap out of her, to scare her. But who? Not many had her phone number. So what? She didn't exactly have anonymity, and there were ways to find out all kinds of information on the Internet. No, Jonas hadn't called her, but some person in her past. Someone jealous or pissed off had tried to get their jollies by leaving the weird message in the middle of the night.

"Get used to it," she told herself as she drained her cup and reached for her jacket. "I won't be gone long," she said to Rhapsody, who had raced to the door in anticipation of a jog. Guilt cut through Kara's already pain-filled brain. "Later," she promised. First, she was going to track Margrove down and find out how she could contact Jonas.

Why?

She didn't answer the question, because she had no good response. Yes, he was her sibling, a member of her family, but he'd never responded to her letters, refused to see her the two times she'd visited Banhoff after she'd turned eighteen. The prison's massive concrete walls, razor wire and stone-faced armed guards had convinced her that she never wanted to be incarcerated, and she'd wondered how Jonas had survived all this time without going insane.

Maybe it had been a short fall to insanity for Jonas. Because a boy who had been capable of killing his entire family had already slipped over the edge.

And now he was out.

A good thing?

Or bad?

She guessed she'd find out.

"He didn't do it," she reminded herself, and snagged her keys and purse before heading to the garage. She slapped the button for the garage door opener, then slid behind the wheel. As the door cranked noisily open, she started the SUV. Placed her hands on the cold steering wheel.

Her cell phone buzzed again and she glanced at it. No name. No number. "Forget it," she said aloud, her breath fogging as she rammed the Cherokee into reverse and gunned the engine as snow had piled on the driveway. The Jeep lurched backward, her tires bumping over the icy berm, a gray daylight starting to illuminate the streets.

"Hey!" a startled voice yelled.

Thump!

From the corner of her eye, she spied a man leap from the driveway to the side yard.

Jesus!

She'd hit him?

What? No!

She stood on the brakes.

"No. Oh, no. Oh, God!" she whispered, ramming her Jeep into park.

She threw open the door. Flying out of the driver's side, she prayed the man wasn't dead.

She rounded the back of the Jeep, her boots sliding, panic surging through her brain.

He lay in the drive, half buried in six inches of icy white powder. Jeans, heavy jacket, boots, dark hair. Face turned to one side.

Unmoving.

She nearly heaved. God, was he dead?

"Hey," she yelled. "Hey!" She slid onto her knees ready to take his pulse, aware she saw no blood.

With a groan, he rolled over, blinking, two blue eyes peering up at her.

"Are . . . Are you all right?"

"Yeah." He lifted his head, snow clinging to his near-black hair.

"Hey . . . don't—No! You shouldn't move."

His head fell back into the depression in the snow. "Wow."

Oh, God, oh, God, oh, God! She swallowed hard, reached for her phone to call 9-1-1, but she'd left her cell with her purse on the front seat. Glancing down the street, she saw it was empty, no one out, the only evidence of life a yellow tabby cat stepping through a snow covered yard slowly, lifting each paw carefully as it made its way to a sedan parked in the driveway and sliding beneath it. But other than that, the yards were quiet, the streetlights still glowing, a few windows bright from interior lights, a couple of houses glowing with strings of Christmas lights.

He sat up. Brushed his face with gloved fingers.

"Stay." Holding out a hand, palm out, fingers splayed, she scrambled backward, still searching the empty street for anyone who could help. No one. Just the cat. "Don't move, just . . . just stay," she ordered. "I'll call an ambulance."

"No," he said around another groan, and winced. "I'm . . . okay . . . just give me a minute."

"What? No!"

"I need a sec."

"But—"

He held up a finger and she was grateful that he was conscious, seeming coherent and could move, that his color seemed okay—normal. And that there was no dark red stain seeping into the snow. She still couldn't stand the sight of it. "I said a second," he repeated. Rolling onto his back, he gazed up at the sky, where morning light pierced the sluggish clouds moving slowly overhead. He let out his breath. "I'm okay. I'll be . . . I'm okay."

Was he? Shouldn't he see a doctor? Or at least an EMT? What about internal injuries?

But she was already backing up, heading toward the open door of her Jeep. "I think we should call someone who—"

"Don't!" he barked. Then a little more calmly said, "Look, I'm okay. Really." To prove his point, he rolled to his knees, then pushing upright, was able to stand, thank God. He didn't even sway.

That said, she was still freaked out, her own blood buzzing with the adrenaline, her mind racing with all the horror that could have happened. She could have killed him. Maimed him. Even now there could be other injuries that weren't visible or . . . or . . .

And then she recognized him.

Damn.

"Man," he said, and glanced at her. For the first time she saw him full in the face and thought he might be familiar. Near-black hair fell over his forehead, beneath thick eyebrows which guarded those stark blue eyes. A hawkish nose and beneath three or four days' growth of beard, a strong jaw and . . . Oh. Crap.

Her heart nose-dived.

Anger flooded through her.

Wesley Friggin' Tate. The damned reporter. Son of Edmund Tate, the cop who'd rescued her from the lake all those years ago, the man she'd run from, the man she'd thought was the monster who had slaughtered her family. Bristling, she said, "What're you doing here?"

He did seem none the worse for wear. But she'd hit him. She'd heard the thud, felt the impact.

Right?

"You weren't answering the phone or my texts."

"And so you what? Were trespassing? Snooping around? For God's sake, I could have killed you!"

It was a big leap, but she took it.

"Wait a minute. You just nearly ran over me!"

"But I didn't."

"Close and you did hit me."

"Did I?" She wasn't convinced. Had she really struck him with the Jeep? Knocked him to the ground? Or had that been only the bump of her tires spinning over the berm of snow? Had she just been played? Had he pretended to be struck? But she'd heard the impact of her bumper hitting or at least grazing his body. Or had she? Was it too crazy to think that he could have thumped the side of the Jeep with his gloved fist as he'd sprung up and then fallen to the ground?

Had he, in fact, faked her out?

Why? For a damned interview? Really? If so, that was sick. "You came here to talk to me?"

"Right."

"When I haven't returned your calls or texts?" Her mind was spinning with distrust.

"I thought I could persuade you," he said, and he smiled, white teeth flashing in his dark beard.

Oh, great, now the charm was coming. Now the guy thought he could flirt with her? "You thought you could 'persuade me'? By pretending to have me run you over. That was your plan?"

"What?" His smile fell away. "No!"

"But you were hoping to talk to me, to get an interview."

"Well, yeah, but—"

134

"But nothing." She eyed him up and down—long legs, broad shoulders, and attitude, all kinds of attitude. "You're not the first to try and trick me into talking to you, you know. There have been dozens who've tried. And why? To get to 'the truth'? Right? No! Each and every one was trying to make a buck off my story, my trauma, my family's tragedy." She felt herself winding up again, years of frustration beginning to boil over. "There have been articles, so many I've lost count, and a couple of books and even a special type of true crime show that ran on cable a year or two after the murders." She advanced on him, holding tight to her anger. "I know that there's all kinds of renewed interest in the story. Because the twenty-year anniversary is coming up, the cable channel is dusting off the program and running it again, probably twenty-four/seven just in time for Christmas? Isn't that what you want to watch during the holiday season! Sit down with the kids and a big bowl of popcorn."

"Whoa, that's not what I'm all about."

"No?" She cocked her head, disbelieving, a gust of cold wind catching in her hair. "What are you about, Wesley Tate?" she asked, then lifted a finger as if an idea just popped into her head. "Oh, right, you have a different angle on the story, don't you? A personal take as your dad was there and he died saving that pathetic, freaked-out little girl from the lake after scaring her half to death!"

"Wow," he said, almost under his breath.

"Yeah, wow." She took in a deep breath, then let it out slowly, trying to pull back on her out-of-control emotions. She looked down the street, where an old guy in striped pajamas, a bathrobe and horn-rimmed glasses was standing near the garbage can at the corner of his garage, his eyes trained on Kara and Tate. The last thing she needed was a nosy neighbor poking his head into her business. She turned back to Tate, who was still staring at her. "You're okay, right? So this is over."

"You hit me."

"You were standing in my drive. And I didn't."

"I was crossing to the front yard."

"But cutting behind the garage? For the love of God, didn't you hear the garage door roll up, me start the car, the engine turn over?"

"I yelled," he said.

Did he? Yes. Just before the thud and she felt a thump in the car. She eyed the rear bumper. Not a scratch and the damned open door was still dinging. "This is crazy," she said, returning to the Jeep, reaching inside and cutting the engine. "Where did you say I hit you?" she asked, her eyes narrowing as she closed the Jeep's door. "On your hip?"

"Yeah."

"But not too bad."

"I told you I tried to jump out of the way."

136

"Yeah, so you said." She remembered the thud and his leap to one side. Fake. She was sure of it. "I didn't hit you."

"You sure as hell did."

"Don't think so."

Tate shook his head, disbelieving. "If you hadn't been on your phone—"

"What?" she cut in. "Unbelievable." Shaking her head, she said, "So you really thought that this little act would guilt me into talking to you?"

"Wow. That's crazy."

"Well, isn't that what they say about me? That I was so traumatized as a child that I'll never be right? That I'm on the edge of a nervous breakdown every day? That I can't be trusted to—" She suddenly shut up; knew she'd already divulged too much. "You work for a newspaper?"

"Freelance."

"Ah. I see. And now, because I 'hit' you with the Jeep, you think I would feel guilty enough to give you an interview. Maybe an exclusive." She glanced up the street to see the neighbor still standing in his slippers, salt and pepper hair sticking up at odd angles, and staring. Oh, crap, was he reaching into his robe for his cell phone so he could take a picture?

Tate said, "The least you could do is talk to me."

"What?" Once again her attention was focused on the reporter. "Are you out of your mind? Why would I talk to you?"

137

He had the audacity to smile again, one side of his mouth lifting. "Well, you did almost kill me."

"Because you were in the way! Holy Christ, you planned this? You hoped I would hit you so that you could get an interview?" she asked, her mind spinning at the lunacy of it all. How nuts was he?

"Of course not. You came barreling out when I was crossing to your house."

"That's the worst excuse I've ever heard," she said, and the headache she'd tried to keep at bay was pounding a painful tattoo across her brain. "Look, go away. No interview. If . . . if you have any serious injuries, you can call my lawyer. I'm done with this." Fury blooming, she stormed to her Jeep, climbed inside, and yanked the gear shift, forcing the Jeep into reverse. "What an idiot!" she said, disbelieving.

Tate was still standing at the side of the drive. Well, let him hang out there all day if he wanted to. It was freezing out. She hit the remote button for the garage door and watched it roll down completely, all too aware that the reporter was just five feet away and staring at her. When the door finally shut, she checked the rearview and backed up, leaving him on the snowy sidewalk. As for the neighbor, he was walking through the door into his house.

Good. Maybe he'd gotten a picture.

Maybe not.

It didn't matter, she'd weathered worse. Far worse.

Her fingers tightened over the wheel as she thought about the reporter. Wesley Tate had a lot of nerve. A lot.

But he did lose his father in the tragedy. You weren't the only one who suffered a loss that night. Remember. Edmund Tate died because he saved you.

She felt that same bit of remorse she always did when she thought of the off-duty cop who'd chased her through the frigid forest that night. She reached the end of the street, slowed for the stop sign at the corner, and took one last glance at her drive. He was still there, watching her leave, long legs spaced apart, arms crossed over his chest, eyes following her.

Well, let him look all he wanted.

And let him come up with some new lunatic scheme to try to force her to talk to him.

She wouldn't do it.

No interview.

Not with Wesley Tate or any one of the dozens of others who were calling. Despite the fact that her brother was now out of prison, that part of her life was over. O. V. E. R.

CHAPTER 9

He was losing her.

Tate thought fast, and started walking even faster.

He would have to play it for all it was worth, so he limped a little, as if his leg were bothering him. Bending down to rub his knee, he glanced up and saw the back of her car as it crested the hill.

Then brake lights.

Maybe she had second thoughts. Hadn't she seen him in her side-view mirror? As the SUV disappeared over the rise, he straightened. He'd lost her. "Damn it." He started walking as he heard an engine a distance down the block behind him and looked over his shoulder to spy the nose of her red Jeep appearing from behind a hedge.

Her SUV.

Coming around the corner behind him. She'd circled the block.

He felt a smile curve his lips and quickly bit down, turning his expression into a grimace, as if he were in pain.

And he kept walking, but now with a visible limp.

He heard the Jeep approach, then slow. She rolled down the driver's side window.

"So you're not okay?" she asked.

"I'll be fine." At least that wasn't a lie. He kept

walking but could see her in his peripheral vision.

Her eyebrows had drawn together over the tops of her sunglasses. "You're sure? I mean . . . maybe you should see a doctor."

"I said, I'm—"

"I know what you said, but you're limping."

"It'll work out."

"What the hell were you doing anyway? Where's your car?"

He was ready for that. Time to blend fact with fiction. "I was coming to see you, but I didn't want to draw any attention to it. You know, like nosy neighbors or reporters."

"Other reporters," she reminded him, keeping her Jeep alongside him, barely moving as she talked through the open window.

"Right. Anyway, I parked a few blocks over, thought the exercise would be good for me."

"And you could sneak up on me," she guessed.

He stopped. His eyes narrowed on her. "Yeah, that was part of it. But I really thought—and still do—that we could help each other."

"I don't see how."

"Then there's nothing to say." He started walking again, then sucked in his breath, making his knee start to buckle before he kept going.

"Oh, for the love of God, get in," she said. "I'll drive you to your car. Where is it?"

"Just a couple of blocks. I'll be okay."

"Get in, Tate!" she ordered, and he decided this

was his opportunity. He'd made his point. If he argued any further, she might just take off, and he couldn't risk losing the chance to talk to her, to convince her to confide in him. So, while her Jeep idled, he hobbled around it, keeping a hand on the hood as he made his way to the passenger side and got in.

She saw the way he'd scurried quickly. "Did you really think I'd hit you again?" she asked as he yanked the door shut.

"What?"

"You watched me the whole time you were getting in," she accused. "Like you expected me to step on the gas. You looked ready to vault out of the way."

"Do you blame me?"

She rolled her eyes. "Because of earlier? I thought I already explained; it was an accident." She rammed the Jeep into gear.

"Was it?"

"Of course! I mean, my part was. I'm still not convinced you didn't fake it." Raising a skeptical eyebrow, she slid a glance at his bent knee as the SUV started moving again. "And just so you know? I'm not buying the limp." Before he could argue, she said, "So, okay. Where did you park?"

He hooked a thumb toward the east. "Off Winchester. At the old church lot. I think it's Lutheran."

"Got it." She took a right at the next cross street. "So why don't you tell me why you wanted to see me? Oh, wait, let me guess! You want an exclusive interview with the girl who survived the McIntyre Massacre."

"I thought we'd already established that."

"Let's do it again, just to be clear." Again, she skewered him with a look that indicated she was pissed.

"It's pretty simple. You and I have unique perspectives on what went down that night and we both suffered losses; both of our lives were changed forever. I think that not only could I write the definitive story about the massacre, but also, if we worked together, we might actually find out what happened. The details are murky and we were just kids at the time, and both of us think justice was never served, right? You don't believe Jonas killed your family. You still think there was an intruder. You've said so. And I'd like to find out what really happened, not just for curiosity's sake, but because my old man died, too."

Her lips tightened a bit, and a hint of guilt shaded her eyes. "But then there's the money," she pointed out as the church steeple came into view, a tall spire rising above the surrounding trees with their skeletal branches, black limbs seeming to reach to the sky as if in supplication.

"Yes." No reason to lie. "Then there's the money." He rubbed the back of his neck.

"We could work out some arrangement and—"

"Not interested." She slowed for the final intersection, then drove into the icy parking lot butting up to the white clapboard church with its broad porch, now-closed double doors, and windows of stained glass.

His SUV had collected a dusting of snow, the windshield covered. He slipped on a pair of Ray-Bans and tried to come up with some other excuse to get her to see things his way, but he had nothing.

Kara drove into the near-empty lot and slid into a spot next to the RAV4.

Finally, he said, "I think we would work well together."

"Oh, yeah, right," she mocked. "We'd be great together. Just friggin' . . . awesome!" She didn't bother to hide the sarcasm lacing her words. As the Jeep rocked to a stop, she added, "We're here." She motioned to the passenger door.

"I'm serious."

"No." She shook her head. "No, you're not." Leaning across him, her body radiating heat, her breasts brushing his legs, she pushed his door open and a gust of icy air swept into the interior. "This is where you get out," she said, straightening, her cheeks a little flushed. "Now."

"Kara—"

"Now!"

He took the hint and slid out of her Jeep. This time he didn't bother grimacing against any faux pain. She'd see right through it. He paused, holding the door open for a second, and said, "I just want to find out the truth, Kara. I thought, maybe, that you did, too. Maybe I was wrong."

He slammed the door shut before she could respond, and climbed into his Toyota, started the RAV4, backed up, then rammed it into drive and spun out of the lot. Checking his rearview mirror where his father's dog tags hung—a reminder of the man who had given his life for Kara McIntyre—he saw that she hadn't made a move to leave.

Good.

Maybe she'd think about it.

Maybe deep down she really did want to know the truth.

He hoped to God she did.

The coffee wasn't strong enough.

Not by a long shot.

Detective Thomas gulped the dregs in his cup and decided that this morning, there just wasn't enough caffeine to keep him going.

Maybe there never was enough, Thomas thought, but he needed a jolt. Especially today. He left his cup on the kitchen counter, then headed to the bathroom, where he opened the medicine cabinet and retrieved a half-full bottle of modafinil. He held the small bottle in his hand, unscrewed the top and dropped a pill into his palm. As he closed the cabinet door, he caught his reflection in the mirror.

Red eyes, deep crow's-feet at the corners, tousled hair that seemed a little duller than yesterday, unshaven jaw that was still tight. He looked like he'd pulled an all-nighter.

Close enough.

To bed at 2:00 a.m.

Asleep by three.

Up at six forty-five.

And tossing back pills at seven o'clock.

Great.

This was not his usual routine. He usually was up earlier and worked out, but not today. He'd broken his self-imposed regimen for the first time in weeks.

The medication was legit. A prescription. Though three years old. For insomnia. His jaw tightened as he remembered the doctor, a woman with a kind smile and white coat, Indian heritage visible in her dark eyes, jet-black hair and slight accent. "These will help you get through the day," she'd said kindly while dashing off the prescription. "Once things have stabilized and you're sleeping again, then you can taper off."

Trouble was, things had never stabilized.

He wondered if they ever would.

He tossed back the tablet, stepped into the shower and let the bracing cold water run over his body. That was a shock. It helped. Icy needles pummeling his skin and running through his hair. Slowly he increased the temperature and within five minutes, he was fully awake and could get on with his morning. He threw on clothes, retrieved his service weapon from the safe and was at the door when he noticed his free weights and bench left unattended near the treadmill, where he'd tossed his jacket last night. *Tonight,* he promised himself, and left any shred of guilt behind him as he walked out the door and into the stairwell.

In less than two minutes he was in his SUV, threading through traffic. He grabbed a triple espresso and a sausage roll from a drive-through kiosk, where the barista, all of eighteen with a messy bun, bright smile and a tattoo of a rose vine crawling up one arm, handed him his breakfast in a white sack while saying "You have a good day" around a smile that was just too perky at this hour of the morning.

"You too," he'd said by rote, echoing the platitude.

Fifteen minutes later, he was at his desk when the station was still on the quiet side, but that would soon be over. It was nearly time for a shift change, the day crew coming on to replace the few officers and staff that held down the fort during the early-morning hours.

His phone vibrated.

He glanced at it and recognized Sheila's number.

Hell.

He picked up. "Hey."

"I thought you might be avoiding me," she chided softly.

"I might be." He imagined her with her intense brown eyes, pale, freckled complexion and wild cloud of red hair that never seemed tamed. Though forty, she looked ten years younger and kept herself in top athletic shape with some kind of intense boot camp–type fitness regimen that the army would envy.

"Look, I just thought you could give me some insight on the McIntyre Massacre. You know, now that Jonas McIntyre's a free man, what's the department going to do?"

Good question, he thought.

"I mean, are you going to look for the real killer?"

"You're assuming that Jonas McIntyre's not guilty."

"He's going free."

"On a technicality."

"Because the cops screwed up," she said.

With effort, Thomas held on to his temper. Because she was right. There apparently had been a mistake in handling the evidence. The admission of that fact had sent the slow-grinding wheels of justice into reverse. But didn't get Jonas McIntyre off the hook, not in Thomas's mind. Sure, he couldn't be tried for the same crimes, as double jeopardy prevented him being convicted again, but a man like McIntyre, a cold-blooded killer who'd spent over half his time locked away with felons? What were the chances that he wouldn't fall back on his homicidal ways? The odds were zero to none.

"Is the department reopening the case?" she persisted.

"Listen, Sheila, I don't know anything yet, and even if I did?"

"I know, I know. You wouldn't say. Protocol and all that crap."

"Yeah, all that crap."

"I just thought I'd give you a chance to say what the department's going to do. I'm already talking to some of the other people who have a stake in the case."

"What'd'ya mean?"

"Other sources. Witnesses."

She was baiting him. He knew it but couldn't help asking, "Who?"

She laughed. "I believe you call them 'persons of interest.' "

"Sheila—?"

"News at eleven," she said, teasing. Or was it a veiled threat? With Sheila, you never knew.

Her voice lost any hint of banter. She said, "You owe me, Cole."

And there it was. The favor that he knew she would call in someday. His jaw tightened. "I thought I'd paid up."

She barked out a laugh. Completely without

humor. Sadly. There had been a time when she'd laughed spontaneously, when she'd flirted and giggled and been sexy as hell. A time when she'd challenged him to strip chess, and he'd ended up sitting stark naked in her dining room while she was wearing everything other than a charm bracelet and her dangling earrings. And a time when she and he had discussed world issues along with the subtle differences between Oregon microbrews. And now this, the hard-edged laughter and her killer instinct. He knew she'd go for the jugular to get a jump on this story. Hence the mention of the favor.

"Where's Jonas now?"

"I don't know."

"But someone does. He's been out of prison for what? Eighteen hours or so? Don't tell me the cops aren't watching him."

That was probably true. "If so, I'm not in the loop."

"Yet."

Another email popped up. From the lieutenant. His superior.

"Holy shit, Cole, if you don't know, who does?"

Another good question. He read the email. Lieutenant Gleason wanted a meeting in fifteen minutes.

"Look, when you find out," Sheila was saying, "I'd appreciate a heads-up."

"I can't do it."

"Sure you can. It won't be the first time you broke the rules."

"I don't know anything," he admitted. "If you want more—"

"Hey. No." She cut him off. "Don't even think about peddling me off to the PIO. Not this time, Cole. This time I need something more than a canned speech by the department."

"And I'm telling you I don't have it."

"Even though you're the senior detective. You work homicide. And before you start saying the case is cold or too old or whatever, don't. Save your breath. I know better. As I said, check the news today. You might find it interesting."

And with that, she hung up just as Johnson appeared.

Peeling off her jacket, she said, "I just passed Lorna's desk. The lieutenant wants to see us in ten."

Lorna Driscoll was the lieutenant's secretary.

"I saw. Email." He hiked his chin at his computer monitor, then checked his watch.

She paused and took a quick assessment of him. "You okay?"

"Yeah, why?"

With a lift of her shoulder, she said, "I dunno. Looks like you're a few quarts shy."

"Of—?"

"Oh, don't tempt me." Her eyebrows drew

together over dark eyes that sparked with humor. "I could come up with lots of things, but let's just say shut-eye." She tossed the jacket over her arm. "Let me guess: Jonas McIntyre."

He sent her a look, but she was already heading to her desk.

Watching her leave, he couldn't help but wonder about her. There was more to Aramis Johnson than met the eye, a lot more. Yet she was secretive. He chalked it up to her being a private person, but maybe it went deeper than that. Maybe she was hiding something.

And then he stopped himself from going down that lonely, forbidden path. She was a cop. Duly vetted. Dedicated to the department. The truth was that he was becoming jaded from years on the force, and that was dangerous; he was becoming suspicious of anyone he met.

Even his own partner.

Ridiculous, he told himself as he pushed out his chair; he was jumping at shadows.

But no matter how hard he tried to bury them, his doubts had a nasty way of always cropping up again, like weeds gone to seed in fertile soil.

He'd just have to deal with them.

But he'd watch his step. Johnson, like everyone else in his life, would have to prove herself before he trusted her.

CHAPTER 10

A few minutes later, Thomas met Johnson outside the door to the lieutenant's glassed-in office. Lorna, a fussy sixtyish woman with a dour expression and rimless glasses, waved them inside.

The lieutenant gestured them into the two empty side chairs facing his old metal desk and got down to business. Which was his style. A man of few words, efficient work ethic and no patience for nonsense, he'd worked in the department for over thirty years, was a recent grandfather, and followed the Portland Trail Blazers religiously. He was bald and clean-shaven, his slacks forever creased, his boots spit-polished to a mirror shine. There were bits of basketball memorabilia in his otherwise austere office, two pictures, one of him and his wife on a beach in front of palm trees, the other of two toddlers in striped pajamas and Santa hats, along with the faint tinge of a recently smoked cigarette in the air. At six foot six, he used his height as a form of intimidation when he needed it and though he'd gained forty pounds since his days as a college star forward, he was still a force to be reckoned with. He knew it and used it to his advantage.

"Let's get down to it." He slipped a pair of

153

readers onto the end of his narrow nose. "You're up to speed on the McIntyre case." He glanced up.

Johnson said, "Yes, sir," and Thomas nodded.

" 'Course you are. Isn't everyone? The whole damned world. I've already started getting calls, and Norah will hold a press conference." He sighed and shook his head. "I guess we need to go through the motions." He glanced over the tops of his half-glasses. "Waste of time, if you ask me. I worked the case, you know."

"I saw your name in the file," Thomas said, and Johnson gave a curt nod.

"Worst thing I've ever seen. And I've seen a lot in twenty-eight years on the force. Car wrecks, natural disasters, hunting accidents, but . . . a family like that. All of 'em hacked to death—" His lips flattened and he shook his head. "Anyway, the way I see it, the case was solved, suspect found, arrested and convicted a long time ago. Case closed." He gnawed at his lower lip and his eyes narrowed. "Or I thought so. But now . . . the higher-ups want us to reopen it. Mainly because of public opinion and the fact that we screwed up way back when. It's a publicity nightmare, y'know?"

Again he checked for acquiescence and got it.

"Good. So, we'll reopen. You"—he motioned to Thomas—"are in charge. It pisses me off that this happened, but there it is. The press and public are going to demand that we find another killer, and that's . . . well, let's face it, that's most likely impossible. We got our man and we know it." He nodded, agreeing with himself. "But let's go through the motions. And by that I mean, look through everything. Check the evidence, statements, autopsy reports, photos, whatever . . . go through it with a fine-tooth comb. Interview witnesses if they're still alive and if they've moved, call them."

"But you don't think we'll find anything?" Johnson ventured.

"You mean anything new?" Gleason frowned. "Nah, nothing significant. So there was a mistake in the handling of the weapon. Doesn't mean we got the wrong guy." He let out a huff of disgust. "And it's not as if the entire case is closed, right? There's still the missing girl, the sister, uh, Marilee—" He checked his computer screen. "No. Marlie. That's it. What the hell happened to her?"

Thomas had spent most of last night wondering the same thing.

"Let's find her. Or, more likely, her remains." Gleason glanced up again. "Again, it's probably impossible. A wild-goose chase. I know. But technology has come a long way in twenty years. Who knows? Something might turn up." He meant bones. A skeleton. Or at least part of one. They all knew it.

"It might," Thomas allowed, though he doubted it.

The lieutenant asked, "Are there any other persons of interest still around?"

"Possibly," Thomas said.

"Check them out." Gleason's lips were compressed as he skimmed the information. "We're gonna be crucified by the press; they'll be saying we were tunnel-visioned about Jonas McIntyre."

"We weren't," Thomas said. "And no one's saying he didn't do it; he's out of prison because of a break in the evidence chain. In my mind, he's guilty as sin."

"Glad to see you've got an open mind," Gleason said as his phone buzzed. He glanced down at the screen. Ignored the text.

"It is what it is." Thomas was unmoved. "Facts are facts."

"Yeah, okay. I know. But"—Gleason was nodding—"we just need to cover our asses." He glanced over the tops of his readers. "Without his fingerprints all over that sword, the case against McIntyre was pretty thin. He was, after all, a victim."

That was the part that had always niggled at Thomas's brain and created his five percent of doubt. Jonas McIntyre had injuries himself, wounds that he could have self-inflicted, but would he have? Had he been that desperate? That enraged?

Gleason asked, "Did anyone ever check to find out who would have benefitted financially from the deaths? What about the partner? What was his name?"

"Silas Dean. He was there that day. Rumored to have had it out with Samuel Senior, but the only people who told us about it were Jonas McIntyre, and he was trying to push blame on anyone but himself, and Dean himself."

"What about the little girl?" Gleason glanced between the two detectives.

Thomas nodded. "She confirmed, I think. But she was only seven, just about to turn eight."

Johnson said, "In her testimony she said, 'Daddy was yelling at Mr. Dean.' Merritt Margrove made a big deal of it in court, but the prosecution shot him down as Dean had been at the house hours before the attack and had an alibi. And he wasn't in the will, nor was there any life insurance where he was the beneficiary."

Gleason asked, "So, what happened to McIntyre's share of the business?"

"Dean bought out the estate's share. It was all handled through the estate's attorney."

"Merritt Margrove," Gleason guessed, glancing out the window. "Run that down. See what happened there." He leaned forward again, his chair creaking loudly. "I'm assuming the kids inherited everything?"

"Right," Johnson said.

"His and hers?" Gleason asked, leaning back in his chair. "All—what was it?—six, no, five kids, right? Divided equally? Nothing specific for her kids versus his kids?"

Thomas nodded. "If both parents were dead."

"So the only ones left to inherit were Jonas and Kara McIntyre." Gleason stated it as a fact.

"Except there was a caveat," Johnson said. "If you were convicted of a crime or involved in drugs, you were out of the will, at least temporarily. So while Jonas was in prison, he was barred from inheriting."

"And Kara was too young. Comes of age within a couple of weeks," Johnson said. "How's that for a coincidence? About the time she's going to inherit, her only surviving sibling is going to be released from prison."

"I don't like coincidences," Gleason said, tapping a finger on the desk. "If the whole family died, kids included, who was next in line?"

Johnson said, "Samuel McIntyre didn't have any siblings and his parents were dead, but his wife had—or has—a sister, Faiza Donner."

"And she ended up being Kara McIntyre's guardian?" Gleason asked, his brow furrowing as his phone rang again and he glanced at the screen, then sucked air through his teeth in irritation. "Damned things never leave you alone."

"Faiza had an alibi," Thomas said, bringing the conversation back to the McIntyre Massacre.

"She and the boyfriend were supposed to come to the mountains for Christmas Eve dinner, but they canceled. Something about the boyfriend, Roger Sweeney, not being welcome. Kind of a 'family only' affair and even though Faiza had been with Roger for years, they'd never gotten married. Faiza and Roger alibied each other."

Johnson added, "And everyone already thought Jonas McIntyre was the killer."

As if they hadn't checked it out too hard. Thomas said, "He was. Is. That hasn't changed."

Her chin jutted a bit and she argued, "But the case has changed. The evidence that it hung on, the sword, it's as good as gone."

She was right, but it bothered him, as if she were subtly grandstanding, showing him up.

She said, "I finally got through to Randall Isley's wife. I wanted to talk to him about what he knew, why he brought up the problems with the evidence chain on the sword now, but we might not be able to speak directly to him. Isley is in an ICU ward at a hospital in Omaha. Congestive heart failure. She's not certain he's going to pull through."

"What?" Thomas said in a breath. Why hadn't she told him?

"Jesus." Lieutenant Gleason sucked in his breath. "God, that's too bad. I worked with Randy. Good cop. Decent guy. Our kids went to school together." He frowned and rubbed the back of his neck, derailed for a second.

"I've already asked for another look at the DNA," Johnson said. "From hair and blood samples collected at the scene, cigarette butts, glasses, whatever. I figure testing has come a long way in twenty years. Maybe something will turn up."

Gleason was nodding. "Good thinking."

"I told them to put a rush on it," Johnson added.

"Great. Double-check everything." Gleason moved a finger back and forth, indicating both detectives. "And I mean everything."

"We will," Thomas said, unable to hide his irritation. "We will."

"And locate the sister. Marlie. Talk to the ex-girlfriend who testified and the younger girl, Kara, as well as her guardian."

"Faiza Donner," Johnson supplied.

"Right, and while you're at it, see what all those ex-wives and husbands of the murdered couple have to say. I know the kids were set to inherit millions, but my guess is that Johnson, here, is right." He nodded to Thomas's partner, who had the good sense not to smile. "There were probably lots of other people waiting in the wings, hoping to get their hands on that fortune." When Thomas started to argue, Gleason held up a big hand. "I know. We think we got our man. I agree. Just check out other possibilities. They'll probably be dead ends or circle right on back to Jonas McIntyre, but let's prove it."

"Again, you mean," Thomas clarified over the sound of a huge truck passing on the street outside, then stopping in a hiss of brakes. "You want us to prove it again."

"Right." The lieutenant nodded. "And yeah, he can't be convicted for the same crime, but at least he did twenty years of his sentence and the department will look good, like we covered all our bases."

Thomas said, "Or our asses, as you said." Again noise from the street, this time the steady beep of a large vehicle backing up.

"And that's the goal? Appearances?" Johnson asked just as the exterior noise quieted again.

"One of many." Gleason managed a cold grin. "Jonas McIntyre, he's got a legion of fans, y'know. And they're vocal." Gleason's lips twisted as if he thought what he was assigning was the biggest waste of time on the planet. "And more importantly, they vote. Both the sheriff and the DA are up for reelection next year, so we do what we have to." With a sigh he leaned back so far in his chair that it groaned in protest. "This doesn't mean we let up on the rest of the work. God, no. We just add this on, because it's flashy. It makes headlines, but the other cases, they can't be ignored. The good news is that right now, things are quiet, right? Not a lot going on? No homicides since Labor Day, right? And there haven't been all that many assaults." He lifted his

161

broad shoulders in a shrug. "But the bad news? The holidays are right around the corner, and that means families and friends get together, have drinks, celebrate, all that good cheer, right? And it always turns out that suicides and homicides take a little bump. Stress of the holidays, or whatever." He glanced out the window to the slate-colored sky beyond. "The upshot is, this just means we all get to work harder. So"—he flashed a humorless smile—"Merry Christmas."

The attorney wasn't picking up.

Her texts—eight of them counting those she'd written yesterday after she'd heard Jonas had been released—remained unanswered.

She drove to the redbrick building that housed his office. The parking lot hadn't been plowed, so she parked across the street, then punched in Merritt Margrove's number for the third time this morning. She was immediately shuffled to voice mail. Again.

"Fine," she muttered, even though it wasn't. Nothing was.

She flung open the Jeep's door, waited until traffic had cleared a bit and dashed across the street, her boots slipping slightly as she stepped into a puddle of slush at the far curb.

Though she knew it was an effort in futility, Kara tried the door. Locked. She rapped loudly beneath a tattered awning, but no one, not anyone in the few rented offices or a maintenance man, appeared. All remained quiet and dark within. The building was obviously only partially occupied, a huge FOR LEASE sign posted in the window confirming what she already guessed. She rapped loudly again, then saw a bell and pushed the button, but nothing happened and she suspected the doorbell didn't work.

Nor did anyone in the building apparently.

All going to seed.

Like her lawyer, she thought, shivering.

Whereas Margrove had once been a famous attorney, nationally known, he'd slipped into near obscurity, his fortunes either gambled or otherwise wasted away, his B- and C-list celebrity friends having long disappeared into the woodwork, like so many cockroaches scuttling away from the light. After his failure to save Jonas McIntyre from a guilty verdict, Margrove's fortunes had spiraled downward in a series of bad marriages and worse investments, his flamboyant lifestyle catching up with him, to the point he'd become a shell of his former self, a small-town lawyer scrabbling for clients.

"Sad," she said aloud, but Margrove wasn't the only victim of misfortune after the murders of her family. Just one more piece of roadkill on the highway of bad karma that had been the aftermath of the McIntyre Massacre.

Kara didn't want to dwell on that now, didn't

see that it would do any good. Camping out here and waiting made no sense, so she returned to her car and fired up the engine. What now? Drumming her fingers on the steering wheel, she glanced in the rearview mirror and caught her reflection: pale, eyes still red, brown hair lifeless and untamed.

She cut a quick U-turn when traffic allowed and after grabbing a large coffee from a kiosk near a local shopping center, she pulled into a slot near the north end and waited. It didn't take long. At ten minutes to nine she spied Celeste, Merritt's wife, pull up in an older black Corvette. Celeste climbed out, a huge coral-colored bag slung over one shoulder, her platinum hair streaked with pink and piled on her head, her body trim and taut in a short coat, black leggings and over-the-knee boots. After locking the car remotely, balancing keys and phone in one hand and a large collapsible water bottle in the other, she made her way to the door of Allure Salon and let herself in.

Kara followed, stepping inside just as the lights came on, and Celeste, who had discarded her jacket, was turning over an OPEN, WALK-INS WELCOME sign that hung at eye level on the door. "Oh, hi," she said. "I'm sorry. I have a nine o'clock who must be running a little late . . . Oh." Her bright smile disintegrated as their eyes met. "Kara." Celeste sighed. "Kara McIntyre. Dear Lord. I heard you've been calling my husband."

She moved to a small coffee stand pressed into a corner in the back, near a door marked RESTROOM and boasting a unisex door sign.

"Merritt hasn't returned any of my calls."

With a shrug, Celeste pulled the glass carafe from the coffeemaker and threw the remains of yesterday's brew down one of the sinks lining the opposite wall. Between the mirrors mounted over the individual basins were shelves filled with hair care and skin products, even candles and herbal teas, the floral scents mingling with that of day-old coffee. "I kinda knew that. But we have a deal, my dear husband and me. He doesn't interfere in my business and I do the same." She glanced up as she refilled the pot, again from the faucet of one of the aligned basins. "It's called giving each other space. It happens in marriages. If you ask me, it's a necessity."

"Jonas was released yesterday."

"I heard."

No news there. Anyone who watched the news or read a morning paper had been apprised of the fact that the McIntyre Massacre Killer was now a free man. "Did Jonas call Merritt? Or meet with him?"

"Again: unknown." She was tossing old grounds trapped in a soggy filter into a trash can with a foot pedal, then as the lid clanged shut, reached into a cupboard, found a canister of ground coffee, and measured tablespoonfuls into a fresh filter. With the press of a button, the brewing machine was gurgling to life. "I don't think I can help you, Kara. And really this is my place of business. I don't feel comfortable talking to you about . . . you know, about *it,* what happened. My clients wouldn't understand."

"In a beauty shop. All anyone does is gossip."

"Not when—" She hesitated, then hoisted up her pointed chin. "Okay, so I was going to say, 'Not when a victim is here.' That would, you know, hit too close to home. Be a real downer."

Unfortunately, Kara did know. Maybe even understood, but she had her own mission. "Is Merritt at home? I can go to your apartment—"

"No!" Celeste snapped, irritated. And then more calmly, "He's not there."

Kara waited and saw the agitation in Celeste's features. Her makeup was perfect, smooth skin without a blemish, pale eye shadow, plucked, arched brows over impossibly thick lashes and full, glossy lips tinged with just a hint of color. But the whites of her eyes showed a few tiny red veins, and now her chin wobbled slightly. "Okay, so I guess you have the right to know. I'm worried about him. He's been . . . obsessed lately."

"With Jonas?"

She waved a hand, lilac-tipped nails flashing. "With the whole damned thing. He's slaved over this case for years. Years. Long before I met him, and now it's all come to fruition and . . . well, he's holed up in the trailer."

"The trailer?" What was Celeste talking about?

"A mobile home he inherited from an uncle. Not one of the cooler, newer ones. I'd kill for one of those, let me tell you. But ours? It's old. Piece of shit, if you ask me. Up on Mount Hood. Sawtooth Road." Her neatly plucked eyebrows drew together. "I've been calling him for over a day now, but he's still not answering his phone, well, you know that. He blew you off. Right?"

"I guess."

"That man." She shook her head as the smell of brewing coffee filled the small interior. "Won't take a call from his wife? Cripes! Pisses me off. Well, I suppose he's not alone there, now, is he? It's the way he gets when he is really into a project or needs some 'me time.' " She made air quotes with her fingers. "And he's been obsessed with what happened to your family and that brother of yours forever." She let out a sigh and pulled a black apron off a hook near the exit to a back room. "But, I'm telling you, he doesn't take care of himself. Nuh-uh. If it weren't for me, he'd have been dead ages ago. Ages." She sent Kara a knowing look. "If I'm not taking care of him, you know? He's a disaster. No exercise. Doesn't eat right. I've tried to get him into yoga and a healthier lifestyle, but no way. He's too stubborn. Set in his ways. He drinks and smokes behind my back." She rolled her eyes. "As if I can't smell him coming a mile away. Who does he think he's married to? I've got a nose like a bloodhound. For the love of God, does the man think I'm an idiot?" She looked beyond Kara, through the glass front of the building. "Uh-oh, my nine o'clock's here. Right on time: ten minutes late."

Kara glanced over her shoulder and spied a Cadillac roll into one of the spots in front of the shop while Celeste strapped on the apron, black plastic now covering her tunic. "Look, that's really all I can tell you. My day is booked solid, and the other stylists show up just before ten." There was worry in her eyes. "I can't afford to have anyone recognize . . . Wait. Here." She reached into a small flat dish positioned near her station, plucked off a business card, and handed it to Kara. "That's got my cell on it. You can call me," she said as the door opened, a bell dinged and a plump fiftyish woman swept through.

"Sorry I'm late, Celeste!" she said breathlessly. "Oh, thank the Lord, you've got coffee going!" Unwrapping a scarf and hanging it and a long coat over a hook near the coffee table, she let out her breath. "You wouldn't believe the morning I've had! A nightmare! With Chuck and the kids? I'm telling you, it's a living nightmare!" She was already pouring herself a cup of coffee from the half-full carafe and didn't even cast a look in Kara's direction. Which was probably

168

good since Kara's picture had been in the papers and on the news and she wasn't in the mood for a discussion of the McIntyre Massacre with Ms. Nine O'Clock, who sloshed some of the coffee, drips sizzling on the hot plate of the coffeemaker.

Kara took the hint and left, pushing out the glass doors to the cold day beyond, but she couldn't help but think, as she slid behind the wheel of her Jeep, that Celeste's client had no idea what a living nightmare really was.

Unfortunately, Kara did.

CHAPTER 11

He'd blown it.

His one big chance to nail an interview with Kara McIntyre, and Wesley Tate had flat out blown it. He finished his breakfast burrito in the corner café, scooted his chair back and, slipping on his ski jacket, walked outside into the cold, all the while mentally beating himself up. He should have gone at her another way, he thought as he melded with a thin stream of pedestrians walking briskly under the awnings of the stores lining the street, their breaths mingling in a visible cloud.

As Tate crossed the street, he passed a couple of teenage girls bundled in thick coats, hats and gloves. One was eating a donut, crumbs clinging to her glossed lips, the other was deep into her phone, scanning the small screen as she walked, somehow avoiding people hurrying in the opposite direction. Both girls' noses were red, their cheeks flushed from the cold, though they seemed unaware of the temperature.

It was freezing. An east wind blasted through the canyon, whipping along the jagged river, creating whitecaps before slicing through the streets of Whimstick and rattling windows of some of the original buildings built upon its shores. The town had been originally erected at the bend in the river, the first buildings circa 1840, huddled around what had been a single-lane bridge built for horses and wagons. Over the course of nearly two centuries, the population of Whimstick had steadily grown, buildings encroaching on the surrounding hills and sprawling around the point where the river curved backward on itself, like a snake that hadn't quite coiled.

Tate's family had lived here for four generations. He figured that was long enough and had sworn at his high school graduation that he was moving out and moving on, heading to college in California and from there? Who knew. All he'd been certain of at the time was that he was never returning.

And he'd been wrong.

Dead wrong.

So much for idealistic dreams and teenage declarations, he thought as he rounded a corner near what had once been a mom-and-pop grocery but now sold antiques and "gently used" furniture. He sidestepped a man walking a dog, some kind of beagle mix that nosed every crack and cranny in the building's façade.

Tate had fantasized that by this age he would be a famous photojournalist who jetted off to all of the hot spots in the world, reporting on wars and military coups and juntas. Or, failing that, a sports reporter.

Instead, he'd settled for crime journalist and

returned to Whimstick when his sister had called and informed him that his mother needed help. She'd been in a car accident that had crushed her pelvis and broken both legs while trying to take care of his stepdad. Darvin had been diagnosed with dementia for three years when she had been in the near-fatal accident, so she'd needed help. Badly. His sister, at the time, had two jobs, a kid under two, and had been separated from her loser of a husband.

That had been ten years ago.

Now, he was still here in the converted warehouse with its unique view of the river.

Once inside his loft, he peeled out of his jacket and hung it on the hall tree that served as a closet. The apartment was austere with its concrete walls, tall windows, and exposed pipes. He'd furnished it with a couch, recliner, and an area rug he'd picked up at a garage sale when he'd moved back to Oregon. His table doubled as a desk. He'd bought the old claw-foot at a flea market, along with his filing cabinet, which was really an old TV console, circa 1950, built of sturdy blond wood and now devoid of the television and stereo that had once been the guts of it.

He did have a bed, pushed into one corner, and a flat-screen dominated one wall. But that was it. When he'd rented the loft, he'd thought this place would be temporary. So far, he'd been wrong.

Just like he was about so many things.

Including his attempt to get an interview with Kara McIntyre.

"Idiot," he said to himself as he dropped into his desk chair and rolled it closer to his monitor, a large screen that connected to his laptop. He pushed aside the various legal pads, newspaper clippings and printed reports that were scattered over the surface.

Tate had foolishly thought that if he could see Kara McIntyre face-to-face, if he could find some way to gain her trust, that he might have a chance for an interview. Not only did he want to find out the truth and expose what had really happened on the night of the massacre, but he also had plans for a book of his own on the subject, told from the unique perspective of the son of one of the victims. Kara's take on what happened, as she'd been the prime witness, a kid herself, would add to the whole concept of the "kids as survivors" theme.

Of course, she didn't trust him, but he'd figured he would be able to gain her confidence, if only she'd give him a chance.

So he'd played it for what it was worth.

Feigning being injured.

In that split second when she was backing up, he'd made the decision and thumped the side of her Jeep with his fist before throwing himself down in the pile of snow.

It had been a quickly concocted ruse.

173

And she'd seen right through it.

Let him know it on the ride back to his parked SUV.

So now, he wasn't even back to square one. He was at square minus eleven or so. "Idiot," he said again. The only injury he'd sustained was the serious wound to his male pride. He should have just gone up to her front door. That had been the original plan. And then when he noticed the garage door rolling upward, he'd taken advantage of the situation and the whole thing backfired spectacularly.

He'd have to tread carefully.

And he might need help.

Someone who had military training, someone who was a techno wiz, who had the skills and connections to help him in his attempts to gain information that seemed locked away from him.

And he knew just the guy.

Pulling his phone from his pocket, he second-guessed himself, then decided he was tired of hitting brick walls. It had been twenty years. He was stuck in this damned town again. Jonas Frickin' McIntyre was a free man. And the competition for this story, *his* story, had just gotten a lot tougher.

Time to pull in the big guns.

As long as they were concealed weapons.

He pulled up his contact list, found the number, and punched it in.

. . .

Driving through the mountains, Kara checked her watch—nearly ten thirty—just before she spied Sawtooth Road, barely a lane cutting through dense stands of fir and pine. Only a series of ruts and a faded, iced-over sign indicated where what had once been an old logging road intersected with the county road. Visibility was difficult, the flurries of fat flakes turning into a near-blizzard as she'd driven ever higher into the mountains.

A lap blanket was tossed over her legs as the damned heater had given up and she hadn't yet bothered to fix it. Now she was paying the price as the defroster, blowing cold air, couldn't keep up with the condensation constantly building on the inside of the windshield.

Swiping at the fogged glass with her gloved hand, she tried to find Merritt's place. A mobile home, Celeste had said.

Creeping along the tire tracks, she squinted, searching through the veil for mailboxes or names on the cabins hidden deep within the trees and undergrowth. A sparse few came into view, all appearing to be uninhabited. No vehicles parked close by, no recently broken paths in the snow, no smoke curling from chimneys, just old cottages, stark and dreary, windows shuttered, snow drifting on forgotten woodpiles.

A good place to get lost, she thought as the wind

picked up, high-pitched keening, slicing through the branches. Kara felt her nerves tighten.

Which was ridiculous.

She reminded herself that Merritt had once been her ally and if his current wife didn't have the time of day for her, his second, Helen, had been close to her, being more of a mentor and mother-figure than Aunt Faiza had ever hoped to be. Merritt, too, had helped her along the way, even as his own life and career had spiraled downward, especially after Helen had died suddenly, the victim of a rare virus.

Why then was she so nervous?

Because of Jonas.

You know Merritt kept Jonas's secrets. Attorney-client privilege.

Her stomach twisted as her mind went to places that she'd never allowed herself to consider. What really did the lawyer know? Had Jonas told him the truth, or had he perpetuated a lie?

What really was the truth?

She thought about Wesley Tate and his accusation that she didn't want to know what had really happened on that horrible night, but that wasn't true. She did. That's why she was driving through the mountains, determined to find Margrove.

As for Tate, she wanted to dismiss him. She remembered him as a boy, but he no longer looked like the pudgy, freckled-faced kid with wild, untamed hair, glasses, and braces. Nope, he was all grown up now. Dark hair, bladed features and a dimple she hadn't noticed way back when. His glasses had been replaced with reflective shades, his teeth straight and white, his awkward boy-child innocence having given way to a hard edge evident in the set of his jaw and the tight corners of blade-thin lips.

Stupid that she'd noticed or even remembered leaning across him in her own damned rig, his breath warm against the back of her neck as she'd flung the passenger door open, her heartbeat quickening.

Don't think about him now. He's not worth it. You're just hyped up because Jonas has been released and Tate reminds you of that night. Adrenaline. That's all it was. Nothing more. And you have more important things on your mind. Remember that night, what happened. Tate's wrong. So wrong. You do care about digging up the truth, no matter what!

She bit her lip as she took a corner a little too fast, the back end of the Jeep sliding as she hit a spot of ice, then righting as the tires dug in.

Her heart leapt to her throat and she slowed a bit, her mind turning back to Christmas Eve so long ago. What had happened to Marlie? Why did she know to protect her younger sister? Why had her clothes been laid out on the bed as if she intended to leave? Why the hell had she been so scared? Had she somehow been a part of the slaughter?

"No," Kara whispered out loud, not daring to believe what so many had insinuated in the articles, true crime reconstructions on televisions, and more recently the blogs and Facebook groups dedicated to the murders.

But someone knew.

And she needed to find out.

Her fingers clenched around the steering wheel as the towering firs, needled limbs laden with snow, flashed past.

Kara had always suspected that Jonas or Merritt, or both, knew more about her sister's disappearance than either admitted, but she had no proof.

There's that paranoia kicking in again.

"Oh, yeah? Then why haven't I heard from Jonas?" she asked out loud.

Maybe you already have. Maybe he sent you that text last night suggesting that Marlie's alive.

"If it was about Marlie," she said aloud.

Who else?

The Jeep shimmied, tires slipping again, and she realized she was driving across a short, single-lane bridge that spanned a now-frozen creek.

Still the tracks continued.

How far did this road go? She squinted through the shroud of snow.

Around a sharp bend, she spied a single-wide that had seen better days. The mobile home was wedged in a grove of fir trees, needles and snow collecting on the roof, icicles pointing like crystal daggers from the edge of the overhang near the front door. Kara might have missed the mobile home altogether except for the fact that she'd seen the recent tire tracks visible beneath the new-fallen snow and had caught a glimpse of a crumpled red fender through the trees.

"Here we go," she said, recognizing Margrove's aging BMW. The car was barely visible as it, like the trailer, was partially covered in snow.

Fingers tight over the wheel, she tried to ignore her apprehension, but the place was so isolated, Kara second-guessed herself. She parked next to the old Beemer, then cut the engine and braced herself. Obviously Margrove wouldn't be all that happy to see her; he'd been avoiding her even though he'd known, according to Celeste, that she was trying to reach him. Feeling her nerve slipping away, she glanced at the glove box, then opened it, dug behind the owner's manual and a box of tissues, until she found two airplane-size bottles of vodka.

"Liquid courage."

Pulling off her gloves, she didn't think twice, just cracked open a bottle, tossed back the alcohol, felt the familiar burn in her throat and the warming sensation in her stomach. She repeated the process, capped the empties, and threw them back into the open compartment and snapped the lid into place.

Eyeing the beat-up mobile home, she set her jaw and pulled on her gloves again. "If the mountain won't come to Muhammad, then . . ." She opened the door of her Cherokee and stepped into the storm.

The path to the front door was deep in the snow, pounded by footsteps leading directly from Margrove's BMW, though now several inches of snow covered the tread. She followed it to the stoop, which consisted of two steps and a covered landing, all constructed of rough-hewn graying boards. The door was shut, but a flickering blue light was visible around the edges of a window shade that wasn't quite shut.

She pressed the doorbell.

Heard nothing and decided maybe the bell wasn't operational.

Shivering, she knocked.

Waited, pulled the coat tighter and stomped off some of the snow from her boots. Still she heard no footsteps, no heavy tread from inside.

"Come on," she muttered, then knocked again, rapping hard. "Merritt?" she called through the rusting metal door. "It's me. Kara."

Again, nothing.

Was he asleep? Well, too bad. Time to get up!

"Merritt?" More pounding.

But silence from within.

"Oh, come on. It's freezing out here." And though the vodka was beginning to take the edge off, she still wasn't buzzed; probably hadn't drunk enough to even smooth out the rough edges in her mind. Most likely it had been a bad idea.

"Another one," she told herself, pounding once more and hearing no response. Well, she was over this. Freezing on a dilapidated stoop wasn't her idea of how the morning should go.

She tried the damned door.

The knob turned easily in her hand. As if it had been oiled.

Good.

She pushed and the door swung inward without a creak.

"Merritt?" she said again as she peered inside and her eyes adjusted to a shadowy, shifting darkness. A burst of warm air that smelled of cigarette smoke and booze wafted out. No wonder Merritt wasn't answering. Obviously he had tied one on last night.

This wasn't the first time she'd had to rouse him from overindulging.

Nor is it close to the first time that he did the same favor for you.

"*Touché*," she told the nagging voice in her head. As she stepped inside, she heard the quiet murmur of the television that was casting the eerie bluish light into the room.

"Merritt?" she said again as a new prickle of anxiety trickled down her spine. For a second she thought she heard footsteps.

Running.

Outside.

But when she stopped and listened over the rapid beating of her heart, she heard nothing.

But the television. The sound must've emanated from the television.

She took another step.

Stopped short.

Her heart froze.

"Oh. God."

First she noticed the dark stains on the carpet.

Then Merritt Margrove. Wedged between the futon and coffee table. She let out a scream and jumped back, her eyes riveted on the unmoving body. He was sprawled on the dirty green carpet, his face pale, a red gash slicing his throat ear to ear.

Blood, so much blood, pooling beneath him, dark red and coagulating. "No," she whispered, backing up. "No, oh, no . . . no!"

Was there a chance he was alive?

No—impossible.

He was just so . . . dead.

His skin where it wasn't sprayed in blood was gray, his eyes fixed, no breath rattling from his lungs, no bubbles of red gurgling from his throat where the blade had severed his flesh.

No. No. No!

Her stomach lurched.

Hyperventilating, she backed toward the door.

You can't just leave him like this! You have to check. There's a chance he's still alive.

"He's not," she whispered aloud, but forced herself forward, her boot slipping in blood as she reached the unmoving body and bent down. Unable to find a spot to touch on his neck, she reached for his hand and felt for a nonexistent pulse on a cold, cold wrist.

Nothing.

Of course.

She dropped his fingers and leapt backward, but her gaze was fixed on the dead man she had known, the *murdered* lawyer she had trusted.

Someone had come here and slit his throat?

Why?

Jonas!

Of course it had to do with her brother's release!

Her entire body quivered, her stomach churned. Flashes of Christmas Eve twenty years ago cut through her mind. Sharp, painful shards of memories, glittering and jagged like pieces of glass, all stained red with the blood. Mama. Daddy. In their bed, red stains on the bedclothes, their eyes open and staring. And in the living room, the bodies of her brothers, strewn in front of the smoldering fire, their sightless eyes open and wide, their bodies covered in the same dark red, the Christmas tree toppled, the music, that continuous song playing over and over.

Gagging, she inched backward through the open door. The second she was on the stoop she couldn't keep the meager contents of her stomach in place a second longer. Hanging on to the rotting porch rail, she heaved what little she'd eaten, bile and vodka hurling into the deep snow near the porch.

Merritt was dead.

Murdered.

And the killer . . . ?

Nervously, her heart trip-hammering wildly, she glanced at the surrounding woods, felt the kiss of cold wind on her cheeks.

Had she heard footsteps? Did she catch sight of a shadow darting behind the pines?

Oh, Jesus.

Frantic, breathing hard, she searched the forest, eyes straining against a curtain of snow, heart clamoring in terror as she saw shadows moving between the trees.

Was he here?

Was he watching?

Lurking and biding his time and staring at her and gripping tightly in his fingers—a long, bloody blade?

Was it a knife?

Or maybe a machete?

Or an antique sword, like before?

She was backing up, fear sizzling through her bloodstream. One hand was in her pocket as she scrabbled for her keys. She had to get out of here. She had to get out now! Stumbling, she clambered down the steps.

Then she ran.

Through the drifts of snow.

Cold air slapped at her face.

Snow blinded her.

Fear propelled her ever faster.

Just like before.

CHAPTER 12

Her gloved fingers scraping the door handle of her Jeep, Kara bit back a scream and scrambled inside.

As the engine fired, she hit the gas, reversed crazily, then rammed the Cherokee into drive and took off. Freaked, her insides quivering, the image of Merritt lying in his own blood kaleidoscoping with vibrant pictures of her own slaughtered family. Mama. Daddy. Donner. Sam Junior. All dead. Blood surrounding them. Red spray on the walls. Staining the carpet. Smeared on the handrail of the stairs. And now Merritt . . .

"Oh . . . oh . . . no . . . no!"

Get a grip. For God's sake, Kara, pull yourself together!

But she couldn't.

She was shaking and hyperventilating and out of her mind. Tree branches scraped at the sides of her SUV, screeching along the glass as the tires slid and she twisted the wheel, the entire Jeep bucking over a ridge of ice.

Calm down. Calm the hell down.

Get control of yourself!

Frantic, the horror she'd witnessed screaming through her mind, she drove by rote, pressing on the gas where the rutted tracks ran straight, braking around curves and trees, feeling the entire chassis shimmy as she hit potholes, keeping her foot pressed hard to the gas.

She thought of Celeste at the salon, believing her husband was ignoring her. Not dead. Not *murdered!* "No . . ." She blinked. Tears were running from her eyes. She took a corner too fast and slid onto the bridge, the back wheels fishtailing. She didn't care, just drove as if Satan himself were chasing her.

You have to call someone. The police. Let them know. Or Celeste. Dear God, Kara, the killer could still be in that mobile home. Didn't you think you heard someone?

"Oh, God, oh, God . . ." Did she have Wi-Fi up here? A connection? She reached for her phone, still on the passenger seat. A tree loomed in front of the Jeep and she cranked hard on the wheel. The phone skittered onto the floor! Out of reach.

Shit.

Then she got her head together. "Call nine-one-one," she yelled at the dashboard, and prayed for a connection as the snow came down faster and she increased the speed of her wipers.

She heard the phone ring at the other end of the connection.

Thank God.

"Nine-one-one. What is your emergen—"

"He's dead. I think . . . I know he's dead. There's blood everywhere." Just like *before!*

"Oh, Jesus!" she murmured under her breath, then, getting a grip, becoming a little calmer, "Just listen. I want . . . I want to report a murder. It looks like a damned murder! Merritt Margrove, the attorney. He's the victim. Someone killed him. I mean, it looks like it. Send someone!"

"Ma'am? Can I get your name and your location?"

"What? No. I mean, I'm driving."

"Your name?"

"Kara McIntyre and I'm on Sawtooth Road and—oh, crap!" The road turned back on itself and she swerved to avoid hitting a branch that had snapped and fallen partially in the roadway.

"So you are reporting a murder on Sawtooth Road."

"Yes! Yes!" Was the woman dense? "I don't have the address, but it happened in his house. Margrove's home. It's . . . it's located on, oh, what—?" She had no idea of the direction with snow continuing to fall. "Maybe the east end of Sawtooth Road, Merritt Margrove, the dead guy, the victim, he owns the place I think."

"If you'll just stay on the line at the scene."

"I'm not there! Okay? Didn't you hear me? I'm driving and I'm not going back there. No way!"

"Ms. McIntyre—"

Kara's mind was racing as she squinted past the windshield that was fogging, wipers on overdrive. "Send help! Just send help!"

"If you'll please—"

"No!" With that she cut the connection and trod on the accelerator, her tires spinning around the corner, the rumble of the Jeep's engine barely audible over the jackhammering of her heart. No way would she sit here in the snow, waiting for the cops and EMTs and whoever else to arrive while a dead guy lay in his own blood and a murderer was on the loose. Not again. Not ever!

She thought again of her brother.

This had to be because of Jonas. Had to be.

Because he was now a free man.

Otherwise it was just too damned much of a coincidence.

And where the hell was he? Her fingers tightened over the steering wheel as her pulse pounded.

Why hadn't he contacted her?

Was he hiding, avoiding the press, or . . . ?

For a split second she thought of the possibility that maybe he'd met with Margrove and somehow things had gone wrong and . . .

"No!" Her denial rang through the interior of her Jeep. She'd always believed in Jonas and wouldn't stop now. Even though Merritt, like her family, had been murdered with a blade. Someone had gotten close enough to him to slice his throat open.

She swallowed hard.

Someone he knew?

Or . . . someone connected with the murders of her family. Someone who was triggered by Jonas's release and all of the new publicity, the renewed interest of the press.

Her thoughts tumbled to Marlie.

What had she known that night?

How was she involved?

Why in the world had she spirited Kara up to the attic that night?

The same old questions that had plagued Kara all of her life spun wildly through her mind. She remembered being awakened. Marlie's clothes folded on her bed. The sound of Christmas music and the grandfather clock chiming off the last seconds of their lives.

Marlie's words replayed through her mind:

"I just have to make sure it's safe . . . There's something . . . something really bad, Kara."

"Where are you?" Kara asked aloud, as if her sister were in the passenger seat. "What happened?" She swallowed the lump in her throat as she remembered the late-night text. Two simple words:

She's alive.

Marlie. Whoever had sent it had meant Marlie. Right?

From the floor her cell phone buzzed, but she ignored it. Kept driving. Hit the main road that had been plowed and finally let out a breath. She drove slowly through the pass and caught up with a white Subaru as it crept along the road that had once been plowed but now was covered in snow again as the damned stuff just kept falling from a gunmetal sky.

Kara was nervous, the road serpentining down the mountain as it followed the natural flow of the river far below. Forested mountains rose on the passenger side of her Jeep, the oncoming lane narrower than in summer because of the snow that been plowed and left to freeze on the shoulder. The tops of fir and pine trees poked over the snowbank, deceptive as they grew a hundred feet from the canyon floor.

Her nerves stretched tight as the taillights of the Subaru she was following winked a watery red through the curtain of snow. Her cell rang again and she glanced at the screen on her dash.

Unknown number. But she recognized it as belonging to Detective Thomas. She hit a button on the steering wheel and answered, "Hello."

"Kara McIntyre? Detective Cole Thomas."

"Thank God!"

"Where are you?"

"Driving. About an hour—maybe a little more—from town."

"Are you okay?"

Had she ever been?

"Okay? No! Are you kidding? I just found a dead body, for Christ's sake! A murder victim! Someone I know who had his throat opened up

191

ear to ear." She let out a breath and it came with a sob. "What do they say? It's like déjà vu all over again." She couldn't stop the tears nor keep her hands from shaking. She grasped the wheel even more tightly.

"I think you should pull over. We'll have someone come to you."

"No . . . forget it." She didn't want to see anyone. And slowly she was calming down. The more distance she put between herself and Margrove's trailer, the more in control she felt. Or at least she told herself she did and dashed her tears aside with one hand. "I am *not* going back there."

"I need to talk to you. Face-to-face. About what happened, what you saw."

"What I saw was a dead body. Merritt's body." Margrove's blood-soaked corpse appeared behind her eyes again and she shuddered, the horrifying image burned into her brain.

"Nothing else?"

"No! Just . . . just him."

"What were you doing up there? Did he contact you?"

"No . . . no, I was looking for Jonas and figured Merritt might know where he was, but Merritt wasn't answering my calls or texts, so I tracked down his wife and she told me about this place in the mountains. When I got here, I found him." Her voice squeaked and she sniffed. "That was it.

End of story." She was crying again, tears raining down her face, blurring her vision. "It was like before," she admitted, gasping. "Like that Christmas." Blinking, she tried to focus, but the images swirled in her mind. Donner lying dead, blood staining the carpet beneath the leaning Christmas tree; Sam Junior near the fireplace, the embers still glowing; and Jonas, looking up at her, rasping out, "Get help," as "Silent Night" played over and over.

"Kara!" Thomas's voice cut into the reverie and she saw that she'd let the Jeep drift into the oncoming lane. Her heart nearly stopped.

"Kara," the detective ordered, "pull over!"

She jerked on the steering wheel. Over-correcting. Edging toward the sheer cliff on the passenger side. The Jeep seemed to float as she eased off the gas, her heart knocking, her throat closing in on itself.

"I'm sending a deputy—"

"No." She shook her head as if he could see through the wireless connection. "No, no, I'm fine," she lied, gaining control of the vehicle again. She just wanted to get home. No matter how irrational that was, she wasn't going to wait by the side of the road for some cops to come and what? Take her with them? Haul her to the station to ask a kajillion questions? Make her leave her Jeep unattended here in the middle of nowhere? No way. No fricking way! "I'll be . . . I'm okay."

There was a long pause on the other end of the line and in the silence she heard the first sound of sirens in the distance, getting louder, heading up the mountain on this very road. "You'll go straight home?"

"Yes."

"I'll stop by after I check out the scene."

She realized that the Subaru in front of her had disappeared around a far corner, its taillights no longer visible in the snow. When had that happened? Where? She'd been so caught up in her conversation that—

Another vehicle appeared, headlights cutting through the snowfall, roaring up the hillside. A pickup with a camper top. Hauling ass.

"As long as you don't ask me to go back there. To the trailer," she bartered with Thomas. "Because I won't. I can't. And I don't need any lectures about the fact that I should have stayed there, with the body, you know. He was dead. I checked. Even though I knew he was dead, I felt his wrist. Couldn't find a pulse on his neck because his damned throat had been slit." She choked out a sob, remembered the awful gash, a macabre red smile that had cut deep.

"I think you should find a spot and—"

"I said no!" she said firmly, her hands aching from their grip on the steering wheel. "You can come to my house. That's . . . that's fine." It wasn't, but it would have to do. Kara ended the call and kept driving, fast and steady, not missing a beat when three cop cars screamed by, their blue and red lights flashing through the snowfall.

Only then did she let out her breath.

Only then did she relax her grip on the steering wheel.

Only then did she hear a rustle, the sound of movement in the car.

What?

Her heart glitched.

Anxiously she glanced in the rearview mirror.

Oh. Dear. God.

Hers weren't the only eyes in the reflection. Another pair, deep and dark, glared back at her in the glass.

CHAPTER 13

They met in the park near the overhang of the falls just as they had in the past. Though it had been years ago.

Here, where the river rushed over the cliff, casting up spray as it crashed into the roiling water below. The clouds overhead were parting, sunlight piercing through a thin veil to reflect against the snow thick on the branches and forest floor.

Tate spotted Connell's pickup as it wheeled into the near-empty parking area of the viewpoint and slid into a spot on the far end of the lot. Seconds later, Connell was out of the cab and heading in Tate's direction.

Tate started walking along the path, up the slight incline to the park as the water, icy gray, crashed over rocks and tumbled wildly down. Water spray mingled with the falling snow, the roar intense as Connell caught up with him.

Five-eight and fit, Connell was dressed in jeans, hiking boots and a down jacket. A baseball cap covered most of his brown hair, and sunglasses covered his eyes. Several days' growth of beard covered his jaw and he was, as always, all business. "Okay, what's this all about?" he asked without preamble and they walked, side by side, the path winding through tall evergreens with drooping, snow-covered limbs.

"I need your help."

"Surveillance?"

"Yeah."

Connell shot him a glance. "You know, I'm out of the business."

"I heard." But Tate wasn't convinced.

"I'm kind of into God and country, helping out those who are . . . you know, less fortunate."

"Really?"

"Really." He nodded. "Got involved with wounded soldiers—veterans who're coming back to the States."

"And so you've given up surveillance."

Connell smiled. "I've given up walking that thin line that separates legit from non-legit. Too tricky of a balancing act. And it was time for me to give back a little."

"If you say so."

"I do."

"Then we're okay."

A beat and the waterfall's deafening roar filled the silence. Connell made his way to an ancient rock wall that had been reinforced and heightened by a steel railing. He leaned over the barrier, seeming to study the roiling river below. "So I won't be breaking any laws?"

"Look, same deal as before. No questions asked."

"You're sidestepping the questions."

"How you do your job is your business."

"Job?" He let out an amused huff. "Business? Haven't you been listening? Didn't I just say that I'm done with all that?"

Tate nodded. "I heard. Let's just say this is for the greater good, all right?"

"So it's not personal?" Connell couldn't hide the skepticism in his voice. He knew Tate, had known him for years. Their fathers had worked on the force together and though Connell was in his fifties, nearly a generation older than Tate, they'd known each other when Tate was a kid, and he had reconnected with Tate a few years back. "This isn't like a personal vendetta. Right?"

"Nope." That was the truth. For the most part.

"But there's a personal element to it," Connell surmised, and Tate didn't argue. Couldn't. Connell would see right through it. Not only had they been close so he could read Tate like a book, but Connell was sharp, supposedly had a genius IQ, and possessed skills to go with his brains. Skills possibly honed by the CIA or NSA, though Connell never admitted as such. Nonetheless, they were skills Tate needed. Above all else, Connell had connections and could keep his mouth shut. "So let's cut to the chase. What is it you want, Wes? I'm guessing it has something to do with Jonas McIntyre's release." He stopped then, where the path had serpentined back to the river, just above the falls, sharp hazel eyes assessing. Daring Tate to try and lie.

"I need to find out more about that night."

"What? You know more than anyone—maybe even the cops." Connell's eyebrows drew together. "I helped you with this before."

"It's been twenty years, man. A lot has changed. Everything's more sophisticated. DNA testing, cameras, digital files. Guys who've been locked up for years are finally free because of new testing. Criminals are located the same way, if their DNA is found in the system. Old camera footage is enhanced. Cameras themselves or microphones are tiny and can pick up sounds and images from incredible distances, digital files are added to or changed electronically . . . well, you know. I can go on and on."

"So what do you want?"

"Your expertise," Tate said.

Connell was unique in his knowledge, all of which he'd absorbed like a sponge, from working in stores selling electronic equipment all through college to being a communications specialist for a cable company and expanding his own company specializing in cyber security.

Connell's eyes narrowed as they turned back along the slope, heading downward. "I told you—"

"I know, I know. Look, Jonas McIntyre is out of prison on a technicality."

"I read."

"Then you know," Tate said. "He swears he didn't kill anyone, but we all know cons all claim their innocence. Now we—you—have the chance to prove what really went down that night."

"By hacking? Breaking the law?"

"Think of it as serving humanity or justice or just your own curiosity. You've always said you wanted to know what really happened that night. Now's your chance to find out."

Connell thought about it as they stopped at the viewpoint again. He stared at the frigid water tumbling over the stony edge of the falls, at the geysers of spray creating an icy mist that filled the air with prisms of light refracting and reflecting from the sun's wintery rays.

"The McIntyre Massacre is the worst crime that happened around here in years. In decades. And there's always been this air of mystery around it. Of evil. Even when Jonas McIntyre was locked away, there were so many unanswered questions. Five people died that night, including my old man. Maybe six, as no one knows what happened to Marlie Robinson. She could be long dead. Probably is. But double-check with her father, Walter Robinson, if you can find him. The last time I checked, he lived at the coast. Seaside. Moved there sometime after Jonas's trial."

"Okay," Connell said. "Will do."

"And what about the other people who'd been

at the house that night? Her boyfriend—Chad Atwater? See if you can find him."

"You don't know where he is?"

Tate said, "What I know is that he moved away about two years after the tragedy." He glanced up, met Connell's gaze. "The press wouldn't let up on him."

"Meaning you?"

"Meaning the press in general, I was still a kid." Tate thought about all the people who'd been close to the family. "Another person to look into is Silas Dean, he was Sam Senior's business partner. They'd met in the military, I think, and then formed a partnership that lasted a lot of years before it went south. Dean had been at the house earlier in the day. They got into it. A big argument over some kind of land development. Silas wanted to buy the property and Sam Senior was dead set against it. So they had it out that day."

"On Christmas Eve?" Connell asked.

"Yeah, earlier in the day, and Silas Dean has a temper. Some domestic abuse charges were filed six months earlier. By his wife. At the time they were rumored to be on-again, off-again."

Connell's eyebrows shot up.

"The case never went to trial."

"Why not? Why did his wife back down?"

Tate felt his lips twist. "Same old story. He apologized. Swore he'd never raise his hand to her again. It was an accident. He'd had too much to drink . . ."

"She might know something," Connell theorized, nodding to himself, as if turning over the suspects and witnesses in his mind, people who may have forgotten what they had seen or heard. A person who had lied.

"The exes of the victims, too. Word was that neither of Sam Senior's previous wives—he had two—were thrilled with him taking up with Zelda. The same is true of Zelda's first husband."

"Robinson."

"Yeah, Marlie and Donner's father. He'd gotten into it with Zelda earlier in the day." Tate was on a roll now, remembering all the people who were players in the tragedy that had become the McIntyre Massacre. "And don't forget Zelda's sister, Faiza, and her boyfriend . . . his name is . . ." He snapped his fingers to remind himself. "Roger Sweeney! That's it! A musician. Plays in some kind of band that does gigs on the West Coast, I think. Dear old Auntie Faiza and her deadbeat boyfriend didn't waste any time moving into her dead sister's mansion. According to rumor she was always jealous of her sister and especially her money."

Connell was watching him, about to say something, but held his tongue as Tate ranted on, his voice loud enough to be heard over the roar of the falls. "Then there were the people who kept up

202

the place. Samuel McIntyre had groundskeepers and maids and a chef on his payroll, though none of them were at the 'mountain cabin' that night." He made air quotes with his fingers as the "cabin" was a mansion by anyone's standards. "They could have seen something or overheard a conversation or been confided in."

"But they were all interviewed by the police."

"Right. The cops. The same group who lied and covered up about the transfer of evidence? What does Randall Isley have to say?"

"He's the cop who is coming clean about the evidence chain?"

"Right. He goes by 'Randy.' I'm thinking maybe his memory can be jogged and he'll come up with some other detail he forgot in his original testimony."

"Speaking of testimony. You've heard it all, right? Read the transcripts?"

"Yeah. And one always bothered me."

"Just one? Like Kara McIntyre's?"

"No—she was too young. Yeah, what she said was scripted and obviously rehearsed, but the one that got to me was Lacey Higgins, Jonas's girlfriend who slept with his brother."

"Stepbrother."

"Right." Tate scratched at the beard beginning to shadow his jaw. "What was that all about?" He remembered how she'd almost demurely admitted that her boyfriend would take an axe to her lover before killing her. "Check her out."

"Haven't you?"

"Working on it. But I've come up dry," Tate admitted, not bothering to hide his frustration. "Lacey Higgins is married now. Has a couple of kids. It all seems on the up-and-up, but dig a little deeper if you can."

"Do you really think you can learn more after all this time?" Connell walked to the railing, gloved fingers working as he thought. "Books have been written, true crime episodes aired about what happened in that mansion on the mountain. I even heard that someone's working on a podcast now that it's the twentieth anniversary of the crime, along with a revisiting of the event by the production company that first aired the story."

"So maybe that will help. Now that McIntyre is a free man, people who were involved, witnesses who testified and those that didn't, they might be thinking about the case and might remember something they'd forgotten or weren't asked about in their depositions or at the trial."

"A long shot."

"My shot to take."

Connell nodded. "Okay, so you want what? Me to chase these people down? Ask them questions, or just observe and maybe tail them. GPS tracker? That kind of thing?"

"Whatever you've got." Tate rested his hips on

the railing. "Poke around. See what you can dig up. See if you find anything irregular."

"Like what happened to Marlie Robinson?"

"Especially what happened to her," Tate said, remembering the older sister who had flat out disappeared. "I figure she's the key."

Wayne Connell frowned as snowflakes piled onto the bill of his Padres cap. "Irregular how? In the phone records, bank statements? Computer records? Emails?"

"I said you do it your way. Nothing illegal or anything you're uncomfortable with, okay? But come on. Wouldn't you like to be a part of this? Maybe break a twenty-year-old case wide open?"

Connell snorted. "Don't try to con me, Wes. I get it." He turned away from the view to face his friend again. "You want justice for your father. That's normal. I'll work on it, okay, but I'm not making any promises and as I said before, I'm not breaking any laws. Got it?"

"Got it." Tate figured he could handle the illegal stuff himself. "One last thing."

"Yeah?" He paused.

"See if you can locate a woman named Hailey Brown from Modesto, California. Could be a fake. Or her maiden name. It's used online on a fan website for Jonas. You'll see it. I think she's a phony."

"Talk about a needle in a haystack. Common first name and surname."

"I know, but if you can locate her, that might help."

"Why?"

"Just a feeling."

Connell snorted. "Great. Anything else?"

"Not that I can think of. That's it for now."

"Good." Squaring his hat on his head, Connell turned toward the parking lot, but stopped after taking a couple of steps, as if he'd had a sudden thought. "And, Tate?" he called over his shoulder.

"Yeah?"

"Take care of yourself." His eyes held Tate's for a second. "Revenge or obsession, or whatever you want to call it, can eat you alive. Don't let it."

"If you say so."

"And don't do anything stupid."

Too late, Tate thought. *Too damned late.*

He watched Connell disappear through the snowfall, slipping like a ghost through the veil of icy flakes.

Tate smiled to himself. Slipped his sunglasses over the bridge of his nose.

Despite his objections, Connell had taken the bait.

Could be that Connell had wrapped his acquiescence in all kinds of do-gooding rhetoric, but the truth of the matter was that Connell was intrigued. Mystified. And there was nothing more he liked than figuring out a puzzle—through legitimate means or not. Yeah, he was definitely on the side of justice, which was just fine, but he was intrigued.

Stuffing his hands deep into his pockets, Tate stared at the water as it tumbled and fell over the time-worn stones below the surface.

Whether he knew it or not, Wayne Connell was in.

CHAPTER 14

"Jonas?" Kara whispered, fear nearly strangling her.

Her heart knocked frantically against her rib cage, her lungs tight. Fear sliding down her spine as she drove ever downward, the steep cliffs rising on the passenger side of the car, a sheer canyon on the other, two narrow lanes carved into the packed ice and snow.

Her brother was in the Jeep with her? Her ex-con of a brother?

Hiding in the back seat like they do in all those stupid horror flicks?

For a split second she wondered if he had a weapon. A gun or a knife or . . . or . . . God, whatever it was that sliced Merritt's throat.

Trying not to freak out, Kara kept one eye on the road, the other on Jonas, lurking in the seat behind her.

"Drive, Kara," he commanded.

"What the hell are you doing here?" She grasped the steering wheel in a death grip, trying to force herself to concentrate on her driving. The pass was treacherous. Narrow. Cut into the side of the mountain with sheer rock rising on one side and a deep canyon on the other. All that separated her Jeep from that dark, yawning abyss was a slice of icy pavement, a short guard rail and the tops of giant firs, branches glistening with ice. She had to drive. Had to keep the Cherokee on the road, but she was panicking, her pulse was skyrocketing, her mouth dry as cotton and her mind spinning in desperate circles. This couldn't be happening! Merritt couldn't be dead, his throat slashed so violently. Jonas couldn't be—

Stop it. Get a grip. It's all real. Deal with it, Kara.

"What am I doing here?" Jonas repeated. "What does it look like? Oh, shit." He dropped out of sight.

Another cop car sped by, lights blazing, siren blasting, only inches separating the two vehicles.

Kara gasped, her heart knocking crazily, the sound of the siren fading.

She glanced in the rearview again. "You're hiding from the police?"

"Hell, yeah, I am. You were in Margrove's trailer. You saw him. I heard you call the cops. What do you think they'd do if they pieced it together that I was there? Just out of prison and my attorney ends up dead. Murdered." His gaze held hers in the mirror. "And just so we're straight about it. I didn't kill him. I know it's what you're thinking, but I didn't kill him." He let out a sharp breath. "Son of a bitch. Son of a goddamned bitch. This is a nightmare. I mean, I'm finally out. Finally, and now . . . now . . . fuck!"

"Merritt is dead," she reminded him. "This isn't about you!"

"Isn't it? Hey, watch the road!"

"I am." She slowed slightly as the road jogged, the downgrade steepened. "You scared the hell out of me!"

"Couldn't be helped."

"Of course it could have been! You didn't have to pop up in my car like some serial killer in a slasher movie, for Christ's sake."

"A slasher movie," he repeated, and she immediately regretted her words.

"You know what I mean." She was still trying to calm down, to bring down her racing pulse, but adrenaline was firing her blood and anger was seeping in. "So where have you been, Jonas?" she said, catching his eye in the mirror. "Why the hell were you at Margrove's? Why didn't you let me know you were up there?"

"Margrove wanted to meet somewhere private. You know, just him and me."

"In the middle of nowhere? Why?"

"To avoid the press."

She squinted through the windshield, adjusted the defrost, the fan whirring loudly. If what Jonas was saying was true, then there was some sense to it. Margrove could hardly have found a more isolated spot. Even now, they'd hardly met a car on the road, the landscape muted, but still—

As if he could read her thoughts, Jonas muttered something unintelligible under his breath. "You don't believe me."

"I don't know what to believe." And that was the God's honest truth.

"I didn't kill him," Jonas said from the back seat. "That's what you're thinking, isn't it?"

She opened her mouth, but before she could ask another question, he repeated himself. "I didn't kill him, okay? He was dead when I got there."

"And when was that?"

"Like ten, maybe fifteen minutes before you showed up," he said. "I just told you we had a meeting."

Don't believe him, don't believe him, he's a liar! You know *he's a liar. And what if he did kill Merritt? Who says he didn't? Just Jonas, and he was in prison for murdering the family. Right? You've defended him, but you've always had doubts. Who wouldn't? The jury convicted him. Remember that!*

"A meeting?" she repeated, her mind racing.

"Yes, for Christ's sake. He's my . . . was my attorney. And not a great one, if you want to know the truth. Why did it take him twenty years, half my damned life, to find this cop who finally admitted that the police had screwed up? Huh? Why couldn't he have found the guy before the trial or anytime in between? Trust me, Margrove was no saint. He was paid and paid well." That

211

much was true. She knew it. Hadn't that money come out of the estate? "Between Margrove and your aunt, they pretty much helped themselves to every last dime, right?"

"I don't know."

He snorted. "You're supposed to inherit, right? The bulk of the estate, soon. If I were you, I wouldn't count on it. It's gone."

"How would you know?"

"I make it my business to know. And now that I'm out, my conviction thrown out, I'm an heir, too. I checked."

"How? You were . . ."

"Locked away? Behind bars? Cut off from the world?" He snorted. "There are ways, Kara, trust me." Jonas was working himself up. "You should have been on top of the money."

"I was eight!" The snow was falling so fast, she had to up the tempo of the wipers.

"Yeah . . . well, they took advantage of you. Of us." Tapping his fingers on the edge of the window, he asked, "What happened to the house? You still live there?"

"No . . . oh, no." She shook her head violently, saw the curve up ahead and slowed, the Jeep shimmying slightly. "I have my own place."

"Lucky you."

"Jonas—"

"Was it sold then? The house?"

"No . . . it couldn't be." She eased around the

curve, felt the tires slide a bit. "Not according to the trust."

"So?"

"Aunt Faiza lives there."

"What! Faiza? Shit!" He let out a long breath. "You're fucking kidding!"

"I thought you made it your business to know these things."

"I guess Margrove had his reasons to keep that little fact from me." He glowered into the night, his fingers still tapping rhythmically on the glass. "I wonder how much else he hid? How much he bled from the estate?" She caught his grimace in the mirror, his lips razor thin. "I want it."

"What? You want the house?"

"I figure it's owed to me. It and a whole lot more."

"If you say so."

The tempo of his nervous tapping quickened, and the interior of the vehicle seemed to shrink. "Look, just so you know, and you're not disappointed. You shouldn't expect any big payout when your time comes to inherit. I'm pretty sure that between Faiza, our loving aunt, and that fucker Margrove, there isn't much left."

Her stomach knotted at this unexpected turn in the conversation. "I don't know what to expect."

"As I said, I'm taking the house. I don't care who I have to sue."

"Auntie Fai, okay, but Margrove—"

"Was an incompetent clown. A has-been!" Jonas said emphatically. "It took him years . . . *years* to get me out. While the cop with the conscience, that Randall guy who ratted out the rest of the cops, was right under Margrove's goddamned nose!" Jonas thumped the armrest in frustration. "I spent half my fuckin' life locked up because he was so incompetent! Jesus H. Christ, could he have been any worse?"

"He stuck with you," she argued, though the points Jonas was making were valid, if sharp enough to cut deep, make her reexamine her beliefs. Another curve as they headed downhill, the beams of her headlights reflecting on the swirling snow.

"Cuz no one else would have him. And, it seems, because he was skimming from the estate. I shoulda known. Shit, I should never have trusted him."

She didn't like where this was going. "I thought you turned all religious, that you found God or something while you were in prison."

He shot her a look in the mirror. "I did."

"Doesn't sound like it. You aren't exactly turning the other cheek."

"Didn't you hear me?" he spat. "*Twenty* fucking years. You try that on for size."

She wondered. Jonas seemed angry, tough and, yeah, scared. Like she was after finding the body, but she saw nothing of the spiritual, calm man he was supposed to have become. She passed a sign warning of a steep downgrade and her palms began to sweat on the wheel. "How'd you get to Margrove's?"

"A ride."

"With who?"

He hesitated, then slashed her a dark look in the mirror, his features shadowed. "Mia."

"Who's . . . who's Mia?" Jonas had a girlfriend?

"Someone who cares, okay?" He glared at her. "Unlike everyone else."

She knew who everyone was. Not just her and Margrove. Jonas felt completely abandoned; she'd heard that from the attorney. His mother, Daddy's second wife, Natalie, had fled the area after the murders and her only son's arrest. Kara had no idea what had happened to her. As for Lacey Higgins, who had been Jonas's girlfriend at the time of the massacre, the girl whom Jonas had supposedly found screwing around with Donner, she had testified against him and never spoken to him again. At least that's what she'd heard Margrove say to his wife once when Kara had been staying at his house for a weekend. She'd snuck down to the kitchen for a soda, and Margrove and his wife Helen had been in the den, the TV on, a fire burning in the fireplace. "The kid feels completely alone. Even his own mother won't visit. And that girlfriend of his?" Margrove had let out a disgusted sigh. "First, she screws his stepbrother, then that testimony."

"It did sound bad," his wife had admitted.

"I know, I know, but he was just an angry kid."

"An angry kid who had trouble with the law before. And hadn't he broken a kid's arm in grade school, when they were wrestling?"

"That was an accident," Margrove had snorted.

"Maybe, but hadn't he gotten into a fight with Donner Robinson just the week before the massacre?"

He'd sighed. "Brothers."

"Stepbrothers," she had reminded him. "Full of raging hormones—too much testosterone. What do you always call it? 'Piss and vinegar'?"

Silence.

"If you ask me—"

"I didn't."

"Too bad, you need to hear this. Jonas McIntyre took things to the next level. You know it. I know it. And the judge and jury knew it. I wouldn't blame Lacey Higgins one bit for not wanting to hitch her wagon to him, if you know what I mean."

Again Margrove had snorted and as he'd clicked the remote to up the volume on what appeared to be an episode of *Law & Order*, Kara had tiptoed up the stairs with her purloined bottle of Coke.

Now, though, she was driving through a damned

blizzard, Jonas probably armed and definitely dangerous, his fury palpable, riding in the darkened contours of her Jeep. It was surreal driving through the darkness, trees towering overhead, the wind whistling over the steady thrum of the engine and Jonas glowering in the umbra.

Her fingers were clenched around the steering wheel. "So this Mia, the girl who supposedly cares about you," Kara said, "she just dumped you in the woods in the middle of a blizzard?"

"That's the way I wanted it," Jonas insisted. "I told her to leave me. At the cabin. She wanted to stay, but I made her take off." Under his breath he added, "Yeah, she's not like Lacey!" He spat his ex-girlfriend's name as if it tasted foul.

"Mia is your girlfriend?"

"Does it matter? For Christ's sake, Kara. Did you not see Margrove? Someone butchered him. Who knows who's next. Me? You?"

Looking into the mirror again, Kara thought she saw more than anger in his dark eyes, some deeper emotion reflecting in the glass, and with it came a prickle of apprehension that raised the hairs on the base of her scalp. What was Jonas really doing? How dangerous was he? What was he after?

Tate was taking a chance.

A big one.

So he had to work fast.

217

He tried the door to the old brick building on the edge of town, but as expected, the handle didn't move. Locked tight.

He knocked and checked the awning that covered the entrance, searching for a security camera in the rafters where paint was peeling and an old bird's nest was visible. Yeah, there was a camera, but he knew from experience that it was a fake, the kind bought online to deter trespassers.

No one answered.

He heard no signs of life from inside the building where Merritt Margrove had made his office.

Good.

Though it was early afternoon, the gray clouds and continuing snowfall gave him some kind of cover. Not much, but some. And he didn't have time to wait for nightfall. He intended to get in and get out.

Using picks to open the front door, he slipped inside the musty old building and waited, just in case someone was inside, but again, nothing. Good.

He walked silently through the empty reception area, his boots covered with disposable shoe covers he'd picked up at an open house several months earlier and, of course, a pair of tight-fitting gloves.

Nerves taut, he clicked on the flashlight app on

his cell phone and quickly made his way down a short hallway to Merritt Margrove's office. Again he made short work of the simple office lock, let himself inside and left the door slightly ajar behind him. Once more he paused, straining to hear any sounds of life, but heard nothing but the rattle of an old furnace keeping the interior of the building barely above freezing and occasionally the sound of a vehicle passing by.

The area where Margrove worked was a compact, cheaply paneled room with one exterior window, a massive desk, two faded client chairs and bookshelves filled with dusty tomes that appeared to have not been touched in ten years and what seemed like dead air tinged with the scent of stale cigarette smoke. One wall was covered in cheaply framed photographs of Margrove in his heyday where he posed with B-list celebrities, many of whom were now dead. One at a golf course, Margrove holding a putter and surrounded by his foursome, all in golf caps and loud outfits; another at a restaurant table, half-full drink glasses and ashtrays in front of Margrove and a beautiful woman whom Tate recognized but couldn't name, an actress in movies now considered classics. On the wall behind his desk, proudly displayed were various degrees, certificates and diplomas.

But the whole place seemed disused.

Abandoned.

An empty work space for a once-high-profile attorney who had spiraled downward into obsolescence through a series of bad choices aided by alcohol, divorce and gambling. And the case that had brought him his most fame or, possibly, infamy? His defense of Jonas McIntyre in the slaying of his family. It hadn't mattered that Jonas had been found guilty, Margrove had caught the media's attention for a brief moment in time. And in his "fifteen minutes of fame" he'd been a bright, charismatic star before self-imploding.

So, R.I.P.

It was over now.

First, Tate tried the file cabinets, all standing in a row, like metal soldiers along the wall near the door. All locked tight.

No surprise there.

Next, Tate stole across the room to Margrove's massive desk with its wide, well-used blotter and slid back the worn executive chair and glanced at his watch. He didn't have much time. News of the attorney's death was already getting out. He'd heard about it from one of his sources, a deputy who was close to retirement who had worked with Tate's father back in the day.

He turned on the computer.

The screen lit and immediately demanded a password.

Not surprised, he tried the desk drawers. Fortunately, they all opened easily. The narrow tray drawer in the middle of the desk held nothing but pencils, pens, paperclips, two pairs of scissors, rubber bands, three lighters and an opened carton of cigarettes, several packs missing.

But no keys or passwords.

"Damn it," he said under his breath.

The other drawers held a gym bag with a change of clothes that was so unused it was dusty, papers and supplies, a half-drunk bottle of Irish whiskey, but nothing worthwhile and no set of keys. He didn't want to break into the file cabinets even if he could, and he couldn't very well steal the desktop computer so he was stuck.

But Margrove had been old school, had grown up and completed his education and law degree before the widespread use of personal computers and the Internet. And in recent years, he'd had no secretary or legal assistant or junior partner. Margrove was an old one-man show. An old one-man show who once had a thriving firm filled with a staff eager to do his bidding, younger associates and aides who'd been tech-savvy and would have handled the mundane day-to-day routines of the suite of river-view offices located in downtown Portland.

So now, alone, alcoholic and aging, would he have trusted himself to remember his own passwords?

Maybe.

Maybe not.

He shined his light under the space where the desk chair had been tucked into and searched for a list of passwords taped to the underside. All he found was a brass plate with the name of the manufacturer, CAL'S CUSTOM FURNITURE, and the phrase PROUDLY MANUFACTURED IN OREGON SINCE 1966 etched into the metal. On impulse he touched the plate and it moved, the panel unlocking and becoming a wide wooden tray on a hinge that clicked into place to provide additional desk space. Tate half expected to find a list of personal information, client names and phone numbers and the like adhered to the smooth wood surface, info that Margrove could have accessed while working on the computer.

But no luck.

Maybe the old guy had been sharper than Tate thought.

He tried a couple of passwords—easy numerical sequences, or the word *PASSWORD,* or a combination of Margrove's initials and dates on the certificates lining the walls, all to no avail.

"Crap."

It was useless.

He decided to file this illegal break-in under Barking Up the Wrong Tree, when he thought of the hidden tray he'd discovered and the fact that this desk was "proudly" custom-made. If one secret panel, why not others?

Once more, Tate searched the drawers of the desk.

Again he found nothing.

He was about to give up, figured this was all a wild-goose chase, when he stopped short and eyed the blotter again. It looked small on the massive desktop, and he realized the long drawer in the center of the desk wasn't as deep as the desk itself, even though there was no overhang on the side facing the client chairs.

Just the design? Or . . .

He pulled out a side drawer and the center drawer.

The side drawer was about six inches longer.

Why?

Using the flashlight app on his phone for illumination, he checked inside the center drawer again, shoving aside the carton of cigarettes, and discovered a small metal indentation in the back corner. Even under the harsh beam, the depression was hardly visible.

Tate reached in and pressed.

Nothing.

"Son of a—"

He tried again. Harder. Pushing the tip of his gloved index finger into the slight dimple.

Click.

The drawer slid open another six inches and there in a long, narrow cubby running the width of the drawer was not only a small leather-bound address book but several zip drives. All hidden away.

Tate hesitated a second.

He heard the sound of a truck's engine and caught the glint of headlights showing through the space where the door was cracked.

Every muscle in his body tightened.

Had someone seen him? Or was the camera he was certain was fake, real? Or had there been another small security camera hidden in the building, one he'd missed?

It didn't matter.

He heard the engine die.

Tate didn't think twice, just scooped up everything in the small niche and stuffed the zip drives and address book into his pocket as he heard a car door slam, then a faint voice, from outside, as if someone was talking on a phone, but close to the door.

Shit.

He didn't want to get caught.

No doubt if the police found anything disturbed they would start looking at security footage for this building and the surrounding businesses and street cams, but it was a risk he felt compelled to take.

Yes, he'd crossed a moral, ethical and legal line, but he wasn't backing down.

He heard keys rattling in a lock, probably the front door.

With a creak, the door opened.

Crap!

Quickly, he closed the office door and slipped to the window, opened the sash, took out the screen and slid to the ground. Reaching up, he pulled the window down. It slid and landed with a soft thud. He left the screen in the frozen bushes and then, moving stealthily, leaving footprints he hoped the falling snow would cover, he cut through back alleys and side streets to the neighborhood where he'd parked his SUV. Once inside, he pulled off his gloves, started the engine and used the wipers to swipe the glass clean of the layer of snow that had collected.

Pulling away from the curb, he knew it was probably only a matter of time before the authorities were on to him and figured out that he'd broken into Margrove's office, so he'd have to work fast, taking pictures of the notations in the attorney's address book and downloading whatever information he could find on the zip drives, then possibly returning the stolen items— if he could pull it off.

Slowing for a red light, he thought about Margrove's locked file cabinets and wished he'd had time to go through them.

Perhaps another day, he thought as the light changed and he stepped on the gas.

He'd broken enough laws for one day.

CHAPTER 15

From the floor Kara's phone buzzed.

Still shaken, Kara glanced at the small screen. Caught a glimpse. Recognized the number. "It's Aunt Faiza."

"What the hell does she want?"

"Only one way to find out," Kara said, eyeing the phone. "I can answer—"

"Shit, don't!"

She leaned a little farther to try and snag her phone and as she did, the Jeep slid to the shoulder. Ice scraped the driver's door. Gravel crunched beneath the tires.

Jonas flung himself forward, wedging his body into the space between the front seats and, stretching one arm, he snatched the phone.

"Hey!" The Jeep bounced into the narrow oncoming lane.

"Keep your eyes on the road!" he ordered, hitting his head as he returned to the back seat. "Jesus! You can call her back later."

She eased the SUV to the middle of the once-plowed surface again.

"And don't use the hands-free option. Okay?" She caught his reflection in the rearview mirror again. He was rubbing his crown. "Just forget it and fucking drive."

"I'm not 'just driving'!" She was suddenly pissed—her emotions stretched to the breaking point, her nerves fraying by the second. "You need to tell me what you and Margrove were planning, why you hid in my damned car, and why the hell I haven't heard from you since you were released!"

"So now you want to know what I've been up to? Unbelievable." He leaned back in the seat and she saw him shake his head. "Where have you been, Kara? In the last twenty fuckin' years, where the hell have you been?"

"Wait . . . what?" How had the conversation turned like this?

But Jonas couldn't stop himself and as the icy landscape whizzed by, he ranted. "I could count the times you showed up at the prison on one hand, and that's if I'd lost three fingers!" He was angry. Enraged. In the reflection, she saw the flush crawl up his face. "How many times did you show up? Huh? Twice. Twenty fuckin' years in prison and you came twice with that freak show of an aunt. Like a million years ago."

"She was my guardian."

"I thought Margrove was."

"It . . . it . . . fluctuated." She thought of her lonely years with Aunt Faiza and how she'd escaped to Margrove's house in Sellwood. How with Merritt and his second wife she'd felt safe. Cared for.

"Oh, geez." Disgusted, Jonas let out a harsh laugh. "Just forget it! Drive!"

"I came. To the prison. But you wouldn't see me!"

"Once—no, no, twice," he said, and glanced out a side window. "Two damned times. Big fuckin' deal! And you never bothered to show up again." He said it derisively and a needle of guilt pierced her heart.

Don't fall for this. You can't trust him. Can NOT. He was a manipulator before prison, you heard Donner and Marlie accuse him of it, so don't let him work you.

Was he a killer? A cold-blooded murderer? Had he really slit Merritt's throat in the same manner that Donner was killed? The grade sharpened and she tapped her brakes, felt the Jeep slide a bit, tires hitting ice beneath the snow.

"Jonas, I'm sorry if—"

"Don't. Okay? Just . . . don't. It's too late for apologies and come on, you don't mean it. I bet I'll hear the same from my own damned mother. She gave up on me, too."

"I never gave up."

"I said don't! Shit." He let out a breath through his nose. "Just fuckin' drive, okay. Take me to 84." He was looking out the side window, swiping at the fog and studying the frosty landscape as if trying to get his bearings.

"I-84? The interstate?"

"Duh. Isn't that what I said? There's a truck stop west of The Dalles. Hal's Get and Go. You can drop me there."

"I can't. We missed the turnoff."

"There's another one. Just turn north at Kreb's Corners."

"Where?"

"It's still a few miles west. Smaller country road."

"And it goes through?" She didn't like the sound of this.

"Curves back a little, but yeah."

"Is it plowed?"

"How the hell do I know?"

She tossed him a look in the mirror. "You seem to know a helluva lot."

"But not enough." He let out a beleaguered breath. "Come on, Kara, you've got four-wheel drive. It'll be a piece of cake."

Nothing about this was a "piece of cake."

"So, let me get this straight: You want me to just leave you there? Even though you were at the murder scene." She was thinking ahead, certain that what he was doing was illegal, what *she* was doing was nearly as bad. "I can't. I'm meeting with the police."

"Right after you drop me off at Hal's."

"They'll find out."

"Not if you don't tell them," he pointed out.

"It's just not smart."

"And talking to the cops is? Think about it, Kara. From my perspective."

What she thought about was that he most likely had a gun. Would he really use it on her? His own sister? Then she remembered Merritt's ashen face and the gory red gash across his throat. The horror of the night in the mountains. A jury finding Jonas McIntyre guilty of multiple murders. She swallowed hard, her fingers clenched over the steering wheel, her nerves stretched to the breaking point. What did she know about her half brother? How could she even imagine what he'd been through in the last two decades?

"All the cops are gonna do is railroad me, like they did before. Did they even look at anyone else?"

"I think—"

"No," he cut her off, nearly spitting, he was so angry. "They didn't. And there were plenty of other suspects, y'know. Marlie disappeared, right? So what about Chad, huh? The 'love of her life'? The guy that didn't seem all that broken up about her going missing. In fact, I'm pretty sure he had another girl, ya know, on the side."

"Another girl?" Kara couldn't believe it. "Marlie was so in love with him."

"Yeah, but that girl who was his 'friend,'

remember? She was his alibi? He ended up marrying her, right?"

"Right."

"You think that happened *after* that night? Come on, Kara. Grow the fuck up!"

"But . . . but she was only a kid then."

"Fourteen."

"They didn't get married for years," she said, trying to remember.

He let out a disbelieving breath. "Wow, are you naive or what?" And then, "Well, what about this, then?" Jonas went on, ignoring Kara's argument as he was on a roll. "Maybe Walter Robinson? He *hated* Dad, y'know, for stealing his wife away? Dad and Zelda had a hot affair behind Walter's back, and Dad got her pregnant with you. Besides, Walter had been in the military—would have been good with a sword."

"But you didn't see him?"

"Not enough to ID him," he said, using the same defense he had all those years ago, that he'd only caught a glimpse of the intruder in the dark, a masked figure whom he struggled with but couldn't identify, a fierce attacker who had somehow gotten hold of the sword and left no fingerprints on the weapon, probably because the assailant was wearing gloves at the time.

"And the cops, they didn't even look at Silas Dean. Dad screwed him over, or at least he swore

231

it. And they fought. I saw them, earlier in the day, screaming at each other."

So had Kara. Dean had been a short spark plug of a man, bald aside from a ring of jet-black hair and thick horn-rimmed glasses covering his eyes. Kara had seen her father, a good six inches taller than Dean, ushering him out the front door. "Leave it alone, Silas. It's done."

"And it's cost us thousands. *Me* thousands."

"Ancient history."

"You're a fucker, McIntyre. You knew this was how it was going to go down and you'll live to regret it. I'll make sure of it," Silas had said.

"He . . . he left." The court had heard Silas's threats, but his alibi had been tight and he'd sworn he'd driven home and cooled off.

"Yeah, right, I know," Jonas said with a huff of disgust. "But he could've come back to the house! And who would be the wiser? His fingerprints were already there." Jonas was working himself up even further, years of pent-up anger spewing out. "And who's to say it was a guy. What about Marlie?"

"What?" Now he was grasping at straws.

"Why the hell did she run, huh? Did you ever ask yourself that?"

"No, that's not possible," Kara said, one eye on the road, one on the mirror where she saw his darkened silhouette. "Marlie would never—"

"You don't know that! She was vindictive,

232

Kara, and she didn't like me, and she was pissed that Zelda and Dad didn't approve of Chad. Dad even paid Chad to break up with her. Did you know that? I bet not!"

"No." Was that possible, or was Jonas just spitting out half-baked theories he'd concocted while spending year after year behind bars?

"And let's not forget Natalie." He was seething now, fury emanating from the darkened back seat as the snow-crusted landscape passed by in a blur and the tires hummed over the icy pavement.

"Your mother," she said, disbelieving. "You think your own mother . . . ?"

"Why not?"

"For one thing she had an alibi."

"But she could've hired someone. And she loathed the fact that Zelda had sneaked around behind her back and carried on a hot affair with Dad. You know, it was exactly what she'd done to Dad's first wife, so to have the tables turned? To have Dad cheating on *her,* she never forgave him and even had a short, hot affair with Walter Robinson, did you know that? The two exes consoling each other. God, what a shit show."

Everything he said was meant to shock and it did. She had pieced together much of the story about that tragic night over the years, read the books and articles, seen the made-for-TV episode on a true crime program. Of course she didn't know all of the truth, no one did, but still, she didn't buy into Jonas's twisted, malicious theories.

"Nothing became of the affair, though. It was just a way to get back at Dad for getting involved with Zelda," he said. "So it died a quick death."

That didn't sound right.

"But you think your own mother could have set up the murders and let you take the fall? Go to prison?" That was nuts.

"You know how she is. It's all about Natalie. The sun and moon and stars revolved around her. She doesn't give a shit about anyone else. Including me." His laugh was ugly.

"But you're her son."

"She gave up on me years before. At the divorce. That's how I ended up living with Dad. Didn't you think that was weird I wasn't with my mom?" he said with such venom Kara's skin crawled. "It was her choice."

"She defended you," Kara said, remembering seeing footage of Natalie in tears that her son was being arrested.

"All for show."

She remembered Walter Robinson being interviewed by a television crew, how he'd denounced Jonas, claimed Jonas had killed his only son, Donner, and was the reason his daughter went missing. "He's a bad seed," Walter, a tall, broad-shouldered man, had claimed. Clean shaven, he hadn't flinched, but stood soldier-straight as he'd stared straight into the camera's lens. "He knows what went down and he's not saying. Just to save his own miserable, cowardly hide." Then his eyes had narrowed and he'd addressed Jonas directly, as if Jonas could hear him. "What happened, you murdering bastard? What the hell happened, and where is my daughter?"

Kara thought of Merritt lying in his own blood. Deep in her heart, she didn't believe Jonas hadn't killed him, she really didn't know what he was capable of, did she? Winding him up, bringing all the anger that had simmered for twenty years to a boil seemed dangerous. She needed to take it down a notch, so she changed the subject and asked, "What's at the truck stop?"

"I told you: a ride."

"To . . . ?"

"Wherever," he said brusquely. "And don't give me any crap about talking to the cops again."

"They'll find you. And they'll think you ran."

"I am running."

"But you need to talk to them," she said, catching his eye again. "To tell them why you were at Margrove's trailer."

"Sure I do," he said sarcastically, his smile—cold and deadly—visible in the mirror's reflection. "My first priority."

"You have to explain."

"Explain what? That I was supposed to meet

him up there? It was all arranged. And I showed up and he was dead, his damned throat cut ear to ear?"

"Yes!"

"Like they would believe me." He snorted his disbelief as Kara took the first part of an S curve a little too fast. She hit the brakes for the opposing turn and felt the back end of the Jeep shimmy before straightening out. "Hell, you don't even believe me."

She opened her mouth to say something and he cut her off, leaned forward so far that his breath ruffled her hair. "I didn't kill him. You got that? I did *not* kill him. He was dead when I got there. I knocked. He didn't answer. I figured maybe he got wasted or something; it's not like that's been unheard of. I saw that the TV was on and that the door was open, so I let myself in. Like you. And I found him on the floor. Already dead."

She glanced again in the mirror as a phone rang. Not her cell. Jonas's. He already had a phone? And someone was calling? Who? She watched in the mirror as he answered, thought about the text she'd received from the unknown number. She's alive. From Jonas?

"Hi. Yeah . . . I'm on the road," he was saying in a hushed voice. "Yeah, yeah, I *know* . . . Look, it's a long story. I'll tell you when—" He glanced up then, caught Kara looking at him, and his face flashed with anger before his expression turned

236

to horror. "Watch the damned road!" he yelled. "Holy shit, Kara, watch the goddamned road!"

From the corner of her eye she spied a deer bounding from the woods. It stopped, poised for a split second in the piled snow at the side of the road. Ready to leap. "No!" Kara said. "No, no—!"

A flash of movement. The forked-horn buck sprang—a blur of brown fur, big eyes and long legs.

"No, no!"

Kara stood on the brakes!

The deer landed in front of her.

Kara screamed.

Cranked hard on the wheel.

The Jeep started to spin.

The deer leapt into the oncoming lane.

"Fuck!" Jonas swore from the back seat. "Kara! Are you nuts?"

Still the Jeep rotated, almost as if in slow motion.

Oh, God, oh, God, oh God! Kara was shaking, her pulse pounding, her fingers curled over the steering wheel as she tried to drive away from the oncoming lane, where the cliff, beyond a low barrier, dropped deep into the river's gorge.

"Get control!" Jonas said, panicked. "Turn into the slide, turn into the fucking slide!"

Through the windshield, she spied the semi. A huge monster of a rig bearing down on them.

"Oh, no!" She eased up on the brakes, hoping beyond hope there was enough time to get out of the huge truck's path.

"Oh, shit, oh, shit, oh shit!" Jonas was screaming. "Kara! Pull over!"

Headlights, two huge glowing eyes, closed in on them.

The driver honked the truck's horn.

Long and loud.

Echoing through the woods.

Still the Jeep spun out of control.

Panicked, she tried to right it, to find her lane.

"Kara!" Jonas rolled over the back of the front seat. Jostling her. Her hands slipping away from the steering wheel as he shouldered closer.

"Watch out!" she cried.

He grabbed the steering wheel.

"No—are you crazy?"

"Fuck." Leaning over her, he jerked on the wheel. He was twisted over the console.

"Don't!" she cried, seeing only swirling snow in the windshield, feeling a cold terror. This was all wrong!

Another blast from the truck's horn.

Terror clawed at her heart.

Close! The truck was close!

Oh, God, so damned close.

As the Jeep spun wildly, she peered through the curtain of snow and pressed hard on the brakes, standing on them.

They had to stop, to find a way—

Jesus, was that the semi's huge grill bearing down on them? Above the massive hood, the driver in the cab was chalk-faced and working the steering wheel.

"Get out of the way!" Jonas screamed as if the trucker could hear him. "Get the fuck out of the way!"

Too late!

They were going to hit!

The driver, so close, was blasting them with the horn and cranking the steering wheel hard.

"Shhiiiiit!" Jonas yelled.

Kara braced herself.

Screamed.

Eighteen wheels thundered through snow that had collected at the edge of the road. The top of the trailer skimming the lowest tree branches, ice sheering, limbs snapping, snow and needles and shards of wood flying over the truck, scattering across the road.

With a squeal of brakes, the tractor trailer seemed to move in slow motion as the cab swept past, the Cherokee still out of control, the back end of the truck swinging as the rig jackknifed.

"Fuck!" Jonas yanked even harder on the wheel.

The Jeep jerked, careening to the side of the road, just as the back end of the trailer clipped the SUV's rear bumper.

Reeling faster and faster, the SUV spun crazily toward the piled snow on the edge of the road and the canyon beyond.

"Hold on!" Jonas yelled as the SUV tore through the snowbank, ice and snow clods flinging in all directions. Flying into the abyss, hurtling forward, the Jeep went airborne.

Branches snapped, scraping metal.

The tires landed, the whole vehicle jarring.

A huge fir tree loomed.

"Kara, watch out—"

Bam!

The Jeep shuddered as it crashed into the tree, steel groaning as it crumpled.

Emergency airbags inflated.

Glass rained into her hair.

Cold air surrounded her.

Jonas screamed in agony, but she couldn't move, couldn't think.

From far away, as her eyes closed, she heard the honk of a huge vehicle's horn. The sound was steady and mournful, a one-note funeral dirge drowning out the sound of her brother's moans.

"Jonas . . ." she tried to say, but the sound was a whisper. She was going to die. Right here on this frozen mountainside. Maybe if she could find her phone and call . . . the thought crossed her mind, but only for a second and then everything went dark.

CHAPTER 16

"Wouldn't you know?" Johnson said as the body bag carrying Merritt Margrove's corpse was slammed into the back of the ambulance. "The lieutenant finally hands you the case that has consumed you for years and a primary witness, the damned attorney for the man convicted of the crime, has his throat slit before you even have a chance to question him. How's that for irony?"

"Or convenience," Thomas said as he eyed the trailer where the attorney had lost his life. The place that probably had looked peaceful, an aging single-wide mobile home nestled in the snowy woods, was now crawling with cops, vehicles parked between the trees, yellow tape strung around the perimeter, the quietude disturbed. Inside the aging mobile home was a bloody crime scene, the forensic team and ME already having examined the mobile home and surrounding area. All the while, snow just kept falling, disturbing any footprints and tire tracks.

And it was cold as a mother up here.

Despite his down jacket and gloves and hat, he felt the chill, the bitter wind harsh against his face.

Johnson didn't seem to notice as she studied the grounds, watching the ambulance roll away.

Things had been tense between them since the meeting in Gleason's office when he'd felt as if his own partner had been holding out on him. He'd confronted her in the hallway, telling her that she'd crossed a line with him, that either they were a team of equals who shared info and worked together, or they weren't.

Johnson hadn't seemed chastised as they'd walked down the crowded hallway, jostled by a steady stream of cops heading the opposite direction. Instead, she'd thrown him a disbelieving look. "We *are* a team," she'd said, skirting a potted plant in the reception area. "We share information, but that doesn't mean either of us is looking over the other's shoulder. I guess I should have told you about asking for new DNA results. I thought you trusted me."

"We just need to work together."

"I was just being efficient. I figure that's a good thing, right? We weren't just spinning our wheels."

"But you didn't let me know."

"Oh, Christ, Thomas, I wasn't keeping anything from you! Jesus! It's just there's a lot going on and we were called in to report to the lieutenant before I could share." She'd let out a huff. "Get over your bad self. Let's just solve the damned case. Together."

"That's all I want."

"Is it?" She'd pushed open the outside door,

letting in the cold air before he'd had a chance to open it for her. "Then open your mind. You and Gleason both. It could just be, you know, that Jonas McIntyre isn't the killer."

"You weren't here then."

"Precisely," she'd said. "Fresh eyes. Could be the department could use a pair."

"Just don't undercut me again."

"Ouch. Undercut? Seriously? Is that the sound of wounded male pride I'm hearing?" She'd reached his SUV. "Wow."

And then, before they'd had a chance to drive to Kara McIntyre's place to interview her, Thomas had received the call from dispatch after Kara had phoned 9-1-1. They'd ended up here at Margrove's mountain retreat. It had taken them longer than anticipated because of some accident that had clogged the main highway and they'd been diverted to a secondary road that had barely been plowed.

As Kara McIntyre had reported, the lawyer had been murdered, his throat sliced, bleeding out in the space between his coffee table and a couch. A cigarette had smoldered in the futon, though the place hadn't burned down, the TV was still on low, a near-empty bottle of scotch on the table with an ashtray full of butts, a paper plate with the remains of a slice of pizza, just the nearly burned crust.

But there were things missing.

Important things.

Blood spatter had stained the coffee table, red beads visible on a pair of glasses, the ashtray, glass and bottle, the greasy paper plate, even a pen. But there were clear spots where the marred table showed no signs of blood, a square patch about the size of a laptop computer, a smaller one that could have been where Margrove's cell phone had rested, and then a larger area, not as defined. Notes? A legal pad with some pages having been torn out. Maybe.

He hadn't been robbed.

His wallet was still in his jacket pocket in the parka hanging on a hook near the front door, his wedding ring and another one, with what appeared to be diamonds, still on his fingers. And a small safe in the bedroom hadn't been disturbed. It had been closed, but unlocked, a loaded pistol and a bag of marijuana left, though there had been no personal documents.

"You think this is Jonas McIntyre's work?"

He hesitated. Rubbed a hand around the back of his neck. "Not sure. But it seems a little too pat. Yeah, someone close to McIntyre was killed, the weapon of choice being a blade of some kind, like before, but it seems almost like a setup. First of all, why would Jonas McIntyre kill his lawyer? After all, the guy was the one person who stood by him, worked for a couple of decades trying to get Jonas out, so why turn on him?"

"Anger issues?"

"I don't know." Thomas wasn't buying it. "The word is that Jonas McIntyre is a new man, found God and all that."

"Maybe an act."

"Maybe." But it didn't wash, not with Thomas, and most likely not with Johnson either. She was just playing devil's advocate.

"And how did McIntyre get up here? Did he have an accomplice? A driver?"

"Where is he?"

"Good question."

"No sign of forced entry," she reminded him. "Either he knew the attacker or the guy got the jump on him."

"If he knew him, he didn't offer him a drink. Only one glass. And he was attacked from behind."

The front door that opened directly into the living area and the back door off the kitchen were both unlocked. The windows were closed, but the bathroom window hadn't been latched and seemed broken. There were few screens, and the two that existed were frayed. Not exactly tight security. The prevailing theory was that the killer had entered through the kitchen door, possibly while Margrove was dozing or in the bathroom, or somehow distracted, then waited for the opportunity to come up behind him and kill him quickly as there hadn't been an indication of a struggle. Margrove hadn't had time to defend himself. Not only was the gun in his safe, but there had been a baseball bat in the living room, practically at arm's reach. So the killer had acted quickly. Time of death, the ME thought, was the early morning hours.

He chewed at his lower lip, his eyes narrowing as he stared at the single-wide mobile home with its rickety porch and rotting railing. What had Margrove been doing up here? Had he known his killer? Thomas's mind kept returning to Jonas McIntyre, but why would he kill the lawyer who had worked so hard to set him free? He would know he would become Suspect Number One.

The move was a stupid one.

One thing Jonas McIntyre was not?

Stupid.

Before he'd murdered his family, he'd been applying to get into Stanford, his father's alma mater. His SATs, essay and high school GPA all pointed to a brilliant teenager, but that was before his trouble with the law, someone who had turned out to be a cold-blooded killer.

Thomas believed that Jonas McIntyre, all of eighteen that Christmas long ago, had been hopped up on teenage adrenaline and jealousy. What had turned into an argument had escalated to a savage massacre, and no one had been able to stop him. Bloodlust. Testosterone and adrenaline fueling his fury. Not that the case had been totally without question.

Why kill his parents?

Because they had punished him for his earlier fight? Grounded him?

Because they were witnesses to the crime?

That part had never set quite right with Thomas.

And what happened to Marlie? Why was there never a trace of her? Why had her clothes been so neatly folded, her bed unmade?

Then there was Kara. Saved by her missing older sister. The girl whose testimony had been twisted around enough to send her brother to prison.

The whole case had been manipulated. Not that Thomas didn't believe Jonas McIntyre was guilty as sin. The kid had been a hothead, volatile and brutal. He'd killed his brothers. They'd all gotten into it and things had escalated out of control.

But the parents?

Killed first, it seemed, as Jonas had been found clinging to life in the living room with his brother and stepbrother.

"Hey!" Johnson broke into his thoughts. She was striding toward him as she shoved her phone into a back pocket. "Just got off the phone with dispatch. The highway up here that was shut down and diverted us? Turns out there was a major accident."

"Yeah?" They'd known that much.

"Don't have all the details yet, but a truck jackknifed, and another vehicle was involved.

A Jeep registered to Kara McIntyre. Couple of hours ago. Three victims."

"Three?"

"Driver of the semi," she said, holding up a gloved finger. "Then the driver of the Jeep, IDed as Kara McIntyre." Another finger shot up as Thomas's stomach plummeted. "She had a passenger with her. Male, thrown out of the vehicle."

"What?"

Her third finger joined the first two.

His gut tightened. "Fatalities?"

"Not yet, but it's iffy. None of them are in great shape, of course, but for the most part lucked out. The guy with Kara?" she said. "No ID. Bruised and battered but miraculously not critical, at least that's the report at this time."

Thomas felt a deep-seated and dreaded certainty that he knew the answer when he asked the question, "Who is he?"

"They're not sure. He hasn't come around."

But he read the answer in her eyes. "They think it might be Jonas McIntyre."

"That's their best guess. Right height and build. His face has been plastered all over social media and the press. Super recognizable. Except right now, the guy thrown from the Jeep's face is kind of a mess, scratches and bruises, and enough of a jolt to knock him out. Like I said, it's a miracle he survived or isn't clinging to life in ICU."

"I heard he found religion. Seems like God was looking out for him."

"Or he just got lucky. Either way, until they take his prints, or he wakes up and tells them who he is—or Kara does—they're not saying for sure."

"It's Jonas." Thomas was certain of it. "Damn it." He eyed the trailer where the crews were still working. "Somehow he's involved in this."

"Looks like," she admitted.

He started for his SUV, but her phone jangled again. "Wait," she said, and answered, her face growing grim. "Shit." She let out a slow breath and shook her head. "I knew it. I just knew it!!"

Thomas paused, the wind whipping through the canyon, shaking snow and ice from the branches of the surrounding trees, the cold sinking deep into his bones.

"Yeah, yeah, fine. I know . . . we'll meet you at the hospital ASAP," Johnson said, then cut the connection.

"What?" he asked, dreading the answer.

"I lied," she said, her expression grim as she pocketed her phone. "I told you there were no serious injuries in the accident. Well, that just changed. One of the victims went into cardiac arrest on the way to the hospital, but they managed to revive him. For now. But it doesn't look good."

Kara opened a bleary eye.

Dim lights.

Hushed voices.

She tried to focus but failed.

All she knew was that she was lying on a bed. A narrow bed.

". . . when she wakes up, she could be released," a soft female voice said. "All her vitals are normal."

"Even with that gash on her head and a concussion."

Concussion?

"That and a few contusions and that bruise where the seat belt held her." A harsher voice. "That's going to hurt."

They were talking about her. Again, Kara tried to wake up.

"She's coming around," said one of the whispered voices, belonging to an older woman, it seemed. A shadowy image approached the bed. "Kara?" she said a little more loudly. "Ms. McIntyre?"

Kara couldn't answer.

She tried. Moved her lips, but her tongue wouldn't comply and she couldn't force any breath to form the words.

"You're here. In the hospital. Whimstick General." The same older voice. "Ms. McIntyre?"

But Kara faded away.

Didn't care where she was or who the pushy woman who was now touching her shoulder was.

Hospital?

She was injured?

She felt the warmth of the blackness surround her and though she didn't understand why, she was grateful for the cloak of unknowing, of just letting go and forgetting. Sleep that had been so elusive to her for so long enfolded her in its dreamless and empty fog.

And then again.

How much time had passed she couldn't guess, didn't want to.

But unbidden, bits and pieces of the accident swirled through her mind, cutting through the fog, like spinning shards of glass, memories cut deep into her brain, first in one place, then the other. Painful little pictures causing her to wince.

She'd been driving.

Oh, God, had she been drinking?

A huge truck had been racing toward her vehicle, a roaring monster with glowing head-lights, bearing down on her. On them.

Crap! Someone had been with her.

Jonas! Yes, yes, hiding in the back seat! Popping up like a gruesome doll in a jack-in-the-box.

And then spinning—wildly rotating over the edge of the cliff.

Screaming!

Twisting, shrieking metal!

Glass splintering. Raining on her.

Thick branches crashing through the wind-shield!

Her heart raced as she remembered.

Or had it all been a dream? Oh, God, she hoped beyond hope that it was a dream, that *this*—the hospital—it was all a bad, bad nightmare.

She blinked. Eyed her surroundings. Trying to clear her head, to think rationally, to come to grips with where she was.

The room—small, dimly lit but sterile—two women hovering over the bed, the quiet, steady beat of some kind of monitor.

Kara's heart sank. It was real.

"She's coming to again," the woman, a nurse most likely, was saying. "Ms. McIntyre? Kara, how're you feeling?"

"My head," she whispered.

"You were in an accident," the younger nurse said. Kara blinked, saw the name DANI RUTGERS, RN pinned to the nurse's scrubs. She was definitely in a hospital room, and there were two nurses nearby. An older woman, brown hair starting to silver, was eyeing the monitors, while a petite woman in her twenties with short dark hair and oversize red glasses—Dani Rutgers—was talking to her. "You've got a few cuts and scratches, a major bruise from your seat belt and a head injury."

"A head . . . ?" Then she remembered the slamming of a tree branch through the broken windshield.

"That's the concussion," the older nurse said.

Kara reached up, winced a little as she felt some pain in her shoulder, then tenderly touched her forehead, where a bandage was taped. "Six stitches." The older nurse was curt.

Nurse Rutgers added, "But your CT scan didn't show any sign of skull fracture."

"If you're lucky, you might not even need plastic surgery," the older nurse observed with a smile that didn't quite reach her eyes.

At the moment, plastic surgery was the last thing on Kara's mind. She was shaking off the cobwebs, starting to feel more alert.

"I'll call Dr. Ortega and let her know you're awake," the older one said, and was stepping toward the door. "She can let the police know."

The police?

The younger nurse, too, turned from the bed, but Kara reached out and grabbed her hand, holding her fast despite the IV embedded near her wrist. "Why are the police wanting to talk to me?"

"I don't know," Nurse Rutgers said, and the older one snorted.

As she left the room, she muttered under her breath, "Maybe they want to know who murdered that lawyer and what you were doing up there and why an ex-con was in your car." She glanced over her shoulder through the ever-narrowing space between door and jamb, as if to make sure Kara got the message.

She did.

But the door clicked closed before Kara could respond; her temper was rising, a million questions boiling to the surface. "My brother," she said suddenly before the younger nurse, too, could leave. "He was with me. Jonas McIntyre. Is he okay?" Oh, God, what if Jonas had died in the accident?

"I really can't discuss another patient."

"So he's here." And obviously alive. Kara felt a moment's relief. "I want to see him."

"That's . . . that's not possible," the nurse said, her eyes kind.

"Why not?"

"Well, first off, you need to stay in bed until the doctor releases you."

"And when is that?"

"Not sure. Because of the head injury, Dr. Ortega wants you to stay the night."

"I can't. I have a dog to take care of."

"You can call someone. There's a phone." She pointed to the tray next to Kara's hospital bed.

"There is no one."

Small creases appeared between the nurse's eyes, only partially obscured by the frames of her glasses. "What about your aunt? She's been calling and asking about visiting you."

Faiza. Oh, God. No. Kara's heart sank. She couldn't deal with her. Couldn't imagine the questions—no, accusations—from the aunt who had been named her guardian but basically abdicated her duties to Merritt Margrove. "Where's my phone?" she asked suddenly.

"You didn't come in with one."

Of course not. It had been in her Jeep.

"My purse?" Kara asked, already guessing the answer.

"No."

She didn't have to ask what happened to it. The police were involved, they'd no doubt impounded the car and it was at some garage somewhere. The cops had her personal items or the garage did. "I'm leaving."

"You can't."

She wanted to bite out "watch me" but held her tongue. This nurse was still on her side, or so it seemed, and she couldn't chance her calling someone. She knew she'd have to talk to the police—dear God, hadn't she all her life?—but right now, she wanted to make sure that Jonas was all right. She thought of Merritt Margrove, lying in a pool of his own blood staining the old carpet of his trailer. Jonas had been there, and some girl . . . God, what was her name? Her head ached as she strained to remember. Mia something or other . . . had Jonas even said . . .

Kara sat up quickly, felt a stab of pain in her neck, but ignored it. "Where are my clothes?"

"In the closet, but as I said, you can't leave. Not without the doctor's orders."

"I think I can. I'll sign a release. Whatever." She slid to the side of the bed, felt the IV in her arm tug against her skin. Wincing, she ripped off the tape holding the IV in place.

"What're you doing!"

"I said I'm leaving, so this"—she held up her arm with the tubing attached—"this needs to be removed and"—she glanced up and hooked a thumb at the monitor glowing over the bed—"however I'm tangled up with that? It needs to come out, too!"

"You can't just—"

Kara pulled on the needle still stuck in her arm.

"No! Stop! Okay, okay! Don't rip it out! You could injure yourself. Dear Lord, are you nuts?"

"You tell me."

Shaking her head, her lips compressed, Nurse Rutgers removed the IV quickly, then dealt with removing the electrodes for the heart rate monitor. "It's a good thing Dr. Ortega ordered you to be disconnected," she said a little frostily, all of her earlier friendliness dissolving. "But still the doctor needs to see you."

"Why?"

"Hospital protocol."

Kara didn't have time for red tape. She thought of Jonas possibly near death in another room. Again remembered Merritt Margrove, lying on the green shag rug, his lifeblood spilled out around him. She felt in her bones that he was killed because Jonas had been released. Otherwise it was too much of a coincidence.

Had the killer known Jonas was going to show up there?

Was Jonas, too, the murderer's target, or was she jumping to conclusions? Why did she even believe her brother? The most likely scenario was that Jonas had slit Merritt's throat. But why? And why then steal into her car? Nothing was making sense. And she didn't feel safe. Not that she ever had, but right now, all the danger she'd felt lurking at the edge of her life seemed to be moving closer. And here, in the hospital, she felt like a sitting duck. If the news teams hadn't reported that she was a patient, the driver of the car, they soon would. It was only a matter of time. Her throat even drier than before, Kara felt an intense case of claustrophobia.

And now a nurse was telling her she was forced to stay here and offering little information on Jonas.

"Where's my brother?" she asked. "What room is he in?"

"I can't say," the nurse said.

"But he made it? He's going to be all right?"

"I told you, I really can't comment on his injuries." She placed a bandage over the spot on Kara's wrist where the IV had been inserted.

"What about the other guy?" Kara asked, remembering the accident again, the huge semi roaring toward them, its massive grill looming. "The truck driver?"

The nurse's jaw knotted as she tossed packaging for the bandage into the trash.

"Is he here, too?" Kara's stomach twisted at the hesitation. "In this hospital?"

Rutgers shook her head. Her voice was low. "He's not here."

"But he's somewhere. Another hospital?"

Rutgers's eyes behind the red-rimmed lenses darkened. "In Portland."

"Is he . . . is he going to be okay?"

"Okay?" she repeated. "It's really too early to tell."

"What do you mean?"

"Just that. I can't really say."

"Oh, God." Kara let out a breath, stunned for a second, her heart sinking. Obviously the driver of the truck wasn't in good shape and though the nurse hadn't said it, there was a chance he wouldn't survive.

Her heart ached.

There were no words.

Nothing Kara could say.

She had no connection to the driver other than the twist of fate that had caused him to be behind the wheel of the eighteen-wheeler at those crucial seconds. A flood of questions rushed through her, a newfound need to know more about the man who appeared to be holding on to life by a thread. Was he married? Did he have children? God, what was his name? Her heart squeezed and guilt pricked at her brain.

Despite the storm of emotions roiling through her, the guilt, anger and sorrow, she forced herself to push them aside. She had to think clearly. Keep moving. There was time enough for answers and grief and recriminations and what-ifs later. Right now, she needed to ignore the guilt and focus. On Jonas.

"I really need to see my brother," she said again. She had to see for herself that he was all right and she had a million questions for him. What was he doing up at Margrove's mountain place? What were his plans? Who was this Mia woman? How did he think he could wrangle the house away from Aunt Faiza? Did he know anything about the call and text that she'd received? Were they about Marlie? But first and foremost, she had to find out what he knew about the night their family was slaughtered. He was out of prison now, couldn't be sent back for the same crime, so maybe, finally, he would tell the truth.

If she could just talk to him.

"As far as I know, I'm Jonas McIntyre's closest relative, so surely someone here should be able to tell me about his condition."

"You'll have to talk to his doctor."

"But . . . he's not in ICU or anything? He's going to survive?" she said.

She felt the nurse weighing her options. "I heard his injuries weren't life-threatening."

"Good." Relief washed over her. "So I can see him," Kara said, her head beginning to throb.

"That's up to his doctor."

She checked her phone. "Looks like you're in luck. Dr. Ortega will be here shortly and then you can discuss your release."

"Good." Kara flopped back onto the pillows. "Then maybe she'll understand that I'm not kidding. I need to leave."

"I'll let her know." Thank God. Finally, the nurse seemed to get the message that she was serious. What Nurse Rutgers didn't know was that Kara would do it by any means possible.

All she needed was a ride.

CHAPTER 17

Allure Salon was buzzing with conversation as Johnson and Thomas entered. Three of the four stations along the wall were occupied, the acrid scent of some hair dye tinging the air. A manicurist's chair at a small table was empty, tiny bottles of colorful polish glinting under the lights.

The first beautician was clipping an older woman's gray pixie cut, the second applying goop to hair that she wrapped in pieces of aluminum foil. Celeste Margrove's area was near the back of the salon. She was taking payment from a client who was chatting up a storm about her plans for Christmas and what a "nightmare" her sister-in-law's family was.

"I'm telling you, I don't know how I'll get through it." The thirtysomething with streaked blond hair and tinted glasses was nodding but, as the police approached, glanced nervously at them as she handed Celeste a credit card. "Be sure to put a tip on there—the usual." She made a sweeping motion with her hand. "Fifteen percent."

"Got it," Celeste said, but it took her several swipes of the card before she could finish the transaction. "Call me about your next appointment."

"After the first of the year," the client with streaked blond hair and tinted glasses said as she pulled a puffy coat from the rack on the wall, pulled out a pair of gloves from a deep pocket and hurried out.

The other two clients and their stylists stared at the detectives in the reflection of the mirror that lined the wall over the sinks. Conversation died to the point Thomas heard the smooth jazz playing from speakers mounted high overhead. The beauticians stopped working.

That's the effect cops had on people—innocent or guilty. Everyone froze. No more snipping. No more applying the dye. No more conversation.

Thomas and Johnson made their way to the last station, where Celeste, too, had stopped talking and was watching them. "Can I help you?" she asked.

"Celeste Margrove?" Thomas said quietly. "I'm Detective Thomas and this is my partner, Detective Johnson." They showed their badges.

"Is there something wrong?" Her expression had shifted to one of concern.

"It's your husband," Johnson said. "Merritt."

"Oh, Lord." Celeste's face drained of color. "No . . . oh, no," she whispered, shaking her head, tears springing to her eyes. "Oh, no, no, no."

Thomas asked, "Is there somewhere private where we can talk?"

"Oh, God. Jesus, no," she whispered, tears running from her eyes, mascara streaking her cheeks. "I knew it, I just knew it. Something's happened to him. Something awful. Is he going to be all right? In the hospital? What?" Her chin wobbled and the nearest stylist dropped her scissors on the counter and came to give her colleague a hug.

"Maybe you should go in the back room," one of the stylists suggested. She was a pretty woman with streaked hair, worried blue eyes and a kind smile. "Roxanne and I can handle things."

"But–but I have more clients. Belva . . . Uh, Mrs. Hightower and then . . . God, I think it's Heidi Willis or . . ."

"Got it," Roxanne, the woman who was working with the aluminum foil, said. In her fifties, with white hair and an easy grace, she glanced back at Celeste. "Seriously, Celeste. Donna and I can handle everything." She managed a smile that was full of empathy and locked eyes with the other beautician. "I'll reschedule her. For . . . sometime next week. And the others. They're booked online."

Celeste leaned hard on the back of the chair.

"You can talk back here," Donna said, motioning to the cops and opening a door marked EMPLOYEES ONLY. Celeste didn't protest, and Donna ushered them into a tiny back area filled with a stacked washer and dryer, baskets of folded towels and boxes of hair products. Wedged by the back door was a coffeepot and two folding chairs, and another door with a unisex sign indicating a bathroom. "We're right out here if you need us," she said, her eyes holding Celeste's. "Okay?"

"Yeah. I-I'll be fine." But Celeste steadied herself against the dryer.

"What happened? Where's Merritt?" she asked, as Donna returned to the main salon and closed the door discreetly behind her.

"We're sorry," Johnson said. "For your loss."

"Sorry . . . For . . ." Celeste seemed confused.

Thomas said gently, "He's gone."

"Gone?" she repeated, but understanding crossed her features. Her face fell. "You mean he's gone as in . . . as in dead? You're saying that he's not hurt somewhere, that he didn't have a heart attack and is at the hospital and—"

"He was found today in the mobile home in the mountains," Johnson said directly. "He'd been murdered."

"Oh." She gasped, all remaining color draining from her face. "Murdered?" And then it hit. Her entire body crumpled as she dropped into one of the folding chairs and let out an animal cry of pain. "Ooowwwwooo . . . no, no, no!" Tears flooded her eyes and she dashed them away, using the back of her hand. "Damn it." She sniffed. "I just knew something like this would happen," she squeaked, and found a box of tissues near the coffeepot. She plucked one and blew her nose. "How many times did I tell Merritt to give it up, that the Jonas McIntyre case would kill him? Huh? How many?" She dabbed ferociously at her eyes.

"You think someone connected to the case killed him?"

"Well, who else? He lived and breathed that case for twenty damned years."

"He had other clients," Thomas reminded her, but she waved a hand, like she was swatting at a bothersome fly. "Ancient history. I need to see him. Where is he? Oh, dear God."

Thomas thought about the condition of Merritt's body, the jagged red smile slashed across his neck. "He's been taken to the morgue."

"Then let's go there." She read the hesitation in Thomas's eyes. "What happened to him? He was . . . killed how?"

"His throat was cut."

She gasped again, a hand flying to her mouth. "Who would do something like that?" Again her face scrunched as much in revulsion and horror as sadness.

"That's what we're trying to find out," Johnson said. "Did your husband have any enemies?"

"Only the ones associated with *that* case."

"We'll need a list."

"Fine. You can start with Natalie McIntyre," she said. "Or, wait—her name changed. Natalie—

oh, it will come to me." She sucked in her breath, then snapped her fingers. "Natalie Brizard. That's it. Some fancy French name, I think. Her maiden name. Doesn't matter. But she, Natalie? She ran Merritt ragged with her calls and clues. It was weird, ya know?" Celeste looked up from her chair and was apparently warming to her subject. "It wasn't as if she was all that into her son, if you know what I mean. Never visited him. Got involved with someone else pretty soon after the trial. I think her connection, the reason she kept calling Merritt, was the money. When Sam died, he left a pot load of assets. Stocks, bonds, property, interest in oil wells or off-shore drilling or whatever, and when she and Sam divorced, she thought she got the shaft. 'A pittance.' That's what she told Merritt."

"You think she would kill your husband?" Thomas asked, remembering the brutal murder.

"Oh. No." She'd finally collected herself. Rubbed her eyes. "You asked about enemies and there was no love lost between Natalie and Merritt. He was Samuel's divorce attorney, but, no, I don't think she would . . . She isn't capable of . . ." But Celeste couldn't finish the sentence as she thought about it. "You said Merritt was in the morgue. I-I need to see him."

"First," Thomas said, "let's go to your place. We'll need to search through Merritt's things, look for clues, you know. And maybe we can talk there. I would advise you to wait to see your husband."

"It's that bad?"

"Not pretty," Johnson said.

Celeste's lips pursed as she thought. "Fine. Roxanne and Donna can deal with my clients. They have their numbers. As for clues at our place—good luck. Merritt kept everything digitally, on his phone and laptop, oh, and his iPad, too. But he took all of them with him. There's nothing at the house except old, old files in the attic."

"What about a desktop computer?" Johnson asked.

"Nope, got rid of it years ago." She popped her head through the connecting door to the salon, had a quick conversation with Donna, then slipped into a jacket and picked up an oversize coral bag. Unlatching the back door, she said, "Let's go this way. I don't want anyone seeing me like this."

"Are you okay to drive?" Johnson asked as the cold slapped them in the face.

"Yeah, fine." And she did seem it. For as destroyed as she had been upon learning the news, she now seemed to have pulled herself together, a determined look in her eye as she marched in three-inch heeled boots along the snowy alley. Flipping up the hood of her coat, she said, "This is Jonas McIntyre's fault." Her breath fogged in the air as they walked briskly to the corner of the long building, snow continuing to fall, the wind brittle. "His sister came in earlier—oh, God." She stopped dead in her tracks at the corner of the building. "Kara. She was going up to see Merritt this morning."

Johnson, in lockstep with her, said, "She's the one who called us."

"What? Kara? No wonder she wanted to know where he was. Is . . . is she okay?"

"At the hospital." Thomas was checking his phone, hoping to hear that Kara McIntyre had come around. He wanted to talk to her, as she was the person who had called in Merritt Margrove's murder. What else did she know? For that matter, what did Jonas McIntyre know and why was he there? Was it possible he killed Margrove? That didn't make any sense. Yet it was a damned coincidence that Jonas showed up in Kara's wrecked Jeep and was now injured.

Again, Celeste appeared shocked, her red-rimmed eyes rounding as they crossed the sparsely filled parking lot. "Kara was attacked, too? Or wait—did she get into it with Merritt?" Her neatly plucked eyebrows drew together as she took in a swift breath. "Oh, shit. Did she kill him?" Panic started to rise again, her eyes round with the horror of the thought.

"Accident," Thomas said quickly. "She called it in. We don't know what happened. Won't until we talk to her."

Celeste nodded, but didn't seem convinced and sighed, looking up at the heavens as if seeking some kind of divine intervention. "When it rains, it pours, ya know, and when it snows? It's only worse." Blinking against tears again, she fished into her massive purse and withdrew her keys. Just as his phone buzzed. Squinting through the snow, he saw it was from a deputy at the hospital. Kara McIntyre was awake. He texted that he'd be there within the hour.

Johnson said to Celeste, "I'll ride with you and fill you in on the way to your house."

"Good. I want to know everything." As they reached the front of the strip mall she pressed a button on her keyless remote. A sleek black Corvette responded, its lights blinking, a beeping sound audible.

Thomas pulled Johnson aside. "Kara McIntyre's awake. I'll meet you at Margrove's after I talk to her. Don't want her slipping back into a coma before I get some details."

Johnson nodded, then caught up with Celeste. "I can drive," Johnson offered again.

"Oh, right," Celeste mocked, shaking her head as she reached the driver's side and opened the door. "No way in hell. You can ride shotgun." Celeste hitched a chin toward the passenger side of the sports car. "No one drives my baby but me."

CHAPTER 18

Whimstick General was a madhouse.

As expected.

Tate parked two blocks over as all the nearby lots were full. Once he'd slid his RAV4 into a spot near the icy curb, he double-checked information on his phone, skimming news stories and the social media platforms dedicated to the release of Jonas McIntyre.

Not only had the news of Merritt Margrove's murder and the near-fatal accident in the mountains rippled through the local restaurants, cafés and shops of Whimstick, the information had spread like a wildfire in tinder-dry grass. The ex-con's fan pages on social media had erupted with concern, "prayers," "good vibes," and emojis and memes filled with sad faces and hearts and praying hands. Apparently there was already a vigil staged near the hospital, the most active of his fans who lived nearby collecting at Whimstick General. The news outlets were buzzing about the accident and the fact that McIntyre and his sister were survivors, though there was little information on the driver of the other vehicle. The story of the accident was not just local but showing up online throughout the Northwest. God only knew how far it would go.

Probably national and, nowadays, of course, likely viral.

The good news was that Kara McIntyre, who was driving her Jeep, hadn't been seriously injured. Thank God. Even though he barely knew her, there was a part of him that found her intriguing. Yeah, he wanted to interview her and needed her help in his quest for the truth, but there was more to it than that. More than he wanted to admit.

As for her brother, so far it seemed that Jonas McIntyre had survived.

Tate hoped so.

And he hoped the son of a bitch was coherent enough to give one last interview.

No time like the present to find out.

He checked his watch. 4:48. Perfect timing for a shift change. Though some of the nurses worked ten- or twelve-hour shifts, a majority of the staff, admin workers and the like, including some of the nursing and clinical staff, worked the 8:00 a.m. to 5:00 p.m. schedule. After grabbing the small satchel he'd packed before leaving his apartment, Tate locked his car and hiked through the snow-crusted sidewalks to Whimstick General.

About forty or fifty people had gathered on the walkway, the beefy security guard and the makeshift barricade holding them away from the sliding glass doors while others lobbied to get inside.

There were more milling around in the building. Through the wide glass windows, Tate spied patients in wheelchairs or on crutches, loved ones hovering nearby. The vestibule with its long couches and chairs situated between potted plants and small tables was full; the information, registration and admission desks surrounded by people. He thought he caught glimpses of some of the people he'd seen online, those who had clamored for Jonas's release, members of his Internet fan club, but he couldn't be certain.

Since he didn't want to deal with the crowd, he headed toward the emergency entrance located on the far side of the building. It, too, was being patrolled, a security guard posted inside, another bundled up outside and posted under the portico, making certain the lane for emergency vehicles was clear.

Tate hurried along the concrete pathway that rimmed the building. Though it had recently been cleared of snow, a thin film was already collecting over the path, piling thick on the surrounding shrubbery and stretches of grass separating the walking paths.

He knew this hospital all too well. Not only was this the place where his own father had been brought, dead before the emergency room doors had slid open, but Tate himself, due to his own injuries—a bike accident that screwed up his ankle, a broken arm from falling out of a tree and an emergency appendectomy—had landed here while growing up. But that wasn't the reason he knew all the ins and outs of Whimstick General. Nope. Only later, when he'd returned to help out his mother, had he learned about the ins and outs of the hospital.

He'd not only pushed his mother's wheelchair along the glossy floors shimmering under the fluorescent overhead lights of the hallways, but he'd spent hours within these halls. During Selma Tate's lengthy stays and continual visits for tests and rehab appointments, Wesley had discovered the shortcuts and tucked-away elevators, the back stairways and connecting rooms between the clinic, labs, cafeteria, locker rooms and rehabilitation areas. He'd even located the mechanical rooms and the morgue in the basement, along with restricted areas where equipment and supplies were kept under lock and key. He'd had hours to explore and he'd taken advantage of the free time, once looking up the schematics for the plans of the hospital. The original building was eighty years old, the south wing added in the sixties and the north at the end of the eighties, which created a little bit of a hodgepodge and more than a few odd spaces and connections. Wesley Tate knew most of them, and now decided to use that knowledge to his advantage. Otherwise he would be shut out from Kara McIntyre and her brother. He knew it. And this—their tragedy—was his story. *His.* His father had died saving Kara. The way Tate figured it, she owed him. Big time.

As he knew the hospital like the back of his hand, he slipped into a side entrance that opened to the hallway connecting to the wing housing clinics, then took a back hallway that converged with the surgical section of the hospital. Rounding another corridor, he made his way behind several operating rooms and ended up in a wing that housed a bank of elevators and beyond which was the cafeteria. One story below housed the morgue, the two stories above were dedicated to patient rooms. Somewhere on one of those floors was Kara McIntyre. And, he suspected, in a more isolated area, her half brother. He doubted it would be hard to find Jonas; there would probably be guards posted outside his door because, no doubt, he would be a prime suspect in Merritt Margrove's murder, though that didn't make much sense to Tate. Kara would be more difficult, but he figured he could handle it.

He went to the basement and found an unlocked closet wedged between the mechanical room and the morgue. He pulled a set of scrubs and a fake ID tag from the bag, changed quickly and emerged, careful to avoid the major hallways. As far as he knew there were cameras posted in the main corridors, near the elevators and at every major entrance to the building, but he didn't think all were monitored 24/7, or that there was surveillance in the minor areas or any of the patient rooms due to budget concerns and privacy laws.

But he couldn't be certain.

He strode confidently, as if he belonged inside the building, slipped through a doorway marked STAFF ONLY, then took a set of back stairs two at a time. At the third floor, he opened the door and peered down the hallway. As expected, he spied a uniformed deputy seated in a chair near the doorway of a room at the end of the hallway. The deputy was around twenty-five and doing a deep dive into his cell phone.

No way to get past him.

Tate slipped into the stairwell again and descended to the second level, where he suspected Kara might be housed. He stepped into the hallway, all too aware of the cameras mounted in the ceiling. He knew there was a good chance he'd be found out, but he hoped to put it off as long as possible, so he walked confidently, checking his clipboard, avoiding looking at the cameras or coming into contact with anyone. However, he couldn't locate her room and so returned to the stairwell, made his way to an area off the cafeteria where he knew a lot of the staff convened, bought a soda and a sandwich from the deli counter, then took an empty table near a group of nurses. His back to them, and while pretending interest in his phone and a newspaper he'd grabbed from a table on the way in, he listened to their conversation.

Since Jonas McIntyre was the news of the day, Tate was certain to hear something. It didn't take long.

"It's flipping chaos out there," the male nurse was saying over the buzz of conversation and clatter of utensils. "Like this is just what we need—chaos at the workplace." Tate saw him and the rest of the table from the corner of his eye. The nurse took a bite from an apple. Tall and reedy, with a nest of receding gray curls and thin-rimmed glasses, he was tanned despite the fact that it was the middle of winter in the Pacific Northwest.

"Things will die down," one of the women replied, brushing her bangs from her eyes. She was a short redhead with freckles and rosy cheeks who opened a small bag of chips.

"Not if that freak show group has anything to say about it. They've been calling the hospital ever since the word got out."

"What group?" The third woman, in her mid-thirties, Tate guessed, with doe eyes and thin brown hair scraped back into a ponytail, was already picking at a salad and sipping from an oversize cup of some dark soda.

"Some fans, I think." Male Nurse took another bite of the apple.

"What?" The redhead wrinkled her nose. "Fans?"

"I know. Really? It's an Internet thing, I think. This group of people—women, mostly—think he was falsely accused and convicted and have been trying to get his conviction overturned. For years. Real nutcases, if you ask me. The guy cut up his whole damned family."

"Nuh-huh." Thin Ponytail was working through her mound of greens drizzled with thick dressing. "Imprisoned incorrectly."

"Yeah, right. Tell that to his dead attorney and the poor bastard driving the semi who has been fighting for his life." He took another bite of his apple and leaned back in his plastic chair. "The way I figure it, whatever happens, it's his damned fault."

"And that doesn't count his family," the redhead pointed out as the male nurse tossed his apple core into a nearby bin and the rosy-cheeked nurse with the ponytail mowed through her bowl of limp-looking lettuce.

"A shame, that's what it is," Redhead said. "If you ask me, he should never have been released."

"Lots of people agree." Male Nurse was nodding as he unwrapped a toothpick and started working on his teeth. "Except for the fan club. They're all about him being free. You know, for justice."

"Give me a break." Redhead crumpled her chip bag in a small fist.

"Tell that to the entire McIntyre family."

"Uh-oh. I gotta go—duty calls," the nurse with the ponytail said suddenly. She forked a final bit of her salad into her mouth, then scooped up her tray and scraped back her chair, nearly pushing into Tate.

"Sorry," she said without even looking in his direction.

"Break's not over for another ten," the male nurse pointed out while tapping the face of his watch.

"I know, but I have to call the sitter." Ponytail held up her phone. "Problems at the old hacienda." Rolling her eyes, she tossed the remains of her salad into a garbage container. "She just texted me for, like, the third time. Jake's cold is worse. He stayed home from school today and now he's crabby." She made a face. "Besides"—she leaned over and stage-whispered—"I *need* a ciggy. Don't tell Darlene, okay? She's already on my case."

He laughed. He said, "I'll come with. Trying to quit, but you know . . ." Together they headed out and the redhead managed to say, "See you in a few," but never looked up from her cell.

Tate felt like a sitting duck as he noticed two cameras covering the wide dining area with people clustered around plastic tables, talking, eating, reading or hooked into laptops or phones. He caught bits of conversation over the rattling of trays and shuffling of feet, but if anyone was talking about the accident in the mountains and the infamous patient on the third floor, he didn't catch it.

He was clearing his tray when he spied two security guards file through the line and grab diet sodas and packages of snacks. Both were male, one short and stout, the other a little taller with the physique of a bodybuilder, his shirt stretching at the shoulders, his expression hard.

Tate lingered for a couple of minutes, then stood. He hoped he didn't appear too obvious sorting his recycling from his trash at the bins as the guards took chairs at a table across the room. He didn't want to draw attention to himself, but he wended his way through the tables and took a seat nearby, clearing the table of trash someone had left.

No one seemed to notice as the cafeteria began to fill, people began stacking up, trays in hand, the smell of Italian herb mingling with the lingering scent of fish. Burgers sizzled on a grill and customers yelled their orders over the general buzz of conversation.

Tate pulled out his phone and pretended to text, but watched the two guards from the corner of his eye.

And he hit pay dirt.

"I know. It's a frickin' shit show," the shorter guy said. He was bald, his pate shining under the lights, a three-day growth of reddish beard covering his jaw, a chocolate-covered donut and bottle of pinkish vitamin water on his tray. "They never should have let that cocksucker out, if you ask me."

Tate swallowed a smile. Obviously they were talking about Jonas McIntyre.

"But they did and he's here." Bodybuilder dug into what looked like a ham on rye sandwich. "But won't be for long."

"You think? Is that what you heard?" The bearded guy cracked open the bottle and took a sip of the pink liquid.

"Yeah. Even though the prick wasn't wearing a seat belt, he lucked out, got banged up, has maybe a busted rib or two and a slight head injury or somethin', but not much more. Lucky SOB, if you ask me. Would've been better if he just woulda died in the accident. Serve him right for what he did to his family. Prison's too good for him." He washed down another bite with a swallow of Diet Pepsi. "The way I see it, the loser should either die or end up a vegetable."

"Geez, man—"

"It'd be cheaper for the state if he just checked out, if you know what I mean." As if he realized he was talking too loud, he took a quick look around and wiped a bit of mustard from his chin.

"What about the other one—the woman on two?"

"The sister?" Bodybuilder asked, eyebrows drawing into one thick line.

"Yeah. Her."

"Head case."

"What do you know about her?"

"A lot."

"You do? How?"

"I read, man, I read. You should try it."

"I read."

"The sports page doesn't count." Bodybuilder took another long swallow from his can. "And I've seen all the documentaries and specials about it, ya know. My old man? He worked for the department when it all happened, one of the deputies first on the scene up at that bloodbath. It was all he could talk about for weeks. So yeah," he was nodding to himself as he crunched into a pickle, "I took a major interest. And the woman in 234?" Tapping a thick finger on the tabletop, he added, "Trust me. She's certifiable."

"If you say so."

"Not just me. It's all over the media. It was big news then, and maybe even bigger now cuz, ya know, the Internet and all. Anyway, a cop lost his life saving that little girl's. Pissed off my old man. Big time." He polished off the first half of his sandwich and said around the final bite, "The cop who died that night? He was on vacation with his family. Not even on duty. But he had to help out, ya know? In his blood."

Tate froze.

The room seemed to shrink, the buzz of conversation receding to a dull hum as he strained to listen.

"That right?"

"Uh-huh. Tate, his name was. Some of the other guys who worked the scene afterward, checking for evidence and shit, they think he saw something."

"You mean, he saw something other than the girl who almost drowned that night?"

"Oh, yeah. He ran through that house, saw all those bodies—man, that must've been something. Gory as hell. Then he took off, chased the little girl onto the pond and fell through the ice." He picked up the second half of his sandwich and glanced around, his gaze skating over Tate. Lowering his voice, he added, "That cop. Tate? He said something to the rescue worker as he was loaded into the ambulance."

Tate froze. Strained to listen. Even though he'd heard this story before. They were talking about his father.

"What'd he say?"

"The EMT, he wasn't sure, but it sounded like, you know, like fee or fie . . . maybe it was fee, fi, fo, fum . . . or backwards. Who knows? It probably don't mean anything. The cop was probably delirious. On his way out, if you know what I mean. Had himself a massive heart attack and was out of his head." In three huge bites, he polished off the remainder of his sandwich as his partner chugged down the remainder of his pink drink.

Tate remembered the stories about his father's death. Even now he felt a familiar pang in his chest at the memory. He slid a glance at the guy. Saw his name tag: LESTER ALLEN.

"Hey, you gonna eat that?" Allen the body-builder was eyeing his companion's plate.

"What? My donut? Hell, yeah, I'm gonna eat it." To prove it, he took a big bite of the chocolate-covered pastry, then licked the brown drizzle from his lips. "If you want one, go through the damned line and get your own."

"Nah, don't need it. Too many calories—all carbs, sugar. Trans fats."

"Whatever."

Allen finished his drink in one long swallow, then crushed the can in one meaty fist just as his cell phone jangled. Glancing at the screen, he scowled. "Hey, we gotta go," he said, his voice lowered.

"Why?" His partner shoved the donut into his mouth.

"Not really sure. But something was caught on camera."

"That idiot fan club, I'll bet. I'm telling you, those females who think McIntyre is, like, the

283

Second Coming or something? They're nuts. And rabid."

"Don't know, but it didn't sound like a mob. Anyway, the lieutenant wants us to meet up. Check it out."

"Shit."

Tate's insides clenched and he kept his back to them as they scrambled away, kicking out their chairs, leaving their trays and striding to the main door. Maybe the call was about someone else, but maybe not. He couldn't take a chance. Didn't want to blow his cover. Nerves strung tight, he waited, precious seconds ticking by. He didn't have much time. Not only had he already been discovered, but there were the cameras filming the area. If Lester Allen was as much of a McIntyre Massacre devotee as he claimed, he might recognize Wesley as Edmund Tate's son. Right now, Tate didn't want to take a chance on blowing his cover.

Scooping up his phone, he headed toward a side door and, keeping his face averted from cameras or anyone he came across, found his way to a stairway and climbed to the second floor. Adrenaline fired his blood and he kept a lookout as he slipped into the corridor—empty except for a janitor's push cart left near a closet. He moved quickly and wondered if even now Allen and his partner were watching from a secure location as they eyed over a dozen screens with camera views of the hallways.

Rounding the corner, he nearly ran into an orderly pushing an elderly man in a wheelchair at the elevators. Pretending to be talking on his phone, his head down, he walked quickly past and with a glance over his shoulder saw them disappear into a waiting elevator car. Thankfully no one stepped out.

He found the door marked 234, paused to listen for voices and, hearing none, quietly pushed the door open and stepped inside.

CHAPTER 19

Kara expected the doctor.

Or the damned police.

But who was it she got? Wesley Frickin' Tate. Dressed in scrubs, for God's sake. Like, oh, sure, he was a hospital employee. "I should've known," she said, unable to keep the disappointment from her voice. "What are you doing here?"

"Looking for you."

"Me? Why? You can't be in here."

"It's okay."

"It's definitely not okay!"

He held up a hand as if he expected her to scream.

"What do you want? Oh, wait, let me guess. An interview." She let out a huff of exasperation. "I can't believe this!"

He didn't deny it. "How are you doing?"

"How do I look like I'm doing?" she threw back at him as if he were dense. "I'm in the frickin' hospital! And you didn't come here in a damned disguise to ask about my health. For the love of God, Tate, I'm not an idiot."

"Never thought that."

"Good. And since you asked, I'll live." Some of her anger dissipated as she caught a glimpse of what appeared to be real concern on his face. She didn't believe it for an instant, of course. And she didn't have time for small talk. Sooner or later a real medical person, nurse or doctor, would slip into her room and she needed information and possibly even help.

"Look," he said. "I know I'm being pushy."

"Well beyond pushy."

"Okay, but you're not the only one who lost family members that night. My dad didn't make it either."

She felt that old, familiar jab of regret, but vowed not to let it slow her down. "So now what? You're going to try and guilt-trip me into helping you?" Before he could answer, she set her jaw. "No way. I'm sorry for your loss, for your dad dying trying to rescue me," she said, fighting against a storm of emotions when she thought too long or hard about Edmund Tate and how she'd run from him, how she'd fallen through the ice, how the cop whom she'd thought was a monster had sacrificed himself for her and saved her life. She swallowed against a sudden hard lump filling her throat.

"He didn't just try. He did save your life." Tate's eyes, an intense, deep blue, held hers. For a second too long before she looked away, before a profound sense of guilt squeezed her heart so tight she couldn't breathe, before that same sense of guilt clouded her thoughts. She cleared her throat before meeting his gaze again. "Do you know where my brother is? A nurse let it slip that he was in the hospital, but I don't know anything about his condition."

"He's on the third floor. Under guard." For the first time since she'd roused, she felt a moment's relief.

"ICU?"

"No . . . don't think so. I overheard some guards talking. It doesn't look like Jonas's injuries are life-threatening. At least that's what they were saying. Something about cracked ribs and a head injury—no, a 'slight' head injury, whatever that means."

"No one will tell me anything," she complained, frustrated. "They act as if it's for my own good, but I think it's because the police have been here and told them to keep quiet."

"You've talked to the cops?"

"Not yet. But I get the feeling that I'm a suspect."

"Or that you know something."

"But I don't! Jonas was hiding in my car; I didn't even know he was in there."

"At Merritt's place in the mountains," Tate clarified.

"Right, that's where—" She clamped her mouth shut. Had already said more than she intended, but, at this moment, he appeared to be her only avenue of information, her only ally. "Look, I assume you know about Merritt Margrove, right? That he's dead? Was murdered?"

"The whole world does."

"Great." God, what a mess. "Do you know anything about Jonas?"

"Not really. Just that he's definitely under guard, and the guards seemed to think he might have a cracked rib, maybe a head injury, but that he was going to be okay."

"I figured." Her relief that her brother was still alive washed away as quickly as it had come. "I want to see him."

"You and the rest of the world."

"Including you?"

"Oh, yeah. Definitely."

"Then let's go." She pushed herself upright and winced against a sharp pain piercing the back of her neck. "Ooh."

"Maybe you should rethink that," he said, concern again visible in his eyes. "I don't think it's a good idea."

"Oh—and what is? Running around the hospital in scrubs?" she snapped, then leaned back on the pillows, her frustration intensifying. "Is that"—she pointed at him and rotated her finger to indicate his attire—"your idea of a disguise?"

"It's temporary."

"Good."

"So you drove up to the mountains, to Margrove's place, and what? Found him already dead?"

"Apparently a habit of mine," she admitted, flashing back to the horror of that bloody Christmas Eve.

Don't go there. Do not!

Tate cut into her thoughts. "And Jonas was there . . . at Margrove's house?"

"Not in the house. Didn't I just say he was in my—hey wait! What is this?" She stopped before she answered any more of his questions. Wesley Tate was no friend, not a confidante, certainly no one she could trust.

"I just have a few questions."

"A few?"

"Okay, a lot."

Her eyes narrowed. He seemed earnest, but then didn't they all? She'd had her fill of reporters long ago. "I'm not answering any. I think I told you that before."

"When you almost ran me over."

"So you think I owe you, is that it? Even though I'm pretty sure we established that you jumped behind my car. Let's make that clear." Again she swung her legs over the edge of the bed and gritted her teeth against another stab of pain.

"You've had a little trouble behind the wheel recently."

Quicksilver slices of memories of the accident cut through her mind—massive tires slipping, the huge semi jackknifing and sliding sideways on the icy mountain road. "Bad luck," she said, and ignored the pang of worry she felt for the truck driver.

For a second she flashed on the two small bottles of vodka she'd downed to fortify herself before discovering Merritt's body. Alcohol coupled with bad weather and her brother scaring the life out of her, then grabbing the wheel. None of which she wanted to discuss with the police. Not now. Not until she'd talked to Jonas herself. "I need to get out of here," she said suddenly, wondering if he could be an ally, one she could use. "Can you help make that happen? Give me a ride?"

He hesitated. "Now?"

Footsteps approached in the hallway outside.

Kara froze and waited, her pulse skyrocketing as Tate stepped farther into the room, closer to the window. The footsteps slowed.

Oh. Jesus.

She exchanged a frantic gaze with Tate before the footsteps passed by, moving out of earshot.

"Right now," she said, letting out her breath. There was no time to lose before someone actually did enter her room. Quickly, before she could change her mind, she slid off the bed, her bare feet hitting the floor. "And if you're wondering what's in it for you?" she asked, anticipating what he was probably thinking. "You help me get out of here, and then maybe I'll talk to you. Answer some of your damned questions."

"Maybe?"

"It hasn't happened yet, right? But once you have, then okay, for sure." He might not be the best option to help her, but right now, he was about the only one. She decided to run with it. For now. "Look, the interview you want so badly? You've got it." She saw the skepticism in his expression, as if he were trying to figure her out, see if she was for real. "Don't look at me that way. There's something more than a ride in it for me, too."

"The proverbial catch." he guessed.

"Think of it that way if you have to, but I expect you'll share."

"Share?" he repeated.

"I want to know everything else you find out about Margrove and about the past, the night my family was killed, all about the trial, all of the suspects and what happened to my sister." She shot him a glance as she slipped from the bed, thought about telling him about the anonymous text, then changed her mind. She wasn't ready to trust him with everything. Not yet. "This isn't a one-way street. Right?"

"Right." But he didn't seem convinced. Nonetheless, she was running out of options and decided to take a leap of faith and trust him. If only for the moment. "Okay, then. Let's go." She was holding the back of her gown closed with her good hand.

"The doctor is on board with this?"

"Of course not. But I don't care." She arched an eyebrow. "I'll bet the doctor and the staff and security here aren't on board with you impersonating a hospital worker either." When he didn't respond, she threw out, "Am I wrong?"

He didn't answer. Didn't need to. Asked instead, "You can walk?"

"Yeah, I'm fine. Twisted a muscle in my neck, got a couple of bruises, compliments of the airbag, a bruised shoulder, but I'm good."

"And your head?" He pointed to the bandage on her head.

"Just a bump. They only had me up here, in my own room, to run some tests and make sure I was okay."

He hesitated, eyes narrowing as if he didn't believe her.

"We don't have a lot of time," she reminded him.

"Fine. I'll get my car."

"No. Wait," she added. "One more thing."

He paused.

"I want to see my brother first. Before we leave. I need to talk to Jonas."

"I can't make that happen." He was shaking his head. "I told you, he's under guard."

"I figured as much, but . . ." She thought for a moment. "All we need is a distraction."

"A distraction?" He wasn't buying it and pointed out, "This isn't a spy movie."

"Funny you should say that," she remarked, remembering her own nearly identical thought in the car when Jonas had appeared in her back seat. "You know, seeing as you're the one in a disguise."

His lips tightened.

She expected him to argue further, but he didn't. Instead, he gave a curt nod. "Okay, fine. But hurry. I'm pretty sure I've already been seen."

"Great." This was actually working out. "You go make the distraction and I'll meet you. Where are you parked? Not in the lot, I hope."

"Five or six blocks over. Washington Street between . . . Pine and Larch. Near the old Catholic church, the one they use for meetings and receptions. Not the new one on the next block."

"What is it with you and church parking lots?"

"They're empty," he said. Then winked. "And it's Christmas."

"Very funny." Not. At least not how she felt about this time of year. "Shouldn't they be full? You know, because it's Christmas?"

"Not 'til the weekend. You know where the church is?"

"Yeah, yeah! I've got it." She remembered the place with its brick siding, triple spires and tracery windows. "I'll be there in fifteen minutes."

"Make it ten."

"Fine."

He reached for the door. "You're serious?" he asked.

"Yeah," she said, meeting the questions in Tate's eyes. Someone killed Merritt Margrove and she didn't think it was Jonas. But who? And why? Someone was calling her, hinting that Marlie was alive. "You bet I'm serious. Dead serious."

"What the hell's going on?" Thomas, climbing out of the department-issue SUV, eyed the main entrance to the hospital, where, despite the freezing temperatures, a crowd had gathered. Dressed in thick jackets or coats, wool caps and gloves, earmuffs and boots, fifty or sixty people, mostly women in their thirties or forties, standing near the doors, some with backpacks, others with strollers, many with signs that read:

FREE JONAS!

Isn't he already free?

WHO'S THE REAL KILLER?

Well, if not McIntyre, who knows?

WHERE'S MARLIE?

Good question.

JUSTICE FOR JONAS!

Oh, give me a break!

They were chanting and yelling, some actually on their knees in prayer while a couple of security guards were trying to keep them at bay outside the building, snow falling around them. One woman in blond dreadlocks yelled, "We want to see him! Justice for Jonas!"

Another, braving the cold in short sleeves and a vest, with tattoos down two arms and a mop of black hair, yelled, "Free Jonas! Free Jonas!" The chant continued, growing louder; a thirtysomething with a brunette ponytail, who looked like a soccer mom, screamed, "We want Jonas!"

"Yeah!" another voice chimed in, and the crowd started shoving forward, a wave of people in wool hats, winter jackets, scarves and boots screaming to get inside.

"These are Jonas McIntyre's fans," Johnson told him as she eyed the crowd.

"I figured."

"Apparently there are legions of them, not just in this country but worldwide thanks to the Internet."

"Holy shit." Thomas couldn't believe it. The man was a stone-cold killer, the embodiment of evil, a person who had slaughtered his family in a bloody massacre.

"A fan club on Facebook called for a rally here," Johnson was saying. "Twitter, too. Other sites. Like TikTok and Instagram. Where all sorts of crazy conspiracy theories run rampant."

"Like what?" he asked, locking the SUV

remotely as they made their way through dozens of people who were surrounding the main doors of the hospital, creating a raucous, energized mass. Some appeared calm, others angry, a few much louder than the rest. Those who shouted tended to be closer to the hospital doors, while onlookers hung back. Already a van bearing the logo of a Portland TV station was parked in the crowded lot.

Snow continued to fall. Small flakes swirling and dancing with the wind, catching on hats and in hair, melting on already-red faces.

"One of the theories is that Jonas McIntyre isn't really here," Johnson was saying. "That he's being held by the government in some secret spot."

"What?" He twisted his head to stare at her.

"You know, conspiracy theories. The government is lying to us."

"You mean like Roswell, New Mexico, and UFOs?"

"Or who really killed JFK," she said. "There's a rumor going around that he's somehow going to come down from his room to talk to them."

"From some secret government spot?" he asked, raising an eyebrow.

She nodded. "Remember, some of his fans think he's like some spiritual prophet or god or something."

"He's not coming down. Spiritual god or not, he's under guard."

297

"Doesn't matter. They believe what they believe."

Thomas wasn't having any of it as he eyed the mass of people. "If he's so god-like, why did he allow himself to be locked up for twenty years?"

"Because he chose to?"

"Oh, shit, that's completely nuts." He was moving closer to the hospital, Johnson beside him.

"For most people, yeah. But some of his followers think—"

"Followers?" He threw her a glance as they tried to ease through the shoulder-to-shoulder people in the horde, most with cell phones and cameras recording the action.

"Followers. Fans. Whatever. They think Jonas being released from prison is like the Second Coming." Johnson had to shout to be heard and noticed that traffic around the lot was slowing, more and more vehicles arriving, more women dashing over the berm surrounding the parking lot to join the ever-growing throng.

"Oh, for the love of God," he muttered.

"Exactly! That's what they think." And he saw it then, some of the placards with Biblical phrases or Christ's image along with Jonas's.

"This is sick!"

"That doesn't always mean what you think it does."

"You know what I'm saying," he bit out.

Johnson shook her head as the chanting continued, the crowd getting louder. "I'm just sayin'."

"Hey!" One of the guards, a burly Black man with a badge identifying him as Bertrand Mullins, was keeping the crowd at bay as Thomas and Johnson pushed their way through the undulating mass. "You the cops?" Mullins asked. He was sweating despite the frigid temperature. "Help us out here, will ya?"

"We're here to see Jonas McIntyre."

"You and the rest of the damned world. Hey, hey, hey!" He turned to a scrawny woman with bleached hair who was trying to wriggle past. "Ma'am, unless you're a patient you can't go inside."

"Then I'm a patient," she threw back, her eyes blazing.

"I don't think so," Mullins argued.

Johnson said, "She's on something."

As Mullins was dealing with the thin woman, two other security guards, one so muscular his uniform was stretched over his back and biceps, another shorter, a spark plug of a guy with a thin red beard, appeared. They charged through a side door and started trying to hold the mob back. The bigger guy was on a walkie-talkie, the shorter one inserting himself between the building and three women with signs.

Jostled, Thomas asked Mullins, "You called the PD?"

"Ten minutes ago. And you all took your damned sweet time!"

Thomas shook his head. "We didn't take the call. Hey—" He felt an elbow in his back, whirled and faced a man in a flannel jacket who had pushed past him but was stalled by the throng ahead of him. "Sir, you need to leave. Now."

"What? Who gives you the authority to tell me what to do?" The guy, clean-shaven with wire-rimmed glasses and a pinched expression, tried to stare him down.

It didn't work. "Detective Cole Thomas." He flipped out his ID. "Hatfield County Sheriff's Department. I suggest you leave now."

The guy managed a beatific smile. "My authority comes from God," he said disdainfully. "Only God. And you"—he motioned toward the guards—"you all need to leave us be. I know what I can and cannot do." There was a hard edge to his practiced piety. "The last I heard freedom of assembly was still valid in this country!"

Thomas stepped closer to him and, eyes narrowed, said sternly, "I'm asking you to leave. And I'm asking you politely. That might not last."

"And I'm telling you to butt out." All of the guy's faux serenity fell away. "I know my rights." His muscles tensed and for a second Thomas thought the guy might throw a punch. Well, come on. He was spoiling for a fight.

Apparently Thomas radiated that feeling

300

because the blow never came. Instead, the sanctimonious prick spat on the ground at Thomas's feet before spinning quickly, edging past a determined, heavy-set woman. He bumped into her and she yelled, "Hey! Watch it, moron." She was holding a yellow picket sign with Jonas's name emblazoned over a field of tiny crosses.

Thomas was about to take off after the jerk.

"Let it go," Johnson warned, a hand on his elbow.

"The Whimstick Department said they are sending backup," Mullins said, his voice raised to be heard over the din, his eyes still scanning the crowd. "There's already a couple of cops here, so maybe we can get some of them to disperse. If the leaders do, the rest might follow."

"Other cops?" Thomas repeated. "Here . . . at the hospital?"

"Yeah, a couple of deputies."

Thomas's stomach clenched. As far as he knew, the only other officers at the hospital were supposed to be guarding Jonas.

Mullins was looking around over a sea of capped heads. "So where the hell is the backup? Shit!" A woman in a long overcoat and bangle bracelets pushed forward, trying to slip past Mullins. "Hey, lady," he said. "Why don't you please turn around and go home."

"Fuck you!" she spat, and shouldered her way past.

301

"Goddamn—"

"The cops that are here now?" Thomas said, recapturing Mullins's attention. "Why were they here?"

"Assignment. Guarding McIntyre."

"Shit." Thomas caught a glimpse of Johnson on her cell, holding a finger to one ear and instructing whoever was on the other end to get to Whimstick General ASAP. "That's right. I mean now! This is about to become a riot!"

And she wasn't wrong. The crowd's mood had turned from anticipatory to impatient and rebellious. Beyond angry. A shifting and undulating energy pulsing through the wintry air. He saw a couple of uniforms exiting the elevator and racing toward the door. Deputies he recognized. Deputies assigned to guard Jonas McIntyre.

Fuck! This was all wrong. He felt as if he was being played.

"We need to break this up," he said to Johnson just as the sound of sirens split the air.

"The cavalry," she said as the wail of the sirens increased.

"The cops! Someone called the cops!" a woman in a bright yellow beret announced furiously.

Another woman in jeans and a down vest cried, "Jonas is coming! He's coming down to see us!"

"How do you know?"

She was beaming, cradling a coffee cup. "I

just talked to a doctor and he said Jonas is being brought down. Here. To see us."

"That doesn't sound right," an unseen skeptic said as Thomas noted the camera crew disembarking from the van in the lot, a reporter he recognized from Channel 3. Sheila Keegan, in a heavy red ski jacket, her curly hair catching snowflakes, was scanning the crowd as she hurried forward, a cameraman on her heels. He, too, was in the red Channel 3 jacket, a bulky camera hoisted onto his shoulder.

"He's coming! Jonas is coming!" other voices chimed.

At that the reporter looked up sharply and zeroed in on the vested woman.

And the first woman, breathless and starry-eyed, nodded. "A doctor just told me: He's coming!"

"That's impossible," Mullins said. "The guy's sedated. McIntyre, I mean." He held up his hands as the crowd pushed forward. "No one goes inside unless they are patients of Whimstick General and—"

"He's coming! He's coming!" another couple of women cried, rushing the doors.

What the devil? Why would the crowd think Jonas was being released? His eyes narrowed on the surge of faces, all ruddy and eager, and the news crew trying to set up, an elderly couple huddled near a car in the lot, everyone intent on getting into the hospital, except . . . he caught a glimpse of an intern hurrying the opposite direction, still in scrubs and a jacket, hurrying across the parking area.

It seemed wrong to him.

Out of place, though he couldn't put a finger on it, just followed his gut instinct. "I'll be right back," he said to Johnson as he started wending his way through people, moving faster, but getting nowhere as the crowd seemed to congeal around him. The intern paused again, long enough to say something to a woman in a black puffy coat, and her face lit up. "He's coming," she cried, juggling a cup of coffee from a local shop. "Jonas is coming down!" She rushed forward, her face glowing.

"Son of a bitch." Thomas took off after the intern, but the crowd swelled forward.

"Hey, Thomas, you gotta help us out here!" Mullins pleaded.

"I will." At that moment a determined fan, a petite redhead, was having none of it. Swinging her sign to clear a path toward the doors, she pushed past Mullins and rushed forward. "Jo-nas! Jo-nas!" A drumbeat.

"Jesus H. Christ!" The guard was on a walkie-talkie in an instant.

His partner tried to hold the door but was unceremoniously shoved to the ground under the portico. The crowd pushed forward, through the first set of glass doors, holding them open as more people poured through the second set leading to the wide reception area.

People rushed by, some sidestepping her, others tripping over her.

"Oh, shit. Don't go for your weapon!" Mullins commanded, staring at his fallen partner, trying to reach her. "Don't go for your weapon!"

But she was reaching for her sidearm and Thomas, closer to her, struggled to get to her side. "Don't," he said, more quietly, placing his hand over hers before she pulled her pistol. He saw her name tag: MADGE PETROSKI. "Come on." He held out his hand as some eager bystander knocked into him, but he managed to remain standing. "Back off!" He helped her to her feet. "You okay?"

"Yeah, I think so." Then her face squeezed together. "No." Dark eyes flashed as she surveyed the mob. "They're frickin' crazy! Lunatics," she muttered, her fury palpable. He didn't blame her. Petroski was right. The mob was incited, an angry moving curtain. They were all hyped, certain they were about to see their beloved icon. The damned murderer. With these frenzied women of all walks of life idolizing him. She surveyed the crowd. "This is gonna get ugly."

"It already is." But the sirens were screaming closer.

"Detective Thomas!" a woman's voice yelled.

305

"Cole! Cole Thomas! If I could talk to you?" Sheila Keegan was waving one arm aloft, trying to get his attention, her cameraman at her side.

Thomas's stomach dropped a notch. He didn't have time for an interview.

"Just a few words." She was trying to move through the throng, but he was ignoring her, searching for the intern who had been nearly jogging away from the scene, as if he were hurrying to get away.

Or maybe just moving quickly because he was late. Or cold.

Too late to find out. The guy was long gone. Had disappeared into the night.

Thomas bit back a curse. The intern hustling away seemed out of place, and Thomas knew from experience that wasn't a good sign. Who the hell was he? As he turned back to the hospital and caught Sheila Keegan's red jacket out of the corner of his eye, he thought about the hospital cameras. Maybe there was an image of the intern. If the guy turned out to be legit, so be it, but if not, maybe he could be identified.

For the first time that day, Thomas allowed himself a smile.

If only on the inside.

CHAPTER 20

Tate was true to his word.

Kara didn't know how he'd managed it, but the security guard was no longer posted at the door to Jonas's room. The folding chair was vacant, a jacket slung over the back, a magazine left on the floor near an empty paper coffee cup.

She didn't wait.

Knew she didn't have much time. She'd used up precious seconds yanking on her clothes, all of which she'd found in a closet in her hospital room.

Then, barely daring to breathe, she'd slipped past the nurses' station without being seen. Only one of the nurses was at the desk and she'd been on the phone, staring at a computer screen, deep in conversation about a patient, her back to Kara, her head bobbing as she'd listened to someone through a headset. As she nodded, she twisted a lock of long dark hair and studied some chart.

Kara eased into the hospital room and found her brother lying faceup on the bed, his eyes at half-mast, bandages over one side of his head, bruises showing beneath both eyes. His gaze slid groggily to the side. He blinked as if in slow motion, his dark eyebrows drawing together as he attempted to focus on her. He licked his lips slowly as if it was a great effort. "Kara?" His voice was a rasp. Barely audible.

"Hey. I'm here."

Tubes ran in and out of his body, an IV stand was nearby. A monitor was suspended over his bed, a black screen displaying his vital signs and logging his heartbeats. His skin was sallow above his beard.

"I . . . I . . ." He forced his gaze to the window, where the sky was sullen and dark, the coming night brooding while snow was falling, collecting on the sill, as the heart monitor gave off soft beeps. "I . . . need . . . get out."

She took stock of the tubes and wires, the pallor of his skin, the bandages and dull sheen in his eyes, and heard the steady beep of the heart monitor. "I don't think I can do that." She inched nearer the bed. "You need to get well. Heal."

His gaze locked with hers for an instant. She saw the anger etched in the set of his jaw, silently arguing with her. His voice when he spoke was a rasp. "They're gonna try to pin this on me, too. They'll never let me out." His jaw tightened. "But . . . but I didn't do it. I didn't kill Merritt, and I didn't kill Dad and Sam and . . . Oh, shit." His mouth tightened and his eyes narrowed on her. "You put me in that place," he accused, and her heart sank. "Your testimony."

She wanted to defend herself, to say that she only answered the DA's questions honestly, that the way they were peppered at her and her confusion as an eight-year-old on the witness stand contorted her testimony, twisted her words, but she didn't. She'd tried to explain long ago and Jonas had turned a deaf ear to her explanations, to her apologies. The expression on his face suggested his attitude hadn't changed. If anything, it had hardened.

A cart rattled in the hallway and Kara jumped.

Soon, very soon, the missing cop would be discovered, or he'd return and Kara would be trapped in Jonas's room. Time was running out.

"Did Merritt say anyone was after him?"

Jonas just stared. "What do you mean?"

"Who would kill him?"

"I don't know. He had other clients. Maybe one of them or—" He lifted a hand, then let it fall. "Someone he pissed off. I don't know."

"But it has to be connected, right? To what happened at the house that night. That's why he wanted to see you."

"Maybe."

"It's too much of a coincidence that the day you're released someone kills Merritt. Why? Did he know something? What did he tell you? Why did he want to meet?"

"He didn't say. He didn't get the chance."

"But you had your own reasons for going," she said, remembering how Jonas had said he thought Merritt, along with Aunt Faiza, had drained the

309

estate. "You wanted a reconciliation, right? You wanted to see if there was any money in the estate."

"Yeah."

"How . . . how did you know there might not be?"

"Just little things Margrove said. Nothing explicit, but just remarks he made about how expensive it was to keep the case alive, how much it costs for you and your education, how some investments had gone south. I wanted to see for myself. I expected a complete list of every dime he'd spent over the last twenty years."

"Did he know that?"

"Yeah, and he backpedaled, you know, talking about how 'grateful' I should be to be getting out, that kind of thing." He was seething again, and she heard noises outside his door. Voices. She looked around the room, searching for a spot to hide. Found none. She was about to bolt when the voices receded, but her nerves were strung tight.

"Okay, I've got to go," she said quickly, easing toward the door when one last thought struck her and she paused, turned back for a second. "Have you heard from Marlie?"

"What?" he whispered, and slowly shook his head against the pillow. "Marlie? No . . . Why?"

"I got a text and a phone call. Weird ones. Just the other night. It sounded like . . . I mean I thought it might be her."

"A prank."

"Maybe."

"What did she say?"

"She's alive."

"That's it?"

"Yeah."

"She's alive," he repeated. "Then it wasn't Marlie, because she would have IDed herself, right? And said something like, *I'm* alive. Not *she's* alive."

"I thought about that."

"Maybe they—whoever called—they weren't talking about Marlie."

"Who, then?"

"I don't know," he admitted, moving on the bed and grimacing in pain. "You tell me."

"I can't," she said. "I thought maybe you knew something about it."

"Me?" His gaze sharpened as he understood. "Why? Oh, wait. Now I get it! You think I left you the message? Because I was released? Out of prison? You thought I would play some sick mind game with you, is that it? Give me a fuckin' break."

Again, Kara heard a noise outside the door, footsteps coming closer. She froze. What if the cop was back? How would she explain herself and get out? Or what if a nurse or doctor came in to check on Jonas? She couldn't be discovered here in his room. Didn't want to be found out.

Not yet. At any second her empty bed could be discovered and if so, Jonas's room would be one of the first places the staff would search for her. She'd made her need to see him well known to the nursing staff. That had been a mistake.

And what about the police? The nurse had told her the cops were going to return to ask her questions. She was out of time. "I'll be back," she promised, but he didn't seem to be listening, was sleeping again. Carefully, she cracked the door, peered into the hallway and slid out, past the empty chair. She passed a man in a wheelchair rolling down the hallway and the semicircular nurse's desk where the same nurse sat, back turned to her.

Kara moved noiselessly to the elevators just as the nurse clicked off her phone and glanced over her shoulder. Her gaze met Kara's and she stood up quickly. "Can I help you?" she asked, her eyebrows knitting.

Kara froze.

Silently prayed the elevator doors would open. Shoving back her chair, she stood and ripped off her headset as she rounded the desk, phone still in hand. "This floor is off-limits to visitors at this time."

Kara thought about coming up with a quick lie but knew she would be found out. "I'm leaving now."

A soft ding announced the arrival of the elevator car. Thank God!

"What were you doing up here?" the nurse asked as another nurse, a tall male with a wrestler's physique and concerned expression, appeared from a patient's room.

"What's going on?" he demanded.

"I was just trying to visit my brother."

The woman said, "But it looks like you're a patient."

Her bandages! Kara had forgotten the gauze covering her stitches. Crap!

"Your brother? And who is that?" The nurse glanced down the hallway to the empty chair at the door to Jonas's room just as the elevator door opened and Kara, heart thumping, slipped inside. "Wait a sec—"

Too late. Kara slapped the button for the first floor, then punched the door closed as the nurse approached, already speaking into her phone.

Thankfully the door closed and with a clunk the car started to descend. But she'd seen the nurse calling someone, maybe because of her, maybe not, but she didn't want to deal with anyone. Not a doctor, not a hospital administrator and certainly not anyone from security, or the police for that matter. She thought about trying to stop the elevator on the second floor and using the stairs, but it was too late. Maybe she had enough time to—

The car settled on the first floor and as the door opened onto a hallway, Kara tore off the gauze on her head and pulled her hair down so that it covered the injured side of her forehead. She stepped out of the car, one eye on the other elevator door and the staircase beyond, just in case either of the two nurses had decided to follow her.

But the reception area was mayhem: loud conversation, shouts and footsteps and some kind of chanting. About Jonas. Oh. God. She caught a glimpse of the reception area, where a crowd had gathered, a crowd composed mainly of women—mostly under forty, some with babies, others with handmade signs, all about freeing Jonas.

Wesley Tate's distraction.

Security guards and cops were trying to keep the throng at bay while a tall man in a dark suit—probably an administrator of some kind—was speaking with a red-jacketed female reporter, hair wet with melting snow, cameraman at her side. As the cops were trying to herd people out a side door, she took advantage and slipped between a tall woman in heeled boots, wool coat and an updo, and a shorter, rounder woman wearing a ponytail, jeans and sneakers.

Heart drumming, Kara avoided eye contact with the guard as he shepherded their group through the open door to the exterior.

She was almost free.

As she stepped outside, a blast of bitter air slapped her cheeks, but she kept walking along a concrete path where snow had been trampled. She circumvented the crowd congregated outside the wide front doors where women carrying picket signs had gathered. Denied access to the interior, they were chanting.

About Jonas.

It was nuts. A circus sideshow.

Television news crews had set up in the perimeter of the hospital, several white vans emblazoned with logos from stations in Washington and Oregon were parked, and she spied a couple of freelancers who worked for rival papers trying to gain entrance and getting nowhere with the security guard, who was obviously on crowd-control duty as the front entrance was roped off.

Kara scanned the crowd.

So many faces.

A few men scattered in the throng of women, many clustered in knots of two or three.

What the hell were they all doing here?

And then she saw her: a woman standing alone near a bank of tall windows. Her streaked blond hair was visible only at her nape as it was twisted upward into a red stocking cap decorated with white snowflakes. One of her hands was in the pocket of a black ankle-length coat, while a red scarf was wrapped loosely around her neck and tinted glasses shaded her eyes. Nonetheless, Kara recognized the arch of her cheekbones and the sharp slant of her jaw. Even her chin had that hint of a dimple that Kara remembered pressing her tiny finger into a lifetime before. But there was something else, something a bit off, probably the fact that her face was covered in a thick coat of makeup, visible even from a distance.

"Marlie," Kara whispered, her stomach dropping, her breath catching. Could it really be? After all this time?

Kara stopped dead in her tracks.

A female voice shouted "Hey!" just before a woman behind her plowed into her back and together they were skidding on the slick concrete, nearly falling into a redhead pushing a stroller.

"What the—?" the young mother demanded, whirling, just as Kara got her feet under her and the baby started crying.

"Sorry," Kara said quickly, and scrambled around the mother.

"Watch where you're going!" The redhead leaned over the stroller. "It's going to be all right," she cooed, picking up her child.

Kara didn't pay any attention, her gaze scanning the crowd, searching for a red stocking cap, but there were dozens of them in the mass of people, and the woman she'd seen had vanished.

The woman you thought you saw.

Ignoring the doubts in her mind, she eased

around several clusters of people, keeping her head averted from any of the cameras or cops until she reached the spot where the woman had stood. It was now occupied by two teenage girls in pink sweatshirts and earmuffs who were posing in front of the hospital, smiling upward as they held their phones aloft and took a series of selfies.

Teenagers? Here?

They couldn't even have been alive when Jonas had been thrust into infamy. But no Marlie. No blonde in a red and white stocking cap hurrying away.

"Crap." Wending her way through one shouting, agitated cluster to another, she searched frantically for the woman who looked so much like her missing sister.

You're imagining things.

All because you got a weird text and phone call and Jonas is out of prison. It's your mind playing tricks on you, Kara, the weird power of suggestion. Nothing more.

But she wasn't convinced and did a slow three-sixty, searching faces, her eyes narrowing.

She'd been here!

Marlie had been right in this very spot.

And the text and voice mail she'd received had been right.

She was alive!

"Kara?" A sharp voice caught her attention. "Kara McIntyre?"

Kara's stomach dropped and she saw the reporter approaching. An eager, smiling woman in a red jacket, a cameraman following with a shoulder cam, the call sign for Channel 3 visible.

"Kara McIntyre?" someone, a man, repeated. "Isn't she the kid who was locked in the attic? Jonas McIntyre's sister?"

"Oh, God." Kara started to panic.

"Could you spare a minute?" the woman, Sheila Keegan, said, her toothy smile seeming so genuine as she approached.

The answer was no.

A definite and firm *NO*.

"Sorry." Kara took off. Before more people caught on. Before more attention was cast her way. Before it became *a thing*.

"Kara McIntyre's here?" she heard as she hurried away, skimming the perimeter of the crowd, avoiding the pools of light cast, the snow providing a curtain of cover as she tried to blend into the shadows.

She was late, she knew. Tate could already have driven off, and then she'd have to figure out another way home as her crumpled SUV was most likely in a police department's garage somewhere. Not that it could be driven in its current ruined condition, no doubt a totaled wreck.

She couldn't worry about it now as she cut down a side street, parked cars iced over, snow piled on their hoods and roofs. Windows glowing, casting illumination onto the frigid white lawns. Strings of lights winked and blinked around eaves and glowed from beneath a white mantle covering the shrubbery.

Christmas.

Kara's most hated time of year.

And no one was about.

People were tucked snugly into their houses, but the street itself was empty, devoid of life.

Just her, walking swiftly, her boots clicking unevenly on the packed snow of the sidewalk. And yet she didn't feel alone. A chill swept through her and she sensed that someone was watching her, maybe even following her.

Get over yourself. It's just that it's been a hard couple of days. Your nerves are raw and fraying, your senses hyped, that's all. You're always super tense this time of year.

The Christmas season was always the worst.

This year would be even more so.

Twenty years had passed.

A milestone.

The "anniversary" of the McIntyre Massacre. There were already plans to dredge it all up again. Reruns of the TV specials about the brutal tragedy, books reissued, magazine and newspaper articles written back then dredged up again, a brand-new hyping of the Christmas horror show with poor little Kara McIntyre cast as the tragic heroine.

319

"Bullshit," she muttered, her breath clouding as she spied a snowman leaning precariously near a porch decorated with a sagging blow-up Santa and his overflowing bag of toys. As she passed the plastic Santa Claus, it sprang to life.

"Ho, ho, ho! Merry Christmas!" it called, rocking a little as it inflated, the toy sack, too, filling with air.

"Oh, Jesus!" Kara physically jumped.

For a second she thought the sudden animation was a cruel joke, that someone was manipulating the horrifying display. But no, while her heartbeat skyrocketed into the stratosphere, she realized she'd been caught in some hidden camera's eye and inadvertently activated a motion detector sending old Kris Kringle into his full stature. Even so, with a glance at the Santa's shiny face she felt a niggle of fear snake down her spine. His painted eyes seemed outlandishly round and ogling, his red lips beneath a painted-on beard appeared to grin with fake, toothy intensity. Like an evil clown in a house of horror.

Your imagination again.

That's all!

First you think you see your long-vanished sister, now you think someone is playing sick mind games with you.

Just calm the hell down.

Yet her pace increased. Only two more blocks. She prayed Tate was still waiting for her.

Over the rapid beating of her heart, she thought she heard footsteps. Quiet, but steady, muffled by the snow but ever following.

She glanced over her shoulder.

Squinted through the snowfall.

Nothing.

"Get over it," she muttered, still walking.

And then she heard it.

"Ho, ho, ho! Merry Christmas!" in that same robotic voice.

Oh. Dear. God.

CHAPTER 21

Kara's heart nearly stopped.

She whirled on the sidewalk to peer intently through the veil of snowflakes steadily falling from the night sky.

Her breathing shallow as a frightened rabbit's.

Was someone behind her?

Did she just see movement, a shadow quickly disappearing between two parked, frozen vehicles sitting and collecting snow in front of the house with the creepy plastic Santa?

Don't let your fears get the better of you.

It's all in your mind.

What does Dr. Zhou say? "Breathe. Think calm thoughts. Mind over matter. Face your fears."

But the now-silent Santa was still inflated, the whir of its pump loud in the night. Something or someone had set off the motion detector.

"Shit!"

No time to waste thinking about it.

Only two more blocks to the church lot.

Heart pounding, she started running. Faster and faster, her boots sliding a bit, her breathing wild.

It's only your mind, Kara, just your mind!

She didn't care. Wasn't strong enough to turn and wait until her heart rate slowed or someone actually did leap out at her. She wasn't going to take that chance.

Slap, slap, slap! Her footsteps beat a frantic tattoo only intensified by the pounding of her heart.

Flying, she ran through the narrow, empty street.

Slap, slap, slap!

Whether it was her imagination or someone was really after her, she raced toward the final corner silently praying that Tate had waited for her. That he hadn't given up. That—

She slid around the corner and spied a single vehicle in the old church's parking lot, a black Toyota RAV4.

Tate was at the wheel, his face illuminated by some kind of screen that he was reading.

As if he'd noticed her from the corner of his eye, he glanced up just as she dashed across the parking lot and raced to the passenger side of his SUV.

"Let's go," she said, sliding into the warm interior and slamming the door shut behind her. "You know, like now!"

"Trouble?" he asked, his eyebrows slamming together.

"I don't know. Let's just get out of here."

"Fine." He slipped his iPad into the console, then, checking his mirrors, eased out of the empty lot.

Kara swiped a patch of condensation away so that she had a better view of the side street as they drove past. There was nothing. The neighborhood was quiet, no dark figure hiding in the shrubbery or peering out from behind a lamppost. Slowly she let out a breath.

"You look like you just saw a ghost."

She thought of Marlie and the woman who, until a few seconds ago, she would have sworn was her missing sister. "Just a very weird Santa Claus."

"Weird?" He slowed for a stop sign. "Santa?"

"Never mind. It was just one of those odd Christmas displays. Inflatable. Kind of freaked me out. I'm okay." The inside of the RAV4 seemed safe somehow, the dash lights glowing, the heater blowing warm air, the windows and doors locked tight.

Tate was no longer in the hospital scrubs, having changed into jeans, shirt and leather jacket. "Where to?" he asked.

"First my house."

"The cops might be there."

"I'm not running from the police."

"You want to deal with them?"

"No, not yet."

"And there could be reporters camping out."

"I'm with a reporter," she said dryly, and a corner of his lip twitched, showing the hint of a dimple beneath the scruff of beard shadow. His hair was mussed and when he cast her a glance, his eyes held a glint of amusement, as if he found the situation humorous or some grand caper.

"That you are, and you're with the best."

"Certainly the most humble." Then she got serious again. "Look, I have to stop by the house. I'll be quick. I need to check on my dog and grab some clothes."

"Could be trouble," he said.

"More trouble than I'm in now?"

He laughed. "No, probably not."

"Probably not." Folding her arms over her chest, she leaned back in the passenger seat and stared out the window.

"There's a blanket in the back," he said, and before she could argue he snagged a thin sleeping bag, dragging it over the console and dropping it into her lap while driving with one hand. Thankfully traffic was thin. Even so she still flinched when an oncoming vehicle hugged the center line. She was still twitchy from the accident, so recent, so violent.

"What do you know about the trucker?" she asked, tucking the sleeping bag under her chin and smelling a trace of wood smoke and must in its downy folds. "The guy who was driving the semi that jackknifed." In her mind's eye she saw the gigantic grill bearing down on her, heard the crackle of glass shattering, the crumpling of steel.

"That he's in an ICU in Portland."

"Will he be okay?"

He hesitated. "Unknown."

"But maybe not," she said quietly, and swiped at the passenger window where condensation had collected. Kara didn't remember all the details of the horrific accident but felt the weight of another man's life on her shoulders.

"Maybe not." He was serious now, his face illuminated by the dash.

"God, how awful." She swallowed hard against a tide of guilt. No matter what the reason, she should not have been driving so wildly, so out of control, so freaked by Margrove's murder and Jonas in her back seat. If she had forced herself to stay put as the police had suggested, that truck driver would be okay.

Or would he? What were the chances that you would be able to wait for the cops to arrive, Kara? Jonas was already in the back seat. He wouldn't have allowed it. He would have demanded to be driven to the truck stop on the freeway or taken the Jeep himself.

She couldn't let herself go down that dark, twisted path. Clearing her throat, she pointed at Tate's iPad, still glowing on the dash. "What else do you know about the trucker? I figure you've already researched him."

Tate slowed for a stop light, waited as cross traffic sped through the intersection. "His name is Sven Aaronsen. He lives in Boise. Owns two rigs, the one he was driving and another. He's forty-seven, is divorced, a grown daughter who got married last year. Had a couple of busts, a domestic that was dropped nearly ten years ago and a DUI four years later."

"And he's still a truck driver?" she asked.

"Independent. As I said, he owns the company. One other driver."

She felt sick inside. Deflated. Slumping against the passenger window, she said, "Take me to my house."

"You sure? The police might be there."

"Maybe so." She slid him a glance as they passed the hospital, saw the police vehicles, lights flashing against the windows, several deputies trying to disperse the ever-growing crowd of Jonas's fans, some of whom thought he was some kind of new-age messiah.

"That your doing?" she asked, hooking a thumb at the milling crowd spreading under the portico.

"They came of their own accord. I improvised. Just jazzed a few, told them Jonas was coming down to greet them."

"From his hospital room?" She couldn't believe it.

"Best I could do on the spur of the moment. Luckily some of them bought it." He rounded the corner and headed in the direction of her home. "It worked, didn't it?"

"Well enough."

When they reached her home, she instructed him to park one street over. "I'll just be five minutes—maybe ten. If I don't come back in that time, just leave."

And then she cut across several yards and slipped into the back door of her house. Rhapsody about lost her mind. "I know, I know. I'm so sorry," Kara said, wondering at her need to apologize to the dog who was turning circles at her feet. She let Rhapsody out, then put food in her dish and checked her water. As the dog returned, Kara locked the door behind her and dashed upstairs. Her headache was beginning to pound, and she desperately needed a shower. But there was no time. She didn't want to deal with the police, not yet, and was certain they would come calling at any second.

Quickly, her pulse pounding at every sound, she stuffed clothes into an overnight bag and heard the dog bounding up the stairs. "You're coming, too," she said, and after throwing a makeup kit, brush and toothbrush into the open bag, stopped long enough to open the medicine cabinet, find a bottle of Aleve and toss back two gel caps dry. Then she dropped the bottle into her bag, zipped it and flew down the stairs, only pausing to slip on her coat and boots, grab Rhapsody's leash hanging near the pantry, then snap it onto the dog's collar.

Ten seconds later she'd locked the back door

behind her and retraced her steps to the spot where Tate's black RAV4 was idling near a snow-covered laurel hedge. "See that?" he said, pointing to a van parked up the street as she and the dog climbed inside.

"Yeah?" She settled into the passenger seat; Rhapsody curled in the foot well.

"A photographer. Freelance."

"How do you know?" Clicking her seat belt in, she eyed the van.

"I've hired him."

"Oh." She sent him a look. "Great."

"But I didn't this time. Someone else either has already or he's out trying to grab some shots on his own and will try to peddle them." He put his Toyota into gear and pulled away from the curb. "He's just the first to show up."

"You're the first," she reminded him.

"Can't argue with that."

But he was right. All too soon her house would probably be swarming with cops and reporters and photographers. All with a million questions, most of which she didn't want to answer. At least not yet. As they passed the van and she saw a man in a watch cap staring at the front of her house, she knew she would be inundated if she tried to stay at home. Reporters would be camped on her yard, photographers training their camera lenses on her, neighbors and curious bystanders using their cell phones to catch a glimpse of her, and of course the police would come calling. Kara would have to talk to them, of course, but she just wasn't ready yet. "You can take me to the hotel on Wheeler Street," she said, then glanced down at Rhapsody and patted her head. "I mean, if they take pets."

"You don't know?"

"No, and I don't have a phone . . . wait." She dug into her bag to retrieve her iPad. "This'll do . . ." As he drove toward the heart of town, she pulled up the website for the hotel. "Nope. No pets and it's full. No vacancy."

"It's almost Christmas. Places are booked." He adjusted the fan; it whirred more loudly, warm air flowing from the vents while she searched the Internet.

"Here's another one, a motel on the east side and—" She googled the Lazy Daze Motel, pulled up the website and discovered that it, with its amenities of free Wi-Fi and complimentary continental breakfast did welcome all pets, but again was full. "No room at that inn either. Crap!"

"What about your aunt's place?"

"Stay with Faiza?" she said, and thought of her mother's sister and shook her head. "No."

"A cousin then? A friend?"

"No cousins around and . . . and no friends either." That was a sad statement, but true. She'd never made any real friends, just acquaintances she'd met in school, girls whose fascination with her had been based on the trauma she'd suffered, the infamy of it all, as if she were some kind of tragic, tarnished celebrity. And she'd never worked in one job long enough to form any real bonds, never felt a connection deep enough with a coworker to form a real friendship, one in which she could confide all of her hopes, fears, dreams and nightmares. Whether it had been because she'd learned to be standoffish, keeping people and questions at arm's length, or because people naturally avoided the girl who had survived such a savage family annihilation, she didn't know.

"Uh, there's really no one," she admitted, feeling a pang of self-pity. Clearing her throat and her mind, she dismissed the pathetic emotion; she'd learned early enough that dwelling on her heartaches only made them worse. "Surely I can find something," she said, and delved into the Internet again.

"Okay." He slowed for a corner, then ventured, "You could stay at my place."

"What? Your place? No!" Shaking her head, she searched for another motel and found nothing in town. "God, no. Not a good idea, but . . . but thanks." She watched him from the corner of her eye. Really? No way. "Maybe there's something out on 84."

"Forget it. The interstate's partially closed."

"What?" She glanced up at him. "Closed?"

"Um-hmm. A section of the road is shut down. Because of the storm. The Gorge is a mess."

"You're kidding." But she could see from his expression that he was earnest, and she knew that sometimes in winter, blizzard-like conditions of freezing rain or ice or snow could cause the highway skirting the Columbia River Gorge to be closed.

He glanced at her iPad. "Google 'road conditions.'"

She did. Of course he was correct. "Well, crap."

"Look. You can crash at my place until we find something. It's no big deal." He tossed her a smile—the first real one she'd seen, white teeth flashing in the dark interior, his face partially illuminated by the dash lights. "And you lucked out. There's room available and I'm dog friendly."

"Very funny."

"Yeah," he agreed, his grin fading just a bit as he angled through an alley to connect to a street that paralleled the river, "I thought so."

It practically took an act of Congress for Thomas and Johnson to be allowed into Jonas McIntyre's room and when they got there, the patient was reticent, refused to talk.

"We just want to know what you were doing up at Merritt Margrove's mobile home," Thomas explained, but McIntyre, if he did hear them, didn't say a word. He never made eye contact with them and appeared almost comatose lying on the bed and hooked up to all kinds of hospital equipment.

It was an act.

According to the staff, Jonas McIntyre had conversed with the nurses and, it seemed, his sister. The reports were that Kara McIntyre left AMA, against medical advice, in a hurry, and a couple of the nurses on this floor had seen her duck into an elevator, presumably after speaking to her brother while the guard on duty had been called away to deal with the commotion downstairs.

It all seemed fishy, and Thomas had the uncomfortable feeling that he'd been set up somehow. He just hadn't figured out how.

He tried one last time. "Listen, McIntyre, we just need to know what you were doing up at Margrove's trailer. What you saw. Who you saw. Why you were up there in the first place. A simple statement."

No reaction.

Not so much as a flicker in his eyes.

He barely blinked.

Thomas's back teeth gnashed in frustration. Jonas could hear him. He knew it, but the guy, even in pain in a hospital room, wasn't budging. Twenty years in a prison had taught him how to hide any emotion, to keep his emotions in check.

Thomas glanced across the bed to Johnson, who gave a quick shake of her head indicating they were fighting a losing battle. She was right. He knew it, but it pissed him off.

"Okay, let's go," he said, and started for the door. In the hallway the guard was arguing with a petite woman in her thirties with two-toned hair that fell to the middle of her back, pouty lips and pale blue eyes that were flashing fire. "I told you, I'm his girlfriend!" she said, tossing the hair over her shoulder. "I need to see him."

But the guard, who had been reprimanded for leaving his post earlier, wasn't standing down. "No one sees him."

"I'm practically next of kin!"

A nurse was on her way. "We can't have this," she said. "The patient needs his rest."

"The 'patient' is my boyfriend and he's not under arrest or anything, so I need to see him. He's a free man the last I heard." She was wearing black tights, heavy military-style boots, a sweater that just covered her rear, jean jacket and a huge looping necklace comprised of wooden beads and a dangling wooden cross that resembled a rosary. Maybe it really was a rosary. He couldn't tell.

Thomas stepped in and introduced himself. "You say you're Jonas's girlfriend?" he said. "What's your name?"

"Mia." She folded her arms over her chest and

jutted her chin, defiance emanating from her in waves. "Mia Long. I want to see Jonas."

"Not possible."

"Under what law?" she demanded.

"Hospital regulations," the nurse supplied.

Thomas interjected, "And jurisdiction of the county."

"Sooooo what?" Her eyes laden with liner and mascara thinned, Mia pointed a black-tipped finger at Thomas. "You're arresting him again? But he's out. A free man. You can't arrest him again. Not for, well, you know, what happened twenty years ago."

"We're just trying to talk to him," Thomas said. "He's not under arrest."

"But there's a guard here and you're not allowing anyone to see him. Even me." Her chin jutted out and she took a step forward, again pointing accusing fingers. "You people are the ones who set him up, who arrested him and convicted him, so he spent twenty years of his life, twenty fucking years, like half his life, behind bars with murderers and rapists and thugs." So livid she was shaking, she said, "He was brutalized in there. Did you know that? Huh?" She didn't wait for an answer. "Jonas McIntyre was a kid when he went in. He suffered. Like *really* suffered. For *years*. And now . . . now you're trying to railroad him again on some trumped-up charge so that he has to go back!

Well, I won't stand for it. Thousands of people know this was all a big sham because the police were too lazy, too determined to blame him for crimes he didn't commit. We won't stand for it, and we won't rest until he's vindicated."

"Just hold on a second," Johnson said. "No one's charging Jonas with anything. We're just trying to find out what happened at Merritt Margrove's place in the woods."

"Weren't you there?" Thomas asked, putting two and two together as he stared back into her blazing eyes.

She blinked. Surprised. "No, I just dropped him off."

"And then?"

"He told me to wait until he called, and I did, and then . . . and then he said he got a ride and I could meet him at a truck stop on 84. Hal's Get and Go, just outside of The Dalles."

"And you did?" Johnson asked. To Thomas she said, "That section of the road is shut down."

"Yeah! Hey—what is this?" Mia said, a little less sure of herself. "It was before the road was shut down, and I don't know anything about what happened in that mobile home. I took Jonas up there, he got out of the car, and I left. End of story."

Thomas asked, "Did Jonas say anything? About Margrove? About why he was going up to the mobile home?"

"No, he just said they were meeting." She suddenly looked worried.

Johnson eyed the girl. "What about when he called you to say he had a ride? That he didn't need you to pick him up?"

"I called him," she clarified. "I was starting to get worried. I was at Kreb's Corners, at the truck stop, and there was talk that the road was going to be closed, so I wanted to check with him."

"And when you did?" Thomas asked.

Mia shifted from one booted foot to the other. "He sounded kinda freaked, y'know, breathless and . . ." She pursed her lips and angled her chin. "What is this? Do I need a lawyer?"

"What's going on here?" the nurse said, her patience finally running out. "This is a hospital, not an interrogation room. Take this, whatever it is, somewhere else. We've got patients—"

"And what? Breathless and what?" Johnson cut in, ignoring the blond nurse, her eyes laser-focused on Mia.

Thomas told the nurse, "We're about done here, just asking a few questions." And to Mia, "A lawyer is your choice."

Mia glared at them all, as if the cops and nurse were her sworn enemies. "I'm not answering any more questions. Not until I see Jonas."

"That's not happening," the nurse said. "No visitors. Period."

"But they were in the room!" Mia whined as she waved a hand at the officers.

"They have authority." The nurse was growing more and more irritated as a phone at her station began to ring. "Maybe you all want to take this conversation out of the hospital hallway?" Her eyebrows raised over the rims of her oversize glasses. "There are quieter spots, even small conference rooms—?"

"Or the station," Johnson said, obviously tired of Mia's theatrics. "We could go there."

"What?" Mia turned suddenly ashen. "No . . . No, not happening."

The nurse said, "But you all need to leave." Her gaze met Thomas's. "Now."

"I'm not leaving. Not until I see Jonas." Mia planted herself near the elevator bank, her arms crossed over her chest defiantly.

"Fine." The nurse was having none of it and the phone kept ringing. "I've already called security, and these fine officers will escort you out of the building."

"But this is a public building."

"It's private and, whether you believe it or not, we're only interested in taking care of our patients, your boyfriend included, so, come on, let's get a move on." Her face was calm, her voice steely. "I have other patients who need me." And with that she headed to the semicircular desk, reached over and picked up the receiver, all the while keeping her eyes on the small group as the elevator call button dinged and the doors whispered open. "Third floor. This is Evelyn Mathers. Can you hold a second?"

The security guard who stepped onto the third floor was Madge Petroski, the officer Thomas had helped to her feet less than fifteen minutes earlier. And her mood hadn't improved. Petroski's lips were compressed, her muscles tight, her demeanor as serious as a wolf studying a lame, straggling deer. "What's going on here?" she demanded, and didn't soften a bit when she recognized Thomas.

"We need an escort for Ms. Long," Thomas said. To the nurse, he added, "We're leaving, but if there's a problem"—he cast a meaningful glare at the deputy stationed near Jonas McIntyre's room—"let us know."

The nurse nodded tightly. "Will do."

The security guard gave a clipped nod. "Come along," she said to Mia Long and before she could reach for her, the younger woman stomped into the open elevator.

"Thanks," Johnson said to the nurse. "We'll be back."

"Fabulous," the nurse replied, her smile as icy as an arctic blast as she glared at Thomas. "Just . . . great." Then she turned her attention back to the call.

Johnson asked, "Do you always have this effect

on people you meet? This uncanny ability to make enemies everywhere you go?"

"It's a gift," Thomas acknowledged as they waited for another elevator car and gave a wide berth to an orderly pushing an elderly man in a wheelchair heading down the short hallway. "A real blessing."

CHAPTER 22

Kara double-checked the lock on the bathroom door of Tate's condo, then stepped into his small shower, where hot water was already running and steaming up this small space, a corner of his high-ceilinged loft. The needle-like spray felt good, relaxing muscles that had been tense ever since she'd spied Merritt's body, then nearly been given a heart attack with her brother appearing in her car. After that, there had been the accident and waking up in the hospital where she escaped and now was . . . was alone, naked, in the home of a man she barely knew and didn't trust at all.

Good one, Kara. Now what? You're trapped here without a phone, or a car, or even a damned friend you can call. There's Aunt Faiza. "No!" she said aloud, startling herself. *Well, then, how about the police. You need to talk to them, explain about finding Merritt's body and how Jonas stowed away in the Jeep and how the semi came at you, sliding sideways.*

She blinked. Thought of the driver of the truck and her heart twisted. She knew the accident wasn't her fault and Jonas would back her up, but he was a convicted felon, believed to be a liar and a stone-cold killer, not exactly the best witness, and there were the vodka bottles that would be

341

found in the wreckage, tiny little bits of evidence that she might have been under the influence.

But certainly they'd checked her blood in the hospital . . . God, it was all so complicated.

"Hey!" She heard two sharp raps on the door. "You okay in there?" Tate called through the panels.

"Yeah, yeah. Just a minute." She used his shampoo, lathering and rinsing, then applying a conditioner that smelled decidedly masculine, but really, who cared? Certainly not her and not Wesley Tate.

Rotating her shoulders and neck, wincing slightly at the pain that lingered, she warned herself about him again. Sure, he'd stirred up the fans at the hospital so she could make good her escape, but he was still the same guy who put himself in harm's way as she backed out her driveway, all for the sake of getting her story, an exclusive interview. As she turned off the water, the pipes creaking slightly, she reminded herself of that important fact. Oh, sure, he could be charming and helpful, and was handsome in that rugged, I-don't-give-a-damn way, but that wasn't good enough. Not anymore. She'd always been interested in the totally wrong type of man for her. It was her romantic MO and probably had roots in the damned tragedy she'd suffered through.

Dr. Zhou hadn't said as much, but it didn't take

a psychologist to connect those particular dots.

And she wasn't going to end up depending on him. Uh-uh.

No way was she going to stay here even though she'd agreed to use his condo as a landing place, a spot where she could shower, change, and get her head together. Tate was, as they say, the only port in a storm.

A temporary port, she reminded herself as she dried her hair with a towel he'd provided, then after swiping away the moisture that had collected on the mirror mounted over a small, utilitarian sink, checked the stitches on her forehead. The flesh surrounding them was tender, but she'd survive, and she could part her hair and hide the tiny would-be scar that was probably forming. Makeup would help on her face, but she was stuck with the long bruise that had developed across her shoulder and down her chest compliments of her seat belt.

That discoloration would take weeks to fade.

Nothing she could do about that, and she didn't have time to think about it as she pulled on a pair of clean jeans and an oversize sweatshirt. Then, still rubbing her hair briskly with the towel, she stepped barefoot into the main living area, a wide room with soaring ceilings, exposed pipes and windows that stretched along one wall and offered a killer view of the river where it bent back on itself.

She reminded herself again, this wasn't a place to stay. Not at all. Just a quick landing spot where she could hopefully get her head together and screw up her courage so she could talk to the police.

When she was ready.

Whenever the hell that might be.

Rhapsody, though, had made herself right at home, even settling onto Tate's bed with its navy-blue quilt and military-tight corners.

As she dried her hair, Kara thought of her own messy bed with its wrinkled duvet and wine bottles left on the nightstands in a cozy if messy bedroom. This huge, stark room was certainly at odds with that.

Tate didn't seem to mind that the dog had pawed his pillows into a different position before curling into a ball and staring at him as he worked. He'd ditched the jacket and flannel shirt, but was still in a long-sleeve black T and battered jeans, his hair unruly. Leaning over the table, a cell phone jammed to his ear, he was staring at an open laptop, his eyes scanning whatever he was reading on the screen.

He didn't look up but must've sensed she was in the room because he motioned with his free hand toward the kitchen area, where she spied a coffeemaker complete with pods for different flavors and types of coffee or tea or hot chocolate.

But no bottle of wine had been left open to breathe.

No bottle of vodka or whiskey set on a bar with an ice bucket and chilled mixers at the ready.

She told herself she didn't need a drink, but a tiny voice inside her head insisted she was a liar.

Just a taste, it urged.

Come on.

Something to calm your nerves, that's all.

No big deal.

However, there was no evidence of any liquor visible even though she took another quick look and scanned the shelves and countertops, mentally calculating where, if he had alcohol, he might stash it.

Since she couldn't very well root through his cupboards, she settled on black coffee and eavesdropped as she took one of the cups set out, selected the strongest blend and pushed a button. As the water gurgled, steamed and streamed into the cup, she heard Tate's end of the conversation. "Yeah, okay . . . text the addresses and phone numbers . . . That'll work . . . We're heading over to Margrove's place . . . I know, but I called. She's got copies. Digital . . . uh-huh . . . don't worry; she's no fan of the police." A pause, then, "Yeah. Fine. Just make sure the addresses are still valid. Yeah . . . tonight. We need to get a jump on this ASAP . . . What?" A beat. "Right, right. Start with anyone still around. Face-to-face is best."

The coffee machine had quieted. She picked up her cup and took a tentative taste, her stomach rumbling. God, when was the last time she'd eaten? She flashed on the wine and cheese and crackers from the night before.

It seemed like a lifetime ago.

Tate was still talking. "You got it. Confirm those who have moved . . . what?" A lengthy space where Tate listened, then grabbed a pen from a nearby cup used as a holder for writing implements and scribbled a note to himself on the already full first page of a legal pad. "Yeah, got it." Nodding, Tate ripped the note from the pad, took a quick picture of it and stuffed the jagged yellow strip into a pocket. "Okay. Yeah. Keep me posted."

He hung up and twirled his chair around to face her. "Better?"

"Marginally."

"How's the pain?"

"Manageable."

He said, "I have ibuprofen."

"I'm okay. Really."

Tell him you'd like a beer or a glass of wine.

"Hungry?" As if he'd read her earlier thoughts.

"Is it that obvious?"

He grinned. "Maybe. Anyway, I'm starved. So let's do it!"

"Well, yeah, I could eat, but more importantly, I need to get a phone, at least a temporary one,

one of those burners, I guess, until I get mine back from the police. And then there's the whole rental car thing."

"Through the insurance company."

She'd already thought of that. "Eventually, but I need wheels ASAP."

"You've got ID? You'll need it."

She groaned. "Again—"

"With the police?"

"Right."

"Okay." He frowned. "Well, first things first. I've already called for delivery. From a mom-and-pop deli just up the street."

"Great."

"And we can stop at a store to pick up a phone, but I'm pretty sure you'll need ID."

"Shit."

He stood. "The police should release your cell back to you but like it or not, you're gonna have to talk to the cops sooner or later and get your stuff back. Driver's license? Keys?"

"I vote for later." She buried her nose in her cup and took a long swallow. She didn't want to think about being grilled by the police, having to answer question upon question about Merritt. About the past. About anything.

"If you want your belongings and to start dealing with getting a new car, that's the fastest way possible."

"I know, I know." She'd already told herself

the same as she'd washed her hair in the shower. "I just need a little time."

"Emphasis on 'little,'" he said as a buzzer sounded, and he hurried down the stairs.

The second he'd disappeared she made her way over to his computer to take a peek. She tapped a key so that the display appeared—a screen saver requiring a password. Of course. As for the scribbles on his legal pad, the only words that leapt out at her were names:

Marlie
Donner
Samuel
Zelda
Jonas
Sam Junior
Kara

But not just the names of family members.

Others associated with the family and that brutal, hideous night were included. Skimming the list, she saw notes about her mother's sister, Faiza, and her musician boyfriend. Both of her parents' exes and, of course, Lacey Higgins and Chad Atwater, with whom Marlie had supposedly been in love.

And she had been.

Head over heels.

Kara remembered.

"He's just so . . . so awesome, Kara-Bear," Marlie had confided on Thanksgiving night at their home in the city. Located in the West Hills of Portland, the McIntyre estate was composed of nearly two sprawling acres cut into the forested slopes. Their huge, rambling home that Mama was forever redecorating was positioned so that the back of the three-story home with its bank of windows had what Daddy had called "a million-dollar view" overlooking the city sprawled upon the banks of the Willamette River far below. Beyond the city, far in the distance, stood Mount Hood, a jagged peak that towered on a ridge of mountains and, on bright summer mornings, was backlit by the rising sun.

This Thanksgiving night was clear, a million stars winking overhead, the glittering lights of the city visible through the trees surrounding the grounds.

The sisters had slipped outside, escaping the noise of the house: a raucous game of Risk the boys had been playing and the argument between Mama and her sister that had escalated through the evening fueled by after-dinner drinks.

Unannounced, Auntie Fai had brought her latest boyfriend to the family dinner. Mama hadn't been happy with Faiza's "ingratitude and arrogance" and had let her sister know it. Faiza, defiant and "bullheaded," had been unfazed, even smug as she'd introduced Roger Sweeney, a struggling guitar player in a local band, as they'd arrived. Mama's small chin had become rock hard, her smile fixed, her eyes glittering with indignation. For his part, Roger hadn't said much but taken in everything with his deep-set, pale eyes above a hooked nose and thin lips surrounded by a neat little beard and moustache. An earring had sparkled from one of his earlobes, his hair was turning gray and had been clipped back into a thin ponytail, and both of his middle fingers had been tattooed with an image of a wolf's head. Though he'd been quiet, Kara had felt that Roger, too, had enjoyed seeing Mama seethe and Daddy try to smooth her ruffled feathers by smiling tightly and mixing drinks.

"Let's get out of here!" Marlie had said, slipping through one of the French doors. Kara had eagerly followed.

The huge house with its lingering scents of roasted turkey, pumpkin pie and cigarette smoke had felt claustrophobic because of the seething emotions.

"God, they're pathetic," Marlie muttered under her breath as she closed the door behind them. Outside, the air was cold, a breath of wind rustling through the trees. Dry leaves skittered and danced across the path that cut across the backyard to the pool, now covered with a huge tarp.

Marlie had taken Kara's hand and pulled her

farther away from the house, where lights glowed in the windows, creating patches of light on the yard. Grinning widely, Marlie whispered. "Can I tell you a secret?"

"Sure." Kara loved secrets.

"You have to promise, though. You can't tell anyone."

"I won't," Kara had vowed, grateful that her older sister was entrusting her with something she didn't want shared.

"Pinky swear?"

"Pinky swear." For a brief second they locked their smallest fingers. "For sure."

"Okay. Good."

"So what is it?" Kara asked.

"I'm going to marry him," Marlie announced, hunching down so that her face was close to Kara's. "I'm going to marry Chad!" She straightened, wrapping her arms around herself and twirling, her silhouette visible against the lights of the city winking in the distance.

"For real?"

"For real!" Marlie stopped whirling long enough to pick up Kara and swing her over the frosty grass and the night had spun around them, Marlie beaming and Kara giggling wildly. "I'm going to be Mrs. Chad Atwater!" She'd stopped twirling and been dizzy, her legs wobbly. Both she and Kara tumbled together on the grass, Marlie breathing hard as they stared into the night-dark sky where thousands of stars glittered.

Kara said, "Do I have to call you that?"

"Mrs. Atwater?" Marlie asked, laughing. "Nah, you just call me Marlie and I'll call you Kara-Bear. Just like now. That doesn't change. Okay?"

" 'Kay." Kara felt better.

"Good girl." Marlie had clasped Kara's hand again. "Oh, Kara, we are going to be so, so happy."

"But you'll still live with us, right?" Kara had asked.

"No." Marlie got a little more serious. "But we'll be close. I'll make sure of it. We'd like a farm or a ranch with dogs and horses," she confided, dreaming.

She'd always been an athlete and had loved animals almost as much as she loved competition. In an effort to keep up with her brothers, she'd taken up archery and target shooting, just to prove she was as good as they, that girls could keep up with boys. "Actually, I'm better than all of the brothers," she'd confided in Kara just last week. "They just won't admit it."

Now, gazing up at the stars, Marlie said, "Maybe we'll go up to the lake, you know, maybe Dad and Mom would let us keep the place up. But whatever, it's going to be so, so cool."

Kara didn't like the sound of her living as far away as the mountain house, but Marlie didn't notice that she'd gotten quiet. "Just remember:

This is our secret. Right? You can't tell a soul. Not Mama or Daddy, not Jonas, not Donner or Sam or *any*one!"

And Kara hadn't.

Not to this very day.

A sadness stole through her as she thought of the sister she'd lost, a sibling whom she had been closer to than her own mother. And now she was getting messages about her.

You don't know that. The text and voice said, "She's alive." You decided that whoever is behind it is talking about Marlie. That's a leap, Kara. A big leap.

But who else?

She glanced back at the notes again, to the names Tate had listed. Her father's one-time business partner, Silas Dean, had been written on the yellow page, as well as her parents' ex-husbands and wives. Leona and Natalie, both married to Kara's father, and Walter Robinson, her mother's ex-husband. So many marriages, so many names. Each with his or her own agenda.

And then there was Marlie. Who someone insisted was alive. Could she tell Tate about the text and voice message? Could she trust him with that information? Could she confide to him that she'd thought she was being followed? To that end she walked to the tall window and stared outside to the desolate night. The streets were nearly empty, the river a dark swath with whitecaps reflecting white from the vaporous illumination of the streetlamps near its banks.

For an instant she thought that someone, anyone, could be looking up at her, her entire body silhouetted by the soft glow of interior light. For an instant her blood ran cold and she took a step backward.

God, she could use a drink.

Swallowing back her fear, mentally chastising herself for being a paranoid ninny, she thought she heard voices rising from the floor below. Oddly, it was comforting to hear Tate talking to the delivery person.

Tonight she wasn't alone.

But he's a virtual stranger to you, Kara. A man with his own purpose. A reporter who wants your story, the son of a man who died saving you. You cannot trust him; not fully. Don't drop your guard.

Uneasily she walked back to his desk and the papers strewn upon it. Again she eyed the list of people connected to the tragedy of her family. She noticed arrows and smaller notes scribbled in the margins, words and phrases she couldn't quite read, but Jonas's name had been circled several times, and arrows connected it with Lacey Higgins and Donner.

Lacey.

Kara traced the name on the paper with the tip of an index finger.

What about Lacey?

A girl no longer, she reminded herself, though she still remembered Lacey as she had been then, a seventeen-year-old in the virginal white dress, her most famous quote about Jonas still burning in Kara's memory:

"He said, 'If I ever find out you were fucking someone else, I'll take an axe to him first and you next. That way you can watch him die before you go to hell.'"

Kara's skin crawled. Did Jonas really utter that ugly, blood-chilling threat? Or had Lacey been lying? At the time everyone believed the calm, wide-eyed girl who'd sat so still and straight in the witness box.

Biting her lip while still tracing the letters of Lacey's name, Kara tried to recall her brother as he had been before the night all the members of her family were so brutally slaughtered. He'd been a hothead, for sure. Angry. Even Natalie, his own mother, had said he was a mixture of "piss and vinegar sprinkled with way too many raging teenage hormones."

Kara had definitely seen Jonas with the sword earlier that day. She remembered spying on him through the open door to his room. In jeans and a hooded sweatshirt, he swung the old, heavy weapon easily. An athlete by nature, he'd practiced his martial arts moves for as long as Kara could remember. So there he was slashing through the air, spinning, and hopping onto the unmade bed in his bare feet. From atop the mattress he jabbed determinedly, his face twisted in a seething fury as if he were slaying an invisible enemy.

An angry, troubled teen who a jury had decided was an enraged killer, an eighteen-year-old hyped up on adrenaline and testosterone who had sliced his own brothers, father, and stepmother to ribbons. As she had a thousand times before, Kara thought back to that night, to the jagged pieces of that horrid blood-soaked puzzle that, try as she might, she couldn't force together.

Why had Marlie woken her? Had she been afraid the killer would come looking for her younger sister? How did she know? Was Marlie somehow a part of the attack? Why had she disappeared? What happened to her?

Was there an intruder, as Jonas had insisted?

If so, who?

Why hadn't the police found him? Wouldn't there be something, a trace of hair or skin or blood that DNA testing could have proven did not belong to a member of the family? She remembered the smeared blood on the walls, the fire hissing and glowing red, its flames reflecting on the dark pools of blood, several Christmas stockings on the floor as the machete had sliced through the mantel and sent the red-and-green socks flying.

But most of all she remembered her brothers, blood-soaked and still, mouths gaping open, eyes fixed as they'd fallen, their bodies splayed garishly over Mama's Persian carpet. Only Jonas had moved, been alive, able to focus on her in a moment of heart-stopping clarity. She'd been rooted to the floorboards of the hallway, her heart hammering, terror gripping her as her mind screamed, *No, no, no!*

Blood-spattered and weak, he'd risen slowly up on an elbow. "Get help . . . Run!" he'd rasped weakly just as a blast of frigid wind had ripped into the room, sending the flames in the grate crackling as a huge, shadowy figure loomed in the doorway.

"Find anything interesting?" Tate's voice startled her.

She jumped, coffee sloshing from her cup onto the desk and legal pad as the horrid memory withered and died. "Crap!" Frantically she searched for something to wipe up the mess.

"Got it!" Tate snapped paper towels from a spindle, crossed the room in three long strides and dabbed quickly at sodden, stained paper.

"Sorry."

"No worries."

She saw he was holding a big paper bag in his other hand as he mopped the desktop.

The scribbled notes on the top page bled into each other.

"Oh, geez!"

"Just my thoughts," he said, glancing at the ruined pages. "Everything's on the computer. It's okay. Don't worry about it." He glanced up as he tossed the sodden towel into a nearby trash can. "Lucky for you I've got a photographic memory."

"Seriously?" That stopped her.

"No." He offered a hint of a smile. "I wish. It would sure make things easier."

"So you're a liar," she said, arching an eyebrow.

"Only when I have to be." He opened the bag, then withdrew two sandwiches. "I was just trying to make you feel better."

"You didn't."

"Okay." He shrugged. "Then go ahead: Feel bad. But in the meantime, come on, let's eat. I don't know about you, but as I said, I'm starved." He cleared a spot at the far end of the table. "It's not exactly five-star, but it'll have to do. Tuna or BLT?"

"Tuna." Her stomach rumbled as she unwrapped the sandwich and tried to remember the last time she'd had a meal. Cheese, crackers and a bottle of wine last night? A splash of Baileys for breakfast? Not that she'd had any time to eat, but it was little wonder that a simple deli sandwich made her mouth water and tasted divine. Even the accompanying dill pickle almost made her sigh.

Rhapsody, of course, had wandered over to

the table, her nose aloft, her brown eyes soft and pleading. Kara shook her head, but she caught Tate tearing off a bit of bacon and offering it to the dog.

Rhapsody snapped the morsel into her mouth and swallowed.

"That's a definite no-no," she said, wiping her fingers. "Feeding from the table."

He grinned. "You know me, always breaking the rules."

She flashed back to him as a youth. Floppy hair and gawky build. Shy smile and teeth that seemed too big for his face; eyes, above a freckled nose, squinting against the summer sun; a boy who'd been a bit of a rebel, she'd heard, though he hadn't held a candle to Jonas.

Tate had definitely grown into himself in his thirties. Filled out. His blue eyes appeared more intense, his hair had darkened to almost black, and peach fuzz had turned to serious beard shadow. He was more good-looking than she'd ever expected. Not that it mattered at all.

"So," he said, "you know you have to talk to the cops."

She'd come to the same conclusion. "Yeah. But tomorrow. I can't face them or Aunt Faiza tonight."

"Your aunt, too?"

"Otherwise she'll worry. If she can't find me in the hospital." She sighed. "It's complicated with her." She thought of how Jonas had suggested that Auntie Fai was interested in her sister's kids only because of the money attached to them. She didn't want to think about all the difficult relationships she had with her family, so she changed the subject. "You live here alone?"

"Yeah." He leaned back in his chair. "Just me. Considered a dog once and a cat a couple of times, but I'm gone too much."

"Ever married?"

One side of his mouth lifted. "Thought about it once, but no." He shook his head, dark hair glinting under the lights high overhead. "Never seemed to be the right time or the right woman." Wadding the paper that had wrapped his sandwich, he asked, "You?"

"I figure you know all about me." She motioned to the computer and his scribbled notes, noticed that the room, with its soaring ceilings and wall of glass, had a warmth to it she hadn't noticed at first glance. Despite the loft's austere walls and mishmash of furniture, there was a lived-in comfort to it, an ambiance that she found strangely inviting.

Don't go there, Kara. Do not. It's trouble, pure and simple.

"I only know what court records show," Tate was saying as he opened a small bag of chips. "Most of the stuff I found on the Internet."

"Most of the stuff on the Internet is garbage.

Rumors. Opinions. Even the made-for-TV movie about that night wasn't all that factual, just a lot of hype and innuendo."

"You watched it?"

"Yeah." *Like once a year just to keep it real. To never forget.*

As if she could.

"So you googled me?" she asked.

"And then some, but I found no marriage licenses and hence no divorce decrees. No engagement announcements."

"That about sums it up," she said, not elaborating about her love life, though Brad's arrogant face sliced through her mind for just an instant.

Brad had left angrily, disbelieving that she would have the nerve to throw him out. "You're a freak, you know that, right?" he'd said when she'd insisted he leave. He'd been gathering his faded jeans, polo shirts and hoodies, along with his much-loved bong and trophies from being a standout soccer player in high school and college. "A fuckin' freak!"

"At least I don't cheat," she'd thrown back at him, along with a pair of soccer cleats, as he'd scrambled out the front door.

"Maybe you should," he'd screamed. "Maybe it would help." He'd climbed into his aging hatchback and roared out the drive, nearly backing over a kid on a bike.

Good riddance!

Now, Tate was staring at her.

She felt the need to explain as she plucked a chip from her own opened bag. "I'm different from you."

He frowned. "Really?"

"Yup. You thought about marriage and decided against it."

Interested, he leaned across the table. "That's right."

"I thought about a dog once," she said, and swallowed a smile, surprised at herself that she was actually teasing him. What was wrong with her?

"Yeah?"

"Unlike you, I committed. Went to a shelter, saw Rhapsody and, as they say, it was love at first sight."

"Ever experienced that before?" His turn to banter with her, the corners of his lips lifting almost imperceptibly in his beard shadow. God, was he flirting with her? Is that what was happening here?

If so, she had to close it down. Break this too-comfortable mood.

"Never," she said, almost icily. "So . . . are we working together, or what?"

"I thought this was already decided."

"Good."

"Then let's make it official. Seal the deal." He

walked to the kitchen, opened a cupboard over the refrigerator and retrieved a bottle of red wine, a Cabernet from a winery in Washington. She recognized the label.

Within seconds he'd opened the bottle and set it along with two stemmed glasses on the table. "I think it should breathe a bit."

"Or not."

"Okay." He poured them each a glass, then touched the rim of his to hers with a soft clink. The bouquet was heady and as she swirled the stem in her fingers, she watched eagerly as the legs of the wine appeared, red drips sliding down the inside of the glass.

Then, despite all of the warning bells clanging loudly in her head, it was done. Wondering if she'd just made a deal with the devil, Kara took a long swallow of wine and found that, at least for the moment, she didn't care.

She didn't care at all.

CHAPTER 23

"So now she's MIA," Johnson said as they waited on the front step of Kara McIntyre's home. Johnson was on tiptoe, trying to peer through a sidelight, but the seeded glass was nearly opaque.

Thomas had rung the bell, then pounded on the door, even called inside, but there was no response.

"She's not home," a female voice said, and he turned to spy Sheila Keegan walking across the snow-crusted lawn. "I've called her, tried to catch her at the hospital and waited around here, and figure she must be with a friend or something."

"Or something," Thomas said, and glanced up the street to where the white news van was parked under a streetlamp and idling, exhaust visible.

"Everyone else left, Cole," she explained, walking closer, her face beneath the hood of her station's winter jacket a little shadowed, but he could still make out the slope of her jaw and curve of full lips.

"Who else was here?" Johnson asked, and Thomas felt his partner sizing up the situation.

Sheila was, as always, way too familiar, and he suspected she did it on purpose with her coy smile and knowing lift of her eyebrows, silently reminding him that they'd once been intimate, that for months they'd shared a bed and ultimately she'd shared a source with him, that he "owed" her.

"Mostly freelancers, though someone from the local paper hung around for a while. I expect some of them will be back. And there will probably be more, once the highway's open again. Portland's a mess—it always is in a snowstorm—but the stations, they'll figure out a way to send crews. This is too big a story to let slide."

He couldn't argue.

"So, is it true that Kara McIntyre didn't even wait for a doctor's release to leave the hospital? Did she really just walk out, past all the guards even though Whimstick General had all kinds of security on-site?"

"You know I can't comment on that," he said, irritated that he'd run into her, even more irritated that his new partner was going to witness the conversation.

"Oh, come on, Cole. What about Jonas? My sources say he's already hired a new attorney and that he, too, is trying to get out of the hospital."

"You'll have to ask him."

Her lips pulled into a tight little knot. "Are you reopening the McIntyre Massacre case?"

"We're investigating Merritt Margrove's death." He figured that was safe. Common knowledge.

"I know. Any suspects?"

He smiled. "You know me, Sheila. Everyone's a suspect."

"Don't try to be cute," she threw back at him, and from the corner of his eye he saw Johnson give him a what-the-hell look. "I heard the nine-one-one call and don't ask me how, but Kara McIntyre called in the murder. Was that before or after she picked up her brother?"

"I can't comment on an ongoing case."

"Like hell," she said, challenging him. "And what about the accident? How did that happen?"

"We're still figuring that out."

"Why were both Kara McIntyre and Jonas McIntyre, barely out of prison, at Merritt Margrove's trailer on Mount Hood?"

"As I said, the investigation is ongoing." Which was the truth. But it was complicated. Jonas had been Merritt's client, his conversations with his attorney privileged.

"Is Merritt Margrove's death connected with Jonas McIntyre's release from Banhoff Prison?" she asked, and waved a gloved hand toward the van parked up the street. "Is he a suspect?"

"We're looking at all angles."

"Oh, come on, Cole." She was frustrated, bordering on angry. "What about Kara McIntyre? How is she involved? Why was she up there? Was it to meet her brother?"

Another quick, frantic wave and the door to the

news van opened, a big cameraman hopping to the ground. He was hoisting the shoulder cam in one arm, while in the other hand he was pressing a cell phone to his ear. He kicked the door shut and started heading their way.

"I can't comment on that."

"And you don't know where Kara McIntyre is?" she said.

"No."

"So she just walked out of the hospital? How? Isn't her car wrecked?"

"I don't know."

Sheila's eyes narrowed, thick lashes thinning. Over her shoulder, she said, "Carl, can we set up here?" And then to Johnson, who was just slipping her phone into the pocket of her jacket, "So she took Uber or Lyft or had a friend pick her up?"

"Don't know."

Thomas's phone rang and he answered. "Detective Cole Thomas." He paused, frowned, then glanced at Johnson. "Come on. We gotta go."

"What?" Sheila's eyes laser-focused on him. Her reporter instincts went into overdrive. "What's going on? Who called you?"

"Official business," he said, and they walked back to the car.

"Meaning what? Does this have something to do with Jonas McIntyre? Or Kara?" Sheila called after them, the cameraman trailing behind. "Well, of course it does or you wouldn't be here."

He kept walking, using his remote to unlock his vehicle. The Chevy responded with a flicker of its lights and a sharp beep.

"Co-le," Sheila said, making two syllables of his first name. She sounded frustrated. "Remember—"

"Yeah, yeah, I know. I owe you. So you've said. Got it."

"You don't want me to . . ."

She let the threat linger and he turned. "What I don't want is for you to threaten me. It won't work." He held her gaze for a brief moment, then added, "You should know that."

She opened her mouth, then closed it again and whispered something to the cameraman.

Thomas and Johnson climbed into his Tahoe.

As he started the SUV, Johnson pulled the passenger door closed and strapped in.

"Thanks." He drove up the slight rise in the street, the beams of his headlights catching the swirling flakes as snow continued to fall.

She lifted a shoulder in a half shrug. "She wasn't going to give up."

"So you called. To give me an out."

"Seemed like the easiest way to get out of a sticky situation." She shot him a glance as he slowed for a stop sign and a big truck spewing gravel onto the recently plowed cross street rumbled through the intersection. Johnson added, "Look. I don't know what went on between you two, and trust me, I don't want to. None of my business. But I gotta say, that woman, Sheila Keegan? She's a piece of work."

That and so much more, Thomas thought, as he nosed the SUV toward the station, that and so much more.

Tate wondered if he was making the biggest mistake of his life. He stared across the shadowy room to his bed, where Kara McIntyre was sleeping, her brown curls splayed upon his pillow, her dog curled next to her. Together they'd knocked off a bottle of wine and probably would have opened another if he'd had it. She'd even offered to go down to the market and buy another, but cooler heads had prevailed—his head—and they stopped at one. He hated to admit it, even to himself as he watched her breathing slowly, her eyelashes brushing her cheek, but he'd considered cracking open a bottle of Crown Royal that he'd gotten from his sister for his birthday, but, seeing that Kara was exhausted and still healing, he'd resisted.

Who knew what would have happened? Would she have opened up even more, told him secrets she'd locked away for twenty years, let him in? And he, would he have given in to temptation and kissed her? He'd thought about it. And there had been a couple of times when he'd caught her looking at him in a way he'd found incredibly sexy, but he'd been sober enough not to make that mistake.

At least not yet.

So he'd convinced her to sleep in his bed while he settled down in his favorite chair, but sleep, for him, had been elusive, and he'd given up all pretense of slumber around four thirty, long before dawn. In the ensuing hours, he'd downloaded the jump drives he'd taken from Merritt Margrove's office.

He'd hoped to find something new and game-changing in the information, but so far, hadn't. He'd made notes, though, and wanted to interview everyone associated with the McIntyre Massacre.

Whoever had killed Margrove had killed him for a reason.

Because he'd finally gotten Jonas McIntyre released from prison?

He leaned back in his chair and glanced at the woman sleeping in his bed. What did he know about her other than what he'd read? Already she was changing his opinion of her. After the massacre, Kara had been placed in her aunt's care even though Faiza and her younger sister, Zelda, had never been particularly close. Nor did she have children of her own, but Faiza had been determined to claim custody of her young niece, and Tate wondered if all of her sudden concern as an aunt had more to do with the fortune attached to her young charge than the girl herself. And though Kara spent most of her time with Merritt and his wife, that marriage had never been rock-steady and Faiza had put an end to any furthering of the relationship at least until Kara came of age. Throughout it all, Faiza and her live-in boyfriend Roger Sweeney had taken residence in the McIntyre home on two acres in the West Hills of Portland and as far as Tate could tell, Faiza had control of Kara's inheritance.

But that was about to change. Kara was about to come of age to inherit, according to the copy of her parents' will that Tate had found in Margrove's files. Well, make that Kara and Jonas, as they were the only surviving children of Samuel McIntyre.

He rubbed his chin and thought. Was it possible that the homicide of Merritt Margrove didn't have so much to do with Jonas McIntyre's release from prison as it did with Kara McIntyre coming of age to claim her inheritance?

Was this why Margrove was killed?

Or was he grasping at all-too-thin straws?

Kara stirred, turning over and cracking open an eye. "What time is it?" she asked around a yawn.

"Five."

"Oooh. Too early." And she rolled over, the dog shifting and protesting with a quiet growl before settling down again just as Tate's cell phone vibrated on the desk and Connell's name appeared on the screen. With a glance at Kara burrowed beneath the coverlet, he snagged the phone and hurried downstairs and through the door to the vestibule, where he hoped he wouldn't disturb her.

"Hey," he answered. "What's up?"

"I wanted to give you a heads-up. I did a series of background checks on people associated with the McIntyre Massacre. A deeper dive."

"And?"

"A couple of interesting things."

"Such as?"

"There are several people with records. First off, the older girl Marlie's boyfriend at the time—Chad Atwater? He'd got caught stealing from his grandfather, if you can believe that, but of course the charges were dropped, the family refused. Painkillers, the grandpa's gun and some cash. Then, about the same time, an assault charge was filed by another kid at school. Both were juveniles at the time, records sealed, but most of the reports suggest Chad was the aggressor in a fight over a girl that escalated. Supposedly the two were friends and the fight was over a girl who just happened to be Marlie Robinson."

Tate thought about it. He'd known the kid had some trouble as a teen, but what teenage boy came out of high school unscathed?

"There were drugs involved, steroids mainly and alcohol, of course. The fight was all hushed up by the parents, nothing more than a 'scuffle,' I think is the way Chad's father described it, but Chad smashed the other kid's face to a pulp on the steering wheel of his Mustang and the kid had to have stitches and plastic surgery. Once again, Chad skated, his parents bailed him out and from that point on he kept his nose clean."

He leaned against the back wall of the vestibule and stared through the glass doors to the dark morning beyond. He'd never really considered Atwater as a serious suspect. "Why would he slaughter an entire family?"

"Don't know. Can't speculate. Just giving you the facts. But there's one more wrinkle with Atwater. He had a girl on the side."

"So he was furious that someone came on to Marlie, but meanwhile he was seeing someone else."

"They were teenagers, what can I say?" Connell said. "Her name's Brittlynn Cadella. She was all of fourteen at the time. They ended up marrying the minute she turned eighteen. So now she's Brittlynn Atwater."

Tate hadn't known this. "Did Marlie Robinson know that he was seeing someone else?"

"Doesn't seem that way."

"Huh."

"There's more," Connell said. "Another

shady character. Roger Sweeney. The aunt's boyfriend?"

"What about him?"

"He's got a record, too. First of all, he had a dishonorable discharge from the Marines. Pulled a knife in a bar fight, cut someone pretty bad. The victim survived, but barely. And then five years later, more trouble. In Nashville. Didn't get along with members of his band. Accused one of them of stealing and they got into it. The fight got physical and Roger pulls a knife, cuts the guy, might have done more damage but the third member of the trio puts a stop to it. He had a pistol."

"So, in an about-turn, that guy brought a gun to a knife fight."

Connell snorted. "The upshot was that no charges were filed. They both get stitched up, but Roger is out of the group. That's about the time he migrated to Portland and took up with Faiza Donner."

"But again, why would he kill the family?"

"Robbery gone bad? The family didn't like him? Faiza wanted her share? Again, I'm just spitballing here and I have no facts to bear any of this out. This was just a first deep dive. I'm still checking out Silas Dean, Samuel's business partner, as well as the exes: Walter Robinson, Leona McIntyre and Natalie Brizard."

Tate thought about it but really couldn't see a

woman hoisting that old sword and killing the entire family and he said as much.

"Just covering all the bases," Connell explained. "And women can have long memories, vendettas and accomplices." True enough, Tate thought as he heard footsteps overhead. "Take Leona McIntyre, Samuel McIntyre's college sweetheart and wife number one. She blamed her husband for their baby's death and then lost custody of her only son, Sam Junior, because Sam Senior claimed she was nuts. It was all probably depression, but Leona has always claimed her husband and his second wife, Natalie, ruined her life. She never got over it."

"It would be hard."

"I suppose. Anyway, she never remarried and became a bit of a loner. Then years later, when Sam left Natalie, his second wife, for Zelda, Leona was supposedly ecstatic."

"How do you know that?"

"An old friend of hers who knew both Leona and Samuel back at the university. I found her on Facebook, tracked her down on the Internet and she was more than willing to talk. Anyway, Leona, upon hearing that Samuel was dumping Natalie, said, 'What goes around comes around, even for bitches who break up a family.'"

"No way would Leona kill her own son, Sam Junior," Tate countered, because he'd gone down this mental path before. "And Donner died that night. That's the primary reason Walter Robinson wasn't considered. He was a great dad, loved his kids. Sent himself to school on the GI Bill or something. Became an electrician. But he had been at the house that day and got into an argument about custody."

"Have you ever thought that there may have been more than one killer?"

"As in a team?" Tate asked.

"Yeah. Or possibly someone who didn't intend to kill everyone, but because he was seen and could be identified, murdered the witnesses?"

Again, this wasn't a new trail, but there was a roadblock. "Sam Senior and his wife were in their bed. Asleep. Both had traces of sleeping aids in their blood. Dead to the world."

"So to speak."

"Not funny," Tate said.

Connell said, "Maybe they were the ultimate targets, but the killer didn't expect everyone to still be up. Could be that all of the killings weren't part of the initial plan, but it went awry."

"They were killed with the same sword. Every last one of them. Blood from all the victims was found on the blade. Two killers—one weapon?"

"Again, I'm just throwing out ideas. I've still got some things I want to dig into. Alibis and motives, I figure the whole money angle should be more deeply explored. Samuel McIntyre was a rich man when he died. People lose their perspective and their moral compasses get all skewed when money's involved."

"But kill the whole damn family?" Watching an older-model Ford Escape slow near the front door of the building, he saw a newspaper being tossed through the driver's open window. The paper landed on the snow-covered sidewalk outside the front door just as the Escape, engine revving, tires spinning, drove off.

"How else would someone end up with the pot o' gold and not have to share?"

"I'm pretty sure the police have looked into that angle. I know I have."

"Wait a minute, you just said yourself you found it hard to believe someone would kill the entire clan for money. I beg to differ. But we'll see. In the meantime I'll send the info I got to you, encrypted, and you can go through it yourself." Which Tate would and compare it with the data he'd collected over the years, as well as what he'd taken from the jump drives he'd lifted from Margrove's office.

"So I'll keep looking," Connell said, and was about to disconnect, but Tate asked, "What about Marlie?"

Connell let out an audible sigh. "So far a dead end. But I'm still searching."

"Good."

"And I've been searching for Hailey Brown in Modesto," he admitted.

377

"And?"

"None of them that I've located in the area match up with the online profile for the woman who's a follower in Jonas McIntyre's Facebook fan page."

Tate already knew this as he'd been checking himself as Jessica Smith, his own alias. The groups were hyped up over Jonas McIntyre's release and hospitalization and were already screaming that he couldn't have killed the attorney who had finally secured his release, that no doubt the police would try to pin the murder on him.

Hundreds of fans had commented or "liked" the posts, but many had been silent, and in that group was Hailey Brown of Modesto.

Tate heard a thump overhead, probably the sound of Kara's dog jumping from the bed to land on the floor. "Gotta go." Tate ended the connection and grabbed the newspaper from the front walk.

By the time he climbed the stairs to his loft, Kara was awake, her hair a brown tangle, her expression far from friendly as she stood over the coffeemaker in a knee-length sleep shirt, the dog dancing at her feet.

"Just so you know, this is waaay too early for me," she said. "Even when I teach, I'm not up before six. Never." She waited as the coffee drizzled into her cup. "I'm a substitute teacher."

"I know."

"Of course you do. You know everything about me."

"Not everything."

"But you will. Or that's what you hope for." She slid Tate a glance as she picked up her cup and blew across the rim.

Tate watched her lips pucker as she chased the steam away, then gingerly took a sip. She eyed him over the rim. "Since you're dressed, would you mind taking Rhapsody outside?"

"Glad to," he said.

"And then, once I get myself together, maybe you could give me a ride to the police station."

He raised an eyebrow.

"Don't even say it. I've had time to think, okay? Like it or not, and yes, I think 'not,' I have to talk to them, explain what happened. Also, I really want my phone and ID, so I can, you know, communicate with people and get around. I can't just hang out here and rely on you, for God's sake."

"No?" He felt one side of his lips twist upward.

She sent him a withering glance. "No." But she, too, smiled, and for just a split second it was difficult to remember that he couldn't trust her.

CHAPTER 24

In the darkness Chad edged to the side of the bed and slid open the drawer of his nightstand. He didn't want to wake Brittlynn, didn't want the fight. Glancing over his shoulder, he saw that his wife had her back to him, was breathing rhythmically, lost in deep slumber as the old furnace rumbled low and steady, the background noise he counted on.

Good.

The bedside clock glowed a soft blue. 3:57. Early. But Britt wouldn't wake for another three hours and by that time he'd be long gone, already in Washington State, and possibly Idaho. Ultimately out of the country.

If everything went as planned.

It had to.

His fingers brushed against the leather sheath of his bowie knife and then the smooth grip of his handgun, a sweet little Ruger 9mm, a pocket pistol with incredible accuracy. He retrieved both weapons, glanced again at his slumbering wife. Then he hurried on bare feet to the bathroom, where he'd left his clothes hanging on a hook near the door—just as he always did. He dressed quickly in ski pants, sweater and down vest pulled over his thermal underwear, patted its pockets to make certain he had keys and three extra clips for his pistol. He left his cell phone. On purpose. Didn't trust Britt not to put a tracker on it somehow and he needed to disappear. Really disappear.

He slipped noiselessly into the second bedroom.

From the closet he pulled out his duffel bag, already packed, then moved the never-used skis and, by feel, located the loose floorboard in the closet. It slid out easily, allowing in a rush of cold air and the smell of the earth. He reached inside, twisting his hand to find the plastic packet he'd duct-taped to the underside of the closet floor. Carefully, nerves strung tight, he retrieved the bag, then carefully replaced the floorboard and skis. So that Britt wouldn't find his hiding spot. Just in case.

Still kneeling, he shined the light on the thick plastic and saw the roll of cash, a burner phone, and several small bags of weed, which would be like cash in states where marijuana was still illegal.

A small stake.

But it would have to do.

He stuffed the bag into a pocket of his vest.

And felt something brush the back of his leg.

He froze.

What?

There it was again—

His heart stilled.

Every muscle in his body reacted before he realized his mistake.

The cat! Shit! Britt's damned cat Jasper had sauntered stealthily into the room unnoticed and was crawling over the backs of his calves. Relieved but irritated, Chad pushed the tabby roughly away, toward the door, and climbed to his feet just as the light snapped on, casting the small, pine-paneled room in harsh illumination.

Brittlynn was standing in the doorway.

"What the hell are you doing?" she asked. "God, you're dressed and sneaking around and . . ." Her gaze landed on Chad's duffel bag gaping open on her grandmother's old brass bed with its hand-stitched quilt.

"What does it look like?"

"Like you're leaving," she accused. Her red hair was a mess, her gaze still bleary from sleep, her oversize T-shirt she always slept in, an old souvenir from a U2 concert, wrinkled.

Chad had hoped he could sneak out without waking her and therefore not being asked dozens of questions. She usually slept like the dead. Not tonight. "Why are you awake?"

"I had to pee. And what does that matter?" Her little pointed chin jutted and traces of yesterday's mascara shadowed the skin around her eyes. "What's going on, Chad?"

He zipped the bag. "What's it look like?"

"Like you're leaving." An accusation. "Again." A beat, and then, "Without me."

"Just for a few days."

"How many is 'a few'?"

"I don't know yet." He tried on a confident smile, but couldn't make it stick.

"You weren't going to tell me." Fire was starting to blaze in her eyes. "You were going to sneak out in the middle of the night and just leave. Shit, Chad, I can't believe this!"

"Of course I was going to tell you," he lied, trying to defuse the suddenly volatile situation. "I just didn't want to wake you up."

"So what were you gonna do? Just leave a damned note on the kitchen table?"

He was starting to get mad. He didn't have time for this bullshit. "I-I don't know, Britt. I just have to get out."

"What about work?"

"I have it covered. Lance needed an extra shift. Could use the money."

"*We* could use the money. What the fuck are you thinking?"

"Just go back to bed, okay? I've got this all handled."

"What? You've got what handled?" she demanded as he slipped the strap of the duffel over his shoulder and forced his way past her. "What the hell's going on, Chad?" she demanded, storming after him to the kitchen.

He stopped at the back door to step into his boots.

"Don't. Don't leave."

"I have to."

"But why?" And then the light dawned and she rolled her eyes. "This is about Jonas McIntyre." She flipped on the lights, illuminating the orange Formica that was stained and chipped near the stove.

"He's out."

"He's in the hospital. I don't think he's much of a threat."

"Gotta go." He laced both boots and straightened just as the cat hopped onto the kitchen counter and Brittlynn scooped the silver tabby into her arms. "Do you honestly think Jonas McIntyre is going to hunt you down? I thought we talked about this already."

"I'm not worried about him."

She wasn't convinced. "I thought you said if he ever got out, he would come gunning for you."

"That's not the problem." He pulled his grandfather's old Winchester from a hook near the back door. "It's the cops. They'll be lookin' for someone to blame."

"For what? You were already cleared for the murders on the mountain all those years ago." A tiny smile lifted one corner of her mouth, and her green eyes glinted with a bit of evil he'd found fascinating from the first time he'd set eyes on her. "I'll still back you up." She petted the cat slowly, almost sensually.

"And what about Margrove, the lawyer?"

"You weren't involved in that." Her gaze fastened hard on his. Her hand stopped stroking Jasper. "Right?"

"Oh, great, now you're doubting me, too? Give me a fuckin' break. I'm just sayin' that his trailer is, like, two miles from here as the crow flies. They're going to come snooping. They've already called work, y'know? Someone called Ted at the lodge checkin' on me."

"So what?" She lifted her shoulders and the big T-shirt slid off of one of her shoulders in a provocative way he found absolutely irresistible. And she knew it, the way she sauntered closer to him, her gaze smoldering as her eyes held his. "I'll say that you were with me all night."

It was tempting. She was tempting. And she knew it. That was the thing with her, she was mercurial, hot one minute, ice cold the next, sweet and warm and oh-so-sexy, until she stabbed you in the back. That's what kept him interested, he'd decided long ago. She always surprised. And intrigued. Even as a girl barely in her teens, Brittlynn had a dangerous side he'd found fascinating.

Tonight he wasn't into any of it. And her plan of lying for him might not work. It could blow up. So far, she'd had his back, for twenty damned years. But she'd been desperate and fourteen, still a girl really, and now she was a woman in her thirties with her own mind, her own agenda.

But he didn't want to piss her off. He said, "Look, I've got to do this."

"Do what? Run?" she accused, pouting now, her lips pulling into a tight little bow.

"Whatever you want to call it."

"So what if the police come here?" she asked as he reached for the door. "What should I say?"

"Tell them the truth: You don't know where I went and when I'll be back."

"What if they want to know about the night that all those people were killed?"

"I don't think you want to do that," he said. "You were a kid then, you're not now and you might be considered an accessory."

"But you swore you didn't kill anyone," she said, her eyes rounding as she thought she might be an accessory to murder. He saw it in her expression, her doubts.

"I'll be back," he promised, and paused long enough to brush a kiss across her temple. And then he left, the lie still hanging in the air between them as the door slammed shut behind him.

The night had been short. Too short.

Thomas pedaled his stationary bike as if his life depended on it, faster and faster and faster in his makeshift gym in his garage. Breathing hard and sweating like the proverbial pig, he kept at it as his muscles began to ache in protest. A towel was draped around his neck and he stared at a flat-screen he'd mounted over his workbench. But he wasn't watching the news as the anchors and reporters went on and on about the coming storm and traffic conditions. It was all just background noise over the steady hum of the bike and the pounding of his heart. Instead, his thoughts were turning as fast as the wheels of the bike. He pushed himself, his legs pumping even harder, the bike's wheels spinning madly while he was going nowhere. Much like the damned case, he thought.

He'd stayed up past midnight with the old files, making notes trying to tie the murder of Merritt Margrove to the massacre twenty years earlier. He'd always believed that Jonas McIntyre was guilty, that he'd slaughtered his family in a wild rage and deserved to rot in prison. Now, though, Thomas had doubts, at least some doubts.

And the case was getting to him. He usually slept like a log, but when a case was eating at him as this one did, his subconscious always interrupted his sleep and played nasty games with him. Last night, Thomas had spent five fitful hours tossing and turning, his dreams vivid. Images of dead bodies, all brutally slaughtered and dripping in blood, had interrupted any slumber he'd hoped to find. He'd finally given up trying to get any shut-eye, thrown on his sweats and worked out his demons in his home gym, which was really the second bay, the space that Daphne's car had once occupied.

On his forty-minute ride, he'd learned the Portland Trail Blazers had lost their third game in a row, plans for construction of a new I-5 bridge over the Columbia between Portland to the south and Vancouver, Washington, to the north were once again stalled, and another winter storm with "blizzard-like" conditions was on its way, bringing with it what looked like a white Christmas for most of the state.

As a commercial for a local car dealership came onto the screen, Thomas hit his goal of forty minutes and climbed off the bike. He swiped at his face and dropped to mats he'd placed over the floor, positioned near the furnace.

He'd left it as it was for a while, until he'd learned that she was moving to Austin, Texas, to be with a guy she'd met online. Then he'd decided he couldn't stand the void of that bay with its oil stains from her vehicle still visible. The emptiness had been a constant reminder of what he'd lost.

Stopping himself at that thought, Thomas finished his routine, fifty curls, a hundred push-ups and then a plank that he held until his entire body trembled. Afterward he wiped the sweat from his face.

He hadn't lost Daphne, he reminded himself. The simple truth was that he'd practically pushed her out the door. She'd accused him of having a mistress in the form of his job, told him she couldn't compete with his obsession with his work and was tired of trying. There had been tears in her eyes and his as she'd hit the accelerator and backed her Honda out of the garage on an August morning three years ago.

She'd never looked back.

He still remembered the shimmering heat rising from the driveway, the leaves of the saplings she'd planted two years earlier already dried and falling, the lawn brown. He'd stood on the front porch and heard the garage door rolling down and landing with a final clunk just as she'd thrown the garage remote out the open window of her Honda. It landed with the sound of plastic scraping against asphalt, then skated across the street as she'd driven around the corner and out of his life.

Angry with himself, with her and the whole damned world, he'd retrieved the shattered remote.

Then he'd waited.

He'd called.

She hadn't picked up.

Texts and emails had gone unanswered.

He'd heard from a mutual friend that she'd met a guy online and moved to Austin, Texas. When the holidays came and went, he finally faced the fact that she wasn't coming back and he'd bought himself the stationary bike, assembled it where it now stood and had used it almost every day since.

He'd added the floor mats and speed bag, even a heavy punching bag that hung in the corner over him, creating a veritable one-man gym that he figured was better than cigarettes, black coffee, rye whiskey, and soulless one-night stands, though, for a time, he'd indulged in all. Hence the fling with Sheila Keegan. He couldn't help but smile when he thought of her. Smart, sexy, fun, Sheila had helped pull him out of angry self-isolation and get over Daphne. Their affair had run hot and heavy for over six months.

Probably a mistake. But there it was.

His latest acquisition had been the TV, where now the screen was filled with pictures of Whimstick General Hospital. A handful of Jonas's fans were still gathered, diehards out on a cold winter morning before dawn. They were shouting and holding signs, and Sheila Keegan in her red jacket and ready smile stood front and center as she interviewed Mia Long, who stood in her faded jean jacket, her pale eyes rimmed with thick mascara, her chin jutted with the same defiance she'd displayed when he'd met her.

"So what do you hope to accomplish?" Sheila asked.

"Justice," Mia said, her face set as she stared into the camera. "For twenty years Jonas McIntyre was in prison for crimes he didn't commit, crimes in which he was a victim."

"But he's out now."

"And he'll never get those years back, will he?" Her eyes flashed. "He gave up half of his life while the real killer has lived a free man or woman and we won't rest until Jonas McIntyre is absolved of the crimes he was charged with." She was shouting now and a handful of people standing nearby hooted and raised their signs and began chanting, a weak performance compared to the crowd the day before.

Sheila asked, "Does justice have a price tag? I've heard that Jonas McIntyre is going to sue the county for thirty million dollars."

Mia's mouth twisted into a cynical smile. "Freedom is priceless."

"You heard it here, at Whimstick General Hospital, where Jonas McIntyre is recovering from injuries sustained in an automobile accident when he reportedly visited Merritt Margrove at his mountain retreat, just hours after Margrove's death, which authorities are calling a homicide. Margrove, who once claimed a list of celebrities as his clients, drew national attention when he defended Jonas McIntyre twenty years ago in the McIntyre Massacre where most of the family was slaughtered. Mystery still surrounds that tragic event as one of the children, a teenager named Marlie Robinson, disappeared that night, neither she nor her remains ever found." Sheila gave a quick report on the old murders and trial while pictures of the McIntyre family and the crime scene flashed onto the screen. When the camera returned to her, still outside the hospital: "The investigation into Merritt Margrove's homicide is ongoing and if you have any information about the crime, please call the local authorities." The number and email address for the department flashed onto the screen as Sheila smiled and said, "Now back to you, Ned."

Thomas snapped off the television and walked up the two steps to the laundry room that connected his bungalow to the garage.

After stripping down, he tossed his sweats into an overflowing basket, walked through the house naked and once in the single bathroom showered, shaved and dressed for work.

The city was still quiet, traffic thin, a snowplow scraping the streets free of ice and packed snow, Christmas lights reflecting on the piles created.

He was at his desk an hour before the change of shift and Thomas made the most of that quiet time where he was alone with his thoughts before the clamor and din of the day intruded. For nearly an hour telephones, fax machines and printers were almost silent, and the sound of footfalls, boots scraping and bits of passing conversation punctuated by laughter hadn't yet interrupted his thoughts.

He'd already asked for one of the tech guys to create an enhanced computerized likeness of Marlie Robinson, aged twenty years from the headshot on her driver's license. The photoshopped picture had come through, and he found himself staring at the image of a beautiful woman with an oval face framed by curly blond hair, her blue eyes large and round over a long, straight nose, a woman who, aside from a slight dimple in her chin, looked a lot like her mother, Zelda McIntyre.

"What happened to you?" he said to the image on the screen even though he believed that the enhancement was most likely an exercise in futility. He believed that Marlie Robinson had died that night, or soon thereafter. Drops of her blood had been found at the scene and matched by DNA to strands of hair recovered from her hair brush. There hadn't been enough of her blood to think she'd been seriously injured, unless she'd stanched the flow and escaped somehow.

How likely was that?

Absently he picked up a pencil and tapped the eraser end on his desk as he considered the alternatives.

Had Marlie gotten away, escaped after locking Kara in the attic? Had she been chased by the killer, slightly wounded in the house, then slaughtered somewhere else? If so, then Jonas McIntyre, himself injured, probably hadn't killed his stepsister.

Thomas twisted the pencil in his fingers. Was that possible? For two decades he'd believed that McIntyre was the killer. Had he and the rest of the force been so wrong?

If Marlie Robinson was dead, where the hell was her body? Had the search teams and dogs missed her trail and her remains decomposed in the forest, her bones and flesh carried off by wild animals? Or had she somehow survived?

He kept coming back to the same question that had nagged at him whenever he'd thought of the tragedy: Why had Marlie Robinson hidden her little sister away? Why didn't she stay in the attic with Kara and save herself? How had Marlie been involved? Had Jonas McIntyre—or another killer—spared her? Why?

Had Jonas McIntyre been telling the truth all these years? Was he really innocent?

Thomas found it hard to believe and scanned Jonas's statement again. His story had never changed, never once faltered: Yes, he'd been "messing around" with the sword earlier, and he had been in a fight with Donner earlier in the week, all over Lacey Higgins, but that night he had not killed his brothers or his parents. He'd been in the living room when an intruder had slipped into the house and attacked him first from behind. Injured, Jonas had lost consciousness. When he woke up, Kara was in the room; he told her to run, to get help, and then he passed out again. He could not ID the killer. Had not seen the murderer's face. Jonas assumed the intruder had been wearing gloves, hence no fingerprints other than Jonas's appeared on the sword. Jonas swore that he had no idea why anyone would slaughter most of his family, and he did not know what happened to Marlie Robinson, his stepsister. He figured Kara lived through the rampage because she was hidden away and he survived only because the killer thought he was dead already.

Thomas leaned back in his chair until it creaked in protest.

It just didn't add up.

And now, after Jonas was finally released due to new testimony, his attorney was killed and the guy who changed his story about the evidence trail of the sword that night, Randall Isley, was barely holding on to life in a hospital fifteen hundred miles away in Nebraska.

How effing convenient.

He dropped the pencil back into its cup, walked to the lunch room, where the dregs of day-old coffee sat in the glass pot, and opted for a can of Diet Coke from the machine in the hallway. Thomas was missing something, something important. Lost in thought, he barely noticed that the day shift was arriving, more voices, more commotion. Sipping from the can, he sidestepped a couple of uniforms heading to the lockers, then settled down at his desk again.

What was it?

How was it connected to Merritt Margrove's death?

Jonas McIntyre had been the obvious suspect. Not only was he convicted for the multiple homicides twenty years ago, but on the first day he was let out of prison, he visited Margrove and the attorney who hadn't been able to convince the jury of Jonas McIntyre's innocence all those years ago ended up with his throat slit.

Just like Donner Robinson.

Revenge? Had Jonas spent half his life seething and blaming the attorney for not being able to keep him out of prison?

Or a setup?

Thomas took another long pull from the Diet Coke.

Was it possible they'd sent the wrong man up the river?

He pulled up photos from the scene of the homicides, noting the positions of the bodies and the wounds inflicted, all from the same antique sword. Zelda's and Sam Senior's throats had been slit, ear to ear, as had Donner Robinson's. Sam Junior had suffered stab wounds to his torso and legs, bleeding out from the femoral artery of his right leg. Jonas's wounds had been primarily superficial, though his left calf had been slashed to his shin bone and he'd hit his head, developed a concussion as he'd fallen. And then there was Marlie. Somehow she'd left a few drops of blood near the fireplace and on the Christmas tree.

But she hadn't died.

Not there.

Not then.

Thomas searched the Internet, watched some of the news reports. He saw officers from the department, most retired, a younger Randall Isley and Archer Gleason, both deputies, both being caught on camera from a distance. Gleason, as tall as he was, stood out, but his hair had been thick then, his physique honed. In one shot he and Isley were talking, both their faces grim as they stood near a rescue vehicle parked near the gates of the McIntyres' mountain home.

The next clip he watched was of Walter Robinson making a plea for the safe return of his daughter. He appeared to be about six feet tall, with square shoulders and a firm jaw, his lips compressed as he begged for the return of his daughter. "Please," he said, staring straight into the camera's lens. "If you know anything about Marlie's whereabouts, call the police." He swallowed visibly just before a picture of the missing girl appeared on the screen. In the shot, Marlie was posed, a school picture, it looked like. Blond hair falling to her shoulders, her eyes twinkling, her—

He stopped short and froze the shot.

He'd seen her.

Goddamn it, he'd seen her.

He brought up the enhanced digitized picture of her and again he was struck with the thought that he'd seen this woman, in the flesh, and recently.

For the love of God, could she really still be alive?

CHAPTER 25

"Where the hell have you been? I've been frantic! Out of my mind with worry, Kara. Out. Of. My. Mind! And you left the hospital against the doctor's orders? What in God's name were you thinking?" Faiza's voice was tight over the wireless connection. "Is this your new phone number?"

"No," Kara said quickly. She was using Tate's phone. She'd called her aunt on it, but, of course, Faiza hadn't picked up. Then Kara had left a voice mail and texted and within minutes her aunt had phoned. "I'm with a friend. It's his phone."

Seated on the edge of Tate's bed, she held the phone in one hand while petting Rhapsody with the other. Her shoulder and neck felt tighter today and the stitches in her forehead pulled a bit, but she'd managed to get dressed and before she went to the sheriff's department to talk to the detectives, she'd decided to bite the bullet and call Faiza.

"*His* phone?" Faiza repeated. "What friend?"

She didn't want to go there. "It doesn't matter. I've got Rhapsody with me and I'm going in to talk to the police and get my phone back."

"And then?"

It was so complicated. "I have to talk to the insurance company, get a rental car."

"And what about your brother?" she said in disgust. "I heard Jonas hired an attorney, well, a new attorney, and he's going to file a lawsuit or something."

"A new attorney?"

"Well, his other one is dead," Faiza pointed out. "And if you ask me, he's involved!"

"You don't know that."

"He was there, wasn't he? He's dangerous, Kara. Always has been."

"But a new attorney? Already? Isn't he still in the hospital? How could he hire a new lawyer?"

"I'm not sure, but I think he has this online fan club and they had something to do with it. I saw some chatter—isn't that what you call it?"

"Wait, *you're* in the Facebook fan club?" This seemed out of character.

"To keep up with what's going on!"

What was the old line from *The Godfather*? "Keep your friends close and your enemies closer." Auntie Fai seemed to be adopting the philosophy.

She was ranting on. "If you ask me, Jonas should never have been let out of prison. That's the problem, you know. If there wasn't all this hype about him being released, if he was still locked up, none of this would have happened. Merritt would still be alive and you, you wouldn't have been in that awful car crash, and that poor other driver wouldn't be in the hospital!" She let out a shuddering sigh. "Your mother never liked him, you know."

"Jonas?" Kara did know. She'd heard her parents arguing, even that night after Silas Dean had been over to confront Daddy and put him in, as Mama had said, "one of his moods." Walter Robinson's arrival where he threatened custody only made things worse. They'd argued in their bedroom, but Kara had overheard them yelling about Jonas and Donner, Mama saying Jonas was on the edge of becoming a criminal, that he was always sneaking out, thinking no one knew and doing only God knew what—either having sex with anything that moved or doing drugs or joining a gang or something. Mama told Daddy that Jonas should go to some military school to "straighten out" before he got into some real, serious trouble, while Daddy insisted that Donner always provoked Jonas, that Donner, not Jonas, was the problem. Then Daddy had spied Kara lurking in the hallway and had closed the door and by the time they'd had dinner, her parents weren't arguing anymore. They were still angry with each other, Mama being polite but frosty, her words clipped, and Daddy being quieter and quieter as he'd had too much to drink. Again.

"Zelda told me that he was—how did she put it? 'Not right. Out of control.' That's what she said, and I think she even called him a 'maniac,' after he attacked Donner. He was her pride and joy, you know. The apple of her eye. Walter, he wanted to take the boy from her when they split up, but Zelda, bless her heart, wouldn't let him. Nuh-uh."

"Walter fought Mama in court?" Kara asked.

"Oh, yeah."

"For Donner?"

"Mm-hmm."

"What about Marlie?"

"Oh, he wanted her, too, you bet he did, but Zelda wasn't having any of it and with Samuel's money, Walter didn't have a chance at custody for those kids. He knew Marlie would insist on staying with Zelda, but he thought he could persuade Donner to go with him. Of course that wasn't going to happen." She let out a snort. "Don't get me wrong, Walter's a good man. Served his country, works hard and does well enough for himself as an electrician, even got into electronics, but compared to your father? It's no contest."

She let out a sigh. "They were good kids, you know. Not like Sam's boys. Oh, the older one, the namesake, he was okay, I guess, but Jonas? Mean. From the get-go."

Faiza had always blamed Jonas for the murders, but she didn't dwell on it now. Instead, she abruptly changed the subject. "So are you coming home?"

Home to Faiza was the house in the West Hills, the mansion where Kara had spent the first eight years of her life, where Faiza and Roger had resided since the killings, the place from which Kara had retreated, preferring to stay with Merritt Margrove and his second wife, Helen. Kara had avoided the huge, rambling estate with its Tudor-like house and magnificent view of the city.

"No, Faiza. I live here," Kara asserted. "In Whimstick. And I'll go back to my own house soon."

"Oh, Kara, this is your home," her aunt argued. "You belong here."

Never. Kara was never going back.

"And soon . . . well, after your birthday, you'll actually own it."

"With Jonas," she said succinctly, and Faiza drew in a quick breath.

"Not if he's incarcerated again. There's a distinct clause in the will that forbids any of Samuel's children from inheriting if they're using drugs or imprisoned."

Kara wasn't surprised that her aunt knew about the estate inside and out and though she hadn't understood it as a child, she'd later realized Faiza, with the help of Roger Sweeney, was skimming off Kara's inheritance, as had, according to Jonas, Merritt Margrove. All of it was a bitter pill to swallow.

"I want to see you," Faiza said suddenly, her voice audibly brightening. "How about I throw you a birthday party?"

"What? No! Are you serious?" The last thing Kara wanted was any more attention drawn to her. "No."

"You could use a little fun in your life, Kara. And really, so could I, not to mention Roger!"

"Forget it," Kara said. "Look, I have to go. I just wanted to let you know that I'm okay. My friend needs his phone back." And before Faiza could argue, Kara ended the connection and decided she needed a drink.

Thomas scanned the statements again, made a few notes to himself and by the time Johnson arrived with a crowd of coworkers, dawn had broken and Thomas had located Chad Atwater, who was a ski instructor on Mount Hood, and Silas Dean, who, now retired, was a snowbird, living the winter months in Scottsdale, Arizona, a suburb of Phoenix, and the summers in Bend, the largest town in central Oregon. He'd expected that Dean was down south but had called and found out that he was actually in the area, back in Oregon to spend the Christmas holidays with his son and grandchildren, who lived in Hood River. Silas had already been here for a week and though Bend was in central Oregon, it wasn't that far from Margrove's trailer, two hours or so depending on traffic and road conditions.

A possibility.

Thomas was ready to roll.

Johnson barely had time to sit down at her desk when he'd approached. "I'm heading back to the hospital," he said, "then I want to go over to Margrove's office. After that I want to talk to Silas Dean, Faiza Donner and Chad Atwater. So far, I haven't been able to scare up Kara McIntyre, but if we locate her, she goes to the top of the list."

"Whoa . . . hold on a sec. I haven't even had my coffee yet," Johnson said around a yawn. She wasn't a morning person, Thomas knew that, but he also knew she worked extra hours, often late into the night, around her son's schedule.

"We'll get it on the way."

"Fine. Give me ten minutes to check email and catch up."

"You got it."

They met in the parking lot, and with Thomas at the wheel and under the gunmetal-gray sky, eased through traffic to a drive-through coffee kiosk five blocks from Whimstick General. By the time he parked in the hospital lot, Johnson was halfway through her latte and in a much better mood.

Until they reached the third floor, where the security guard met them at the entrance to Jonas's room. "His lawyer is with him," the guard said.

"His lawyer is dead," Johnson said.

"Not Margrove. He's got a new one. Woman."

"Already?" Johnson said. "He works fast."

"As I said, she's in his room." The guard hitched a thumb in the direction of the open doorway. "A real ballbuster."

Johnson stiffened. "Is she?"

"Sorry . . . but . . . yeah, she is," the guard said. "She's not letting him talk to anyone."

Thomas didn't wait, just strode through the open doorway, where he found Jonas McIntyre, beard shadow dark over sallow skin, a few bruises visible on his face, lying on the hospital bed, the head of which was partially raised. An IV stand was still connected by a narrow clear tube to his wrist, a computer display at an angle as it monitored his vital signs.

Standing next to him, deep in conversation, was a slim fortysomething woman in a black power suit, pink blouse and matching heels. With sharp features, rimless glasses and short blond hair, she glanced up when Thomas approached and the smile she'd offered Jonas froze icily in place. "This is a private room."

Thomas already had his badge out and was starting to introduce himself. "I'm Detective Cole Thomas and this is Detective—"

"I don't care who you are, my client is a patient in this hospital and as such will grant no interviews. Not to the press, not to the police, not to anyone."

"And you are . . . ?" Johnson asked.

"Alex Rousseau." She fished into a pocket of

her jacket, snapped out a crisp business card and handed it to Thomas. "Not Alexis. Not Alexandra. Just Alex."

"You're from LA?" Johnson asked, eyeing the card in Thomas's hand.

"I've got an office in Portland."

"We need to ask your client some questions about his previous attorney's homicide."

"In good time," she said. "As you can see, Mr. McIntyre is still under doctor's care."

"It's okay," Jonas said, his voice a rasp.

"Oh, no." She was shaking her head. "I wouldn't advise talking to the police until—"

"I just want to get it over with," he said, his gaze holding Thomas's as he pressed a button and with a click and hum, the head of his bed elevated so that he was sitting more upright. "I'm going to give a statement. No questions." He glanced at his attorney, whose lips were pursed into a disapproving knot, but she did give a curt nod.

"I did not have anything to do with Merritt Margrove's death. I was supposed to meet him. It was prearranged. 10:00 a.m. Margrove picked the place and time as he wanted the meeting to be private. I was dropped off by Mia Long, a friend of mine, and I told her to leave. She did. I knocked. No answer. I went inside and Merritt was lying by the couch on the carpet. Already dead. His throat slit. I was about to leave when

I heard a car. It was my sister. While she went into the cabin, I went outside and hid in the back seat. She was driving off the mountain when I let her know I was inside her Jeep. A few minutes later she nearly hit a deer and then there was the accident. We both saw the truck and she hit the brakes. The next thing I knew I woke up here." He paused. "And that's all I'm saying."

"We do have some questions," Johnson said.

Alex Rousseau nodded. "I'm sure you do. And you can ask them later. My client is still recovering, still under doctor's care. His health is his primary concern, so until he's released, he won't be saying anything more. You're lucky to have his statement."

Thomas wanted to challenge her, to assert his authority, but he'd always believed in catching more flies with honey rather than vinegar, and the ensuing investigation would go much more smoothly if Jonas McIntyre cooperated rather than becoming a brick wall.

"Fine." Thomas found his own business card and gave it to the attorney.

"Wait a second," Johnson said, unwilling to step away. "We have authority here. What can you tell us about the massacre?"

"Wait. What?" The cords in Alex Rousseau's neck became visible, her words clipped as she said succinctly, "My client is *not* going to address this matter. He's been absolved."

"He wasn't absolved," Johnson argued, her eyes flashing. "But since he can't be tried again for those homicides, why doesn't he come clean and tell us what really happened that night?"

"Don't answer that." Rousseau shot Jonas a warning look. Then she turned her attention to Johnson. "Get out. Now. Both of you. Thank you for your time and your interest, but Mr. McIntyre needs his rest."

Thomas said, "My partner's right. We do have the authority here, but—" He glanced meaningfully to Johnson before adding, "We'll give Mr. McIntyre a chance to recover."

"Thank you." Rousseau tossed Johnson a last withering glare.

Thomas walked out of the room with Johnson reluctantly on his heels.

Thankfully it wasn't until they were inside the elevator car and descending to the first floor that she exploded. "What the hell was that all about?" she demanded, her dark eyes flashing. "We had our opportunity and you blew it. Just walked away! You know what she's going to do, don't you? 'Just Alex' Rousseau?" Johnson demanded, making air quotes. "She's going to spirit our primary witness away and hide him somewhere! Probably Malibu or Brentwood or some other place in Los Angeles. I'm telling you she's only on this case to get her face in front of a camera."

"Maybe."

"So then we've lost our star witness. And then what?"

"Subpoena. And I don't think Rousseau would haul him over state lines."

"You don't know that!" Johnson was really ramping up. "And what the hell good will a subpoena do if we can't find the bastard?" She threw her hands up in exasperation. "Jesus, Thomas, aren't you the guy who thinks Jonas McIntyre is guilty of murdering his goddamned family twenty years ago?"

"I do."

"Then . . . ?"

The car stopped on the first floor. "Sometimes we have to play a waiting game."

"Oh, right," she said as the doors opened and they had to sidestep an elderly man with a walker. "And twenty years isn't long enough!"

"Not quite," Thomas said, refusing to think he'd made a major tactical blunder in letting Jonas McIntyre off the hook.

He had to go with his gut on this one.

CHAPTER 26

The detectives were waiting in an interview room.

Kara had imagined she would be confined in a small, cell-like cubicle with a two-way mirror, hidden cameras rolling, unseen eyes following her every move, searching for any nuance that might be at odds with what she told the authorities. She'd thought the lighting would be harsh, the ordeal nerve-wracking. She'd heard about the whole good cop/bad cop routine and had expected to be grilled, the detectives intimidating, almost bullying her into saying the wrong thing.

As it turned out, she'd watched too many movies from the 1940s and 1950s.

She was ushered into a cement block room painted a pale gray. A table with four chairs sat in the middle of the room, a line of small windows tucked near the ceiling of one wall, the opposite covered with a double row of framed headshots of police officers in full uniform.

Two officers were waiting for her.

Her stomach tightened. She tried to shake off her anxiety. She wasn't used to being around people, and she'd avoided any contact with the police for years. Yet here she was.

Introductions were quickly made, hands shaken, and she was offered a seat opposite Detectives Cole Thomas and Aramis Johnson. A bottle of water next to an empty paper cup and carafe of coffee had been placed before her.

Thomas, a tall man in an open-collar shirt, navy sport coat and slacks, was more relaxed than his partner. He was clean shaven, his salt-and-pepper hair neatly clipped, his physique slim. His gold eyes were deep-set and intense. Hunter's eyes. The kind that could track a small creature in a dark forest.

Johnson, his partner, was a striking woman, probably around five-seven or -eight, and exuded the confidence of a woman who was born beautiful but had to fight for every bit of respect she'd earned. Her smile was as tight as the band holding her curly hair in a sleek bun, her cheekbones prominent, her eyes so dark as to be almost black.

Kara was offered coffee and water, a soda if she wanted it, was told the conversation would be recorded, and the interview began.

"We've been looking for you," Thomas said.

"I know. I was staying with a friend." She didn't elaborate and was already hoping to get out of here quick. The place was too institutional, the walls too high, and the cops made her anxiety inch upward.

Johnson asked, "What friend?"

"Does it matter? My house was besieged, reporters everywhere! I just needed time to pull myself together."

"You could have called," Johnson pointed out.

"I didn't have my phone. It was in my Jeep. You know that. You must have it. And my purse." Were they playing games with her?

"We do," Thomas said. "You can pick up your belongings as soon as we're done. You'll have to sign for everything."

"I will."

"Doesn't your friend have a phone?" Johnson asked. "Couldn't you have used hers? Or his?"

"I could have," she agreed, and felt the muscles in her back tightening. She fought to appear calm. "As I said, I just needed some time."

Johnson seemed about to pursue the subject, but Thomas said, "Why don't you tell us what happened? Why were you at Merritt Margrove's place in the mountains?"

"I was looking for him," she explained. "I'd been shocked to hear that my brother Jonas had been released from prison and I wanted answers, so I tried calling him. When that didn't work, I started looking for him. He wasn't at his office, but Celeste—she's his wife—she said he was up at his mobile home up in the mountains."

Kara, still inwardly fighting her case of nerves, explained about finding the place, letting herself in and discovering the attorney, already dead, lying in a pool of blood. "I freaked," she admitted. "I mean, really freaked. Seeing him like that." She shivered.

"So what did you do?" Thomas asked.

"I took off." She explained about needing to get away, about driving west toward the city and calling 9-1-1. "And then . . ." she said, taking in a deep breath, "and then Jonas, he pops up from the back seat, just like in those stupid movies. I nearly had a heart attack."

She told them about how she'd almost hit a deer and then the accident with the semi sliding toward them on the narrow road. "All I remember was the truck's grill and trying to turn away from the collision, but that's it. I don't remember hitting, I don't remember the accident at all or the ride to the hospital. When I woke up, I was in the bed, I had stitches in my head and I kind of ached all over, especially my shoulder. The nurses told me that Jonas was there and the driver of the truck was in a hospital in Portland."

"Did you and Jonas talk?" Johnson asked. "On the drive?"

"You mean when he scared the holy crap out of me? Yeah, we talked. Of course we did. He freaked me out." She explained about the conversation. How tense she was, how Jonas, too, had been upset. He'd sworn he'd been dropped off at the place by a girl named Mia and that he hadn't killed Margrove, that when he'd arrived the attorney was already dead. He'd stowed away in her Jeep because he was freaked and didn't have a ride from Merritt's place. He'd wanted Kara to drive him to Hal's Get and Go, a truck stop not far from The Dalles.

"Did he tell you why he was at the cabin?"

"He said he had a meeting with Merritt and when he got there, Merritt had already been . . . been killed." She shivered, remembering the lawyer lying on the old shag carpet. "It was awful." Her voice had lowered.

Thomas asked, "Did you see anyone else there? When you arrived?"

"No, I didn't even see Jonas."

"But you didn't wait for the police," Johnson said. Not really a question.

"No," Kara answered anyway. "I couldn't stay there."

"Had you been drinking?" Johnson asked, and Kara flashed back to the airplane-size vodka bottles that they'd no doubt found.

"That morning?" she asked. "No. But the night before? Yeah."

"And you were driving?"

"While drinking? No." She shook her head. Her blood was pounding in her eardrums. She needed to get out of here!

Johnson's eyes narrowed a fraction, but she let it go. "What can you tell us about the night of the massacre?"

Kara had been expecting this. "Nothing more than what I already did. You have my statement and deposition, everything I testified to in court."

Thomas was nodding, but Johnson said, "You were just a kid. And there were some holes in your memory."

"That hasn't changed," Kara said.

Johnson cocked her head, a friendly gesture intended to say she didn't quite believe it. "Surely over the years you've had time to think about it. And I imagine you did a lot. You've read recounts of it, seen the TV movie, even probably trolled chat rooms about it. Something could have jogged your memory."

"Nothing did," Kara said firmly. She recounted her memories of that horrid, fateful and savage night, just as she remembered them, from the moment Marlie had locked her into the attic, the horror of finding her family members slain, the intruder in the doorway and running through the forest, hallucinating that her bloodied family was chasing her and ending up falling through the ice into the dark, icy depths of the lake. "Then when I woke up I found out that the guy chasing me was Edmund Tate and that he died saving my life."

Neither Thomas nor Johnson had interrupted her as she'd gotten lost in thought, the interview room melting away as she was once again a child of seven, witnessing the horror of the night

416

that had altered the course of her life forever. Memories washed over her, some crystal clear, others so foggy as to be opaque, but all so real that, as she narrated her story, she felt goose bumps rise on the back of her arms.

"Some of it is a blur, even afterward," she admitted. "There were police officers and social workers and . . ." Shivering, she stared straight ahead, blinking to bring herself back to the present.

They asked her more questions, having her repeat her answers, going over every detail until she thought she might go out of her mind. She had to end it. "I think we're done," she said, and scraped back her chair. "Really, I can't tell you anything else."

Johnson seemed about to argue, but Thomas held up a hand. "Thank you. I think we've got what we need."

"But we might call on you again, and if you think of anything else, please phone."

I won't. But she held that in and said, "You have some of my things. I need my purse and phone."

Thomas nodded. "That we do. And you can have them. Of course."

Johnson pushed back her chair. "I'll get them."

Thomas said, "You'll need to fill out a release."

"And my Jeep?"

"We're not quite done with it," Thomas said. "But as soon as it's been completely processed, you can claim it and deal with the towing company and insurance, now that you've filled out the accident report. It'll probably be just a day or two."

Johnson returned with the release and a clear plastic bag. Her phone and purse were visible, along with a pair of sunglasses, a bottle of hand sanitizer, an umbrella, a flashlight and the two empty vodka bottles. Her stomach clenched at the sight of the tiny blue empties, but she didn't remark and signed the release after checking the contents of her purse.

She slid her phone from its plastic bag and turned it on as she gathered her coat. "The driver of the semi?" she asked as her phone came to life. "Sven Aaronsen? Do you know how he's doing?"

"Hanging in there." Thomas opened the door and walked her down the hallway.

"Thank God." Kara didn't realize how worried she'd been until that moment. "He's going to make it, then?"

"All I know is that he's been moved from the critical care to serious and moved out of ICU. A step in the right direction."

She blinked, surprised that tears had formed in her eyes. "Good," she whispered as her phone started beeping to let her know that she had voice and text messages waiting. Faiza's name came up three different times and then a text message from an unknown number:

She's alive.

Kara's knees nearly gave out. Her arm shot out to brace herself against the wall and Thomas grabbed hold of her elbow. "Hey," he said, but her eyes were riveted to the small screen and she noted the time. The text had arrived at 2:37 this morning.

"You okay?" Thomas asked.

"I don't know," Kara admitted, her throat tight as she fought a growing sense of panic.

"What?" There was an edge to Johnson's voice as she caught up with them.

"This is the second time," Kara admitted as a deputy in winter gear hurried past them. "I got this text. Second time. And a call from an unknown number."

Johnson said, "What text?"

"I think . . . I think it's about my sister," she admitted, recovering slightly and feeling a flush climb up her neck that she'd reacted so violently. She saw Johnson staring at her phone while Thomas released her arm. There was no reason to lie. The police could subpoena records from her cell phone company even if they hadn't been able to get into her phone. She bit her lip and pulled herself together. "Someone keeps texting me that Marlie's alive."

CHAPTER 27

Tate waited.

Parked on the street across from the long, low building of the sheriff's department, he sat in his Toyota. While sipping now-cold takeout coffee he picked up from a kiosk two blocks over, he kept one eye on the building where Kara was being interviewed. Even though he was busy, catching up on phone calls, responding to email, researching the Internet, he checked the time every ten minutes.

She'd been inside for over an hour and he was getting antsy, turning the engine on and off to warm the interior as snow began to fall again, big, fat flakes that melted on the hood of his SUV. He would have loved to have been a part of it, but she'd told him it was something she had to do alone. Besides, he was certain the cops wouldn't have allowed him in.

While sitting here, he'd managed a couple of phone interviews, including one with Silas Dean. Samuel Senior's former partner had been livid at the intrusion, at the "insinuation," and had threatened a lawsuit, sputtering, "You, the rag you work for and anyone associated with this damned case will regret ruining my reputation. I mean it. I'm sick to the back teeth from this.

It was bad enough that I was associated with Samuel McIntyre—let me tell you the guy had shit for brains, and go ahead, quote me on that—but that's all there was to it. I wasn't anywhere near the McIntyre place that night and I have witnesses to the fact." He'd then rattled off several family members who could vouch for him. The same had been true for the night Margrove was murdered. The alibis, though thin, had checked out.

Tate scratched Dean from the suspect list.

Next, Tate had pulled up Merritt Margrove's will, a copy of which he'd found scanned to the jump drive he'd discovered in the dead man's office. As expected, everything he owned went to his wife with one exception. Margrove had taken out a million-dollar insurance policy. Kara McIntyre was listed as the beneficiary.

That was odd.

Or maybe not.

Margrove had been skimming from the estate for years, living off Kara's inheritance. Both he and Faiza Donner had submitted bills to the estate with obviously inflated costs for their charge. In Faiza's case, she'd padded the cost of nannies and private schools, dance lessons and horseback riding camps, expensive trips, her own time, the upkeep of both the house in Portland and the one on the mountain and so on and so forth. Margrove's attorney's fees seemed exorbitant and spanned two decades. Added to that the lawyer had made some bad investments with the inheritance. On top of Kara's care and legal fees, Margrove had scraped off attorney's and consultation fees especially earmarked for Jonas McIntyre, and paid for expenses out of the same McIntyre account, charging trips and meals and hotel rooms to the estate as he tried to find a way to get Jonas's conviction overturned. There had even been a new car "noted for Kara McIntyre" when she'd turned sixteen, though the title to the Cadillac had never been registered in Kara's name.

Both Faiza Donner and Merritt Margrove had worked the court system and probably could be sued, civilly and possibly criminally.

Tate drummed his fingers against the top of the steering wheel. It was almost as if they'd been depleting the fortune together. Either separately or in tandem.

Margrove, apparently, had felt some guilt and taken out the insurance policy, then, within two years, had borrowed against it.

"The best-laid plans," Tate said, and turned on the engine again.

He thought about that as traffic passed, vehicles pulled in and out of the county parking lots, and people bundled in jackets, hats, scarves and boots bustled in and out of the buildings.

His phone rang and he saw it was Connell, returning his call.

"You got my message?" Tate asked, clicking on.

"Yeah, I did. So here's the rundown," Connell said. From the sound of background noise, the muffled rumble of an engine and rush of air, Tate figured Connell was driving. "I checked and you're right, the McIntyres' estate has been drained. There are loans against the property in the West Hills, big loans, hard money borrowed from private lenders. High interest. Large payments."

"But the property was for the kids," Tate said as a van for a painting company tried to squeeze into the parking spot in front of him.

"Between Merritt Margrove and Faiza Donner, they had control of the money. It was left to the surviving kids. Jonas had to forfeit his share as he was in prison, and Kara wasn't of age until this year. It was odd in a way, because usually it's twenty-five or thirty, or some multiple of five years, but for whatever reason, her parents chose twenty-eight."

"Doesn't matter," Tate said, but it did, he'd seen the will and the way he'd read it was that if all of the McIntyre kids were deceased or incarcerated, the estate, after paying all expenses, would go to next of kin, in this case, Faiza Donner. Sam McIntyre had no siblings and his parents were dead. Faiza was the only member of Zelda's family who was still alive.

The bad feeling that had been with him ever since reading the will grew as the van wedged into the small spot and the driver climbed out to jog across the road and head into a county records building located in the same complex as the sheriff's department. "What about the house in the mountains?"

"For sale. Outrageous price. Not much interest. Who wants to pay millions for some house where a massacre took place?"

"A rich nutcase with a macabre sense of humor, maybe. Someone who likes to shock or is into trophies of a kind so he's got bragging rights. You know the kind: a freak with more money than brains."

Connell barked out a laugh. "We both know a few of those. So far, though, no one's shown any interest. The place has been with four different Realtors in about as many years, but not a single offer."

"It'll sell. If the price is right."

"Anything will. Look, I gotta go. I'm on the road. I'll check in later." Connell ended the connection, and Tate took a sip of his cold coffee, rolled down the window and poured the dregs onto the street just as a delivery truck belching exhaust rolled past.

As he put up the window again, he checked his watch and wondered for the hundredth time how the interview was going. She had insisted she could handle it, that she had nothing to hide, and that she would do anything she could to see that Merritt Margrove's murderer was captured and brought to justice.

Once again, even though she'd picked up Jonas at Margrove's place in the mountains, she'd defended him, insisting he wasn't the killer. "It doesn't make any sense," she'd protested when, just last night, Tate had suggested her prick of a brother, an ex-con, just might lie. "Why would he kill the man who got him out of prison? And why would he expose himself and get in the car with me?"

"He wanted you to drive him away from the crime scene."

"Do you blame him?" she'd thrown at Tate as they'd stood in the kitchen of his loft. "He'd just gotten out of prison and he hates the cops. And, well, hell, I ran away, too." She'd turned to face him, and he'd been caught again by her beauty. "Jonas didn't have any blood on him, Wes. Not a drop. Wouldn't some of Merritt's blood have been on him if he'd sliced Merritt's throat?" She'd physically shuddered. "Besides, the police would figure that out pretty damned fast, wouldn't they? They had his clothes after the accident. So they know he didn't do it." She'd frowned and studied the wine in her glass. "I know Jonas has issues. He's bitter. Who wouldn't be?"

"That's assuming he's innocent."

"Even so," she'd argued, then tossed back her wine. "Okay, okay, I get it. Jonas is a fraud. I know that. This whole religion thing of his is bogus. No one who's really 'found Jesus,'" she said, making air quotes with her fingers, "would be so vindictive, so greedy, so damned angry. But that doesn't mean he's a killer."

At that point he'd dropped the subject and she'd poured herself another glass.

And this morning, she'd refused to let him join her in the sheriff's office.

Tate had slid his RAV4 into this very spot, and offered only hours before, "Okay. I could come in with you—"

"We already discussed this," she'd snapped as she'd pulled on a pair of gloves, then opened the passenger door. "And you don't have to wait for me. I'll get my phone back, or the cops will take me home."

"Your dog is at my place," he'd reminded her.

"Right. Well, you know what I mean."

"I do. And I'll wait."

She'd sent him a questioning look, as if trying to decipher his motives—was he a good guy or just a reporter bending over backward for a story? "It's freezing."

"I'll be okay."

"If you say so." She'd climbed out, slammed the door shut, hesitated to let traffic clear, then jogged across the street. He'd watched her cross, her hair bouncing, her legs moving so easily and he told himself not to notice how sexy she was. Those kinds of thoughts were way out of line and would only get him in trouble. Still, he hadn't been able to turn away as she'd hustled up the concrete steps to enter the glass vestibule. His view had been cut off by an ancient Volkswagen Vanagon rattling past and when he'd been able to see the steps again, she was gone.

He felt an unbidden pang that stupidly still lingered.

Less than five minutes later, his mother called.

"Don't tell me," she said when he answered. "You're back on the McIntyre thing, aren't you?"

"Hi to you, too, Mom."

"Don't be a smart-ass," she said, and launched right in again. "Damn it, Wesley, can't you let it go?" Her fury emanated over the wireless connection.

She knew he couldn't. They'd had this discussion over and over again.

"I saw on the news that Jonas McIntyre's out of prison and that lawyer who got him out? Merritt Margrove? He was killed. It's everywhere. Newspaper, radio, television, even my damned Facebook feed!" She let out a long sigh. "I've had a reporter call me this morning. That Sheila Keegan woman. Pushy thing. And she's just the first. They'll be lining up, I know they will. There's already been some kind of rally about

Jonas McIntyre. And they're gonna dig this all up again. And you . . . you're right in there with the rest of them."

"It's my job, Mom."

"No, Wesley, it's your obsession!" She paused and then more calmly said, "You need to let it go. What's done is done. I'm not crazy about the fact that Jonas McIntyre is out of prison, you know I'm not, and I feel bad that another man died—was killed—but it's all in God's hands now."

"Merritt Margrove was murdered. I don't think God had anything to do with it." Tate started the engine and cranked up the heat in the defroster as the windows had begun to fog.

"But that's not what this is about," his mother reminded him. "Haven't you spent enough time on this? Give it up, son."

"I've got a new angle," he said, glancing away from his phone and watching through the condensation as two deputies walked out a side door and climbed into a department-issue SUV.

"Look, if I can leave the past behind where it belongs, you can."

"I can't." And that was the God's honest truth. The tragedy had been haunting him for over half his life.

"You're as stubborn as your father was. He wouldn't listen to me either." She let out a long-suffering sigh. "Don't you think this whole thing has done enough damage to our family? And it's been so long. It doesn't matter if Jonas McIntyre is out of prison or not, you need to find a life beyond it."

"So you've said, Mom."

"Okay, okay. Now, there's something else."

He braced himself.

"Dinner rolls and appetizers."

"What?"

"That's what you're bringing to Christmas dinner."

"Wait a minute—"

"Christmas is this weekend, Wesley, and we're celebrating. As I said, we all need to get on with our lives and Our Lord's birthday is the perfect time. See you then. Love you, Wesley."

"Me too, Mom," he said by rote, but she'd already cut the connection. He leaned back in the car seat and replayed the conversation in his mind. It wasn't that she wasn't right. But he couldn't let it go. Researching and writing the book wasn't only cathartic, it would provide answers to questions that had been gnawing at him for two decades.

And being close to Kara McIntyre would help.

"You think your missing sister is calling and texting you?" Johnson asked Kara, obviously skeptical. They were still standing in the hallway outside the interview room, the two detectives staring intently at her.

"No, I don't think it's her. I mean . . . no. Why would she say 'she's alive' if Marlie's calling to tell me she was okay? Wouldn't she say, 'I'm alive'?"

"Maybe to hide her identity," Thomas said as a stern-looking fiftysomething deputy striding in the opposite direction squared his hat over his head as he passed. "Excuse me," he muttered, and they all shifted to one side of the wide corridor.

"Okay, I know it doesn't make any sense," Kara admitted. "But I can't help but feel that . . ." She let her voice trail off.

"That what?" Johnson prompted.

Kara shook her head and felt the stitches in her head pinch a bit. "I want to believe Marlie's alive." There, she'd said it, admitting to the police what was really in her heart, the fantasy she'd held on to for two decades.

"Of course you do," Thomas said, as if he understood.

"So, I see her, you know?" Kara admitted, and rubbed her arms nervously. "Sometimes I swear I see her and then, of course, it turns out it's just some stranger. And the truth is, I don't even know what she would look like."

Thomas said, "Come with me." He started walking down the hallway. "I want to show you something." At the end of the corridor, before they reached the reception area, he turned another couple of corners until he reached a glassed-in office, his office, she guessed, by the way he sat down in a worn chair and fiddled with the computer mouse on his desk. He logged in quickly, his eyes focused on the screen until he located the file he wanted and pulled up an image.

Her breath caught in the back of her throat.

"Marlie," she whispered, staring at the woman on the monitor. "Oh, God."

"Computer-enhanced, aged through a program we've got."

She felt the skin at the back of her neck prickle. "I've seen her," she whispered, thinking back to the group that had gathered outside the hospital and the woman in the red scarf and tinted glasses. "She is alive."

CHAPTER 28

Alex Rousseau wasn't happy as she drove her Lexus into the truck stop parking area, away from the brightly lit canopy and mini-mart to park in the shadow of the big rigs lined to one side.

In fact, when she thought about it, she was pretty damned pissed.

"This isn't a good idea," she said to Jonas, who had pushed the passenger seat into a near-reclining position and had sulked all the way from the hospital.

"So you've said. Like maybe . . . oh, I don't know . . . a million times."

"As your attorney—"

"You do what I say!"

"No," she snapped back. "I advise you on the best course of action. Legally."

"Oh, get over yourself!" He pushed a button on the electric seat and with a soft whirr it began to elevate him back to a sitting position again as traffic on the interstate barreled past Hal's Get and Go. Semis, pickups, vans, SUVs and sedans, all racing on the freeway that hugged the edge of the Columbia. It had been closed earlier for inclement weather.

Now clouds were burgeoning, dark and threatening, snow starting to fall, but it was just a precursor to worse weather. Another blizzard was predicted to slam the Columbia Gorge within twelve hours. But now, at least for a few hours, the vital road was open.

"I don't know how you and Merritt Margrove got along," she told her new client, "but you need to treat me with more than a modicum of respect."

"Modicum," he repeated, mocking her. "Wow, there's a twelve-dollar word for you."

"Is it?" God, he was a dick. If there hadn't been so much exposure and notoriety attached to Jonas McIntyre, she would have told him to go jump in a lake. Considering what had happened years ago, it seemed appropriate. "As your attorney, I'm advising against this—whatever you've got planned." All he'd told her was that he needed a ride to this spot. To meet "a friend."

Jonas nodded and threw her a glance. "Gotcha." Then he reached for the handle of the passenger door.

She tried one more time. "I didn't pull all the strings I did with the hospital just so you could walk away."

"I know." He threw her a cocky grin, opened the door and winced slightly, but seemed to ignore the pain. The sound of engines and wheels on pavement echoed over the quiet ding of the car's alarm reminding her that the car was still idling as the door opened.

"Let's be honest with each other," he said, his face illuminated by the Lexus's dome light and the reflection of the neon lights from the mini-mart.

"We are," she snapped as the odors of exhaust and diesel blew inside on a blast of bitter wind. "At least I am."

"Yeah, sure." He didn't bother hiding the doubts in his eyes, the skepticism. "We both know you're in this for the money, Alex, and the fame. So whether I get out here or do exactly what you want or pretend to be the perfect patient under some prick of a doc's care, it really doesn't matter. Either way you win. No matter what, you get what you want. Airtime. Media attention. This might, I mean probably will, go national, don't you think? So cut the crap. Let this go. I've got things I've got to do."

"You're not a hundred percent."

A hard, sarcastic grin cut across his bearded jawline. "Who is, Alex? Who the hell is?" He stepped out of the car and slammed the door shut.

"Asshole," she muttered under her breath as he hunched his shoulders and jogged, limping slightly, across the parking lot. He started to slip once on the ice but caught himself easily.

Maybe she should follow him. There was a good chance he would run because the cops were going to arrest him for Margrove's murder. It was only a matter of time. He'd been at the murder scene. The victim's throat had been slashed, just like his family members who were murdered in the McIntyre Massacre at Cold Lake twenty years ago.

As far as Rousseau knew, no murder weapon had been found in Margrove's case, but as for motive? Jonas was a hothead, his volatile temper legendary, and he'd already told her that Margrove and his aunt had bled the McIntyre estate dry. That would be more than enough.

She watched as he made his way to a small sedan parked at the far edge of the lot.

Jonas was still rough around the edges, but she'd dressed him well, getting him new jeans and sweaters and jackets, even boots. She'd also bought him a cell phone—one of those temporary burners—and handed him a grand in cash. She needed to be able to communicate with him and would bill him for it, along with her time, as soon as he got even a penny of the McIntyre inheritance. He'd get his share and more of whatever was left, and then they'd sue the hell out of Faiza Donner, Merritt Margrove's estate and his half sister for the rest of what Alex figured was his fair share, but that was just a pittance. The big hit would come when she sought restitution for Jonas being falsely imprisoned. She planned to sue the county and the state and she was just warming up. There could be others . . . oh, the opportunities were endless.

Jonas hadn't been wrong when he'd called her out just now.

It wasn't just the fame Alex Rousseau wanted, she intended to take the fortune, too.

She saw Jonas climb into the passenger seat of the beater car, and as the dome light of the little sedan blinked on, Alex caught a glimpse of the driver: Mia Long. No real surprise there. Mia was his most ardent and loudest supporter. Alex even saw the rosary dangling from the rearview mirror, visibly twinkling until the door was shut and the interior light dimmed.

Mia hit the gas.

Her car sped out of the parking lot to the access road.

For a second Alex wondered if the two were getting together for sex, long yearned for and idealized. If so, the physical act would probably be hot as hell. Until it wasn't. Even still recovering from the accident, Jonas looked tough. Muscular. Sexy. Or was there something else going on? She hoped not. Sliding her SUV into gear, she told herself that she wasn't worried, then eased the Lexus onto the access road, drove across the overpass and turned onto the freeway.

As she increased her speed, she switched on the wipers.

Jonas was right, she reminded herself as she sped past a huge truck that was spraying sludge behind its big tires. If he got himself into more trouble, he'd just become more valuable.

A win-win.

As long as he was her client.

She pressed down on the accelerator, her LX 570 shooting around some muscle car, her wheels humming on the asphalt, the engine a soft, steady purr.

Jonas McIntyre could leave tonight and screw his brains out—or whatever.

But he'd be back.

Alex and the remaining McIntyre son who had survived the massacre and been so wrongly charged were symbiotic.

Jonas needed her as much as she needed him.

Kara slid into Tate's SUV. "Buy me a drink?" she asked.

"It's not even noon. You serious?"

"Just kidding. Drive." She hadn't been kidding. Cooped up with the detectives in the interrogation room had been excruciating. Her nerves were shot and nothing would calm them more than a Bloody Mary or a mimosa or a damned wine cooler.

"Where to?"

"Back to your place to pick up Rhapsody, then I guess I should go home." There was vodka and wine waiting for her in the kitchen and she felt a gnawing ache to taste it.

He pulled into the slow-moving traffic, then glanced her way. "How'd it go with the police?"

"It went," she said, glancing at Tate as he slowed for a red light. "Look, I haven't been totally honest with you."

He didn't seem surprised.

Great. Probably meant he hadn't been honest as well.

"I don't trust reporters, I don't trust men, hell, I don't trust anyone because I have abandonment issues and blah, blah, blah. It's been explained to me by a dozen shrinks."

"Okay." He slowed as traffic was clogged.

"Anyway, I told the police that I think I saw Marlie at the hospital and—"

"Marlie? In the hospital?" He glanced at her.

"No, in the crowd outside."

"You saw . . . ?" He didn't finish the thought, but cast a concerned glance. She held up her phone. "I got this back and . . . well, crap, Tate. I was getting weird calls and texts. I mean when Jonas got out . . . or around there, but before I went to Merritt's cabin, before I found him with his throat slit, before the accident, when Jonas was getting out, and I think they're from Marlie. But then that's not right because she wouldn't talk about herself in the third person, saying she's alive, and I saw a police composite picture of her . . ." She stopped, realized she was babbling, nearly hyperventilating.

"Marlie? You think you got a text from her?"

"Yes! I should have told you sooner," she said. "I know it, but everything's just so weird, so out of control so—"

"Shhh. It's okay," Tate said as he braked for a red light, idling behind a dirty black pickup with a load of firewood beneath a blue flapping tarp. He touched her shoulder. "When we get back, you can tell me all about it. I can stop for coffee. There's a kiosk up ahead."

"Only if they'll add a shot of Baileys or Irish whiskey to it," she said, and sent him a look. "Not kidding." And then she turned her gaze to the intersection, where a young mom was pushing a stroller with one hand and holding on to the mittened hand of a boy of four or five with her other hand. They disappeared in front of the pickup and she glanced to the corner, where a guy dressed in a red Santa suit was ringing a bell and collecting donations. He was shouting "Merry Christmas" and "God bless you" and "ho, ho, ho" ad nauseam. Man, she hated this time of year.

Closing her eyes, she told herself she just needed to hang on, to pull herself together, to do anything but lose control.

By the time they reached Tate's loft and were inside, she was calmer, and it helped that he had taken her at her word by making them each a cup of coffee and adding a healthy pour of Baileys Irish Cream to the brew. No whiskey. She was seated on the couch, Rhapsody at her side, as he handed the steaming cup to her and she accepted it, her fingers trembling slightly before she took a long, mind-calming swallow.

That was better.

So much better.

The warmth of the coffee and the tingle of a little whisper of booze did wonders for the quivering she felt inside.

After grabbing a second cup for himself, he flipped a dining chair around and straddled it in order to face her. "So? What's the big lie?" he asked, sipping from his cup. "We did have a deal, you know. We're in this together."

"Yeah, yeah." She took another big swallow. The alcohol helped calm her frayed-to-the-breaking-point nerves. Being here, out of the police station, eased the tension, but still she was anxious and nervous, felt confined, like a damned caged animal. She needed to get out. Get away. Do *some*thing. "As I said, I've been getting calls," she admitted, and took another big swallow. Then she set the cup down, found her fingers were a little more steady and unlocked her phone. Scrolling through a few calls from reporters and police, she found the voice mail and played the short message that had been left in the thin, papery voice, "She's alive."

"Before you ask, I don't recognize the voice, nor the numbers."

"Probably a burner phone."

"Right. There's more." She showed him the text messages, then picked up her cup and drained it before leaning back on the cushions.

"Who would do this?"

"I don't know." She stood, leaving him with her phone, walked into the kitchen area, brewed herself a second cup and added a healthy shot of the Irish Cream while Tate scrolled through the messages on her phone.

He was absorbed by her phone and she felt a prickle of indignation that he was reading other texts, personal messages. She started across the room to demand it back, then thought: *Why? Who cares? There's nothing in there that is all that personal. And Merritt is dead. Killed.*

"Who's Brad?" he asked.

Using the spoon he'd left on the counter, she stirred her coffee. "My most recent ex."

"He's still texting."

She frowned. "Forgot to block him."

"Your Aunt Faiza seems concerned."

"Talked to her." She was loosening up but still irritated as she, sipping from her cup, returned to the sofa.

"Tell me about the interview with the police," he suggested, handing her back her phone.

Tucking the cell into her pocket, she sat on the edge of the couch, sipped her drink and told him everything she could remember, forcing herself to dismiss any lingering doubts about confiding in him. She needed an ally—even one who might not be the most trustworthy, one who openly admitted his own agenda for seeking the truth. What did she care what his motives were? Was he going to write a tell-all that would expose more of her to the world, strip her of . . . what? Her privacy? Her anonymity? Her pride? Hell, it had all been said before and now, *now* there was a chance Marlie was alive.

So she told him everything she could remember, about her life and what she'd said in the interview. There were holes of course, those empty spots in her memory that she couldn't retrieve, but she bared as much of her soul as she could. Kara explained that Detective Thomas had shown her a computer-enhanced image of an older Marlie, a picture of what Marlie would look like today. "That's when I knew for certain that I'd seen her. At the hospital." Kara stared hard at Tate, hoping to make him believe her. "I tried to get to her, but she disappeared before I could reach her."

"Again," he said. "She disappeared *again*."

"Yes." She took another swallow of coffee.

"And you're sure it was Marlie?" He was skeptical.

"Of course!" she said so loudly that Rhapsody lifted her head and gave off a startled "woof."

Reality settled in. "I mean, I thought I was . . .

seeing that picture of what Marlie would look like now, but . . . no, I'm not sure. Not a hundred percent. I'm not sure of anything right now. The woman looked like her, I mean really looked like her, but she was all bundled up and wearing tinted glasses and I thought, afterward, maybe I was imagining things. I mean, why would she be there? After all this time? Had she been in hiding just to wait to see Jonas? It didn't make any sense and sometimes I imagine things, you know."

"Such as?"

"That I'm being followed, or someone's watching the house or whatever. I'm never not on edge, you know?" She didn't wait for an answer. "Anyway, after seeing Marlie at the hospital, I'd told myself to file it in the Just-Another-Kara-McIntyre-Freak-Out file, but then Detective Thomas showed me the computerized picture. Now . . . now, I don't know what to think. Just that this has to end. Before I go completely insane.

"You're not going insane," he said, his voice calming.

"No?" She raised an eyebrow.

"No."

"Tell that to my frayed nerves and my messed-up memory." She finished her coffee and carried her empty cup to the sink. Ignoring the need of another drink, she walked to the window and wrapped her arms around her middle. Outside, the river rushed past the seawall on the edge of town. Dark and foreboding, it seemed to mirror her thoughts.

So many unanswered questions, so many regrets.

What was it Dr. Zhou had said? Something about needing to acknowledge fear before facing it? Not so easy to do. She was scared of the past; scared to death, afraid of what she might ultimately find out.

However, she couldn't live this way a second longer.

Mia's heart was soaring.

She'd brought Jonas back to her apartment, a one-bedroom unit in Gresham that wasn't too far from the freeway and only twenty-six minutes to downtown Portland. Mia had timed it. She felt a little giddy and a lot nervous as Jonas surveyed the tight space, though to him, she thought, considering that he'd been in a tiny prison cell for half his life, her crammed living room, tight kitchen, single bath and standard apartment bedroom might seem spacious, even airy despite her cluttered counters and bistro table covered in piles of papers, all of which were dedicated to him and his release.

Except he might view her small unit from the eyes of the superrich as he'd grown up with his family having two mansions, each of which could swallow this tiny unit whole.

"So this is what you've been doing," he said, eyeing the papers and newspaper articles before picking up her iPad and scrolling down the Facebook page she'd dedicated to him, where tons of fans had made posts and comments.

"This is only part of it. We've got loads of platforms, not just Facebook. We're on Twitter and YouTube and WhatsApp and Instagram and . . . well, you know. All the sites. Anyplace we can get the word out." She smiled and hoped he didn't hear the baby crying in the next unit. The kid screamed all the time, his colic or whatever so loud through these paper-thin walls that sometimes Mia had to turn her TV or music up to the max, just to hear herself think. She motioned to the screen. "It's all about you," she said, pride tinging her voice. "About the injustice you've suffered."

"Good." He was still scrolling through the comments, studying the posts, his eyebrows pulled together over his oh-so-sexy dark eyes. Some people thought he looked a lot like Jesus Christ—well, the American Christian version of what people thought Jesus had looked like, but in Mia's mind, Jesus looked a lot like Jonas. Only Jonas was rougher looking and a lot hotter, which was a good thing, because Mia couldn't think about sex with Jesus. No way. But with Jonas? Yes, please.

She thought he would jump her the second they

closed the door behind them and slipped the lock through its chain. She imagined him twisting her around and forcing his lips down on hers, and then they would be scrambling, tearing off clothing before he hoisted her off her feet and carried her to the bedroom. And then . . . oh, and then.

But he hadn't.

In fact, he'd barely talked on the way to the apartment, had even drummed his fingers on the ledge of the passenger seat window as if he were passing time—waiting for something. He hadn't seemed to realize that the window glass of her Honda didn't quite meet the car's roof, that cold wind whistled inside the Accord as she'd driven. Worse yet, she'd worn high boots and a short skirt and she'd thought he might reach over and touch her bare leg on the drive to Gresham, but he hadn't even noticed. She'd been practically freezing to show off a bit of bare skin and it was almost as if he'd been somewhere else, barely speaking to her, his thoughts far away.

Shit!

She'd hoped he was planning his seductive next move and was a little shy about being physical with her, but—*Oh, come on, Mia. Who are you kidding? Jonas McIntyre is* not *shy. The man has balls of steel.*

Right?

"You want something to drink?" she offered,

hoping to break the ice, end the awkwardness.

"Sure." He didn't look up. In fact, he didn't react to her at all. It was almost like she wasn't even in the room.

Fuck!

She was about to be angry, but he followed her into the kitchen and as she opened the refrigerator door and leaned inside, she made sure her ass was right in his line of vision. How could it not be? You could barely turn around in the small space. He was forced into the corner between the stove and sink.

She grabbed two beers from the fridge, cracked them open and handed a bottle to Jonas, who was still wearing his damned jacket. Maybe she'd have to be bolder. And the baby next door was cranking up the volume again. The kid wasn't abused, she knew that much, had checked, but the colicky eighteen-month-old picked the worst moments to be upset. The worst. Like now!

"Thanks." Absently he took a pull on the longneck, then eased through the doorway back to the dining area with her flea-market table. He looped one leg over one of the tall café chairs and was once again peering intently at her iPad.

Damn it all.

She was getting desperate.

"I want to show you something," she said in a soft, sexy voice.

"Okay." Again, still focused on the screen.

He'd stopped scrolling at a post from last week and was staring at a comment, then clicked onto the name of the person and Mia died a little inside as Lacey Higgins Swift's profile appeared. Lacey's picture included a tall man with thinning hair, an English sheepdog and two blond boys who appeared to be about two. Twins, dressed identically, in red and green striped PJs.

Mia thought she might be sick.

"Does she post much?" Jonas asked. He pointed a finger at the iPad.

"Lacey?"

"Yeah."

Why the hell was he asking about his old girlfriend? The slut who had fucked his brother, then testified against him. "Not that I've noticed." That was a lie. She'd kept track of Jonas's ex, of course she had. It appeared that Lacey had moved on, went to college, got married, had a couple of kids. Living the perfect life somewhere in Beaverton, on the west side of the Willamette River, not too far from Portland, only minutes from the McIntyre mansion in the West Hills. Mia knew. Mia had made a point of knowing.

He took another swallow from his Coors.

Mia, tamping down a bit of annoyance, leaned across the tall table. "I want to show you something."

"What?" He was starting to turn back to the screen.

"This." She unbuttoned her sweater, exposing her breast, where, just a month ago, she'd added another tattoo. *Free Jonas* was scripted just under her collarbone.

One of his eyebrows raised. "Cool."

"I did it for you."

"Yeah, I get it." A hint of a smile in his beard-darkened jaw. "Cool."

Cool? Are you kidding me?

He dragged his eyes up from the spot where her breast nearly spilled out of her sheer push-up bra. "Hey, Mia, look. I need a favor."

"A favor?" she repeated.

"Yeah, I've got something I need to do. And I need a car. I thought I'd borrow yours."

"You want my car?" She was stunned.

"Yeah, babe, just for a little while."

Babe? Had he just called her babe? Like they were that familiar? "Why?"

"Errands. Hey, I've been locked up for a long while. I just need the car." He lifted a shoulder and she found herself digging in her pocket for her keys. "I'll drive you," she offered. "Wherever you want to go."

"No worries. I got this." He snagged the keys from her hand. "This is something I have to do alone." He was already striding—almost jogging, though limping just slightly, as he headed to the door. "I'll be back."

"When?"

"Don't know." He opened the door and didn't so much as glance over his shoulder. "Don't fuckin' know."

It wasn't until Mia drained her beer and walked back to the kitchen to leave both bottles in the sink when she noticed a knife was missing. She told herself she was imagining things, but no, the closer she looked, the more sure she was that a knife was missing from the block that sat next to the stove—the set had been a hand-me-down from her mother and she knew without a doubt that the largest knife was gone. She looked at the counters and in a nearby drawer, her heart turning to ice. It was gone. The carving knife her father had used to slice the Thanksgiving turkey at every Thanksgiving dinner she'd ever sat through as a child was definitely missing, its slot in the block empty.

CHAPTER 29

"Our bird has flown," Johnson said, stepping into Thomas's office in the late afternoon.

He was on the phone, just ending the call from the assistant ME. He held up a finger, stopping Johnson, and listened to what he already knew: Margrove had died from blood loss due to a wound that had severed his carotid artery and sliced his jugular on the left side of his neck. "I'll look for the report. Thanks." Then he turned his attention to his partner. "What bird?" he asked, but he had a bad feeling he already knew.

"Just got a call from the deputy charged with watching Jonas McIntyre. His attorney, 'Just Alex,' as she so proudly wants to be called, did her legal magic and worked with the hospital staff to get him released. He's already on his way to Portland. The excuse was that he needs to be seen by 'specialists.' "

"For what?"

"Who knows? It's bogus! According to an 'anonymous source,' " she said, making air quotes, "but someone on staff. An aide probably. Anyway, the word at Whimstick General, Jonas wasn't that bad off. The doc was probably going to discharge him today anyway. But his attorney swooped in and off they went."

451

"Shit."

"My thoughts exactly. As soon as he heard about it, the deputy assigned to McIntyre called, but by then it was over. Pisses me off." Obviously agitated, she plopped down in one of the visitor's chairs.

"Portland's not that far."

"Out of the jurisdiction."

"Margrove's homicide is in ours. The Portland PD will work with us."

"If you say so." She wasn't convinced and let out a long, hard sigh. "You find anything more on Marlie Robinson?"

"Not yet." He shook his head, feeling his eyebrows pinch together as he studied some of the shots. "But I pieced together some of the people who showed up at the hospital and connected them to individuals online."

"And?"

"And there are the usual suspects, people who've been vocal about claiming Jonas got a raw deal."

"Like Mia Long?" she suggested.

"Among others. McIntyre's got other pretty rabid fans. Brenda Crawley, she's always got a comment online. The same goes for Simone Hardesty. And there's even a guy, Aiden Cross. I checked the noisy ones out. Simone went to school with Jonas and so did Cross. Brenda, she's involved in any and every cause that comes along." He leaned away from the screen with the pictures on it.

"So?"

"Well, then there's a lot of people who are in the group who don't say a word, probably have given up."

"Yeah? Is there a point to this?"

"By process of elimination, I've taken care of most of them, at least the ones who live within a fifty-mile radius." When she was about to ask a question, he said, "It's a computer app that cross-checks known people and their addresses."

"Big Brother." She eyed him. "There's a reason we get a bad name, you know."

"And a reason we need information. Protect and Serve. Remember."

"Yeah, yeah, so what did you find?" She was intrigued enough to get out of the chair and round his desk to stare at his computer screen.

"There are several pictures of the woman Kara described." He pulled up three group shots where he'd highlighted the woman with long coat, scarf and colored glasses, though in most shots she was turned away from the camera. "There's a resemblance."

"Okay, I guess." She leaned closer, then studied the digitalized picture. "Could be."

"I was hoping to see one of her getting into a car or talking with someone who might know her, just find some sort of connection. Someone we could ID and talk to."

"Did you?"

"No, but if you notice there's this other woman near to her. The redhead with the ponytail. But they're never together, the redhead is in the background, but no matter where she moves to, the redhead is nearby."

Johnson shrugged. "So?" Just then a cell phone chimed outside the doorway and someone said, "Hello," footsteps approaching, then fading.

"Take a closer look at her," Thomas suggested, enlarging the image.

Johnson leaned in.

"Now look at this." He cut the screen in half and scrolled through images taken twenty years before, pictures of the people who had testified or made statements in the McIntyre Massacre trial. Eventually he stopped scrolling at a shot of a teenaged girl with a pixie face and long red hair parted down the middle.

"Oh, God." She glanced at Thomas. "Brittlynn Cadella?"

"Right. Chad Atwater's secret girlfriend, the one he eventually married."

"His alibi." She straightened and trained her gaze on the screen where the image of the Marlie look-alike was.

Thomas pulled at his collar and said, "I can't help but wonder what she's doing at the protest. You'd think she'd want to be as far away from Jonas McIntyre as possible, to lay low."

"Apparently not. She and Chad live up on the

mountain, not far from the ski resort where he teaches lessons. Let's go and see what she has to say for herself."

"And for Chad."

Thomas scooted back his chair and found his jacket hanging on a hook near the door. "Maybe this time he'll speak for himself."

Johnson laughed. "Ten to one she's his alibi again."

"If they need one. I can't see either of them being involved in killing Margrove," he admitted, unable to tie all the loose strings together.

"Unless Margrove dug up something we don't know about, something that Chad is worried will incriminate him in the massacre two decades ago."

Slipping his arms through the sleeves of his jacket, Thomas admitted, his frustration growing, that he felt that they were closing in on something, but he couldn't quite put his finger on it. "I just don't understand a motive here. But there's one way to find out. Want to take a trip up to the mountain?"

She nodded. "Thought you'd never ask."

They were on the way out of the building, Thomas with keys in hand, when they ran into Gleason's secretary, Lorna Driscoll, who was carrying two water bottles toward the lieutenant's office. "Oh, Detective Johnson," she said, "Lieutenant Gleason is looking for you." A glance at Thomas. "You too," she added quickly, hurrying along the short corridor.

"What is it with you and Gleason?" Thomas asked under his breath as they turned to follow Lorna down the short hallway.

"Uncle Archer?" she said, her dark eyes glinting.

"He's not your uncle."

"No, but he and I share a common interest," she said, winking. Then, "Don't get the wrong idea. It's through a charity for disabled kids." She was no longer teasing but didn't elaborate as they walked through the doorway.

Gleason was seated at his neat desk, sports paraphernalia still in place. "I saw the detectives in the hallway, thought you wanted to talk to them." Lorna deposited a bottle on the corner of the lieutenant's desk.

"Right." He glanced at his watch. "I've just got a second. Sit, sit." He waved them into chairs as Lorna slipped out of the office and closed the door behind her. "I don't have time for an update now, but tomorrow morning," he said, "I'll want a full report."

Johnson was nodding. "You got it."

Gleason cracked open the water bottle and got down to business. "I talked to Randy Isley this morning. Cut through a lot of red tape but was actually able to get through on the phone." He shook his head, bald head shining under the overhead lights. "Poor guy. I don't know if he'll make it." Gleason's forehead wrinkled and his mouth pulled into a frown. "Anyway, he reminded me about something, something you should have seen in the old reports."

"Something missed?" Johnson asked.

"Just not paid a lot of attention to at the time. Isley and I were deputies at the time when the massacre happened up at the McIntyre place, and we were there when Edmund Tate was pulled out of the lake. He was about gone." Gleason took a deep drink from the water bottle, then rotated it in his hands. "They'd pried the kid who was screaming her lungs out away from him. I'm talking about the girl, Kara McIntyre."

"Yes," Johnson said, on the edge of her seat.

"And Tate, he was coughing and sputtering, making no sense at all."

Thomas had seen as much in the old statements.

"None of us could make out anything intelligible, but the word he kept muttering and gurgling that was in any way intelligible was 'Simplify.' He kept saying it over and over." Archer chewed on his lower lip as he thought, obviously carried back in time. "He was just so determined to spit it out. He actually grabbed one of the EMT's jackets and raised himself up from the stretcher to say it." Clearing his throat, he snapped back, checked his watch again and pushed back his chair. "That's it. What Isley told me. That and reminding me that we screwed up the evidence chain on the murder weapon, which I'm all too aware of. The only other thing I learned from Isley other than he wants to buy me a drink when we meet again. Now, I'll expect that report in the morning."

And with that, they were ushered out of the office.

As they walked through the corridor to the door to the parking area, Johnson repeated, " 'Simplify.' That's our big clue, the thing we were called into the office for?" He pushed the door open, held it for her.

"You don't have to do that," she said as she stepped outside.

He followed. "Sure I do. I'm old-school." They crossed the parking lot, their boots crunching through a layer of ice that had formed on the snow.

"Amen to that." She slid into the passenger side. "And by the way, next time I'm driving."

"Then who would be checking messages and the Internet? Running down clues while we're on the road and keeping her nose deep into her phone?"

"We all have our strengths."

"And mine is behind the wheel," he said, causing her to roll her black eyes.

"Fine, Ace, so tell me. What's with 'Simplify'?"

"Probably nothing," he said. "Gleason just wants to put his mark on the case and talk to an old colleague before he passes. This way he feels involved. Y'know, on a personal level because he was there that night."

"Yeah, I know." She was thinking, her teeth worrying her lower lip. "But what if the guy wasn't saying 'Simplify'?"

"What do you mean?" He eased out of the lot, merging with late-afternoon traffic, headlights glowing as nightfall came early this time of year.

"I don't know, maybe he was saying, 'Send her to Fai.'"

"Send her?"

"He could've been talking about the little girl. Kara. Isn't her aunt Faiza Donner? Hadn't Edmund Tate seen that Kara McIntyre's entire family had been killed? Hadn't he just rescued her from the lake? So obviously he cared what happened to her. Maybe, in his last dying breaths, he was still trying to save her, so he said, 'Send her to Fai,' or even 'Send her Fai' rather than 'Simplify.'" She cast him a glance as they slowed near a strip mall on the edge of town.

"Then again," she was saying, "it all could be nothing. Just the mutterings of a dying, delusional man."

"Possibly," he agreed, considering flipping on his lights as traffic had snarled, barely crawling past the mall.

One corner of the parking lot had been cordoned off. A choral group on risers was singing

459

Christmas carols. Nearby, in a roped-off area, a crèche was displayed. Actors dressed as wise men, Mary and Joseph, as well as a shepherd and at least one angel, all hovering around a manger with a lifelike doll representing the baby Jesus. A donkey and sheep were caged in the makeshift stable, the donkey braying loudly enough to be heard over the chorus.

Johnson rolled down her window. "I love this," she said. "So Americana." The final strains of "God Rest Ye Merry Gentlemen" seeped inside.

"It kind of puts me in the mood."

"More than trying to solve a gruesome murder?"

"Yeah, but just a bit more."

He was able to jockey around the knot of vehicles trying to go in and out of the strip mall's lot when the beginning notes of "Silent Night" slipped into the interior. Johnson rolled up the window as he picked up speed. Thomas was still thinking about Edmund Tate's last words. Was the guy so out of it, so near death, he didn't know what he was saying? His last spoken thoughts hadn't been "Call my wife" or "Tell my family goodbye." No, according to the EMTs, Edmund Tate's final breath came out as "Simplify."

What the hell did that mean?

"This is the last time," Brittlynn swore, thinking of how many other times Chad Atwater had walked out on her. "No more. This is the end."

She really hadn't believed that he'd leave her, but she'd watched and listened and thought he'd change his mind. But oh, no. Instead, he'd started the old pickup, the engine grinding like it always did before catching, then torn down the driveway, kicking up snow from the big tires.

"Bastard," she'd said. "Dick-wad!" And it was her damned truck. Registered in her name, she'd thought, as she'd observed the taillights, winking red through the trees before disappearing altogether.

So, she was done. *Really* done.

Now she carried the last of Chad's things, his stupid snowboard that he never used, his favorite Oregon Ducks sweatshirt and his precious cell phone that he'd probably left on purpose. It was going to die, too.

Outside the back door, she tromped over a well-worn path in the snow to the fire pit. It was already overflowing with his things—clothes, golf clubs, fishing gear and even his high school yearbook and letterman's jacket. Then she soaked the entire mass in lighter fluid she'd found in the garage before tossing in his precious trophy for playing on some big-deal football team. He was all-state or something. She should remember because he always bragged about it. Get a few drinks in him and it was back to the glory days of BumbleFuck High all over again.

But it was the last time she'd ever hear the time-worn story about that final touchdown. She was through with Chad Fucking Atwater and had already called an attorney, a number she'd gotten from a friend who had already been through two divorces and looked like she was heading for number three. But Brittlynn was going to beat her to the punch and file immediately. She and Chad were history!

When the prick came back, she thought, pouring the last of the lighter fluid on the plush green alligator he'd actually won for her playing a game of ring toss at the state fair about a billion years ago, he'd get one helluva surprise.

If he came back.

There was always the chance that this time he was walking out for good.

"Fine," she said as fat snowflakes began to fall from the heavens. "Just fucking fine." Then she threw the empty bottle of lighter fluid onto the ever-growing pile of all of Chad's things. Using his favorite lighter, an engraved silver thing he'd inherited from his dad, she lit a cigarette, one she'd found from a forgotten pack in his fishing vest. She'd smoked her last one fifteen years ago, at Chad's insistence, but now, she thought, taking a deep drag, she might just take the habit up again. She was a free woman, could do what she wanted for the first time in her shitty adult life.

Cigarette clamped between her teeth, she rolled

a final page of yellowed newspaper, then lit the paper with the tip of the Marlboro and watched as the paper caught quickly, flames rising as the obituary section of the *Whimstick Times* blackened and curled. She dropped the flaming torch onto the pile of his crap that was half as tall as she was. It landed right on the hand-knit sweater his grandmother had given him the Christmas before she died. "Sorry, Granny," Brittlynn said, though she wasn't. Not one bit.

With a whoosh, the lighter fluid caught on the sweater, and flames, small at first, raced around the path of the fuel circling the pyre.

"Perfect," Brittlynn whispered as more newspaper and pieces of dry kindling that she'd scattered throughout Chad's precious possessions caught and crackled, thick smoke rising.

Jasper had wandered outside through the open door of the kitchen. He was tentatively walking through the snow, shaking a paw with each step.

Brittlynn scooped the tabby into her arms and whispered, "Don't worry. We still have each other." Stroking Jasper's back, she stared at the fire with fascination, her smile growing, the heat of the flames warm on her face, melting the snowflakes that were beginning to fall. Within minutes the conflagration grew, rising higher and higher, crackling and shifting in the wind of the coming storm.

Brittlynn stepped back as the fire burned

bright, reflecting on the windows of the cabin. She flicked the half-smoked Marlboro onto the burning mass and thought that she would never again have to watch Chad bite his fingernails and spit the bits onto the floor, nor would she have to put up with his farts and burps, both of which he seemed so proud of. Nor would she ever be disgusted that he could devour a plate of pancakes soaked in maple syrup and look for more before she'd even taken her first bite. And that annoying habit of his of dropping his underwear wherever he wanted or walking into the house with muddy boots. It wasn't ever going to happen again.

He was a pig, she thought, petting Jasper's fur as she stared at the conflagration. "No more," she said. This cabin was hers—kinda. They rented it from her uncle and he'd promised to leave it to her when he died, so Chad had no claim to it. No claim to her.

With an effort she yanked her rings from her finger. Platinum gold on the band, a minuscule diamond on the engagement ring. She hurled both into the burning heap while still holding the cat and watched as black smoke curled skyward, past the tops of the snow-covered old growth firs surrounding the cabin.

Twenty years! Twenty damned years of her life! Wasted! She should never have lied in the first place. One mistake at fourteen, when she was a damned minor just six months out of braces, and the whole course of her life had been changed forever.

What an idiot she'd been! Flattered by an older guy who already had a smokin'-hot girlfriend. A rich girl who had everything Brittlynn would never have, including Chad. But she couldn't just blame her fourteen-year-old self because she'd waited for him, lied for him, felt like she would die for him.

She'd been too young to know what a loser he was.

"Merry Christmas, you fucker, wherever you are!"

At that moment, Jasper stiffened, every muscle tensing. He was peering over her shoulder and began hissing, needle-sharp teeth exposed, ears flattened to his head.

"What—?"

Then he dug in.

Claws slicing into her jacket as he coiled, then leapt to scramble under the house.

Her heart sank. She knew what had happened before she looked over her shoulder: Chad was back. Well, fuck it. She didn't care. He could go straight to hell.

But she was wrong.

She froze.

It wasn't Chad.

Two people were standing between her and the house. A man and a woman in heavy coats and hats. Before the man held up his badge, she'd realized they were cops.

Crap!

She nearly peed herself.

"Mrs. Atwater," the woman said. "We're Detective Cole Thomas and Detective Aramis Johnson and we'd like to ask you some questions."

Damn it all to hell! Wouldn't you know. Brittlynn stiffened her spine as she turned to face them and, she supposed, the music. Son of a bitch! "About?" she asked more calmly than she felt.

"The McIntyre Massacre and your husband," the man said. He was tall and somber, his eyes hawkish and cold. The woman had darker skin and eyes that looked black as coal. Her expression, too, was serious, dead serious. "We'd like to speak with Chad."

"He's not here," Brittlynn blurted out, hoping they would just go away. "He took off this morning." She forced out the words through clenched teeth. "He left."

"Do you know where he went?" The woman with a velvet-soft voice and hard-as-nails expression.

"Nope, he didn't say. Drove off before dawn."

"Why?"

"Don't know."

"Did you have a fight?"

"I'm sorry, is this any of your business?" Brittlynn said, bristling. "I don't think so."

The man took a step forward. "It is our business. We're investigating a homicide."

"What? Homicide?" All the air in Brittlynn's lungs froze. *Homicide? Oh, shit.* "And you think Chad is involved?"

"That's why we'd like to talk to him."

"Well, you're too late. He's gone." The tall cop—what was his name? Cole or something? He looked at the fire and his frown grew darker. Oh, crap, he probably thought she was destroying evidence or something. She could be in trouble. Big trouble. They were investigating a murder, for God's sake. Brittlynn's stomach twisted and despite the freezing temperatures, she began to sweat.

"Are those Chad's things?" he asked.

Oh, God, she'd fucked up. "Some of them."

The woman cop opened up her phone, and scrolled through several screens, probably checking to see if Brittlynn should be arrested. Brittlynn swallowed against a desert-dry throat.

"He has a cell phone?"

Brittlynn nodded and felt as if a noose had been strung around her neck. "He . . . he did. But he left it." She let her eyes slide to the fire, where Chad's possessions were charred and burning, cell phone included. "It's there—" She hitched her chin to the burning mass.

The detectives shared a look and the woman turned away, punched in a number on her cellphone, and spoke softly to whoever was on the other end of the connection. That didn't look good. Not at all.

Suddenly desperate and thinking fast, Brittlynn said, "If there are any of those laws that Chad told me about that, like, I can't testify against my husband or whatever, then it's not a problem cuz I'm getting a divorce."

"That's not an issue," the tall man assured her.

"Okay," she said, sizing up the situation. The cops didn't look stupid, and the man—Cole or Thomas or whoever—was studying the fire, his eyes focused on the contents going up in flames. Oh, God, they probably thought she was involved in some way no matter what she told them. Crap! She had to remind herself these people weren't her friends. She couldn't trust them. As the woman slid her phone into her pocket, Brittlynn began to panic. She could be arrested. Right? Swallowing hard, she forced herself to stay cool, despite the sudden jackhammering of her heart. She'd seen enough episodes of *Law & Order* to know her rights. "Okay, I'll answer your questions, but I want an attorney."

She was not going to jail for anything Chad had done. Nowhere in those hastily written wedding vows had she ever stated, *I promise to love you, to respect you and oh, by the way, I promise to lie for you, to take the fall for you, to go to damned prison for you.* Nu-uh, that was *not* happening.

"No problem," the man said, though the woman's lips pursed almost imperceptibly.

"And," Brittlynn added, pressing her advantage, "I want a deal. Okay? And make sure it's a good deal. For what I'm going to tell you? It better be damned good."

CHAPTER 30

"I think," Kara said, hating the admission as she stared out the window of Tate's condominium, watching the river winding upon itself at the point, then flowing past the town, "I want to go back to the cabin." Her blood rushed in her ears as images of that horrid night spiraled through her brain and the knot in her gut twisted almost painfully.

Tate looked up from his notes. He was sitting at his desk, the dog at his feet, the TV turned to some twenty-four-hour news channel. They'd spent most of the day discussing the past and present, how it all tied together. She'd gone over the police interview and they'd talked about Merritt Margrove's death, Jonas's release from prison, Marlie's existence and how it was all connected. With only a break for sandwiches and to walk the dog, she'd finally come to the conclusion that she would never have all the answers she needed, never have a chance to fill the holes in her memory or be able to put the past to rest until she faced it head on. She'd decided to trust Tate, to confide in him.

"I thought you wanted to avoid that place," he said.

"I do. I mean, I did. But maybe twenty years is

long enough." She offered him a frail smile. She knew she couldn't just stay here forever, hiding out at Tate's place with the dog, feeling safe, but pretending that it—the horror of the past—didn't exist. She glanced back through the window again, away from the river to the town stretched upon its shores and the people on the street, hurrying through the snow, huddled against the weather, bundled in jackets and coats while cars eased past the building to stop at the cross street, headlights and taillights. All the people out there living their lives, not caged by their own paranoia.

Even as she watched the people she scanned the area, looking, searching for whoever it was she felt was always watching her. It had to end.

"I think it's time," she said, feeling the urge to pour herself a drink, or two . . . or seven. She turned back to him and fought the need. "But I definitely can't do it on my own."

"Of course not."

"Good." She let out her breath. She had to trust him. She needed an ally. Even though she knew he planned to write the definitive book on the case, she decided to go for it. Someone would. So why not Wesley Tate, the boy she'd met way back when, the kid who'd lost his father because of her, the man she found attractive? He had a sense of humor as dark as her own, and he would go to great lengths to get to the truth. Whereas she'd hidden from the past, kept to herself as much as possible, tried to deny that she was the survivor of a horrific tragedy that had scarred her forever, he'd run at the past head on. If not embracing the pain and horror, he'd been determined to fight back, to dig up the truth, to escape from the shackles of their shared experience.

It was time, she thought, to deal with it. Even though just thinking about returning to that house caused her stomach to knot. She ignored it. Circumstances were forcing her to challenge the past; she just had to find the courage to outrun her paranoia.

What, Kara? No, no, no! You can't step through that door again.

"I've been avoiding it for too long," she admitted, refusing to pay attention to the coiling inside her, choosing not to listen to that horrid voice in her head and unwilling to fall victim to its venomous fear again. "Maybe if I go there—we go there—something will jog my memory, or those blank spaces will be filled."

Are you out of your mind?

That place—it's evil.

It's where Mama and Daddy were murdered.

All that blood. Do you remember? All the blood?

And the dead bodies and the toppled Christmas tree and the music—the damned music!

Her skin crawled and she thought she might be sick.

No, Kara, don't do this. You will regret it.

"Or," she said, tamping down the urge to throw up as the taste of bile burned the back of her throat. She gritted her teeth and forced a tremulous smile against her growing sense of panic. "Or there's a chance, a pretty good chance, that I'll lose it completely, you know, have a complete panic attack and psychological breakdown." She swallowed with difficulty, fought the fear crawling through her. "What d'ya say? You game?"

"Always," he said, a slow, thin smile appearing as he crossed the room and, once more, touched her shoulder. "You know me, McIntyre. I'm always game for a complete meltdown."

"So we have a deal," the lawyer said from across the table in the sheriff's department interview room. Seated next to Brittlynn Atwater, Robert Cooke adjusted his reading glasses. A thin man with pinched features, brown hair that waved away from his face, he wore an expensive suit and a no-nonsense attitude as he set his phone, ready to record, on the table, next to the department's recording device. Cameras were already videotaping as well.

"That's right." Thomas nodded, waiting, not completely believing that what Chad's wife was going to tell them was the truth.

"Let's get this over with." Brittlynn was

nervous, her skin pale. She'd changed into black slacks and a white sweater, her makeup light, her red hair scraped into a loose bun, her attitude a little less thorny than it had been earlier. And she was chewing gum as if her life depended on it.

It had taken hours to hammer out the plea deal, but the DA had agreed that if Brittlynn Atwater gave her revised statement, the charges that she might have faced as a juvenile of fourteen would all but disappear. Community service was still on the table due to the severity of the crimes, but all in all, Brittlynn would skate.

"Why do you think Chad left? Did he say? Did it have anything to do with Merritt Margrove's death?"

"No." She shook her head. "I mean not directly. And just to be clear: Chad was with me on the night the lawyer was killed. All night. I know. I got up to pee around two thirty and he was still asleep, had crashed around eleven after a long day of ski lessons for kids who are out of school for the holidays. He had nothing to do with it. But he was on edge, y'know, because Jonas was out and once Margrove was killed, Chad couldn't keep it together."

"Why?" Johnson asked.

"Because of what happened. Twenty years ago." She swallowed. "The massacre."

Thomas watched her closely. "What about it?"

"I wasn't there," Brittlynn said. "You know that, right?"

"We do. Tell us what you do know," Johnson suggested, pushing the microphone a little closer to the redhead.

"I was at home, like I said, but Chad had gone there." She looked pained to admit the truth and she fidgeted anxiously. Chewed ferociously. "They had it all figured out, he and Marlie. They were going to leave together, I guess." She shrugged as if it didn't matter to her, but Thomas thought from her sour expression that it mattered, it mattered a lot. "The idea was to run off and, you know, be together, I guess or whatever. I'm not sure. Anyway, Marlie's mom and stepdad didn't like Chad. Of course he wasn't 'good enough.'" She made air quotes with her fingers. "They wouldn't let him come to family functions and that sort of thing and so . . . anyway, they came up with this plan that he would come and get her, and they would take off together. And . . . and I'm not sure if Marlie knew it or not, but Chad intended on ripping the old man off. Marlie had told him where Samuel—the older one, the father, not Sam Junior—kept a stash of cash."

She paused, as if she was thinking how to phrase the next part, rolling the gum from one side of her mouth to the other. "He, um, he got there and waited, but no one was going to sleep. It was cold and he snuck in, went into the back hallway . . . I guess there was this broom closet or something and it had a false wall or secret compartment or something. It was supposed to be where the old man, Sam Senior, kept extra cash when they were at the mountain. Marlie knew about it somehow. Anyway, Chad had some trouble finding the secret spot, and when he did, or what he thought was it, the cubby was empty. No cash. Zero. Either Marlie had lied to him, Sam Senior got wise, or someone beat him to the punch."

She looked from one detective to the next and said, "Chad was pissed and about to leave when he heard shouting. Screaming. Angry threats. He peeked around the corner into the living room and saw Jonas with a sword. Swinging it wildly, like a crazy person. Jonas knocked over the Christmas tree and, like, hit the mantel over the fireplace. Chad said Jonas was out of his mind. Completely out of it, but he wasn't alone in the room. Donner was there, too, and Jonas kept slashing at him, cornering him somehow.

"Chad was freaked. He said it looked like Jonas was possessed by the devil. All Chad wanted to do was get the hell out of there." She paused, even stopped chewing for a second, then said, "I guess, I guess, Jonas said something like, 'I told you to stay away from her, you fucker! I told you what was gonna happen, that I was gonna fuckin' kill you!' "

So they'd gotten it right, Thomas thought. The police had arrested the killer and the jury had convicted him. Thomas felt a sense of relief that all the doubts about Jonas McIntyre being railroaded and unjustly convicted were about to be proved false. Finally. And, thankfully, at least the prick had spent twenty years behind bars. That was something.

"What happened next?" Thomas asked, trying not to sound too eager.

"He swung the fuckin' sword and sliced Donner." Brittlynn closed her eyes. Shuddered.

"Just like that?" Johnson said, her brow knitting.

"Yeah, but, um, Chad couldn't hold his shit together. He made a noise, like caught his breath or something and Jonas heard him, stared at the spot where Chad was hiding and saw him. Even though Chad had worn gloves, he wasn't wearing a mask."

"And, at this point, Donner was still alive?" Johnson asked, to clarify.

"I don't know. I don't think that Chad knew for sure, because Donner was down on the floor and bleeding." She was chewing the gum hard again. "So yeah, he killed him. I just told you."

With what seemed forced patience, Johnson asked, "Was Donner Robinson bleeding from the neck? Did Jonas slit his throat?"

"I-I don't know. *I* wasn't there. Remember. *I*

didn't see what happened. Chad never said. Only that then all hell broke loose.

"Jonas started moving toward Chad just as Sam Junior ran down the stairs, probably heard the commotion, the screaming and falling and whatever. That's when Chad took off. He was sure Jonas would come after him. Kill him for being a witness or something. Chad didn't wait for Marlie and said he even thought he saw her on the landing above, coming down the stairs, too, but he just ran. As fast as he could." She paused. Took a breath. Then added, "I, um, I, um, think Marlie might have followed him."

"Marlie?" Thomas said, feeling a jolt of adrenaline, a sensation that this, at least in part, was the truth.

"And Chad just left her?" Johnson frowned, not completely buying it. "When Jonas was 'out of his mind' or 'possessed by the devil,' and they'd had this elaborate plan to elope and—"

"Not elope. I didn't say elope," Brittlynn insisted.

So that was a sticking point with her.

"It wasn't like he was leaving her," Brittlynn said, but didn't sound convinced. "He told me that he'd parked about a mile away from the house, you know, on the other side of a couple of cabins to kind of hide the car. It was Christmas Eve and people in some of the places were still up, so he had to slow down and be careful. He didn't want to be seen."

Johnson said, "But he wasn't waiting for his girlfriend."

"I don't know! The point is that he was avoiding people and dogs and whoever was up, so he had to slow down, had to wait so that he wouldn't be seen, and because of it, he lost time, a lot of time, he said."

"How much time?"

"I don't know. I didn't ask," she said. "But the thing is, he saw Marlie, he saw her being chased."

"Wait," Johnson cut in. "You mean Kara, the eight-year-old."

"No, that's just it, he saw Marlie."

Thomas said, "And he didn't try to interfere?"

"He was scared out of his mind."

Johnson held up a hand. "So you're saying that Chad saw Marlie being chased by Edmund Tate?"

"No! He couldn't see who it was, he was all dressed in black and had like a mask on, I guess. Cuz I asked. Chad said he knew it wasn't Edmund Tate, the cop, because Chad saw him on his porch. Someone else was chasing Marlie."

"Who?" Thomas asked.

"I told you he couldn't see. Too many trees, but he saw the guy on the porch smoking, because there was light from the inside of the Tates' cabin and his cigarette tip was red."

Was this right? Thomas glanced at Johnson.

"He was sure of that?" Johnson said.

"Look, you'll have to ask him all about it, but that's what he told me."

Was she lying? Thomas asked himself. Or had Chad lied to her? Was there even a whisper of a chance that Marlie Robinson had survived? "Running in which direction?" he asked. "To the lake? Or away from it?"

"I don't know!" she said, exploding. "I'm telling you he said he saw Marlie being chased, but I don't know for sure. Again, *I* wasn't there, but you'd think he would know because he'd dated Marlie for years. They . . . they had a thing. He knew what she looked like, right? And Kara, the sister, she was a lot younger. Even in the dark, he would've seen that she was just a kid."

Thomas leaned forward. "Did Edmund Tate see Marlie being chased?"

"Jesus! I don't know," she bit out. "I'm only telling you what Chad said that night. He could have been mixed up; he was really, really upset. Out of it, kind of. You know, scared out of his mind. I've never seen him like that before or after. He could've been wrong. Like I said, you'll have to ask him."

"We will," Johnson said.

"What about the parents? Sam and Zelda McIntyre?" Thomas asked, backing up a bit, trying to piece the scene together and not get ahead of himself. This was their chance to find

480

out what really happened all those years ago. If they could locate Chad, press him further, and Brittlynn wasn't lying, who knew what they'd uncover? "When 'all hell broke loose,' " he said, "were the parents there? Awake?"

"I don't know. I don't think so. Chad never said a word about them. Nothing. Just that when he finally reached his car, I mean his truck, he drove like a bat to my house. He snuck in through my bedroom window and he was still shaking, his eyes like saucers. He swore he didn't do anything more than try to steal from the old man."

"And witness a murder."

"Yeah." She chewed her gum more slowly, paused, glanced at her attorney.

Cooke nodded grimly, encouraging her.

Brittlynn's voice was becoming a whisper. "So, Chad and I, we struck a deal."

"What kind of deal?" Johnson asked.

"I said I'd tell the cops that he was with me all night. So he wouldn't get caught for the attempted robbery, so maybe then Jonas wouldn't come after him, you know?"

Johnson asked, "And he agreed?"

"Sure. He needed me." Brittlynn almost smiled.

Johnson circled back. "And what would Chad do? What was his part of the deal if you agreed to lie for him?"

Brittlynn looked away and blushed, seeming suddenly ashamed. "I was just a kid. A girl who was in love, you know. Chad was my everything. At least he was at fourteen." They waited until she finally admitted, "He promised to marry me the minute I turned eighteen." Her gaze was level. "He had to swear he'd break up with Marlie, that he'd lie and say they weren't planning to run away and that he wasn't even near that mansion, that she dreamed up the whole thing if she ever testified or was questioned by the cops or whatever. That . . . that she was obsessed with him when he was in love with me."

"When you were the one who was obsessed." Johnson leaned back in her chair.

"He loved me!" Brittlynn hooked a thumb at her chest. "*Me*. Not her." She blinked and a single tear slid down her cheek. Sniffing, she slapped it away with the sleeve of her sweater.

"Weren't you curious as to what happened to her?" Johnson asked, shoving a tissue box toward Brittlynn.

"Sure. Everyone was. For God's sake, it was, like, a national obsession." She angled her chin upward, though her eyes were still bright with unshed tears. Her hands were shaking. "To me, it didn't matter what happened to her. At least not then. All that I cared about was that I had Chad." Her voice faltered a bit. "I won."

Thomas watched Brittlynn's reaction. "Do you believe Chad's story?"

"Yes!" She sniffed again. Ignored the proffered

box of Kleenex. "Oh, yeah. He didn't, like, have any blood on him, and I figured when I read about that massacre that if he'd been anywhere near any of the victims, there would have been blood. Tons of it. And he was scared, like batshit scared. Freaked out beyond freaked out. But not like scared because he thought he was going to be caught for killing an entire family. No, like scared because of what he'd seen. He never liked Jonas, told me that he was 'whacked,' that's the word he used, and from that night forward he wanted nothing to do with the McIntyre family. Nothing."

"So he saw Jonas McIntyre kill Donner Robinson?" Thomas wanted to be certain and the attorney finally broke in.

"She just told you what she knows," Cooke said.

But Brittlynn said, "No . . . I mean, I guess. I think so. What Chad saw was that Jonas attacked Donner—cut him. Bad, I think . . ." She paused. "But I don't know. He could've been still alive or bleeding out or . . . well, shit, I don't know. I'm not sure Chad does. He didn't stick around long enough to find out."

"Someone slit Donner Robinson's throat, ear to ear," Johnson said, leaning forward. "That would take some doing."

Brittlynn glared at her. "I'm just telling you what Chad told me!" She turned to her attorney. "I don't know anything else."

483

Thomas held up a hand, trying to calm her, and silently warn Johnson to back off. They needed all the information they could get from Brittlynn and agitating her wouldn't help. "Did Chad see Jonas kill anyone else or attack anyone else?"

"No, no. I asked him." Brittlynn was shaking her head, her red hair threatening to escape from the band holding the bun in place. "He just saw what I told you, that Jonas attacked Donner, that he swung the sword and cut him, but that's all he saw. Well, at least all he ever told me. And after that first night, whenever I brought it up, he'd shut down. Refused to talk about it. Get mad. He just wanted to pretend it didn't happen."

"So you lied for him?" Johnson clarified.

"Yes." The word was a whisper.

Again, Johnson asked, "And he lied to the police about not being at the cabin?"

"I just told you! Yes!" Brittlynn exploded, angry now, her voice rising. She spat the gum into a tissue she fished from the box. "We both lied, okay? That's why I'm here." She wadded the gum in the thin paper and tossed it into a nearby basket. Then she added, "Just so you know. Agreeing to lie for him just so I could have him and Marlie couldn't was the worst mistake of my life. The worst!" She threw the attorney another glance. They were losing her.

Thomas asked quickly, "What about Marlie Robinson?"

"What about her?" Brittlynn spat back. "I already told you everything I know!"

"Do you know what happened to her?" Johnson asked, as Brittlynn squirmed in her chair. "Does Chad?"

"Jesus, no," she said angrily. "He never said anything else but that he saw her on the stairs that night. And then running. And, believe me, I asked him about her. Just about every time we fought."

"Why?" Johnson asked. "Was he still in love with her?"

"No! God, no!" Brittlynn spat vehemently and her lips pulled into a knot of consternation. "Are we done here?" She glanced at the lawyer. "I don't have anything else to say. I think we're done." And she scooted back her chair so fast its legs scraped loudly against the floor.

Cooke agreed. "I think you've got all you need."

"One more thing," Thomas said. "Do you have any idea where Chad is?"

On her feet, she shook her head. "No. I mean, he kept saying something about we should leave and visit his cousin in Montana. Kind of random, because he never talked about this guy. Not ever. But about a week ago, Chad was like, 'Hey, let's go visit Wilson.' Or, 'You would really like Montana, Britt, we should visit Wilson.' Or, he even said once, 'I think we should go hang out with Wilson, maybe for a month or so. Get away.' And I'm like, 'Uh, no. We have jobs.' And besides, he'd never once in all the time I was with him wanted to visit Wilson. The guy was a jerk. Used to beat up on Chad as a kid, but out of the blue, Chad has a bug up his butt about Billings, Montana."

"And the name of the cousin is Wilson?"

"Yeah, um, Wilson's his first name. Wilson Atwater."

Johnson was already picking up her iPad.

"Now, I'm leaving," Brittlynn said. "I don't know anything else."

"We might have more questions later," Thomas said.

"Well, I'm all out of answers. All out." To the lawyer, "Let's go." And she was out the door while Robert Cooke was quickly gathering his papers and tablet into a briefcase.

Thomas walked them out of the building and then found Johnson at her desk. "I've located a Wilson Atwater in Billings, Montana. I called. No answer. So I let the local authorities know. They're supposed to call me back."

"So you believe Brittlynn's story?"

Johnson sighed. "It's been twenty years, a lot of time for memories to blur and mingle with emotions. I think there's a lot of truth in her story, but she could have twisted it in her mind to satisfy whatever psychological needs she had.

For God's sake, she was fourteen. Fourteen— think what you were like at that age? I was a head case. Didn't know up from sideways but thought I knew it all. And her story is colored by how she perceived it. But yeah, I think she believes she's telling the truth, but who knows? Once we run down Chad Atwater, we might get somewhere." She sat in her chair. "Then again, we may be back to square one."

Jonas clutched the knife as he trudged through the snow.

He liked the heft of it, the way his fingers felt as they grasped the blade's handle.

It all felt so right.

Gave him so much power, so much protection.

To grip a weapon again.

He'd ditched Mia's rattletrap of a car half a mile away, hidden at a mountain cabin that seemed abandoned. It would do. For now. He wouldn't need to hide it for long.

Be cool, an inner voice warned. *Don't do anything rash. You don't want to go back to Banhoff!*

Twenty years of being locked up was enough, he reminded himself as he trudged, breaking a path in the snow. Ducking under low-hanging branches of the firs and cedars, he felt the cold slap of the wind against his face. It ruffled his hair, freezing the tops of his ears.

It felt good.

It felt like freedom.

And he didn't want to lose that.

Even the ache in his ribs was worth it.

He stopped long enough to send up a quick prayer. He had turned to God at Banhoff. The chaplain had convinced him to look inside himself and find the good, give himself up to the Lord, and he had. He believed. He really did. He also knew that he was put on this earth by God to do what was right. His fans, they'd eaten that up, so he'd played to it.

What he hadn't admitted was that sometimes he needed to be an avenging angel. To right old wrongs.

And so he plowed on, through the snow, numb to the cold, on angel wings.

He had unfinished business.

And he planned on taking care of it.

Tonight.

CHAPTER 31

In her office in her home in the West Hills, Faiza skimmed the posts on Jonas's Facebook fan page, found nothing of interest and clicked off. She wondered where that freak was. Samuel's son. Not her sister Zelda's boy. A bad seed. Any way you looked at it. Out of prison and no doubt hell-bent on causing trouble, horrible trouble. No matter what his stupid fans thought. They all seemed to think he was some kind of messiah.

Instead of Satan Incarnate.

And what about Roger, hmmm? Do you think he's so pure?

She could almost hear Zelda's voice telling her to break up with him. "He's a loser, Faiza. Has he ever had a real job? Huh? And wasn't he in prison? You could do so much better. Look at me. I went from Walter to Samuel. Because I wasn't afraid to walk away. Leave him, Faiza. I don't care how much you think you love Roger, he's nothing more than a do-nothing. A leech! Useless!"

But that wasn't true.

Picking her phone up off the desk, she hit the speed dial for Roger and rolled her desk chair back.

Voice mail.

Great. Where the hell is he?

Irritated, she rolled her neck, loosening her tight muscles, thinking she needed a massage. Oh, hell, she needed more than a hot stone massage, she needed a full spa treatment. Irritated, she walked into the kitchen and pushed the speed dial button again.

Once more she was rewarded with a click and Roger's recorded voice.

"Pick up, pick up!" she said, phone to her ear as she stared through the window to the backyard, where the landscape lights were buried, their bulbs glowing beneath two inches of snow. This should be a time of peace. Of serenity. Not the high-octane anxiety that had its grip on her.

Setting her jaw, she texted again:

Call Me.

For the sixth damned time tonight.

She tossed the phone onto the counter and it skidded across the polished marble to bounce off the matching backsplash. She barely noticed as she went back to studying the backyard, where the swimming pool's cover now bore a thick white mantle. Not good. The maintenance on this place was ever increasing and the taxes were always a worry. And what would happen next week, when she couldn't dip into Kara's trust? Where would she be? Where would Roger?

"Ingrate," she muttered, thinking of him now as she retrieved her phone.

She dialed Roger once more.

For the kazillionth time her call went to voice mail, and she dialed again. "Don't you ignore me," she said, phone pressed to her ear as she walked into the den, opened a window, letting in the cold December air and clearing the room of the lingering, ever-present odor of marijuana. God, she hated it. But as many times as she'd bought edibles for Roger, he still preferred to smoke. To her, it didn't matter, but to him it just wasn't the same.

Of course her call went straight to voice mail.

So angry she nearly threw her phone across the room, she stormed into the living room, where the Christmas tree was decorated, ornaments glittering in the soft glow of the tiny lights she'd so carefully strung over the preflocked branches. The room was lit by candles, the scents of pine and mulled wine filling the perfect room with its snow-white carpet covering polished oak floors; a new pale-gray couch offsetting the creamy side chairs and stone fireplace that rose to the height of the soaring ceiling high overhead. A grand piano was tucked into a corner where paned windows sparkled, reflecting the candlelight.

Picture-perfect, she told herself.

She loved it soooo much.

And soon it was going to slip through her fingers.

That's why Roger had left.

Because once more she'd complained about losing it all. He'd been on his favorite old couch in his music room, looked up from his guitar, as he'd been still working on that horrible song, and said in a puff of marijuana smoke, "So deal with it."

"I can't," she'd told him. "It's beyond my control. Kara is turning twenty-eight next week and it doesn't matter that Merritt Margrove is dead. Another attorney will be assigned and they'll start looking through the records and they'll figure out what I've been, we've been doing."

"Which is?" he'd asked so blithely she'd wanted to strangle him with his own guitar strings.

"Which is that there's no money! None left. You know that. Margrove knew it, too, but he was willing to keep his mouth shut because he'd dipped in as well. His bills were outlandish. I showed them to you. He'd padded them to the point of the absurd, all to make up for bad investments and his damned gambling issues."

"There's still the property," Roger said, setting aside his guitar.

"Do you want to move?"

"Calm down, Faiza," he'd suggested in that slightly patronizing, I'm-the-man-rational-and-calm voice, as if she were the screeching out-of-control woman. Ironic somehow, when she was the one who provided everything, every damned thing for them. "I'm talking about the place on the mountain," he explained in his condescending tone. "It's got to be worth a small fortune. Maybe a large fortune."

"It's a damned white elephant. And Margrove borrowed against it. I don't think we're underwater on it, not yet, but no one wants it. No one!" She'd let it all out then. "Don't you get it, Roger? Everything we've worked for all these years. All this"—she made a wide, sweeping gesture with her arms to indicate the house and grounds and their entire lifestyle—"it'll be gone like that!" She'd snapped her fingers. "And worse yet? Now that little shit Jonas is out, and he's going to want his cut."

"So to speak."

"That's not funny, Roger. Get serious. We are going to lose everything. And please, please don't patronize me, okay? Don't tell me that 'I'll handle it,' because I can't. Not this time. And with that psycho Jonas out of jail, things are going to get bad, Roger. Very, very bad."

He frowned then and she'd expected him to turn to his bong. Instead, he'd stood, left his guitar on the couch and in a surprise move muttered, "Well, if you won't handle it, I will."

"What's that supposed to mean?" she'd asked, suddenly worried.

His smile had twisted and his eyes had glinted

in a way that disturbed her, in a manner she hadn't seen in a long, long while. "Don't ask and I won't tell. The less you know, the better off we both are."

Her insides had grown cold. "What, Roger? What are you planning?"

"Shhh." He'd placed a rough finger to her lips.

"Roger . . ."

"I'll be back." He'd turned to leave and offered her a sly, knowing smile. "It's something I've been wanting to do for a long time."

"Don't!" she'd cried, suddenly worried.

He'd shrugged into his leather jacket and looked at her over his shoulder. "Don't what?"

She'd been about to say, "Don't hurt anyone," but her words had come out as, "Don't do anything stupid."

And so now, hours later, she waited, wondering where he was, what he was doing, and worrying and praying that he'd found a way to keep things the way they'd been for twenty years, the way they were supposed to be. And she hoped to high heaven that he hadn't been forced to resort to violence.

But with Roger, she never really knew.

Chad hadn't gotten far.

Fifty miles east of Whimstick, the goddamned battery on the old truck had finally given out. He'd made the mistake of stopping for gas and a Hot Pocket at a convenience store and when he'd climbed back into the truck, the old Dodge hadn't been able to start, the familiar grinding slowing to a defeated *click, click, click* whenever he twisted on the ignition.

He'd wasted hours calling for service, waiting for help, then being delayed again as the battery he needed wasn't in stock and they'd had to send someone to Bend for one that would actually work. He'd ended up wasting most of the day, drinking beer at the one bar in town and eventually shelling out way too much for a new goddamned battery. By the time he'd hit the road again it had been late afternoon.

So now he was here, parked on a forgotten spur of an old logging road that was rarely traveled, not twenty-five miles from where he'd started, drinking from a pint of rotgut whiskey he'd picked up while waiting for the truck to be fixed.

It was a setback, one he hadn't counted on, but he'd deal with it.

He took another swig, then wiped his lips with the back of his sleeve. One part of his plan had worked. When he'd left early this morning, he'd headed east. He'd intended to leave some evidence in his wake, a clue to fool the cops into thinking he was heading to Idaho or Montana and buy himself more time. In reality, he'd planned to double back. That had been accomplished. Enough people in the small town—little more than a dot on the map—had seen him, and he'd made it known that he was traveling toward Billings, where he had a cousin. He might have overplayed his hand a bit because if he were really driving to the middle of Montana, wouldn't he have kept it to himself? Maybe. But the cops would take the bait; he was pretty sure. And he'd called his cousin yesterday, told him he'd be passing through, and he'd always explained to Brittlynn that if they had to leave quickly, they'd make their way to Billings and the airport there.

He thought—well, he hoped—that he'd covered all his bases.

The deal was that he had always intended to turn around and cut north through Washington and drive into Canada. Which he would do tomorrow, leaving again long before dawn and finding a car parked on the street in some tiny town and steal its license plate. He'd probably have to ditch the car and cross into Canada by bus or something, but he'd figure that out tomorrow.

He still had time.

As much as it bothered him, Chad considered the sorry fact that Britt might turn him in.

Man, she'd be pissed when he didn't show up tonight.

But Brittlynn was a smart girl, always interested in saving her own skin, so he figured he was safe, at least for a day or two. She'd expect him to return, tail between his legs, apologize and they would have wild, heart-stopping sex for a while before everything turned to shit again.

He'd always returned in the past whenever they'd had one of their blowout fights and he'd taken off.

She'd be banking on him coming back.

So it gave him time before she called the cops—if she'd actually go that far. Besides, she'd lied and she'd have to own up to that, risk prison time herself, and he didn't think she would make that mistake. At least he hoped not.

Another long swallow and he found the whiskey wasn't burning as it went down, in fact it warmed his belly and gave him a soft, fuzzy feeling. A good feeling.

He'd be okay.

He just needed a little shut-eye.

Night was already falling, the forest around him growing dark. He'd sleep, maybe two or three hours, then he'd be on the road again, making up time. Heading to freedom. From his job. From the past. From always looking over his shoulder. And yeah, if he were honest with himself, from Britt. She was becoming a stone-cold bitch, forever on his case.

Another long pull on the bottle and he noticed the pint was half empty. Shit. He'd better not risk any more as he had to wake in a couple of hours and be sober enough to get on the road. He couldn't afford a DUI at this point. Reluctantly, he screwed on the cap and set the bottle on the passenger seat, then he reclined his seat as far as it would go, pulled the old sleeping bag to his chin and watched as the snowflakes collected on the windshield.

He slipped his hand into the pocket of his jacket and felt the small pistol before closing his eyes and promising himself that he'd wake up long before dawn broke. He had to.

Within minutes he nodded off.

He didn't hear the attacker approach on silent footsteps.

Didn't sense someone stalking him.

Didn't hear the slight click as the magnetic tracking device was removed from the under-carriage.

Caught in a dream where he was having incredible mind-numbing sex with Marlie Robinson, he didn't hear the sound of the truck's door lock click. Marlie was just so damned hot and—

The driver's door opened quickly.

Cold air and snow blew inside.

What the fuck!!!!

Chad's eyes flew open.

NO!

An arm snaked around the back of his neck. His head was pulled back. A blade at his throat.

He started to scream, but it was too late. No one was around to hear him.

Panicking, he bucked.

498

Struggled wildly to get away.

Too late. His attacker too strong.

Just as his fingers found the trigger, the razor-sharp blade sliced through his throat, tearing easily through skin, flesh and cartilage.

Sssst!

For a split second Chad saw the spray of blood on the inside of the windshield, spattering and dripping red against the white layer covering the glass.

CHAPTER 32

"Remember when I told you our bird has flown?" Johnson said as she stepped into Thomas's office.

"Yeah?" He glanced up at her and saw the irritation in her expression. "What?" It was late afternoon, the offices beginning to empty out, the noises of the shift change, people talking, footsteps walking swiftly filtered in through the hallway.

"Well, it gets worse," Johnson said. "He's not just flown, but flown the damned coop. I just got off the phone with the hospital in Portland where he was to be taken. Never arrived." She rounded Thomas's desk and stood in front of it, not bothering to sit. Her arms were crossed over her chest, and her usually smooth face was pulled into an expression of utter consternation. "The Portland PD doesn't know anything about it, nor do the state guys. I tried to phone our favorite attorney Alex Rousseau and she's not taking any calls right now. Convenient, huh?"

"So Jonas McIntyre is in the wind." Thomas shook his head. Just when they were getting somewhere.

"Seems so."

"He left with Rousseau; she knows where he is."

"And now, once again, with Brittlynn Atwater's

statement, he just promoted himself to suspect number one."

"Person of interest," he reminded her.

"My ass. And if Rousseau knows where he is?" Her dark eyes flashed. "Let's go."

"Right. But first, I want you to take a look at this," he said, motioning her to take a look at his computer monitor as a burst of laughter came from outside in the hallway. With an irritated look at the doorway—who could find humor on a day like this?—she circumvented the desk to stand behind him.

"I've seen this," she said, eyeing the screen. "It's a shot of the group that was assembled at the hospital when Jonas was inside, his ridiculous fan club or whatever. This is the one that includes the girl who looks like Marlie Robinson."

"Yeah, I know. But now look at this one." Thomas brought up another picture, a wider angle of the same assemblage, including more of the people who had attended the rally. In this shot Officer Mullins and the thin woman with overbleached hair were front and center. The Marlie Robinson look-alike was caught on one side of the picture.

"Yeah. So?" She was squinting and pointed a finger at the woman in the long coat and colored glasses. "There's our girl again."

"Yes, and over here—I think that's Kara." He indicated a group in the opposite corner where several people were exiting the hospital, and in the group was a woman with a bandage peeking out from beneath her dark hair. Her head was turned slightly, her features not caught in the camera's lens, her body hidden by other people, but in Thomas's estimation, the woman with the bandage was Kara McIntyre.

"Wow." Johnson saw it, too. "They were that close to each other."

"And over here—what do you see?" He pointed to a large man partially hidden by the trunk of a tree. All that was visible of his face was the brim of a baseball hat and the tip of his nose.

"Some dude."

"Yeah, some dude, and what is he looking at?"

Johnson leaned forward for a closer view and her lips flattened. She drew an imaginary line across the screen with her finger. Starting with the man and the tip of his nose and through the crowd to land on Marlie—or someone who sure as hell looked like her. Most everyone else's attention was turned toward the hospital doors, but this man was staring straight at the woman in the tinted glasses and long black coat.

"Recognize him?"

She shook her head. "The tree hides most of his face, as does the bill of his cap." She straightened. "But maybe there's another camera shot, from a different angle, or tape from a security camera or something from the TV stations."

"Or selfies? Pictures posted online from people who were there."

She was nodding. "I'll get right on it."

"And I'll track down Alex Rousseau. Whether she likes it or not, she's going to tell us where she's stashed her killer of a client."

"Alleged killer," Johnson said sarcastically as she was walking out of his office. "Remember that: *alleged.* Innocent until proven guilty."

"Again," Thomas muttered under his breath, and wondered how the hell he was going to get around double jeopardy and charge the bastard again. There had to be a way.

Trudging through the snow, Jonas ignored some of the lingering pain from the accident. He'd lived through worse. Beatings in the prison yard had been infrequent but had occurred, a shiv had once been thrust into his thigh, barely missing his femoral artery. He'd lived through it all, toughened up with exercise until his body was all lean muscle. Physical pain wasn't something he couldn't get through. Emotional pain, though? That was tougher, no matter how devout he tried to be. He wasn't big on the whole concept of turning the other cheek. He preferred the Old Testament ideology: "Eye for an eye, a tooth for a tooth, a hand for a hand . . ."

"Exodus 21:24," he said aloud.

And how many eyes would you lose if anyone tested that theory on you?

He decided not to go there.

He just kept moving through the evergreens with their icy needles that brushed against his face; he thought about Lacey and how she'd lied to him, cheated on him.

He thought about his own stepbrother fucking his girl.

He thought about his parents, how they'd all abandoned him, how they'd punished him.

Samuel Senior had never stood up for him, not like he did for Sam Junior, his firstborn and namesake, the perfect son who never got into any serious trouble. And Natalie? His own mother? That woman had run from him. Had herself a new family, a perfect family, one without a troubled, scandal-riddled teenager. So she'd discarded her firstborn as easy as if he were rotting trash, rarely visiting, barely acknowledging, never so much as helping him get out of that hellhole that was Banhoff Prison.

What kind of a mother was that?

Then there was Sam Junior himself, his half brother. Sam, apple of their father's eye, had never once had Jonas's back. Never once. "Fucker," Jonas growled under his breath, the night air fogging around him.

And finally, of course, there was Kara.

The basket case.

Her excuse for abandoning him had been her youth.

And she'd let their entire fortune be frittered away by Merritt Margrove and her aunt, that vitriolic sister of Zelda's. "Auntie Fai," they'd all called her, but she was a stone-cold bitch who was living in *his* house with her do-nothing musician of a boyfriend. Driving fancy cars. Going on fabulous vacations. Wearing expensive clothes and jewelry. Jonas had learned it all from Margrove, that weasel of a lawyer who was just trying to save his own skin because he, too, had been dipping his greedy fingers into the estate. All that talk about expenses—taxes, fees, maintenance, schooling . . . all horse shit.

He slipped through the gap in the fence around the old house, just as he had as a kid, then he went to the back stoop, reached under the doorframe to that small niche where he'd hidden a key all those years before. Not a key to the front door or even the back door, but a key to the lock that secured the outside door to the woodbin set into a cabinet near the fireplace. It had been his hidden escape route when he'd sneaked out as a teen. The stacked wood had always been an issue, but he'd always been able to sneak out and back in, arranging the kindling and chunks of fir back into the bin so that no one ever noticed, and he'd never been caught.

Rounding the corner of the house, he stopped

before stepping onto the porch. Straining to listen, he double-checked that no one was about. The wind was picking up, rattling branches, whispering through the trees, but he heard nothing and saw nothing indicating that anyone was nearby. And who would be?

He walked past the stone wall of the fireplace to the back side of the bin, where there was a definitive line in the siding. Using his key, he unlocked the latch and the door fell open. He slipped inside, crawling through the close, dusty space where cobwebs caught in his hair and slivers from old chunks of fir scraped his hands. Ignoring the irritation, Jonas slid onto the living room floor, just to one side of the grate, and peered around the gloomy interior.

His ribs protested, pain radiating through him, but he ignored it. He hadn't come this far, spent all those years behind bars to let a few cracked ribs stop him. He gritted his teeth, gutted it out and flipped on his flashlight, the thin bluish beam illuminating, washing over the gray stones and peeling wallpaper and dusty floor.

This is where it had all gone down.

He remembered the blood. The fear. The rush of adrenaline.

But most of all, he remembered the sword, how heavy it was. How sharp. He'd made certain of that because he'd wanted it to do as much damage as possible.

And he remembered Donner in the light from the fire, his eyes rounding in surprise as Jonas had swung, the expression of utter surprise and horror on his face when the blade had made its first deadly slice.

"Jonas! What the fuck! You're insane!" he'd yelled, jumping back toward the Christmas tree. Screaming at the top of his lungs, he'd yelled, "Stop it! Shit! Stop it! Oh, God! Noooo! Help! Help!"

But Jonas hadn't stopped and it was too late for help and that traitorous fucker had died, his blood spilling red on the carpet, him stumbling to his knees and eventually his head dropping with a heavy thud.

It should have ended there, he thought now as he crossed the room, recalling that once Donner was down, how easy it was to tangle his hand in the prick's hair, pull his head back and make the final, purposeful cut across his throat.

Now, reliving that rush, Jonas climbed the stairs to the second floor, hurried down the hallway and paused for only a second at the open doorway to his once-upon-a-lifetime-ago bedroom. As if it were yesterday, Jonas recalled practicing his martial arts moves on the stuffed eagle that had been mounted on the wall, how the head had severed in a flurry of feathers.

Smiling to himself, Jonas hurried to the door to the attic and shined his light up the narrow staircase. It had been years since he ascended these worn steps, he thought, securing the door behind him.

Once on the top floor of the house, he shined the beam of his light over this cavernous space with its high-pitched roof and exposed beams. This attic space was where he'd hidden the cash that he'd stolen from the old man's secret stash. He hardly dared believe it still existed, but this was his chance to find out.

Tate drove into the short lane leading to his family's mountain retreat. The beams of his headlights illuminated the narrow front porch and paned windows of the two-bedroom cottage where he'd spent most of his summers growing up. Built in the 1930s, it was less than a quarter mile from the McIntyre place, and as a kid, Wes had loved it here. Until the night his father had given up his life to save a frantic little girl—this girl, he thought, glancing over at Kara, huddled against the window of his SUV.

Rather than head directly to the house where she'd witnessed the aftermath of her family's slaughter, Tate had brought her here first, to test her, to see if she could handle being so near the house where she'd witnessed so much tragedy and horror. So far she was handling it, he thought, though she'd grown quieter with each passing mile as they'd driven into the mountains.

"We don't have to go inside," he said, but she shook her head.

"I want to." She was already opening the passenger door and stepping into the weather, ready to face the cold as well as the truth.

"Okay, then." And he was out of the Toyota.

Together they made their way to the porch, where he fished into his pocket for his father's set of keys and unlocked the door. She eyed the living room, a small area with the same lumpy couch, rocker and recliner that had furnished the place for as long as Tate could remember. Flipping on the lights, he noticed that one of the bulbs in the old ceiling fixture had burned out and more than a dozen dead insects were silhouetted in the glass.

"No one comes up here much," he admitted. "Mom remarried, but she never felt comfortable coming back to the spot where Dad died. My sister and her kids try to come up once a year or so, mainly to clean the place, fix stuff, but it's not the same. We all say we're going to go up to the cabin 'next summer.' But we never do."

"Why not sell?" she asked, moving toward the kitchen.

"Mom hasn't been able to, she can't quite let go," he admitted, running his fingers over a side table and seeing the dust. "And my sister and I, we don't think she should. It's like the whole family is still hanging on to this place because of Dad." His gaze skimmed over the things that had belonged to Edmund Tate—the photographs, hunting trophies, military paraphernalia—and his heart twisted. "Dad loved it up here." He felt his throat tighten a bit. "We all did."

"Until."

"Right. Until." He walked through the house, caught sight of the military shadow box in the hallway and something niggled at his brain, something he couldn't quite grasp. He stared at the nameplate dead center on the box:

EDMUND W. TATE
U.S. MARINE CORPS
SEMPER FIDELIS

"Semper fi," he said aloud.

"What?" She turned to face him. "What did you say?"

His breath stopped in his throat. "Semper fi," he repeated. As he did he felt a sizzle in his nerves, like an electrical connection, a link to twenty years ago, to the night when he'd lost his father and, for a while, lost his way. His mind spun as he stared at the shadow box.

What was it he'd overheard in the hospital when the hospital security guards in the cafeteria were talking about the last words of his father's life?

"He wasn't sure, but it sounded like, you know,

like fee or fie . . . maybe it was fee, fi, fo, fum . . . or backwards."

But that was wrong. Edmund Tate hadn't been deliriously saying "fee-fi-fo-fum" from some kid's fairy tale, but "semper fi," a phrase dear to his heart, the shortened motto of the Marine Corps, the way it was usually said aloud.

But what did it mean?

Why had his dad muttered that phrase during his dying breaths? He'd served in the marines, yes, but he was also a cop and he would be trying to tell the EMTs what he'd seen. He yanked his cell phone from his pocket and punched out Wayne Connell's number. As Connell answered, Tate said, "Can you check on anyone connected to the McIntyre Massacre who served in the military before it happened? Especially anyone in the marines."

"Sure."

"Good. I'll explain later." Then Tate clicked off and walked through the kitchen and opened the door outside to the back deck, to the spot where his father had first heard the screams from the neighboring property. Kara was standing at the rail, her gaze fastened on the lake, visible through a shifting curtain of snow. "I'm sorry," she said as she heard him approach.

"For?"

"For running from your father," she said, and as he reached her side, he noticed she was fighting tears. "I've been so caught up in my own misery, my own pain, the damned tragedy of my childhood, I've never really considered what anyone else had gone through. No . . . it was all about me."

He placed an arm over her shoulders. "You were seven."

"And now I'm almost twenty-eight. Time, I think, to grow up. You're right. You lost your childhood that night, too."

He folded her into his arms, holding her close while energized that he'd made a breakthrough, that finally he was going to unearth answers that had been hidden for too, too long. "We're going to figure this out," he promised, "and we're going to figure it out tonight."

CHAPTER 33

Kara's heart was in her throat as she stared at the splash of light from the Toyota's headlights against the rusting gate. They were parked on the turnoff to the lane leading to the house—her house—where all of the horror had begun.

On the short drive from the cottage where Tate had spent his summers as a child, he'd told her that he was certain his father had been trying to convey something about what he'd seen that night. Tate thought that Edmund Tate had whispered, "Semper fi," in his dying breath. "It's got to be someone he knew in the Marine Corps. Someone he saw," Wes had said, gripping the steering wheel tightly, his face a mask of steel as the wheels turned in his mind. "I've got someone checking, but we're close, Kara," he'd said. "We're closer than we've ever been."

And now they were here, at the very gates of hell, she thought, and felt a grave sense of foreboding, a feeling that what they were about to uncover would be as disturbing as the past.

Some secrets are best left undisturbed.

Her hands clenched, her stomach was in knots and she had trouble drawing a breath as the beams of Tate's RAV4's headlights bathed the old, rusted gates with an eerie glow. Kara shrank

513

into the passenger seat. What had seemed like a good idea earlier in the day now felt wrong. So very wrong.

"You okay?" Tate asked, cutting the engine, the night closing in on them as snowflakes fell and she heard the wind sweeping through the surrounding forest.

"Am I ever?" she replied as another warning chill slid down her spine. "No, I'm definitely not okay."

"We don't have to do this."

"Don't we?" Ignoring the mounting trepidation, she grabbed hold of the passenger door handle. "We didn't come all the way up here for me to wimp out now." Mentally bracing herself for whatever was to come, she forced herself to push the door open. Air as bitter and cold as the Arctic whooshed inside the Toyota. "We're here now. Let's get this over with." She stepped out of the SUV, her boots sinking deep into the snow, and gritted her teeth. *Enough,* she told herself. She'd been through enough. It was time to end this.

Slamming the door behind her, she walked to the gates. Staring through the grimy bars, she heard Tate get out of the RAV4, then the beep of the remote lock that seemed out of place and jarring in this hushed, frozen forest.

What the hell had she been thinking?

This is a mistake, Kara! Go back to Tate's loft.

Forget this. Have another drink. Have five. You don't have to go back in. Tate said so.

No, she had to go through with it. *Had* to.

A faded real estate sign was still attached to the steel bars, and obviously the electronic lock had given way long ago as a thick chain now held the gates closed.

Tate had come prepared, bringing a backpack full of tools. He snipped the chain with a bolt cutter and pulled one side of the gate open, dragging it through a foot of snow until the opening was wide enough for Kara to slip through.

Once inside the grounds, she started walking along the curved lane that cut through the towering icy evergreens. In an instant she remembered how her mother had strung clear lights from one thick trunk to another, winding hundreds of tiny bulbs between the branches and illuminating the approach to the old house.

No lights now.

None for a long, long time.

"You're sure about this?" Tate asked, catching up with her.

"I told you: I'm not sure about anything. But we're here now. So let's just do it."

Dr. Zhou's advice, "Face your fears," came to mind, though Kara wondered what her shrink would make of this, because being here at the scene of the McIntyre Massacre was definitely

515

her worst and darkest fear. As they rounded a final curve, the trees parted and the house came into view.

Three stories of time-darkened cedar rose in a clearing surrounded by towering hemlocks and long-needled pines. A wide front porch skirted the lower level, where the windows had been boarded, some tagged with spray paint.

Kara squinted upward to the second story and the corner bedroom she'd shared with Marlie. Her stomach dropped as she took in the sight of the once-stately, almost glorious mansion. Even in the surrounding darkness she saw that the roof of the porch sagged slightly, weighted as it was with snow, and the siding was rotting in spots, evidence of rodent habitation visible. Most of the lower windows had been boarded, some of the weathered plywood, too, showing evidence of spray paint.

"Before . . . before what happened that night," she whispered, "I used to love this place. We spent summers up here and everyone seemed . . . happier. The boys were always out in the woods, hunting or playing war or whatever or swimming in the lake and boating and fishing or waterskiing. Marlie too." She bit her lip, remembering. "I was too young for that, but I could ride in the boat with Daddy. And then . . . that year we came up for Christmas. We always did, but it was different," she said, remembering the hostilities, the simmering anger, how everyone was on edge. "Jonas and Donner were at each other and Sam Junior was quieter than he had been, as if he'd retreated within himself. "Marlie was sulking because Chad hadn't been included. Mom and Dad had laid down the law, 'No one but family,' that was the rule at Christmas and it included people who hadn't married in, so Auntie Faiza boycotted as she couldn't bring Roger."

Kara cast Tate another glance. "Really pissed Faiza off. She kept saying, 'Blood is thicker than water, Zelda,' in the weeks before Christmas, but Mama wouldn't budge. At least not for Roger. But that wasn't quite right, because," she struggled to remember, "I think Merritt was here, too. I didn't see him—at least I don't remember seeing him, and he definitely didn't stay for dinner—but . . . but I think I remember catching sight of his car." But was that right? She struggled with the memory, a headache forming as she kept walking toward the house, across the area where everyone had parked, the broad, flat space that butted up to the steps.

"Why would Margrove come up here on Christmas? He had his own family."

"Right." She nodded. "He was married to Helen then," she said, remembering the woman who had helped raise her. "That was his second wife. She was . . . she was great but couldn't put up with his gambling and other women. But I

517

don't know why he was here. Maybe for drinks or maybe because of Jonas, he was always in trouble with the law, getting in fights."

"Including that one with Donner?" They reached the house and Kara paused, staring at the massive double doors, trying to find the will to enter.

"That was bad," she admitted. "So bad that Walter Robinson was threatening to sue for full custody even though they were nearly adults. It was all probably just a stupid bluff, just to get back at her and make trouble. Nonetheless, Mama was beside herself."

"That all came out at the trial," Tate said. "Jonas threatened Donner, said he would kill him. That was your testimony."

"Yeah, I do remember that," she said, her thoughts jumbled, the fights she'd heard from behind the door of her bedroom tangled in her mind. "I know. But I heard it from my room. I wasn't actually downstairs." She thought hard, the cold seeping into her bones. "Well, that's not all of it. I did sneak out into the hallway," she admitted as the blur that was the memory congealed a bit, the edges still fuzzy. "I snuck to the railing above the foyer and Marlie was already there, staring down to the floor below."

The recollection was forming, but incomplete. "I think her father was here." She remembered poking her nose through the balusters and peering to the foyer. The chandelier blocked some of her view, but she saw Mama's white face as she glared up at her ex, who towered over her.

"Don't even say it," Mama had said, her face set. "The children stay with me. That's the deal we made, Walter, and you can't renege. This is all bullshit and you know it. The kids are too old for this crap! But it doesn't matter. Go ahead. Just trust me, I'll take you to court if you keep harassing me and I can afford the best lawyers money can buy."

"It's unsafe," Walter said, standing military straight, his face flushed, his lips pulled back over his teeth. Pointing a finger at Daddy, he snarled, "Your boy tried to kill mine."

Daddy held up two hands. "Oh, come on, Walt. It's just teenagers blowing off steam over a girl. You and I have both been there."

Walter's eyes had turned to slits. "That we have, Sam," he said, and threw another look at Mama. "That we have."

Mama flushed all kinds of red and hissed, "Get out, Walter. Get the hell out of my house or I'll call the police."

"Oh, yeah?" The big man hadn't been intimidated. "Call 'em. The only one they'll arrest is that kid of his," he said, hitching his chin at Daddy. "He's trouble, Zelda. Real trouble." Then to Daddy, he pointed a finger, cocked like a gun. "You keep your boy away from my son."

"Or?"

"Or you'll live to regret it," he'd vowed. And then he was out the door, slamming it with enough force that the whole house had seemed to shake.

Kara hadn't remembered the details she did now, but upon questioning by Margrove at the trial she'd said that she'd remembered Walter fighting with Daddy and Mama, that he was afraid for Donner. The DA had twisted that all around and made it seem that Jonas was the reason Walter was angry and that his threats had been empty.

Marlie had seen Kara out of the corner of her eye. "Go back to your room, Kara-Bear," she'd said, and shepherded her younger sister down the hallway.

"But your dad is mean."

Marlie had leaned down and shaken her head. She'd been ashen faced and her lips had trembled a bit, but she'd said, "Grown-ups get mad just like kids."

Truer words were never spoken, Kara thought now. Walking up the two steps to the porch, reliving the moment, she explained it all to Tate. "So Walter left, but Silas Dean, who had been Daddy's partner, had been here, too." She swallowed. Hard. "Silas and Daddy were in a shouting match in the den. I could hear them from the living room," she said, remembering how

Samuel McIntyre's partner had burst through the door and turned at the foot of the stairs near the grandfather clock. "I swear, McIntyre. This isn't the last of it. What you did could have ruined me."

"It was a bad investment," Daddy had said, but he was mad, his eyes burning into the shorter man. "It's over."

"It nearly wiped me out!" Dean was red faced and spitting. "I'll take you to court and . . . and I'll get even, Sam. I swear it. If it's the last thing I do, I'll get my pound of flesh. Watch your damned back, McIntyre."

"Leave it alone, Silas. It's done."

"And it's cost us thousands. *Me* thousands."

"Ancient history."

"You're a fucker, McIntyre. You knew this was how it was going to go down and you'll live to regret it. I'll make sure of it," Silas had said.

She shuddered at the memory, rubbed her forehead, which was still tender, as she forced herself to concentrate, to pull up recollections that preferred to stay hidden deep in her subconscious. "There was Daddy's business and his trouble with his ex-partner, threats of a lawsuit." She shivered. "Silas Dean was really mad when he left, backed up and hit a tree, I heard it, saw the crumpled bumper. I'd . . . I'd forgotten." Like so many other things, she thought.

"Could that be why Margrove had shown up, because Dean was threatening your father?"

She lifted a shoulder. "Anything could be." And that was the truth. Screwing up her courage, she reached for the handle of the door, tried to pull it open. It was shut tight.

Tate said, "You didn't think it would be that easy, did you?"

"No, but it was worth a try."

"Let me." He set his backpack on the dusty floorboards, unzipped the bag and retrieved two small flashlights. "Hold this," he said, handing her one before delving once more into the backpack and pulling out a small black case from his jacket pocket. "Train the beam on the lock." She did, and he pulled off one glove to hold the other flashlight in his teeth, then opened the case of lock picks. "By the way," he told her, working two thin picks and listening, then hearing the lock click open, "I don't consider this breaking and entering, since I'm pretty sure you own the place."

"Great. That gives me so much peace of mind," she said sarcastically as he put the locks away and pulled on his glove again.

Her insides were shaking as she pushed open the door, then stepped into her past.

Inside, she shined the intense beam of her LED flashlight up the massive staircase, over the wider lower steps, past the landing and upward to the open railing of the floor above. Illumination splashed on the darkened balusters caused shadows to play on tattered wallpaper.

Her throat closed.

Her chest tightened.

She remembered descending the stairs that night with the strains of "Silent Night" and the winking lights of the Christmas tree guiding her.

"Glories stream from heaven afar."

Her insides grew cold.

"Heavenly hosts sing Alleluia!"

Oh. God.

Her insides clenched.

Glancing back at the open door, she thought about running back outside, breathing fresh air, escaping the horror of the past. What was the point? Did she really think she could unlock her subconscious so some long-hidden memory would emerge, that she could change what had happened?

The past was the past.

Dead and gone.

She couldn't alter anything.

Beside her, Tate was moving his flashlight's beam past the scarred floorboards of the foyer and into the living room.

Kara's gaze followed the beam across the floral pattern of the faded carpet. The blood had been cleaned, as it had in the foyer and staircase, but she saw the shading in the pattern and in her mind's eye she saw the room as it had been, the winking lights, the haunting music, the grotesque bodies of her brothers and the blood, all the blood.

"Christ the Savior is born!
Christ the Savior is born!"

Her stomach heaved and she ran outside, down the two steps of the porch, to double over. Vomit rose, her eyes stung with tears as she lost everything she'd eaten that day into the snowy drifts. "Oh . . . oh, Jesus." She blinked and found Tate beside her.

"We really don't have to do this."

"I know!" she snapped, spitting, her mouth tasting foul, her nose filled with the acrid scent of bile. "You keep saying that, but you're wrong." She spat several times. Help me, she silently prayed, then, straightening, she let out her breath and glared at him. "Just forget you saw that and let's go." Steeling herself, she marched up the two steps to the front porch.

Today she was going to face her fears.

Today she was going to deal with the past.

Today, no matter what she had to face, she was finally and forever putting the ghosts of her past to rest.

Footsteps?
Voices?

In the dark attic of the big house at the lake, Jonas froze, his gloved hands deep in the bowels of an old console circa 1963. It was a long, sturdy piece that had once housed not only a bubble-faced television but also a stereo with a hidden, deep-set turntable and slots for records, several in dusty jackets still visible. The long console had been his grandmother's prized possession with its sleek lines and speakers hidden behind panels covered in thin gold cloth. And it had proved to be the perfect hiding place.

All he'd had to do was open the lid, reach inside and unlatch the lock that held the turntable in place. Once released, the turntable, on a huge spring, rose quickly upward, ready to be stacked with vinyl records and leaving below it an empty space, a hidden niche where he'd hidden a fat manila envelope twenty years earlier. He'd half expected the packet to be long gone, discovered either by the police after the massacre or vandals or squatters since. But he'd gotten lucky. The manila envelope, about the same color as the blond wood and fraying fabric of the cabinet, was still where he'd left it hidden by the turntable.

His heart had soared.

Hallelujah! Halle-effin-lujah!

But just when he'd ripped it out and opened it, spying what he knew to be twenty thousand dollars in crisp hundred-dollar bills, he'd heard the click of locks, the creak of a door openand then the scrape of footsteps over whispered voices.

Shit, shit, shit!

He couldn't believe it.

Who would be here?

Why would anyone come here?

Of all the luck!

Of all the damned luck!

The only way out of the attic was down the narrow stairs to the upper hallway. He'd had the presence of mind to close that narrow door, but now he was trapped. He glanced skyward to the single window mounted high near the rafters, where he could see evidence of an owl roosting, whitewash droppings staining the crossbeams, pellets amassed on the floor below. The window was ajar and if push came to shove he might be able to squeeze through it and . . . what? Drop three floors to the ground below? Would the two feet of snow that had drifted around the house be enough to break his fall?

He doubted it.

The voices grew louder.

Damn it!

He strained to hear what they were saying as he considered sneaking out of the attic and into one of the bedrooms on the second floor. From Kara's old room at the other end of the hallway, he could lower himself onto the back porch roof, slide across it and drop the eight feet to the ground. Then he could make his getaway.

Otherwise he'd be found out.

Otherwise he'd . . .

Creaaak!

A floorboard protested and it sounded close.

Not two floors down.

Here in the attic.

But that was impossible.

His blood turned to ice.

He kept his breathing shallow. Listened hard.

Nothing over the sudden thudding of his heart.

Slow down. You're losing it. You've been in much more difficult situations than this. Remember Banhoff? The other cons? The guards? The fights? Hold it together, McIntyre, just fucking hold it together.

He considered praying and decided there was time enough for that later. Right now he had a problem he had to deal with and . . .

Crap!

Did the air in the attic just shift slightly?

The owl. He glanced up expecting to see the wide wingspan of a barn owl, but no bird of prey was roosting.

His imagination.

No, wait!

Did he smell something over the scents of dust and owl feces? The familiar scent of human sweat? Acrid and close? For a second he remembered the prison and the odor of men exercising and the distinct smell of men hyped up on adrenaline and fear.

Every muscle in his body tensed.

A bad taste formed in the back of his throat and he reached for the knife tucked under his jacket, the big blade he'd lifted from Mia Long's kitchen.

Without making a sound, he started to turn, and from the corner of his eye caught sight of a glint of metal in the darkness.

Shit.

He tried to spin. Lifted his weapon.

Too late!

A big, gloved hand closed over his mouth and twisted his head.

He jabbed wildly with the knife but couldn't connect.

Whoever the bastard was, he held him close.

Jonas struggled. Kicked. Tried to scream.

Kept stabbing wildly in the air.

No, no, no! This couldn't be happening. Couldn't.

The voice that whispered against his ear was cold, hard and filled with malice. "You should have stayed in prison where you belonged," it rasped, hot breath against his skin.

His insides curdled. Who? What?

"This is for my son!" the voice hissed.

The blade flashed near his eye.

Shit!!!

No!

Jonas felt the tip of the blade prick the skin beneath his jaw.

"No," he tried to scream, trying vainly to lurch forward.

The knife was drawn quickly and sharply across the base of his throat and in that instant, Jonas McIntyre was gone.

CHAPTER 34

Kara's stomach was still queasy, her nerves tight as bowstrings as she and Tate walked through the gloomy house. It was cold inside, a rush of wind sweeping in from the open cabinet near the fireplace, the bin where, in the past, her father had stacked firewood, now empty, the latch obviously having worn through.

"Let's get on with this, get it over with," she said, and circumvented the living room to walk through the dining area. The room where the family had shared so many meals, the boys hitting and shoving and laughing, was now empty and dark.

Kara remembered her family gathered around the table, the tinkle of cutlery over the sound of holiday music, her father's deep laughter and Mama smiling over a glass of champagne that glistened in the dimmed lights and candle glow. The smells of roasting turkey or ham, cinnamon and cocoa had been ever-present during the winter retreats to the mountains, until that night.

Tears burned the backs of her eyes as she gazed at the long table where once there had been platters of corn, green beans and potatoes and gravy and along with the turkey, roast beef, ham or venison, there had been baskets of bread and bowls of fruit and a sense of gaiety.

Now the table was warped and dusty, covered in carcasses of dead flies, bees, moths and whatever other insect had died here. Cobwebs dangled from the chandelier, and the built-in buffet, long stripped of Mama's Christmas china and silverware, was dirty, the glass panes of the cupboards cracked, the backboards riddled with small, chewed holes, evidence of a squirrel's or rat's nest visible in one corner.

Kara's skin crawled as she walked into the kitchen. It, too, had been stripped bare. No knives suspended from the magnetic strip over the eight-burner stove, no pots or pans visible behind cabinet doors that hung drunkenly from broken hinges, the checkerboard tile floor grimy and mottled. She walked into the adjoining hallway, around the back of the staircase to the entry hall and into her father's den.

The room was empty, devoid of his massive desk, nothing to see. As she stepped through the French doors and was again in the foyer, she turned her eyes to the living room once more.

"I could hear music," she said as the memories tumbled through her, memories that had been locked away for decades. "I, um, I went through the bedrooms. And Jonas's was a mess. His room had some old hunting trophies in it, like a deer's head and an eagle that had been mounted on the wall, but it . . . it had been decapitated and Jonas's room itself looked as if a tornado had swept through it."

"Or someone with a sword had done the damage? Someone out of his mind with rage?"

"Yes," she said meekly, as if she were seven again. "Out of control and"—she licked her lips—"with a bloodlust." In that moment she reverted to her younger self, a small girl padding barefoot along the runner feeling the sticky dampness along the railing. "I knew something was wrong, really wrong."

She viewed the living room as it had been then. "I saw them," she said, her voice a whisper. "The three boys. And . . . and all that blood." Her voice cracked and outside the wind moaned. Overhead floorboards creaked, the sound of the old house settling, or protesting its intrusion.

"I thought they were all dead," she said, "and then Jonas, like a man coming out of his grave, raised up on one elbow and croaked at me to get help. To run." She was staring into the living room, seeing it as it had been with the fallen Christmas tree, the glowing embers in the fireplace, the broken mantel and all that blood. So much blood. "Run, he'd yelled," she whispered, and spun toward the door. "And then there was this huge person in the doorway, like a monster, his face covered in a mask. I ran, oh, God, I ran through the living room and the kitchen and out the back door." She took two steps to follow that path but felt a hand on the crook of her elbow and stopped, her hand on the door handle.

"You don't have to go," Tate said, and she snapped back, no longer a child, but a woman again, creeping around the old house where so many she loved had been butchered. She felt tears on her face and before she knew what was happening, Tate folded her into his arms. "Let's stop this. Now. Bad idea."

She melted into him, her whole body shuddering, her knees buckling, his strength keeping her on her feet. She teetered between wanting to go forward and to run away, to close the door behind her and never look back.

"It's okay."

"It's not, Wes. You know it and I know it. It will never be okay. *Never.*"

"Got him!" Johnson said as she strode into Thomas's office. She spread a series of 8×10 photos on his desk. Different pictures of the crowd that had gathered around the hospital when Jonas had been a patient at Whimstick General.

"That was fast."

"I had someone in the tech department help me with facial recognition, and we were able to match anyone close to the original investigation to people in the crowd at the hospital. It was pretty easy." She was proud of herself. "Also,

I grabbed a lot of shots off the Internet, under the Facebook fan page where a lot of Jonas's followers, if you'd call them that, anyway, his fans posted selfies and pictures of the crowd that had gathered. That's how I got so many different angles and perspectives. Take a look."

Thomas leaned in closer as Johnson said, "The thing is this, quite a few of some of our nearest and dearest suspects were there." She shifted the pictures on his desk. "Let's start here with dear old 'Auntie Fai.' " She pointed out Faiza Donner, who stood separately from Roger Sweeney, parted by a sea of people so that it appeared Faiza didn't know Sweeney was there, and vice versa.

"Now, let's move on. Take a look at this."

In the picture he saw Brittlynn Atwater again, and he recognized Sheila Keegan holding a microphone near to Mia Long. "Right here." Johnson touched another image, of the man in the baseball cap, standing beneath the tree and staring at the woman in the long coat who looked so much like Marlie Robinson. In this picture, from the opposite angle of the first, he stood still hanging back from the crowd, but now he stood in front of the tree, his face in clear view.

Walter Robinson.

Staring at the woman who was a dead ringer for his missing daughter.

And he didn't look the least bit surprised.

"What the hell was he doing there?" Thomas said, the wheels spinning wildly in his mind. Walter Robinson? Joining the crowd rallying for Jonas McIntyre and staring at his daughter or a dead ringer for her?

"Check out his hat."

She showed him an enlarged print of Walter's face and cap. Not a baseball cap as he'd originally thought, but a cap emblazoned with the emblem for the United States Marines.

"Not 'simplify' or 'send her Fi,' " he said aloud.

Johnson was nodding and smiling grimly as he rolled his chair back and reached for his jacket. "Semper fi. Walter was in the Marine Corps."

"As was Edmund Tate. My guess is they knew each other, and Tate recognized Walter chasing Kara that night."

"I thought the attacker was masked."

"He could've pulled it off when he gave chase." The scene played out in his mind, the terrified seven-year-old running through the forest. A huge man running desperately after her. The cop on the porch hearing screams and recognizing the attacker. "Tate wasn't chasing Kara." Thomas reached for his sidearm, slipped it into the holster on his belt. "Walter was."

"Tate just intercepted the chase, cutting across from his yard and running out onto the ice," Johnson said.

"And what happened to Walter? Why did he

back off? Because he saw Tate?" Thomas asked aloud, his thoughts spinning.

"Maybe, or just to get the hell out of there. He might have decided to get as far away as possible before anyone showed up."

"Call the Seaside PD," Thomas said as with a clunk, the department's aging furnace kicked into higher gear. "Have them keep an eye on Robinson until we get a warrant."

"Got it," Johnson said, her eyes narrowing with a self-satisfied gleam. "My ex-brother-in-law is a cop there and we're cool. He's close to my son. I've already texted him while I was on the phone. He'll let me know where that son of a bitch is ASAP."

Thomas should have felt a little buzz of anticipation, the jolt of adrenaline that always came with an impending arrest for cracking a case, but something was off about this one. Walter Robinson was involved, he was certain of that, but it all didn't make sense.

Why would Walter show up at the McIntyre house on Christmas Eve and slaughter the entire family, including his own son?

What had happened to his daughter, Marlie, who, according to Brittlynn Atwater, was supposed to run away with Chad that night?

Where the hell was Chad Atwater? Why did he run?

"Something's off," he said.

"What do you mean? We've got him!"

"Maybe." As Johnson peered over his shoulder, Thomas started typing on his computer keyboard. He pulled up the file on Walter Robinson again, but he was antsy as he read the information, felt as if he was spinning his wheels here at his desk.

He needed to move, get out of the office. *Do something.* Just as Johnson did.

But Thomas couldn't afford to arrest the wrong man.

Thomas read the info. Robinson's current address was still Seaside, where he worked as an electrician. Independent. He had been in the marines, where he'd been a medic, and after being discharged had married Zelda Donner. They'd had two kids, the boy named for Zelda's family, Donner Robinson, and a daughter, Marlie. Zelda and Walter had divorced and Zelda, pregnant with Kara, had married Samuel McIntyre, himself the father of two, his namesake Sam and Jonas, the wild card.

But he'd never been in serious trouble with the law. There was nothing on his record but parking tickets and a fine for poaching, hunting deer out of season.

"He's our guy!" Johnson insisted.

"Yeah, but it's not all adding up."

"We'll bring him in for questioning, put on some pressure, give him a chance to tell his side of the story again. See what he has to say."

"Let's see what we find in his place, once we get the warrant." They were close, but a big part of the case didn't make sense. He studied the pictures that Johnson had left on his desk of the crowd, or Walter Robinson and the girl who could be his daughter. Where the hell was she?

"Fine. I'll double-check with the Seaside PD," she said, and left him to study the footage of Walter Robinson in front of the television cameras, asking for information on his missing daughter. He'd seemed shell-shocked, but he'd just lost his son. Was it all an act? Was he a stone-cold killer just trying to cover his own tracks? Thomas picked up a pencil and tapped the eraser end on his desk. He was missing something, something vital, but what was it?

His cell phone rang, jarring his thoughts.

He picked up. "Cole Thomas."

"Yeah . . . um, this is Mia Long. We met at the hospital."

"I remember."

"I, um, oh, God." She hesitated. "I, um, I think . . ."

"Is something wrong?" His senses heightened as he waited.

"I don't know," she said, and her voice was tight. "I mean, I probably shouldn't even be calling you, but Jonas . . . he took my car. I don't mean he stole it. I loaned it to him and he's been gone a few hours and he's not answering my calls or texts and . . . oh, shit. I'm worried."

"You think something happened to him?" So at least they knew now where he'd been.

"I don't know. But he just got out of the hospital and he's not used to driving anymore and . . . Oh, forget it. Forget I called. This was a mistake. I'm sorry. He's fine. Everything's fine!" She cut the connection and when he tried to call her back, she didn't pick up.

Within seconds he'd pulled up her driver's license information and found the make and model and plate numbers of her car, then put out a BOLO, Be On the Look Out, for Mia Long's fifteen-year-old Honda Accord. Then he grabbed his jacket and sidearm. He'd been looking for a reason to get up and move, and Mia Long's call seemed like the perfect excuse; her apartment seemed like the perfect place to start. Until they heard back from the Seaside Police Department.

When he reached Johnson's desk, he found her on the phone and staring at her computer screen. She must've heard him approach because she held up a hand, listening to whoever was on the other end of the call while he was on one foot, then the other.

"Yeah, thanks," she was saying, nodding and looking over her shoulder. "Tell me what you find when you get in." She disconnected and spun her chair around. "That was my ex-brother-in-law," she explained. "Walter Robinson isn't at his house and not answering his phone, the only one listed in his name or his company's name: Robinson Electric. It's odd because that phone is his business's lifeline, you know, to schedule jobs and such. Voice mail is full. They're gonna go inside. The guys watching the place. Probable cause." When he was about to ask, she said, "No time for a warrant."

"As long as it doesn't screw the case against him."

"It won't." She eyed his jacket. "You going somewhere?"

"To Mia Long's apartment, and I'm going to call Alex Rousseau on the way."

"Because . . . ?"

"Jonas McIntyre was there."

"Oh, wait." She let out a long breath. "Let me guess. He's MIA again."

"Yeah, but this time he's in Mia Long's car. Already got a BOLO for him."

Kara shivered as she stepped into her parents' master bedroom and heard the wind rattling the panes of the windows. An empty bed frame had been pushed against one wall. Water had seeped through a crack in the window, running down the wall and causing the paint to peel and the floorboards to buckle.

This was where Mama and Daddy had been

found, lying in their bed, both dead. Whoever had killed them had moved quickly, able to slice each throat quickly, without a struggle. Thankfully. She silently hoped that the sleeping pills they'd downed had been powerful enough so that they had been out of it, totally unaware that they were being attacked and killed.

Her stomach roiled again.

She wanted to run, to get as far away from this old house with all its secrets, all its horrors, as she could. Instead, she leaned against the doorframe and said to Tate, "This isn't working." A few new fragments, bits of recollection had come to mind, but the images she saw behind her mind's eye, those burned into her memory forever, were of the dead. She thought of them as *her* dead. The family that she'd lost.

No, not lost.

The family that had been violently stolen from her.

Tate placed a hand on her shoulder. "If you want—"

"Stop! Don't say it, Tate. Don't even think it. I don't *want* to leave any more than I don't *want* to be here, but let's just get through it."

"I'm just following your lead."

"Fine," she bit out angrily. He was right. They'd decided back on the drive to the mountain that they would break in and re-create the night of the attack. If Kara could stand it, she would relive the horrid events and talk them out, tell him what she remembered, what she felt, what she sensed. "Just give me a second."

"Okay."

Kara closed her eyes, determined to break through, determined to remember it all.

And if she did, what then?

Setting her jaw, she broke free of Tate's embrace. "Come on."

She refused to be distracted, not by the creaks she heard of the old house settling, not by the wind starting to pick up and buffet the walls, rattling the windows, not by the pounding of her heart and the drumming of her pulse through her brain warning her that she was dancing too near the edge of a greater horror, that danger was nearing with every step she took.

She walked directly to her bedroom and shined her flashlight across the ceiling and down the far wall. "This is where it started for me," she said around a dry mouth. Her twin bed, stripped of any bedding, the mattress seeming to have exploded as the stuffing had spewed through the split covering, stood where it had when she'd been a child, against the wall, the headboard beneath a window where she could look up and see the stars. Marlie's bed had been shoved to the far side of the room, in front of the closet, the bed's mattress intact but stained a dull, dirty gray.

She remembered Marlie, the desperation in

her voice. "My sister told me to be quiet," Kara said, remembering. "She woke me up, I think, and I argued, but she was insistent. I could tell something was going on, something weird, because she was usually a slob and her bed had been made and she had clothes folded on it. It just wasn't like her. I didn't want to go, but I let her take me upstairs."

Kara followed the path they'd taken all those years ago, toward the end of the hall where the attic door was gaping open, hanging drunkenly from its hinges.

Fear curdled her blood, but she pressed forward. Cleared her throat. Ignored the feeling that something dark and evil lurked within these old walls. She couldn't back out now. Wouldn't.

"She was leading me and shushing me, telling me to be quiet."

She paused at the doorway to the crooked, narrow stairs leading upward and for a second she was certain she felt the presence of malice, like the unseen breath of an evil beast skimming across her skin and raising the hairs on the back of her neck.

Don't go up there. It's bad. You know it's bad.

Clenching her teeth, using the flashlight's thin beam as her guide, she began mounting the stairs, Tate a step behind.

The attic was several degrees colder than the hallway below, a sharp breeze cutting through the broken glass of the only window. She remembered that night and staring out the dirty panes, wondering when Marlie would return. Wondering *if* her sister would come back for her.

Inwardly she trembled and the back of her throat turned to cotton.

With her flashlight, she splashed a stream of illumination to the rafters where the window was cracked and the wind rushed inside. Evidence of an owl was obvious, though the bird wasn't hidden in the shadows above. The musty smell of things long forgotten was all too familiar and her insides squeezed with the remembered fear of abandonment.

"She brought me up here and told me it was to keep me safe. Us safe," Kara forced out, and drew her flashlight's shaft of light down from the ceiling to the clutter within. Tate's flashlight, too, illuminated the leftover fragments of lives once lived. Massive piles of furniture and stacked boxes, old vinyl records and tapes and rolled up rugs, all covered in years of cobwebs and dust.

Did she hear something—a humming over the soughing of the wind, or . . . or did she imagine it?

Don't create more problems. Just try to remember and get out. Get out fast.

Trembling inside, she closed her eyes as she recalled that terrifying night. "I was supposed to stay up here. Marlie promised she'd come back for me, but I got tired of waiting. It seemed like hours, but it could have been fifteen minutes. I really don't know. I was just a kid. She . . . she did say there were bad people here or at least one bad person, I can't remember exactly, but she didn't say who it was and then she locked me up here. Locked! Can you imagine doing that to a seven-year-old?" She shook her head, eyes still closed as she said, "I was frantic to escape. Crazy to get out. And then I heard a scream. A bloodcurdling scream."

Kara's heart squeezed and her knees threatened to buckle.

She relived her fear, the panic as she tried to escape her attic prison. "I had to get out. I *had* to." She shivered, not from the temperature in the room but from the memories as they tumbled through her mind. "It took some doing, but I was determined and then the lock sprang, the door opened and I was out. Free." The memories shriveled and shrank away and she found herself once again back to reality, with Tate, in this horrid, hated attic, her eyes opening to the weird darkness, the blue shadows cast by their flashlights.

Once more she thought she heard a humming, so out of place in a cavernous garret.

"Do you hear that?" she asked Tate as he moved his flashlight's beam over the nooks and crannies of the boxes, bags and junk that had been hauled up here.

"Hear what?"

"Something whirring or . . ."

Her phone vibrated in her pocket and she physically started. Retrieving her cell, she saw the anonymous text glowing on the small screen:

Get out. Get out now!

"What the hell?" Kara whispered, her breath clouding in the cold space. She was about to text back. "Tate—it's happening again!"

"What?"

Before she could respond and demand to know who was on the other end of the connection, undulating bubbles appeared on the screen indicating that whoever was on the other end of the connection was typing into his or her cell.

"I don't know, but they're contacting me again . . . Oh, God." The new message appeared in bold type:

Leave now! HE'S HERE!!!!

"He's here? Who's here?" she said, her fear congealing inside her.

Tate asked, "Who knows you're here?"

"Besides you? No one. You know that."

"The text says 'here,' as if whoever is contacting you—"

"Is here," she finished for him, terrified. "In this house!" Dread and fear mingled, coiling her insides, as she glanced around the attic where she'd been trapped all those years before.

"And not alone," he whispered against her ear. "Let's go."

"Someone is here? Up here?" she said desperately, shining her flashlight frantically, its beam jumping from piles of furniture to the rafters to the floor and toward the source of the faint whir.

"Oh, God."

The beam of her flashlight had landed on a stain on the floor. A dark red pool of congealing liquid. Blood. Splattered everywhere. On old books, boxes and vinyl record jackets—Frank Sinatra's face covered in blood drips, The Beatles' album cover smeared in red. She bit back a scream and stared, her gaze riveted to the space beneath the old record console. "No . . . oh, no, no."

"What the hell? Stay here." Tate moved closer to the stereo, opening the lid of the record stand and gasping, his breath sucked through his teeth.

The beam of his flashlight had landed on the crown of a severed head slowly rotating upon an ancient turntable.

Kara swept her light over the front of the console. Through the thin, shredded fabric of the console she saw a head spinning around and around, eyes and mouth wide open, blood still visible on Jonas McIntyre's ashen skin.

CHAPTER 35

Kara ran!

Like she'd never run in twenty years.

Heart racing, blood pounding in her ears, she flew down the attic steps and onto the second floor.

In her mind's eye she still saw Jonas's face slowly revolving, his haunted eyes visible through the tattered cloth covering the console.

Her stomach roiled.

Faster! Faster!

Down the stairs and through the living room, where, flashing through her brain, she saw her brothers as they had been, lying dead, in thick pools of their own blood, the embers of the fire hissing and seething a brilliant glowing red. All the while the grandfather clock in the hallway had loudly counted off the hours over the sound of the Christmas carol.

Bong, bong, bong.

"Silent night. Holy night. . . ."

The sights and sounds of that blood-drenched night thundered through her brain, and she nearly tripped as she slid around the corner and ran through the dining room.

Bong! Bong! Bong!

"Shepherds quake—"

Bong!

"—at the sight. . . ."

Louder and louder, over the sound of running footsteps following after her, chasing her down!

"Kara!" she heard, and she sped faster, seven years old again, racing out the back door, flying down the steps, frantically scrambling through the snow, her heart in her throat, tears streaming from her eyes. Dead! They were all dead!

"Mama," she whispered, her lips frozen. "Daddy." Through the trees she dashed, her feet slipping and sliding, but she plowed forward.

"Kara! Stop!"

Never!

"I love you, Kara-Bear. . . . I'll come get you. I promise." Marlie's words came back to her, haunted her, and just like before, as the frozen branches slapped her face, she saw the ghosts of her family through the trees, peering out at her through the snowy veil, their faces drawn and white. All crying her name over the howl of the wind, "Kara! Kara!"

Mama.

Daddy.

Sam Junior.

Donner.

And now Marlie, distorted, but peering around the rough bark of a fir tree, half hidden by the snow-laden branches.

Oh, God. Oh, God. Oh, God!

She glanced over her shoulder. Through the thick, ever-changing screen of the snow, she spied the man running after her, chasing her down. Tall and looming, his face obscured, he ran with purpose.

She couldn't let him catch her!

The attacker—the killer—running her to ground, a huge man who had so brutally slain her family was bearing down on her.

"Kara!" His voice boomed through the storm. "Kara, stop!"

She blinked.

Tate? It was Wesley Tate? He was screaming at her?

She stumbled at the thought. Something broke within her. His voice was familiar, safe.

Her legs became leaden as she plowed through the snow, the lake barely visible through the trees and snowfall. What had she been thinking? Of course he was following her. But her reality was disjointed and pieces of the past kept slicing into the present, painful, sharp shards of memory cutting into the here and now.

It's Wesley. He's on your side. Kara, trust him.

Slowing, she turned around, breathing hard, expecting him to—

"Run!" he yelled. "Kara, run!"

Tate's voice?

Or Jonas's? As he levered himself up on one elbow to beg her to get help. That was real, right?

550

She was running from whoever killed Mama and Daddy and her brothers—

The scene in her mind splintered again.

Oh, God, Jonas! His head turning on the spindle came to mind and she twisted, ready to run again, her foot hitting a root or rock jutting upward but hidden beneath the snowpack. She fell forward, against a tree, trying to right herself, icy fir needles scraping her face, branches seeming to claw at her, ripping her skin.

"Run!!!" someone screamed.

Tate's voice. Yes, Wesley Tate was urging her forward, and she found her footing for a second, only to slip and see him bearing down on her.

Not Tate.

No!

The man she saw was Walter Robinson, older than she remembered, his whiskered face set, his jaw rock hard, his eyes skewering her in an otherworldly and cruel glare. In one gloved hand he held a pistol, in the other a knife with blood smeared upon its narrow, deadly blade.

Oh. Dear. God.

"Kara! Run!" Tate's voice echoed through the hills.

She scrabbled forward, finding her feet, but glancing over her shoulder.

Not one, but two men chased her. Tate was closer, running a zigzagging course, but Robinson was bearing down fast, the larger man galloping through the trees and swirling snow, making a beeline toward her.

She scrambled forward and as she did, she caught a glimpse of movement, something white and blurry, a pale ghost running parallel with her, hidden by snow and trees.

The apparition turned and faced her for a second.

Marlie?

Kara blinked.

Her long-lost sister was out here?

Impossible!

"Kara, move!" Tate's voice again and Kara looked behind her. Robinson had raised his pistol.

She cut around a tree, a berry vine snagging her jacket, Cold Lake flat and open in the distance.

"Stop!" Walter ordered, and in her peripheral vision she saw him take aim.

Tate leapt out of the woods just as Walter pulled the trigger.

Blam!

Tate's body lurched in midair.

He landed with a hard thud onto the snow.

"Noooo!" Kara cried, sliding to a stop as Walter, too, had quit running. Walking with a deadly purpose, his pistol in one hand, the bloody knife in the other, he took aim at Tate's limp body.

Kara started toward him. "Don't! Stop! For the love of God—"

Blam! Blam! Blam!

Three shots fired in rapid succession.

Blood spurted from Walter's chest. His body jerked wildly backward. Gasping and moaning, he fell to his knees, his fingers still tight over his weapons, his eyes wide with surprise. And then he keeled forward, his face landing in the snow.

Kara staggered back, her knees threatening to give as she screamed at the top of her lungs, her shriek echoing over the frozen water.

The ghost of her sister appeared, stepping from behind a copse of saplings.

"Marlie," Kara whispered as the apparition became real, a living, breathing woman, stepping out of the frozen landscape.

"I'm sorry, Kara-Bear," she said, and Kara wondered if this was all a horrible nightmare where the past blended with the present and the savagery she'd witnessed all those years ago had finally cracked her frail psyche to pieces. "I didn't mean to leave you in the attic; I just wanted to keep you safe." She slid her pistol into her jacket pocket and was walking toward Kara, but it was Marlie. Her face was scarred, slightly uneven, while one arm hung limply at her side, but she was still recognizable.

"But where . . . where have you been?" Kara asked, though her concentration was split. Tate lay facedown in the snow and she forced herself around the bigger man, kicking the gun from his hand.

"Trapped," Marlie spat, anger radiating from her as she stared at her father's motionless form.

"With Walter?"

She nodded, her lips compressed.

Kara found her feet and reeled forward, dropping to her knees at Tate's side. She felt for his pulse and found it. Thank God. "Help me," she said to Marlie, and though the whole scene was surreal, she saw that Tate was coming around, his eyes blinking against the snowfall.

Please. Please. Please. Please let him live, please don't take him. Not Tate. Please. She sent up her tiny, heartfelt prayers to a God she sometimes hadn't believed existed.

She bit off her gloves, then with frozen fingers unzipped his jacket and tore open his shirt, finding the wound, high in his shoulder. "Wesley," she whispered, forcing him to focus on her. "God . . . are you okay?" Her voice caught.

"What the hell happened?" he asked, blinking and wan, 'til he focused on her and a ghost of a smile touched his lips as his gaze locked with Kara's.

"You've been shot. Walter Robinson was chasing me and you . . ." Her throat closed. "You saved my life." Tears filled her eyes and she bit her lip, overwhelmed by emotion. He was alive, but bleeding.

"Let me," Marlie offered, kneeling next to them as the wind rattled through the frozen branches and snow continued to fall. "I know how. I'm good at this. He"—she shot a glance at her father lying still in the snow—"he taught me. We couldn't go to any hospital, of course, and he'd been a medic when he served in the military. So . . ." She worked fast, tearing a strip of cloth from Tate's shirt to bind his wound and stop the bleeding, while Kara, her head finally clear, called 9-1-1. Her teeth chattered, her head pounded, but she was able to rattle off the address. "Just hurry. Walter and Jonas are dead, another wounded!"

Tate was struggling to get to his feet.

"Not a good idea," Marlie warned, holding up a hand. "Just let me finish up here." She wound the strip of cloth over his shoulder, tied it off as best she could.

"Marlie Robinson?" he asked, his head seeming to clear a bit. Grimacing against pain, he leaned on his good elbow so that he could see Walter Robinson lying facedown and motionless in the falling snow. Then his gaze returned to the woman helping him. "You've been alive all this time?"

"Yes," Marlie said, then, "You should lie down. Really."

"I'm okay," he insisted, and offered her a half smile before wincing. "I've been through worse."

"I don't think so," Kara said, and took his hand, then seeing that Tate was going to pull through, asked her sister the question that had been plaguing her for decades. "Why? Why didn't you come back?"

"He wouldn't let me go," Marlie said, still kneeling as she hitched her chin toward her father's still form. Her lips twisted into a dark frown. "Not after what I'd seen." Sighing, she leaned back on her heels to glance at her father. Her hair caught in the wind, billowing away from her face, exposing the scar beneath one eye. As if she felt Kara noticing it, Marlie touched the jagged line slicing her cheek. "This? Dad didn't do it. No, this is compliments of Jonas." She smiled bitterly. Her voice was as cold as the night, and her eyes seemed to deaden. "I made the mistake of getting in my stepbrother's way."

"But what happened? Why did you leave me?" Kara asked. Despite the bitter cold, despite the fact that Walter lay dead and Tate was injured, she had to know. "Why? In the attic? All alone?"

"I had to," Marlie cut in, more than a little defensive. She rubbed her arms and avoided Kara's gaze. Staring into the middle distance, to a place only she could see, she said quietly, "It was all I could think of at the time. I-I didn't know what to do, but I had to save you. I'd seen Jonas kill Donner, because of Lacey. And just as he finished and caught sight of me, Dad—Walter—showed up." Marlie stared into the trees and shuddered. "Oh, God. It was so twisted. Dad had come back to the house to have it out with Mom about custody of Donner and me."

Marlie cast a dark glance at her father's form as the wind raced across the lake, sharp and harsh, causing the snow to swirl and dance, the trees to shiver. Lost in her own vision of that horrible night, Marlie didn't seem to notice. Her voice was low and without emotion. "Dad, he walked in . . . like the door was unlocked, I guess, and he caught Jonas in the act of slicing Donner's throat. The blood spilling, Donner gurgling. That's what he told me."

Kara's stomach lurched at the vision.

Now there was emotion in Marlie's voice. "Dad completely lost it. Snapped at the sight of Jonas murdering his son." Marlie shook her head. "He told me later that the whole world shifted at that moment, that he went back to his days in combat as a marine. He literally saw red and he reacted."

"By killing everyone?" Kara said, disbelieving, her insides shredding as she remembered the ghastly, blood-soaked scene. Tears froze on her cheeks and somehow she was holding Tate's hand, squeezing tight.

"That's how he explained it to me."

"But why . . . why?" Kara whispered. "Dad and Sam Junior and—"

"I know, I know. It's all so horrible. Unthinkable."

And she had lived with that incomprehensible

557

gut-churning, mind-numbing knowledge for two decades, Kara realized.

Marlie let out a quiet sob and the sound was snatched by the wind. Then she stared down at her father's still form. "He told me that he killed Sam Junior instinctively, because Junior was a witness. And then the beast was unleashed. That's how he said it. 'The beast was unleashed.' Like it was with him all the time. He just kept it tethered." She shook her head, as if she were denying her father his excuse for the savagery, the brutality. She said grimly, her voice almost a whisper, "He killed Mom and your dad because he hated them, hated Mom for cheating on him and hated Sam Senior for stealing not just his wife but his kids, too."

Kara imagined the horrid scene, of Walter murdering Sam Junior, then climbing the stairs with his bloody sword to finish his deadly mission. "But why didn't they wake up?" Kara asked. She imagined screaming and yelling, the crash of the Christmas tree as it was knocked over, the splintering of wood when the mantel was hacked in a wild swing of the deadly blade.

Marlie rolled her eyes to the heavens, snow falling on her upturned and disfigured face. "That was my fault," she admitted, a tear sliding from one eye. "I drugged them. So they wouldn't wake up for a long time. I was supposed to meet Chad and we were going to run away. I knew where

Sam Senior kept some extra cash—a lot of it. I'd seen him stash it away. So the plan was to grab the money and take off. By the time Mom and Sam woke up the next morning, we would be long gone. So . . . so, you see. I did my part, too. I contributed to the murders. I was . . . complicit."

Stunned, trying to grasp it all, to understand, Kara shook her head. "You were just a teenager, a girl in love."

"An idiot," Marlie admitted, and her voice held more than an edge of self-loathing. "Don't ever fall in love, Kara," she advised, though Kara was still gripping Tate's hand. "Look what it did to our family. To my parents. To yours. To Jonas. I'm telling you, it's a bad, bad idea."

Kara felt Tate squeeze her hand and far away, over the rush of the winter wind, she heard the welcome sound of distant sirens. "So you . . . you were the one who called me, who texted me?"

"Yes." Marlie nodded and finally met the questions in her sister's eyes.

"But you said, 'She's alive.' "

"I know. She is alive. Marlie is alive."

"But that's you," Kara pointed out.

"Oh . . . yeah. Right." She sighed. "I've been going by a different name for twenty years. Hailey. Hailey Brown. Posing as Walter's niece if anyone ever asked. No one did, much. I didn't see many people. I wasn't allowed and truthfully"— again she motioned to her disfigured face while the sirens shrieked ever louder—"I didn't want to. Until I knew that Jonas was being released. That was what set Dad off. He went out of his mind! Beside himself. So agitated, he left me at the house in Seaside. Locked me up for the first time in years. Until Jonas was set free, Dad had believed I wouldn't leave, wouldn't expose him." She sniffed and her jaw slid to one side as she glanced at the man who had sired her, abducted her, held her prisoner and made her a part of his sick, twisted life. "Unfortunately," she went on, "he was right. For the most part. However, I had my own secrets. In the last couple of years, I found his keys, made a copy and had stashed away one of his burner phones and siphoned off some of the household cash. So, when the time came if he ever locked me away again, I'd be ready. And I was. When he flipped out over Jonas, I couldn't just sit there. And . . . and I didn't have the nerve to call the police, or admit to who I was so that I would be tracked down and have to deal with the cops, so I took the chicken-shit way out, remained Hailey and tried to warn you." She shrugged and snorted, her face a mask of guilt and embarrassment. "That didn't work so well."

"But you could have left anytime you wanted?"

"In the last few years? Yeah." She nodded, then her features grew hard, her scar more pronounced. "But where would I go? My family other than Dad was gone, and I couldn't risk contacting Chad or you without telling the police and turning in my own father. I know it sounds lame," she admitted, a tear tracking down her cheek, "but I was laid up for a while when I was healing and Dad took care of me."

"He locked you away!"

"He . . . he was all I had," she said, her voice cracking.

Kara let go of Tate's hand. Grabbed her sister's shoulder. "Damn it, Marlie. You could have contacted me!"

She sniffed. "Don't swear," she said, shaking her head, fighting against a wash of tears that spilled from her eyes.

"But—"

"You were a child, Kara!" Marlie snapped. "I couldn't." With trembling fingers, she brushed the tears and snowflakes from her face. "In my mind Marlie Robinson is dead." She gave a sad little laugh and pushed Kara's hand from her shoulder. Then added coldly, "And so is Hailey Brown."

"But you'll always be Marlie to me," Kara argued.

"Good. Remember me the way I was."

There was something in her voice, a warning. With dawning horror, Kara asked, "What's that supposed to mean?"

"I can't go back," Marlie whispered, scooting away from Kara. "I can't. I just can't. I'm not

Marlie anymore. She died long ago and I'm not Hailey."

"Don't!" Tate warned, as if he, too, suddenly understood.

"Marlie, please—"

But it was too late.

Marlie extracted her handgun from her pocket and without saying a word, placed it to her temple.

"No!" Kara struggled forward.

Tate lunged.

Blam!

The gun went off, blasting loudly, echoing through the frigid forest.

Marlie collapsed, the bullet exploding through her skull.

Kara screamed. Threw herself forward.

Tate's arms surrounded her, holding her close against the snow-packed and bloodstained ground. "Shhhh. It'll be all right," he said, cradling her head against the crook of his neck, his fingers splayed in her hair as he forced her face away from the gore and she shook; from the inside out, she trembled.

"It'll be okay. Shhh. Shhh. Shhh," he intoned.

But he was lying. She knew that now, staring at her sister's motionless body. There was no chance Marlie had survived. None.

He rocked her slowly, holding her tight as lights flashed, people shouted, the sirens shrieked.

Help had finally come.

Far too late.

Kara was cold inside, a part of her—hope, she supposed—now dead, because tonight in this snowstorm, she'd finally found her sister, only to lose her again.

And this time it was forever.

CHAPTER 36

Kara popped four Altoids, gathered her courage and stepped into Tate's hospital room. The past few days had been a nightmare that she'd gone through numb and zombie-like. Her nightmares had returned and this time she was with Marlie, in the snowy forest, reliving those last shattering moments of her sister's life.

Now, she had to work through it. Find an inner strength. Even pretend if she had to. She plastered a smile onto her face and hoped it didn't seem as fake as it felt, that it wasn't a garish grin forced onto a haunted face.

You can do this.

Tate's near-black hair was mussed, falling over his forehead, his beard shadow dark over his jaw. However, when he glanced her way, his blue eyes were sharp and clear. He smiled, crookedly, as if they shared a private joke.

If not a joke, she thought, then they had shared a twisted, painful lifetime heretofore. "Hey," she said, and pulled the door shut behind her, leaving her demons outside. "Turnabout's fair play?"

"Yeah, meeting in the hospital, not the best plan to keep a relationship going."

"Is that what we have now, a 'relationship'?"

"We've always had one. Maybe not what it is

now, but, yeah, we've always been connected."

She let that slide. "How do you feel?"

"Not like a million bucks, but not bad. They're releasing me today."

"I noticed there was no guard at your door," she said, surprised that she felt the need to tease him. To flirt a bit.

"No one to keep my horde of fans at bay?"

She laughed, though the sound was bitter as she glanced out the window to the parking lot and grounds, where less than a week before a throng of Jonas's fans had gathered. She saw her reflection in the glass, a ghostly image, but she refused to be haunted. Not anymore. She'd do whatever it took to find her way back to a life she was supposed to live, a life her sister had tried to preserve for her all those years ago. Her heart twisted when she thought of Marlie and tried to take solace that finally she was at peace.

She rapped on the wooden windowsill for good luck, then turned around to face this new man in her life. "About those fans," she said, "I guess you're just not popular."

"Fine by me." He quirked a dark eyebrow. "And how are you doing?"

She wanted to say she was okay, that she was doing great, but that would be a lie, and they both would know it. "Managing." She walked closer to the bed. "Still camping out at your place. My house is still a center for the gruesomely curious, those who love the macabre. So I thought it would be best if Rhapsody and I could crash at your place until all the media hype slows down. If it's okay with you."

"It's fine. Great. When I get out of here, you can be my nurse."

"In your dreams. But you can be my shrink."

"Oh. God. That's a dark thought."

"The worst," she agreed but scared up a smile. They had been few and far between in the last couple of days. She'd been shattered on the mountain, losing both Jonas and especially Marlie, but she'd tried in the last couple of days to pull herself together, to ignore the press, to turn off the TV and her phone, to concentrate on the fact that now she knew the truth, as grisly and ugly as it was, and now she could move forward.

With Tate.

Without Tate.

Whatever it took, she would pull herself together.

Somehow.

"So will it?" he asked, sitting up a little straighter in the bed. "Will the hype slow down?"

"God, I hope so. Faiza has been all over my case, begging me to stay with her, at the house in the West Hills, but I think that would only be worse. She's already hooked up with someone in Hollywood who wants to do another story, or a sequel to what happened twenty years ago or something. She's all excited. Over the moon. Her boyfriend Roger found the guy, apparently went looking for him the very day you and I were dealing with Marlie and Walter. He hopped on a flight to LA and connected with a producer one of the guys in his band knew. Since then the producer has talked to Alex Rousseau, the attorney, and Mia Long."

"So are you going to do it?"

"With Auntie Fai?"

"Yeah."

"She sure wants me to. The producer has called, but I think I'll pass." She sidled closer to the bed, thought about how her aunt had used and abused her over the years, but again, pushed those conflicting thoughts aside. For now. "I've got a problem with working with her. You see, I've already committed to a book deal with this reporter. He's a little on the shady side," she said, and saw one side of Tate's mouth lift. "I think he would even go so far as to pretend to be run over by a half-crazed female just to get a story, but there's just something about him that makes me think I should throw in my lot with him." She squinched up her face as if she was thinking really, really hard. Then she snapped her fingers. "Oh, now I remember! Maybe it's because he took a bullet for me." At that thought, of Tate leaping in front of her as Walter had fired, she felt tears collect in her eyes and her throat caught.

She cleared it. "Anyway, I think I might . . . you know, go with him. We had a deal."

"We did," he said and his own voice sounded gruff. "Kara," he said, his voice low. "Stay at the house. Stay with me." He grabbed her wrist, his fingers firm and warm. "We'll figure everything out."

"Everything?" She laughed. "I don't know if it's possible."

"Let's find out." His eyes held hers. "What did *your* doctor say?"

She, too, had spent two nights in the hospital, where she was examined, physically and mentally, and where a psychologist talked to her, a psychologist who had tracked down Dr. Zhou and her associate. Antianxiety drugs had been prescribed and she'd been released, though she was still under a doctor's care. But she played it down. "My doctor?" she repeated. "What does she say? Hmmm. Well, mainly the usual, you know. That I have anxiety issues, and that I should be on medication, that I've been through all this trauma and . . . well, it's nothing I haven't heard all my life, it's just fresh. New stuff to deal with."

"Big stuff."

"Yeah," she admitted. "Big stuff. I'm on the medication. For now. And I have many counseling appointments in my future." She shrugged. "So what else is new?"

"We'll get through it together," he promised,

his fingers tightening a bit. "What about the police? They've had to have been all over you. Despite the docs trying to keep them at bay."

"Yeah, but I talked to them, too. Detectives Thomas and Johnson." In fact, she'd spoken with them for nearly two hours earlier in the morning before heading to Tate's place to check on her dog. Rhapsody had been fine as Tate had a friend, someone named Connell, whom he'd somehow contacted to walk the dog and feed her while they were in the care of the medical team of Whimstick General. Tate seemed to have lots of faith in Connell and had told Kara as much.

"What about you?" she asked.

"Yeah, they talked to me. The nurses and doctor weren't happy about it, but I just wanted it to be over."

"Good. Me too." More than anything, she wanted the horror of it all to be finally put to rest. If that were possible. At this point, she wasn't certain. Then again, she wasn't certain about anything. What had she once heard her father tell Sam Junior one summer? "Life's a crapshoot, son." He'd placed a firm hand on his boy's shoulder. "You never know what the next roll will be." She hadn't understood it at six, but she got it now. *Amen, Daddy. Amen.*

Tate glanced up at her as if he'd suddenly thought of something important. "You know, I'm gonna need a ride. To get out of here."

"I guess it's your lucky day," she said, and held up a ring of keys. "I just happen to be driving your SUV."

"Mine?"

"How else do you think I got here?" she asked, feeling the urge to flirt with him again. "Mine's still not quite drivable."

"You're a terrible driver," he pointed out.

"Not always. And, come on, it's not far." She winked. "I think you'll be safe."

"So Walter Robinson was a busy man," Johnson observed, as she and Thomas watched the frozen body of Chad Atwater being zipped into a black bag before being hauled to the morgue. Two hunters had come across his truck and made the grisly discovery. Chad's throat had been cut with what appeared to be some kind of surgical knife, most likely the same knife that had been used to kill and decapitate Jonas McIntyre. Robinson had a bloody knife with him, still clutched in his hand as he died. And Robinson had a few more stashed in his home in Seaside.

Johnson and Thomas had already made the trip to the coast, where they'd discovered that Robinson's 1980s home was more than just a residence. The residence had a basement with a bedroom, bathroom and mini kitchen on one side and shop for electrical and electronic equipment on the other. The working theory was that he'd held his daughter captive for two decades in the living area and used the other for his surveillance. Tracking devices had been placed on several vehicles, including Chad Atwater's truck, Merritt Margrove's BMW, Faiza Donner's Lexus, Mia Long's Honda and Kara McIntyre's mangled Jeep, vehicles of many of the people connected to the McIntyre Massacre. People Walter could track, and when the opportunity presented itself, murder. So, if the working theory was correct, Robinson had his sights on Faiza and Kara, possibly even Mia. They would never know for certain.

"Too bad Robinson can't be prosecuted." She slid him a glance as the tow truck arrived to haul Atwater's truck to the county garage for processing.

"Really? You'd want the state to spend money on a trial? The way I figure it, we're lucky we don't have to waste our time."

While the tow truck's lights flashed and Atwater's pickup was winched onto the flatbed, she said, "I like to see justice served."

"The daughter he kept captive for twenty years killed him," Thomas pointed out, as he withdrew his key ring from a pocket and with a click on the fob for his SUV unlocked it. "I'd argue that justice was served, and served with a nice slice of irony." He shot her a look. "Come on, let's get out of here. Hungry?"

She tossed a final glance at the tow truck. "Yeah, but let's get back to civilization first."

"I know just the place."

On the outskirts of Whimstick, he pulled into a fifties-style diner complete with black-and-white checkerboard floor, Formica-topped tables and an authentic jukebox that was now playing holiday favorites.

After settling on a booth near the corner, they were served by a waitress with an updo topped by an elf hat. The place was nearly empty but smelled of french fries and grilled onions. Tomorrow was Christmas Eve; the noon crowd had dribbled to just a few patrons at tables decorated with sprigs of holly in small vases tucked near the condiments and napkin holders.

Once they were served and Thomas had taken a couple of bites of his cheeseburger, Johnson said, "Let's talk this over. One more time." She didn't have to explain what she meant; the recent murders had been the topic of conversation all over the state. But Johnson was laying it out. "Jonas killed Donner Robinson and was caught in the act by Donner's father, Walter." She took a bite from her vegetarian sandwich, and after chewing said, "But his daughter, Marlie, who was going to run off with the now-deceased Chad, saw her father—or her father and Jonas squaring off, her brother already dead. She locked her sister in the attic, then tried to intervene while there was a fight for the sword and was sliced."

"Walter was masked at that point, so we don't know if she recognized him," Thomas said.

"Right."

Johnson paused at the Christmas music heard over the crackle of the fryer and rattle of cutlery. "Then Walter went berserk and killed everyone but Kara, who was locked in the attic. The kid got out of the attic, came downstairs and saw the carnage. Walter was still there and chased her down, but spied Edmund Tate, who'd heard something from his deck and took off after the little girl." She swallowed another bite of sandwich, washed it down with vitamin water. "So, at that point Walter peeled off with injured Marlie, while Kara and Edmund ended up in the lake."

"But Edmund recognized Walter and tried to tell the EMTs. Meanwhile Walter gets away and keeps his daughter captive in Seaside."

"That's the weird part."

"Oh, come on, it's all weird," Thomas said. Even sitting here in a retro diner talking about multiple homicides while Christmas music played from the speakers was a little on the outré side.

"Beyond weird."

Thomas nodded. From what they could piece together, Marlie had somehow gotten hold of one of her father's burner cells and found Kara's information on Walter's computer. She'd made the calls and texts to Kara.

Johnson said, "Okay, I follow all that, but what I don't get is why Marlie didn't just leave?"

"She couldn't at first, too injured. Walter stitched her up."

"Because he'd been a medic in the military, yeah, I know."

"But he was no plastic surgeon so she was disfigured, and he also probably convinced her if she ever did leave, she'd be implicated in the murders. Remember, she was totally dependent upon him, had nowhere to turn, or so she thought."

"He brainwashed her." She said it with a grimace. "Sick piece of shit."

"And days became weeks, became months."

"Became two damned decades." She was shaking her head, thinking it over.

"She thought she'd lost everyone. Her mother had been slaughtered, as had her brother, even her stepdad. Jonas was in jail, her other stepbrother killed, and Kara was just a kid."

"Her aunt?" she asked, and the music changed to a country music rendition of "What Child Is This?"

"Faiza. Who bled the estate dry."

"She probably didn't know that," Johnson said as the elf/waitress swept past them to another booth where three teenaged girls had settled in. They were talking over each other while still paying attention to their phones.

"Remember, Walter's her father, he healed her, if she went to anyone, including the police, he would end up in jail and she'd be all alone."

"With scars inside and out."

"Right." He took a long swallow from his Coke.

"But she kept up with Jonas's release when she went online as Hailey Brown. She could hide in the shadows. And that's probably what spurred her on, that he was getting out, and she was afraid he would seek revenge against Kara for her testimony."

"So she stole his phone and somehow escaped."

"After he left to deal with Jonas?" she asked as the teenagers ordered from the waitress.

"Yeah, and a set of keys were on her so she must've stolen those from her father as well." Thomas chewed slowly. He'd already considered all the alternatives. "Maybe by this time Walter trusted her. After all, it had been twenty years."

"I don't know." Johnson paused and finished the rest of her sandwich. Finally, she said, "A lot of holes that we have to fill in." Wadding up her napkin, she shook her head. "We may never know. Too bad about Marlie."

Amen, Thomas thought, and drained his drink. A-effing-men.

"At least Kara survived," Johnson pointed out, "but come on, do you think she'll ever be normal again?"

"Was she ever?" He wasn't being sarcastic. Thomas really felt that she'd never had a chance for a normal life. First the tragedy, then the circus of a trial with her testimony, before being raised by people who were primarily interested in her fortune and exploited her by making money off her story. And then, just about when she came of age, she had to go through another horrific, unimaginable ordeal. His jaw clenched when he thought of all the carnage that one girl had witnessed.

"At least no one else died."

"Other than her sister and brother."

"Jonas?" she said as the waitress left the bill and Thomas swept it up. For once Johnson didn't argue. "The way I figure it, he was dead to her already. Might've been planning to kill her and Lacey, at least if one of his cellmates is to be believed.

"The con claimed Jonas McIntyre hadn't found Jesus at all, and that he didn't give two cents about all his legions of fans, that all Jonas really was after was his share of the McIntyre fortune, which would be larger without Kara claiming her share, and even more importantly, Jonas was out for revenge.

Unfortunately for Jonas, so was Walter Robinson, and Walter had beat Jonas to the punch when it came to killing Merritt Margrove.

"Jonas certainly got paid back." she added. She was talking about the severed head, found in an old record player, slowly spinning, battery powered, compliments of the electrician Walter Robinson. "What goes around comes around."

"Ooooh. Bad," he said, but fought a smile.

"I know. Too far," she said.

Thomas remembered the gore, the headless corpse and the money, thousands of dollars—twenty thousand in blood-splattered bills—next to the torso. Cash that had been stashed and stolen and was now evidence. *Blood money.*

It was still a mystery as to how Walter Robinson had met Jonas in the attic. Had the attack been planned, or was it just by chance, with Jonas ending up losing his life? They might never know.

He changed the subject. "What about Faiza Donner? Was she on Jonas's list of people to get even with?"

"Who knows?" She gave a shrug. "The last I heard she and her boyfriend have hired Alex Rousseau to help them get their hands on the rest of the estate. "Roger Sweeney has some connections to the entertainment business through one of his old band mates." Good old Roger took a flight to LA on the day Walter Robinson was killed and met with some TV personality who wants to do another movie on the case."

"Great," he said sarcastically. "I guess I'm not surprised. I got a call from a reporter who asked about it.

When she gave him a look, he said, "I got a call from a reporter who asked about it." The reporter, of course, was Sheila Keegan, who was still hounding him, reminding him that he owed her. He smiled as they walked outside, where the wind blew his jacket open and icy snowflakes caught in his hair. Maybe finally he'd actually pay his debt.

After all, it was Christmas.

And they were both alone.

"What're you doing for the holiday?" he asked his partner as he slid behind the wheel and she, adjusting her knitted hat, slid into the passenger seat.

"Ooh, it's complicated. I get together with my ex and his family. For my son's sake. You know, my boy's got some issues." He waited. "They're emotional mainly and seem to be improving with medication and . . . and it helps when his dad and I get along, so we do. For Jamie's sake." She threw Thomas a glance. "What about you?"

"I'm working tonight."

"And after?"

"We'll see," he said. "I'll be okay." But he didn't mention Sheila Keegan as he drove Johnson back to the station to pick up her car.

That was his little secret.

And it was best to keep it that way.

EPILOGUE

Kara walked out of the meeting and flipped up the hood of her jacket. Rain was falling from a deep, gunmetal-gray sky. The forecast was for a wet and gloomy holiday. "No white Christmas this year," the weatherman had said when she'd turned on the news this morning.

Perfect.

Enough with the snow for the holidays. Maybe someday she'd feel differently about it. But not this year.

She climbed into her vehicle, a five-year-old Subaru Outback she'd settled on the year before, and drove through the city streets, strings of lights glowing brightly, storefronts painted with snowmen and Santas or Nativity scenes all the while touting end-of-the-year sales. Christmas and commercialism. Never far apart.

Better than Christmas and massacre, she told herself, then angry at her thoughts, turned on the radio and caught the tail end of "The Little Drummer Boy" before the first notes of "Silent Night" wafted through the speakers. "No!" she said aloud. Not now. Probably not ever. She switched the channel to some hard rock from the 70s.

"Dream On," by Aerosmith.

Slightly better.

No, a whole lot better.

And in her warped opinion, more soothing.

She was probably in the minority on that one, but she didn't care and drove along the river, the water nearly black as it reflected the dark, moody clouds overhead. It had been a long year. She was still hounded by the press, and there were details of the trust and estate that hadn't been quite settled, but a new attorney was working on it, a lawyer in his forties, all business, all by the book, about as far from Merritt Margrove as one could get. He was also working with the insurance companies in dealing with the aftermath of the accident in the mountains a year earlier. Thankfully Sven Aaronsen had pulled through after a month in the hospital and several months of physical therapy. Now, she'd heard, he was driving again, even though his blood-alcohol level had been elevated at the time of the crash. And hers—under the limit as far as she knew, but still she felt responsible. She would do right by Aaronsen, but for now, the insurance companies were still haggling it out.

She parked in a space on the street in front of Tate's building, let herself in and was greeted by Rhapsody, who, as usual, raced down the steps, barking and leaping and generally going out of her mind. "I missed you, too," Kara said, ruffling the dog's coarse fur before Rhapsody escaped, running up and down the stairs crazily until Kara reached the loft.

Tate was at his table/desk and kicked out his chair as she appeared. "Hey," he said with a smile, whirling the chair to face her. "How'd it go?"

"It went. Pretty good." She peeled off her jacket and noticed the Christmas tree in the windowed corner of the loft, her first in years. She felt at home here, with Tate. She'd crashed a year ago and never left, even going so far as putting her Whimstick house on the market. Soon, she would list the house in the West Hills of Portland. Now that Faiza and Roger had moved to sunny southern California to chase after the Hollywood dream and Kara was the legal owner, she wanted to get rid of it. Once her childhood home, now an albatross around her neck.

She sauntered up to Tate, fished into the front pocket of her jeans and dropped the coin on the table near his laptop. "One year sober," she said.

His teeth flashed in a roguish grin. "And it's been a great year."

"It has." She straddled him then, wrapping her arms around the back of his neck and kissing him. They'd become lovers the night that he'd returned from the hospital, something that just happened between them, a spark fueled by adrenaline, trauma and the knowledge that in one single heartbeat, a life could change forever.

Rhapsody whined, begging for more attention. "Oooh. Duty calls," she said, pulling away and climbing off the chair. To the dog, "You want to go for a walk?"

"I took her out not an hour ago."

"But it's Christmas and she wants to go again."

"You want me to go with you?" he asked, and there it was again, that unspoken need of his to care about her, his worry about her mental state. Not that she blamed him. She'd been a frightened shell of herself a year ago. And to this day she still counted door locks each night, even though she lived with Tate and he was in the house. It was just a habit she hadn't quite broken. "Nah, I'll be fine." She snapped on Rhapsody's leash. "It'll be a short one."

"I'll hold you to it. And I'll order Chinese for dinner."

She couldn't help but grin. Pointing a finger at him, she said, "Do that. Let's make it a holiday tradition." Donning her jacket, she headed downstairs again, the dog's toenails clicking loudly on the steps.

Outside the wind had picked up, not much traffic on the streets, darkness pressing in, street-lamps glowing through the pelting rain. Holding the leash tightly, Kara jogged to the edge of the river and stared at the ever-moving depths as Rhapsody sniffed at the sea wall. Between the lampposts, strings of colored lights winked in the rain. Only a few cars passed, their tires noisy on the wet streets.

Turning from the river, Kara looked up to the corner windows of Tate's loft. She found his silhouette, a haloed shadow visible next to their Christmas tree, a twelve-foot Douglas fir gleaming in lights and tinsel.

Her heart swelled and the words *One Day at a Time* rang through her mind. He was right. The last year had been a good one. It had started out awash in painful, heart-wrenching memories. The worst was of Marlie. She missed her sister each and every day and probably always would, but she had to admit, each and every day this past year had been better than the last. She crossed her fingers. Hoped her luck would last.

Smiling, she waved up to Tate, then tugged on the dog's leash. "Come on, Rhaps," she said, jogging back to the loft, "we're going home." Ridiculously she blinked against a sudden wash of tears, then repeated, her voice catching, "We're finally going home."

Center Point Large Print
600 Brooks Road / PO Box 1
Thorndike, ME 04986-0001 USA

(207) 568-3717

US & Canada:
1 800 929-9108
www.centerpointlargeprint.com